Standish

Standish

Erastes

P.D. Publishing, Inc.
Clayton, North Carolina

ISBN-13: 978-1-933720-09-8
ISBN-10: 1-933720-09-3

9 8 7 6 5 4 3 2 1

Cover art and design by Cal
Edited by Day Petersen/Penelope Warren

Published by:

P.D. Publishing, Inc.
P.O. Box 70
Clayton, NC 27528

http://www.pdpublishing.com

Acknowledgements:

Kerry — my muse. Also to Ottilie, Irene, Tamanna for coming on the journey with me. Rictor Norton for a fabulous resource (www.infopt.demon.co.uk/index.html) on homosexuality through the ages, and to Douglas Harper for www.etymonline.com which is the most tremendous boon for a historical writer.

DEDICATION

To my mother, who is my greatest supporter
and to Rebecca Day who never lost faith.

Chapter 1

The candle guttered, and Ambrose looked up at it with a frown, the long blond hair falling away from the sides of his face. The scratching of his pen halted briefly. The wick was strong, and the candle had a long way to burn down. He decided that he would write on for another ten minutes, then retire. His sisters were probably lying awake, waiting to hear his footstep on the stairs, and he had promised them both that he would not stay up past ten tonight. He set his pen down and rubbed some life into his cramped fingers, which were long, pale, and elegant. Then, running his fingers through his hair, he took up the quill again, dipped it into the inkwell, and continued to write in a spidery hand.

Since his last bout of ague, he had been sickly and weak. The doctor said it was a bout of brain fever brought on by intensive study, not only during the day but far too often reaching into the lateness of the night. After this diagnosis, his sisters had insisted on his reducing the duration and frequency of his late night sessions. He'd rebelled slightly at this, his study being his driving obsession, but a compromise of sorts had been reached. Maria and Sophy allowed him to continue a lighter regime of study, and he agreed to limit the number of hours he spent closeted alone in the small library.

The clock in the hall began its mournful chime, and reluctantly Ambrose closed the notebook, placed the pen in its holder and shut the roll top desk, running his hands over the silken ridges of the tambour shutter as he had done since he was old enough to sit there on his father's knee. It was almost a superstition with him now; he could no more have left the desk without caressing it than he could interrupt the vicar's sermon on Sunday.

His wise amber eyes expectant, Aries looked up as his master stretched, yawned and absent-mindedly put a hand down and scratched one wiry, floppy ear. The wolfhound groaned in pleasure, pushing his head into his master's hand. Ambrose's eyes were unfocussed in thought, and he found himself staring at the picture of the house on the wall: Standish. His great-grandfather's house. This small box house, the White House, as it was simply called, was merely a satellite of the main building. As they did most nights, Ambrose's thoughts ran to the house, and he allowed himself to imagine the difference in his life, in all of their lives, if they still owned it. If Standish were still theirs, his sisters would be feted and courted, instead of one already an old maid and the other on her way toward a bitter spinsterhood. He himself would... He had no idea what his life would be like; he had nothing to use as a guide. There were no other gentry in the vicinity, and Ambrose had never been to London. The life of the eldest son and heir to a landed estate was completely beyond his experience.

All of his life, Ambrose had been fascinated by the house, which sat in the centre of the parkland like a beautiful Grecian temple. His father had often taken him past it, setting his son in front of his saddle on his daily rides to the village; they would stop at the nearest vantage point and gaze at Standish. His father would tell and retell the story of how it was lost — how his grandfather had wagered his fortune on the turn of a card, and then lost his life in a duel as the result of accusing his opponent of cheating. Ambrose never tired of hearing the tale. "Should have been mine, lad," his father always said, sometimes adding "and yours, of course."

For as long as anyone could remember, a skeleton staff had maintained the property and the grounds. Since it had been won all those years ago, Standish had never been lived in by the owners. It had been let, but not to anyone who stayed very long. Despite its virtual abandonment, Ambrose and his father had never entered the grounds, and Ambrose had kept to that proud tradition, never once walking through the huge iron gates and up the neglected drive. His only view of it was still the one he had shared with his father.

He knew every room intimately, though. His father had described it all to him in great detail: the cavernous entrance hall with the double staircase, the floor paved in stone resplendent with paintings of fabulous beasts; the magnificent ballroom with large arched windows down one side; the withdrawing rooms, the bedrooms, the yew walk, the magnificent conservatory. All were indelibly etched in Ambrose's mind. He often told himself he would go, but he never had.

The clock chimed the quarter hour, and the door opened softly. Maria's mobcapped head appeared.

"Ambrose, you promised!" she said in a hurt and disapproving tone.

Ambrose stood up. "Sorry," he said, "I stopped at ten. I was...thinking." His eyes returned to the portrait of the house above the desk.

"Daydreaming," she snapped. "About Standish again, I dare say."

Ambrose smiled ruefully, his face suddenly alight and irresistibly charming. He kissed her and moved into the hall. "I know, I know. 'The house is gone, and we are ruined, and daydreaming won't pay the baker.'"

In spite of herself, she found herself smiling, too. "I suppose I do repeat myself." She walked ahead of him up the stairs, carrying the candles.

"Just a little," he said. "I know how you worry about money. I will see about getting employment this week." He smiled again at his elder sister as they paused outside his bedroom door.

"You aren't strong enough yet," she said quickly, but Ambrose could see the lines of worry on her face. *It's not fair*, he thought to himself. *She's had to carry the family for too many years. It's about time I started to help.*

"What can you do anyway? Thanks to father, you've trained for nothing. You should have gone into the Church or the army, but I do believe he thought somehow he'd get the wretched house back for you, and in the end — all it did was kill him."

"I'll find something," he said simply. "As you always say, God will provide." Not that he believed that himself; Ambrose didn't believe in God. His studies had taught him there was no heaven in the firmament, nothing but planets and stars. If he needed help, he needed to help himself. He dutifully kissed Maria, went into his room, and shut the door. Aries lay across the doorway and put his head on his paws.

The next morning, Ambrose breakfasted lightly while his sisters opened the post. It was his wont to be taciturn in the morning, silent through breakfast and retiring to his library to read directly afterwards. The women, who adored their little brother, indulged him in his routine, and would not normally have disturbed his peace for the world. This morning, however, Sophy's hand flew to her mouth with a shriek that pierced Ambrose's ears like a knife. His headache, never far away since his debilitating illness, suddenly returned, and he looked up with annoyance.

"Forgive me, brother," whispered Sophy, as Maria glared at her. "We have a letter from Elspeth Whitney. She's in town, as you know. She's met...oh Ambrose, she met Goshawk." She held the letter out for him to take and pointed to the relevant paragraph.

Ambrose took the letter eagerly and read:

"*...and we spent two weeks there. Upon our return, however, we were invited to the Chalmers' once again, this time for Alice's coming out. I wore the gown I had made in Paris, and all eyes were upon me, I am sure. There was one surprise guest, whose identity will interest you greatly, I do believe. Goshawk himself. His arrival caused much furore. As you know, he has been on the Continent for many years, although you would never have guessed it to see him. He was sophistication itself. Mamma confided in me that he had lost his wife whilst abroad, and there was indeed a certain sadness to him, but I was most pleased by his looks. Tall, very dark, but much too serious. He was introduced to all, but he did not smile or dance, which I am certain made all the mammas furious!*

"*Now comes the hardest part to tell, and your dear brother will take this worst of all, I fear. Goshawk told my father that he is now returned to England for good, and sees no reason why he and his son should not move into Standish by the end of the month. He was most interested to discover that we were acquaintances, and says he will call on you as soon as convenient. He gave no indication as to whether he knew your family history, although I assume he does. I can hardly believe that Standish will be a home at last."*

The letter continued with tales of other dances, and Ambrose handed the letter back to Maria; his pale hands shook slightly, and the blood had left his face. He stood up and, neglecting to take his newspaper with him, excused himself and left the room. Reaching the relative safety of his library, he threw himself into a wing-backed chair, and his head fell into his hands. He was being foolish, he knew. Standish was not his, would never be his, but somehow the very fact that it sat empty had given him hope all of his twenty-three years, as it had his father before him. In his very maddest moments, he had allowed himself to believe that maybe his studies would prove fruitful, that he would publish his papers, become recognised, sponsored, and somehow, somehow, he would be able to obtain the money to buy back the house. A boyish dream, one he had clung to all of his life, and one he now realised was worthless.

Rafe Goshawk. The very name summed up the family: venal, predatory raptors. The stories that were told about them were legend. Houses in London, Paris and estates in the Americas, a fleet of ships, factories all won, stolen, or plundered. A name of such wealth and built entirely on sand, forged from the loss and misery of others.

The Standish pride rose in Ambrose, and he sat up. *Well, I will not receive him*, he thought. Then he thought of his sisters, and the poverty under which they struggled. It was beyond hope to think that the widowed Goshawk might look favourably on one of them, but Ambrose was not so ingenuous that he did not realise that their lot might be improved in many ways with the arrival of the fabulously wealthy heir of the Goshawk fortune.

Chapter 2

"Well, it's dashed good to have you back in the country, Goshawk, and that's all I have to say on the matter. Can't imagine what you were thinking, man, spending so many years away from London." Lord Trenberry stood in front of the cheval mirror as two servants attired him in his dress uniform. "Damned place has been dead without you."

The gentleman he was addressing, dressed in deepest black, was stretched out on a chaise at the side of the room, minutely examining his fingernails as he listened to Trenberry's prattle. Long, lean and cadaverous, a narrow face, black-brown hair, tied with an elegant bow. His expressionless black eyes were slanted and lupine as he narrowed them at the speaker. With a small irritated sigh, Rafe Goshawk stood up.

"Sorry to disappoint you, Francis," he said, his voice acidly mellifluous. He knew that Francis' reaction would be unpleasant. "I am not staying in London. I am taking my son to Dorset; we are going to be living at Standish."

Trenberry spun round, flustering the two fitters. "What?" he demanded. "You've only just got here, man! Stay out the season at least! Standish be damned. You've never shown the slightest interest in the place. Why bury yourself in that godforsaken mausoleum now?" Losing his temper with the servants who were attempting to fit his sword, he yelled, "Get out! I'll finish it myself!" The footmen fled.

Francis strode toward the man in black, who was looking at him from under hooded lids. Trenberry's demeanour changed from arrogant lordling to whining youth. "I'm serious, Rafe. I've had years without you, irregular letters, having to trek down to France to see you, being at your beck and call. You finally, beyond all hope, return to me; your wife has been dead for years, and we can be together at long last. Now you calmly tell me you are leaving again?" He put his arms around the taller man's waist and kissed him gently, his voice becoming husky. "Rafe, I long for you. It's been two desolate years."

Rafe very much doubted whether Francis had had two desolate months, let alone years; his libido was only matched by his neediness. He sighed again as Francis continued.

"Stay with me? At least until after the season. Then we'll both go and bury ourselves in your precious Standish." He latched his mouth onto Goshawk's neck and nipped the skin there softly, moved a hand to the front of Rafe's breeches, rubbing the front of them gently with the flat of his palm, then started to unbutton the front panel.

Goshawk remained immobile, allowing himself the pleasure of becoming hard under Trenberry's fumbling fingers, then pulled sharply away from the embrace before more buttons were unfastened. His soulless eyes looked at the vacuous blond officer, who was red faced and panting. *What did I see in him?* he thought, and his memory strayed to a younger Francis, the handsome boy he had met at the Duchess of Richmond's ball, four years before on the eve of Waterloo. In his red jacket, the young cavalry officer had taken Goshawk's breath away, with his laughing eyes and exquisite posterior. *Yes,* Rafe thought, *he had been beautiful.* He'd taken the boy in a brief moment of madness and lust, never expecting to see him again in light of the oncoming battle.

If only he had been killed. He would have stayed with me as a perfect moment, an amber bead of time holding the memory of his peach-like fundament beneath me; the image undimmed and untainted by the years between then and now. Petulant letters, jealous tantrums, demands for time he did not have, money that galled him to send. That perfect moment soured, until there was nothing left between them but bitterness and ennui. Without taking his eyes from his host, he adjusted his clothing. "No, Francis. I am not staying in London, and I certainly am not taking you down to Standish with me. What would your fiancée say? Or your regiment? We grew out of each other years ago." *Or I did him, at least,* he thought grimly, watching the red cheeks pale and the blue eyes widen in shock. *The times I wrote to put him off, and still he journeyed to see me.* He ran a finger over the officer's cheek. "No regrets, Francis. Never any regrets," and without another word he strode to the double doors and departed, hearing the sound of a mirror breaking behind him.

Ten days later he was in his black Park Drag, swaying through the Dorset countryside. They had made an easy journey and had taken their time. There was no rush, after all. Two Dalmatians ran beneath the carriage, and his son was dozing in the seat next to him. Rafe looked down at him. He was too pale. The climate in the south of France had not agreed with him; he had been fretful and indolent in the heat. Various doctors had all agreed he needed to return home. Return. The boy had never been to England. Home was something Rafe had never known.

Goshawk himself had been born in Paris, in 1780, the son of Gordian Goshawk and a Celestine D'Alphonse, an Aristocrat. Born within the *Ancien Regime*, raised in privilege then moulded through fire, death, and The Terror. His eyes were expressionless pits of hell partly because he had seen more horror in his boyhood than most hardened battle veterans had in their lifetimes. He rarely allowed himself to think of it, repressing it as he did most of his memories, and all of his emotions except the love for his son.

Rafe and his father had finally escaped France in 1793 after spending years in hiding, spending a sizeable portion of the family fortune on bribes and sacrificing the life of Madame Goshawk to Madame Guillotine along the way. They travelled extensively across Europe, always moving, keeping away from anyone who might know them. From Portugal to St Petersburg, they had not stopped for many years. Finally, when the Terror ended, they journeyed to England, and moved into the family house in Tavistock Square. His father re-entered society, and Rafe learned about wealth. He saw that the nobility, although holding Gordian in no little disrespect, nevertheless came to his house, ate his food and drank his wine, flattered him, took him into their circles. Rafe learned early that money, influence, and power could get one anything one desired. Or almost anything.

His father had employed a tutor for his teenage son, a Mr Quinn, a tall, slightly effeminate but erudite blond fellow, with a stammer, shabby clothes, and a slight stoop. His task was to teach Rafe Greek and Latin, Literature, Mathematics, and Science. Rafe found the dead languages easy. He already spoke French and Italian fluently, together with a fair smattering of Spanish and Russian. He hated mathematics and was bored with most of the sciences. Quinn's passion was literature, particular the Greek myths. He introduced Rafe to Perseus, to Achilles and to Odysseus. The Adventures, mixed with Quinn's enthusiasm, addicted Rafe to the stories, and he learned the languages quickly to read them for himself. After that, he found that Quinn had a talent for making even Sciences interesting, and Rafe learned anything and everything Quinn showed him.

For the first time in his life, the boy realised that he cared for another human being. He respected his father, but he did not like him. He was cold and forbidding. Rafe could not remember his father ever holding him, touching him, and he had felt nothing but pity and contempt for his spoiled and sickly mother.

But that had all been a very long time ago, and Tomas Quinn was yet another thing that he rarely allowed himself to think of.

After his father died, Rafe, by then at Oxford, came down before the end of his studies and took up the reins of the mighty Goshawk business empire. But his childhood memories of the house at Tavistock Square were unpleasant, and he found that he could not settle there. It had never felt like a home to him, and so, restless and unfulfilled, he travelled. He had been to Standish once only. He had travelled down to see the house in his twenty-first year and had stood in front of it for an hour. It was more beautiful than he had imagined, and he did not feel worthy of it. He vowed then and there he would provide a dynasty for it, for nothing else would do. He did not enter Standish that day, but left promising only to return when he brought it an heir.

It took eight years, but he finally found a woman who did not revolt him. Catarina Sofia Bonifazia Veneziano was the only daughter and the last in a line of faded Venetian aristocrats who could trace their bloodline back one thousand years. Their line dwindled and their fortune almost gone, they lived in a huge crumbling Palazzo on the Grand Canal. Rafe had met the father in business, arranging for shipping in the city, and the old man was only too eager to introduce his daughter to a man, who, if not of noble blood, at least held himself in a manner that suggested nobility, and was so rich the old man could not grasp the breadth of his wealth. Rafe had been charmed by Caterina's quiet elegance and had married her with almost indecent haste.

She deserved a better husband, but she fulfilled her role as Signora Goshawk admirably. Rafe found her company tolerable and sometimes even enjoyable. Her greatest gift, though, was his son, and Rafe was in love with the boy from the moment he took him in his arms.

"We shall call him Sebastien," he had whispered, his eyes on the tiny, perfect infant, "and Louis, after your mother and our poor murdered King, D'Alphonse in memory of your grandmother."

"No tribute to your father, Rafe?" his wife enquired in a weak voice.

Rafe's eyes went dead and cold. "It is enough that he bears his surname, and I would change that if I could." His wife died within the week, and her parents shortly afterwards, from grief and plague.

As the carriage rattled its way towards Dorset, Goshawk's eyes came back to life as he turned them to his beloved son. His heir. His head fell back against the leather upholstery, and his eyes closed. He clasped his son to him and allowed the rocking of the carriage to lull him, if not to sleep, then into a relaxed state without thought. As the sun hit the horizon, the footman tapped the roof of the coach. The horses slowed and stopped. "We are at the gates, sir," came a muffled voice. Rafe didn't open his eyes. He knew he could not see the house from the gates. Like Ambrose, Rafe had grown up with the vision of Standish imprinted in his mind's eye. He had known his grandfather before the revolution, the man who had won the house and grounds from the Standish family, and he had enraptured the young Rafe with his descriptions of the fabulous mansion. He had stolen, won, and embezzled his away across most of Continental Europe and parts of the Americas. He told endless stories about the slave ships, the card games, the duels, the murders, and how he had won his greatest treasure — this house. Rafe had believed every word. To him the old man was a legend and a romantic hero. It wasn't until he was much older that he realised the harm that had been done to the countless families his grandfather had afflicted.

Which brings me back here, Rafe thought. *To the Standishes.* He was not yet sure how he was going to deal with the family; he had had his fill of patronage. *I hope they are not going to be a problem*, he thought, frowning. He felt the carriage turn sharply left, and he opened his eyes and allowed himself to look out of the right hand window at the house that he knew would now be in full view, facing west over the parkland. The sun had transformed its classical façade to an amber radiance, the huge portico ablaze, windows on fire, shouting to the world that Rafe Goshawk had finally come home. He had brought his heir; he had fulfilled his vow.

Chapter 3

"Well, let's see the chestnut, then," Rafe barked, and an extremely nervous ostler darted toward the stable block and brought out the pony. Less of a pony and more a miniature horse, the small, elegant gelding obviously had some Arab in its veins. Rafe stepped up to the animal and ran a practised eye over the withers, the rump, and the deep chest; expertly ran his hands down each slender leg, feeling for splints or strains. "Run him up," he ordered, his eyes narrowing as he watched its action carefully. It moved away from him in a brisk trot. When the pony came back, Rafe opened its mouth.

"He's rising four, sir," stammered the ostler.

"He's nearer six," snapped Rafe, "but that's no bad thing; he won't be as skittish. Yes, I'll take him, too. So, that's the black stallion, the four Cleveland bays, the matched greys, and this fellow here. Have them sent to Standish." He turned on his heel, pleased with the day's results. Sebastien would love the little chestnut; he had been heartbroken to leave his scruffy little pony behind in France.

Horses were Rafe's passion, and without a fixed home he had been unable to indulge it in the manner he wished before now. Now, with the acres of parkland and time enough at last to do nothing, he intended to own a string that would be the envy of the equine world. He was considering branching into racing, but that was a dream yet to be realised; first, his son needed a tutor.

As he sat in the barouche on his way back to the house, he found that he still winced when he thought the word. Tutor. Maybe it was the sun making him drowsy, or maybe it was the pleasure that buying the horses gave him, but for the first time in possibly fifteen years, his thoughts ran away with him, and suddenly Tomas Quinn's face was before him.

Quinn had touched Rafe's mind in ways it had never been touched before. His knowledge of the past was encyclopaedic, and he taught in a way that brought the dead to life. When he spoke of the wars of Roman and Greek gods, of battles on long forgotten sites, his hazel eyes blazed. He would stand behind Rafe, his hands on the boy's shoulders, and together they would gaze into space, their minds recalling the glories of Odysseus and Agamemnon.

For his part, the youth was hotly in the throes of his first crush, and this was when he realised that money might not be able to buy him everything he wanted. He loved and wanted Quinn. He had read the tales of Zeus and Ganymede, of Apollo and Hyakinthos. He knew of Socrates; Socrates had said "Gnothi seauton," and Rafe found that he did indeed "know himself". He wanted to be as naked as one of his father's marble statues and to have Quinn pressed naked to him. He had studied the portrait "The Death of Hyakinthos" and longed to be held in Quinn's arms in such a tableau. He didn't really think further than that, as the mechanics involved seemed too crude for his young, romantic mind. In bed alone at night, he would re-read the love of Achilles and Patroclus, and his hand would lift his nightshirt, caress his slender, boyish penis, and dream that the hand that fondled him belonged to the tutor. His youthful ejaculations were violent and over very quickly. Desperate to please the man, he studied hard. He brought Quinn books of mythology and poetry, left fresh flowers on his desk every day, but if the tutor noticed the boy's attentions, he never said a thing.

But he had noticed.

Upon his appointment at the Goshawk's, he had liked Rafe from the first. The boy had a fine mind, although he was headstrong and understandably indulged. Quinn, who loved beauty in all things, was quickly hypnotised by the wolfish eyes, the half smile, the lustrous hair. He knew his thoughts were wrong, very wrong, but he soon found his day could not begin until Rafe had smiled at him. He told himself every day that he would give notice, make some excuse to the senior Goshawk and leave the temptation of Rafe behind him. But every day passed, and he did nothing about it.

As his fascination grew, he found he made a game of taking every opportunity to touch the youth. He would stand by Rafe's shoulder as he read and would put a hand on his back, revelling in the heat that came through the fabric. Occasionally he would, very casually, brush dust from the boy's shoulders or tidy a stray wisp of hair from his face, his fingers burning from the silken feel of it. Best of all though, were the astronomy lessons, when he would go to the boy's room at night and wake him. Sometimes the boy did not stir when Quinn entered the chamber, and Quinn would find intense joy in watching the long, pale face in sleep, the beautiful shining black hair spread on the pillow. Then what joy it was to reach and touch the slim arm and shake it gently, to see the endless eyes open and the soft beguiling smile that appeared every time the boy saw his tutor.

Quinn would follow the youth up the narrow attic stairs, drinking in the sight of his boyish form outlined in light breeches and a shirt. Once in the darkness of the night, on the flat roof there was a large and elaborate telescope, and standing behind Rafe, he would put his arms around him, while he adjusted the mirrors and explained how the mechanism worked.

He almost imagined that Rafe was aware of his shameful

thoughts, and sometimes he allowed himself to think that he could feel that the boy was deliberately pressing back against him. He knew it was madness; it was simply co-incidence and his own sinful wishful thinking. He truly believed that he deserved damnation for imagining that an innocent boy could share his lustful fantasy.

Six months after coming to Tavistock Square, another star gazing lesson loomed. Quinn was in his small, cell-like room, which contained only a single bed and a table and chair. He anticipated the joy and the agony of that brief moment when he held Rafe in his arms. A bottle of wine was on the table, and he had had more than his normal one glass. *I have got to leave here*, he thought. *I cannot continue to teach that boy. Another starlit night with that slender body pressed to mine, and I will lose my control, my employment, my reputation.* His member was hard, achingly hard, as it always was before going to wake his young charge. He always had to wait for the longing to recede before knocking on his door.

Unexpectedly there was a soft rap, and Quinn leapt to his feet, his hand coming away from the front of his breeches where it had been resting, almost unconsciously. "Who is it?" he said.

"It's me, Quinn," came the boy's soft, beloved voice.

Quinn felt his stomach turn over at the sound of it. He took a deep breath and opened the door. Rafe stood there, his eyes wide and questioning.

"I was worried. You were so quiet at dinner, and then midnight came and went and you didn't come..."

Quinn grabbed Rafe's arm and pulled him into the room, the feel of the bare forearm, exposed from the flowing shirt that was pushed up to his elbows, seemed hot beneath his hand. "Come in, you f-fool," he stammered, losing control of his speech impediment in shock. "Anyone could see you. The last thing you need is to be seen entering my room in the middle of the n-night."

Quinn's voice was uncharacteristically angry, and Rafe looked hurt, and then disdainful. "As if I care what servants think," he boasted.

"You m-may not," said Quinn in a calmer tone, quickly turning away and putting on a frock coat to hide the very obvious bulge in his breeches, "but you do not have a character and a position to lose."

Rafe was not unobservant. He had seen the sign of the tutor's desire and his own hardness throbbed at the thought of it. Could this mean that Quinn loved him as much as he loved his tutor? In his youth and romantic innocence, lust and love were very much the same thing. He smiled happily, his agile brain formulating a plan.

"Come on then, Venus won't wait all night," Rafe said, moving toward the door and smiling again as the implied double meaning registered on Quinn's face, then led the way up to the roof. Quinn appeared quite ill at ease when they arrived there and distractedly talked of the planets and stars and their relative positions. When Rafe stood up to the telescope, he waited patiently, but Quinn made no move to assist him. Finally, he had to turn round to the man in the darkness. "She's moved," he said softly, meaning Venus, "and I cannot find her." Quinn had no option but to put his arms around the boy and move the eyepiece accordingly. Rafe acted quickly; instead of leaning back against the tutor as he had done many times, he spun round and swiftly put his arms around Quinn's waist.

Quinn took a sharp breath in but he didn't move. "Rafe?" he said dazedly.

"What?" Rafe's head only came up to Quinn's chin, so tall was he. "It is better this way, though, is it not?" and he held his body against Quinn, grinding his hardness against the older man's leg. The spell shattered, and Quinn backed away, panting and shaking from head to foot, one hand outstretched as if to ward the boy off. Rafe stood where he had been left; hurt and tears of rejection sprang into his eyes. Seeing this pain he had caused, the boy's agonised expression, Quinn's heart and resolve finally broke, and he moved back to Rafe and embraced him, one arm around his back, the other hand on his hair, pulling the head to his shoulder, murmuring his name over and over, stroking him and soothing him.

"You love me...you do love me..." muttered Rafe, almost stunned that his fantasies of Greek lovers were coming true, loving the feel of the arms around him; Quinn smelled delicious, chalk and wine and sweat.

Quinn knew he had made a mistake, and summoning a courage he didn't know he had, he realised that he had to finish the encounter. He took hold of the boy above the elbows and shoved him backwards. He kept his voice deliberately harsh; he had to hurt the boy now, for both their sakes. "Rafe, what you are feeling is not love. You cannot love another man in the way you mean. God created love for marriage, for procreation. You simply have mistaken your feelings of comradeship for what you will eventually give to a woman."

All the while he spoke the traitorous words, his own heart was stabbed through and through, and his member throbbed beyond anything he had felt before. Every instinct told him it would be so very easy, so very easy to pull the boy to his arms, to lower his mouth upon those beautiful red lips, to reach into the boy's breeches and... NO! He tried not to imagine Rafe naked, but his blood was screaming its lust in his loins, and for a fleeting moment the vision of the two of them entwined on a bed branded itself upon his brain. He gave a wordless, choking sob and turned away to the tower steps, tore open the door and fled, leaving Rafe weeping angry, bitter tears.

After the night on the roof, Rafe and Quinn became icily polite to one another. Rafe retreated into aristocratic arrogance, and Quinn became business-like and more severe than Rafe had ever known him to be. He was unrelenting in his lessons, coaching him unremittingly in his least favourite subjects. He refrained from touching the boy at all, never even looked directly at him. The only astronomy they studied was from huge illustrated books, although unbeknownst to Rafe, Quinn returned to the roof night after night and sat in the darkness trying to rid his brain of the unnatural thoughts which were becoming more frequent rather than diminishing. He sat on the roof, leaning against the parapet, and knocked his head against the stonework as if trying to force the thoughts from him. The headaches he suffered as a result of these vigils helped him to remain impassive and harsh through the day's lessons.

Quinn became frantic. He knew that such perversions were punishable by the full force of the law; pillorying and imprisonment were the lightest one could expect if one were caught, but he could not help himself. Whenever he closed his eyes all he could see was Rafe in his arms, as he had been in this place, smiling, his lips parted, expectant for the kiss that Quinn longed to bestow.

Rafe was furious and hurt. It was all so simple to his boyish mind. He loved Quinn, and Quinn had proved to him that he was equally aroused, so he could not understand why the man was rejecting him.

This sorry state of affairs might have continued for some time, and indeed their feelings might eventually have cooled, but for Rafe's impatience and determination. He had never been denied anything in his sixteen years of life, and the thought of failure never entered his mind.

One Sunday afternoon, confident in being able to break through Quinn's resolve, Rafe sat beneath the stairs. He was an excellent hunter, and under his father's tutelage Rafe had learned the patience to hide in covert downwind, sometimes for hours. It was the tutor's day off, but Rafe knew he would be spending it in the library, and the only key was in his own pocket. Crouched in the shadows, he watched, hawk-like, as Quinn passed by and entered the library. Rafe counted slowly under his breath. Quinn had to get to the other end of the library, find his books and get settled. Five hundred heartbeats should be enough. As he counted, his breath became more rapid, his pupils dilated as the anticipation of the hunt excited him. Quinn, although older, taller, more authoritative, had become his prey. The hunt was even more delicious to the boy, spiced by sexual frustration. He had been hard for just the thought of Quinn for so long, and no matter how much he tried, masturbation seemed to give only a temporary relief.

Finally, he stepped out of the shadows, opened the library door, stepped through, and silently locked it behind him. He kept to the rugs to eliminate noise and peered around the line of bookcases. Sunlight streaming through the full-length French doors showed every mote of dust in the air.

Rafe's voice was soft and low. "You in here? Quinn?" He could see the tutor at the end of the room, and Quinn's head shot up like a startled deer's. Seeing Rafe, Quinn's stomach gave a familiar lurch, and he stood up clumsily. There was a look in the boy's eyes he had never seen before, the wolfish expression predominant. His head was slightly bowed, and his lips were parted as he stalked down the corridor of books toward Quinn. The tutor moved around the table and met the boy as he reached the end of the room. "Rafe," Quinn started, "you know you shouldn't disturb..."

Instead of speaking, Rafe kept coming, and Quinn, startled, retreated. Feeling one of the upright reading chairs behind his legs, he had no option but to sit. Before Quinn could think, Rafe threw his leg over the tutor and straddled his lap, his expression still one of menace and determination. Without words, he took the tutor's head in his hands and kissed him on the mouth, his lips closed, his breathing ragged.

Conquered, Quinn surrendered his soul. He was dazed, defeated. His arms flew around the slender form and crushed the boy to him. There was nothing — no past, no future, no time. Just the beloved body of Rafe, the smell of soap and sandalwood, the silken hair, long and loose over the shoulders. Quinn opened his mouth with a moan and Rafe thrust his tongue into him, possessing him, their tongues duelling, mating.

Rafe was ecstatic; he'd won. He'd won at last. The feel and taste of Quinn's mouth, so new and exciting, the hard bulge in the tutor's breeches which was pressing against his buttocks, the feel of his own heart roaring in his ears: it made him dizzy and delirious. Quinn broke free, and Rafe buried his mouth against the man's neck, licking and biting him gently, kissing the pale skin as Quinn's head rolled back and he murmured Rafe's name. With eager fingers, Rafe undid Quinn's stock and threw it aside, then ran his tongue over the man's Adam's apple. Quinn groaned aloud in pleasure, which made Rafe's insides melt away.

It was far more exciting than Rafe had ever dreamed of, and he knew he could not stop; whatever he needed to do, he had to see it through. Keeping his lips on Quinn's face, he tore his own waistcoat off and undid the strings of his shirt. Quinn's eyes flew open, and the raw, naked lust in them nearly made Rafe ejaculate. He had been expecting shock, disapproval, guilt, remorse, or disdain, not eyes that were hazel and gold infernos, terrifying in their need and arousal.

Quinn tore the shirt from Rafe's body, kissing his bare shoulders in passion, then pulling him further up his lap, stood up, picking the boy up with him. Rafe wrapped his legs around the tutor's waist, and Quinn carried him to the library table and sat him on the edge, then knelt down in front of him. With trembling hands he removed Rafe's shoes and hose.

Rafe looked on in amazement as Quinn kissed his naked feet. Rafe unbuttoned his own breeches, and Quinn gently pulled them off, together with his smallclothes. Quinn sat back on his heels and looked up at Rafe in worship. Tears rolled down the tutor's face.

"Rafe," he said in a broken voice. "Rafe." He had no words to describe how beautiful he found the boy. Except for his love of literature, he would have been at a complete loss. He began to quote Solomon's Song, murmuring the words like a prayer. "His head is as the most fine gold, his locks are bushy, and black as a raven. His eyes are as the eyes of doves by the rivers of waters, washed with milk, and fitly set. His cheeks are as a bed of spices, as sweet flowers: his lips like lilies, dropping sweet smelling myrrh. His legs are as pillars of marble, set upon sockets of fine gold: his countenance is as Lebanon, excellent as the cedars. His mouth is most sweet: yea, he is altogether lovely. This is my beloved."

Rafe's eyes were wide and rapturous; this was how he imagined it would be — a Greek love, filled with longing and poetry and he held out his arms for Quinn. Quinn stood up and started to unbutton his waistcoat.

There was a roar and a terrible crashing of glass. Quinn's eyes flew past Rafe, and Rafe's head shot around to see his father climbing through the shattered French doors, which he had broken with a pickaxe, now lying amongst the broken glass. Goshawk senior was shouting almost incomprehensibly; as he reached the naked boy and trembling tutor, the words were clearer.

"I suspected you were up to something like this, you unnatural sodomite! I knew you had been luring him to your room, but by God I'll see you hanged for this!" Without a glance at Rafe, he grabbed the tutor and threw him onto the ground, "How dare you touch my son? How dare you?" Using his cane, he beat the man about the head and body. Quinn curled into a ball as the blows rained onto him.

Rafe threw on his breeches and shouted at his father, "Leave him alone; it was me! I started this!" He tried to get between his father and Quinn, absorbing the blows himself as he attempted to wrest the cane away from Gordian.

Gordian paused in mid-stroke and looked at the boy as if he had never seen him before, then his eyes glazed as if he were looking straight through him. He was breathing heavily, and his face was suffused with blood, but he stopped beating Quinn.

Gordian's voice was icy. "Get out of my house this instant," he said to Quinn, who lay sobbing on the floor. "You will get no character from me and no salary, and if I hear you are tutoring any other man's son, trust me in this, I will allow the law to take its course, scandal to my family or no." Rafe moved to help Quinn up, and Gordian turned his full rage on him. "He has bewitched you, boy! You will not touch him! He is unclean! Filthy! Unnatural!" Once more, Rafe tried to get to Quinn, but Gordian called to the garden staff who were at the French doors. "Hobbs, take this piece of filth," he spat, indicating Quinn, "and throw it into the gutter where it belongs. You need not be gentle. Adams, take my son to his room, lock him in, and return this key to me."

Hobbs and Adams leered unpleasantly. Adams, the heavy-set gardener, grabbed Rafe by the arm and dragged him off. Desperately turning his head, Rafe saw Hobbs kick Quinn twice before yanking him to his feet. There was blood streaming from the tutor's nose and mouth, and with that last vision Rafe was dragged through the broken doors, which slashed at his bare legs and feet. Adams manhandled him through the house then threw him into his bedroom, and as the key turned in the lock, Rafe flew to the front window, sobbing with grief and loss, desperate to catch a glimpse of Quinn. He was rewarded only by the sight of both Adams and Hobbs dragging a clearly unconscious figure past the front gates and dropping him onto the street like a meal sack.

It was now pouring with rain, and from the window Quinn looked dead. Rafe tore open the window and screamed the tutor's name, his voice torn and broken, tears blurring his vision. As he stood there sobbing, there was a noise behind him as Gordian entered the bedroom, a horsewhip in his hands.

Rafe never spoke another unbidden word to his father from that day to the day he died three years later.

Two weeks after Quinn's departure, another tutor came to the house, and Rafe was allowed out of his room. The new tutor, Simon Mauvaise, was a puritanical, vile and violent man with a taste for blood and castigation. Gordian made no objections to the practices he performed on the boy. Rafe was brutalised, beaten, and humiliated. The youth lost all interest in learning, which goaded Mauvaise to worse punishments. Rafe was sullen and uncaring about the beatings; in his heart, he felt he deserved them for being the cause of Quinn's destruction, but he railed against the injustice of it. Mauvaise beat him for the slightest thing — being slow in a Latin declination, or translating a word incorrectly. On the few occasions Rafe answered back or showed rebellion and fire behind his eyes, he merited Mauvaise's particular favourite form of torture. The new tutor had discovered a lockable box in the disused icehouse at the back of the house, and his extreme punishment was to strip the boy, march him through the garden, and shove him into the small wooden box. There was barely enough room for Rafe to crouch, and as he grew in stature, the pain of being forced into a space too small for him was crippling. There were rats that crept into the holes of the box and being unable to move, he could not chase them away, and they had bitten his feet, his hands, his ears. He grew up with a horror of rats.

Winter or summer, snow or rain, it mattered not to Mauvaise, and several times he had opened the box on a sweltering day or a frosty night to find Rafe unconscious. Rather than producing any sympathy, the fact that Rafe's mind had escaped the punishment made the tutor violent in his rages.

One snowy morning as he dragged himself to his feet, blood dripped from his naked back onto the white snow beneath him. As he looked up at the windows of the house, dark like the Goshawk eyes, Rafe saw his father watching him, his face impassive and cold.

After three long years of this mistreatment, Rafe was changed almost beyond all recognition. He appeared quiescent and pliant, with both his father and his tutor, but beneath his breast his heart beat with a rythm of vengence. One day, he vowed, he'd repay Mauvaise — and his father — if it took a lifetime. When the time came, he went up to Oxford — not for the love of learning, but to be free of the horror of Tavistock Square...and tutors.

That thought brought him sharply back to the present. He loathed the idea of Sebastien being exposed to anything other than a genuine enthusiasm for learning. He would not countenance the thought of the child being sent to boarding school. He did not feel that Sebastien was strong enough for that, having inherited his mother's sickly constitution. Like it or not a tutor must be engaged, and woe betide any tutor who mistreated his son. Rafe was determined that it would at least be a kind man, and his brow furrowed again as Quinn's smiling face forced its way into his mind. "Stop at the village," he ordered the coachman.

As the fields passed, Rafe wondered what had happened to Quinn. Several times in the intervening years, he had tried to find him, but the tutor had vanished without a trace. For all Rafe knew, he was dead. The village came into view, and Rafe repressed it all again, his eyes shutting and his face becoming its usual beautiful mask.

Chapter 4

Rafe entered the solicitors' small offices, bending slightly under the low door. It was dark and cool inside, away from the sunlight. Having recognised the barouche through the large bay window, a clerk was rising to meet him.

"Mr Goshawk," he said unctuously, holding a hand for Rafe to shake, which Rafe ignored. "Such an unexpected pleasure! How can we be of assistance?" His eyes gleamed, anticipating the coup of obtaining the mighty Goshawk as a client.

"I wish to see your principal on a matter of business. Kindly tell him I am here." Turning away, he threw himself with casual elegance onto the large divan by the window. Ignoring the clerk totally, he gazed out at the sunny street, watching a group of young ladies of the village as they noticed the barouche. They huddled together, their bonnets touching, and then they looked around the street, obviously expecting Rafe to appear at any moment. When they eventually came level with the solicitors' window, they spotted him staring at them, burst into giggles and scuttled off. *God grant me strength*, he thought, thinking of the ball he was going to have to hold at some point to announce his arrival. The thought of a ballroom full of giggling frights such as those made his blood run cold.

The inner sanctum opened, and the clerk bustled out. Rafe stood, and the clerk ushered him into the solicitor's office. Crabtree was a large, red-faced man with a white powdered wig. Rafe took his proffered hand and shook it, then sat where indicated, declining the offer of refreshment.

"How may I assist you, Sir?" Crabtree said.

Shows the proper respect, Rafe noted, *but judging by the lack of paperwork around this tatty office, he's obviously desperate for clients.* "I will come straight to the point," he answered. "I am thinking of buying some land south of the park and hope that you can handle the transaction."

At the potential for receiving a lucrative commission, Crabtree's face lit up. Rafe gave him the details about the current owner, then when the man was well and truly his creature, he stood up and added casually, "Oh, and there is one other thing you could oblige me with. I need a tutor for my son. He is only eight, so the level of the man's knowledge does not have to be phenomenal — mathematics, Latin, Greek." He shut down his thought processes and refused to say the word "literature". He flashed his disarming, half smile at the fat, sweaty man. "Of course I could advertise, but I thought, as you undoubtedly command an important influence in the local area..." Seeing the man puff himself up, Rafe grinned inwardly. A local tutor would also be cheaper than some London based man with letters after his name, and possibly less inclined to perversions.

Crabtree didn't hesitate. "Well, you are in luck, Sir," he preened. "You have the ideal candidate on your very doorstep — young Standish, Ambrose Standish. He was in here not three days ago, asking my advice on how he might find employment. He is a little delicate, as he has been ill, but he is well on the way to recovery, and I know the family are in straitened circumstances..." He trailed off, embarrassed. The fall of the house of Standish was a well-known story in the small town. "If you will permit me, I will let him know of your needs."

Rafe's face maintained its icy composure. Everything always came back to Standish. Still, if the man was suitable for employment, it would help relations between the households, and Rafe would surely not be expected to patronise an employee. He realised with a shudder of irritation that he should have been to see the family before this, but he had been procrastinating, delaying the moment that he knew would embarrass them all. This lucky chain of events would at least prevent that. He thanked Crabtree with politeness and agreed that he would call at the White House the next afternoon. His mind a whirlwind, he allowed himself to be escorted to the door.

Ambrose had indeed been to see Crabtree, who had been the family solicitor for many years. The Standishes had not had recent occasion to use the firm for any purpose other than the Probate on Ambrose's father's will. Even as impoverished as the family was, they were gentry in the eyes of the townsfolk and were treated with respect and kindness by most people. Crabtree had known Ambrose's father very well, and Ambrose himself since he was a babe. When Alexander Standish was alive, Crabtree had constantly urged him to send Ambrose to Oxford, to outfit his son for some profession. *"By God, man, if anything were to happen to you, the boy would have to support the family. With his mind, he could be a doctor, a solicitor, a barrister. At the very least, consider the Church."* But Alexander did nothing, had the boy privately educated at an expense he could ill afford when Ambrose could have gained an Oxford scholarship with ease.

Now Ambrose was in Crabtree's office, untrained, shabby, and asking for help to earn a tutor's pittance. It made Crabtree's heart bleed. *The boy is the spitting image of his mother*, thought Crabtree sadly. The two girls took after Alexander with his dark hair and round features, but Ambrose, although he had the height of his father, had inherited Caroline's aquiline features, dark blue eyes, and silky blond hair. He was normally quiet and serious, the years of study and long months of illness having taken their toll on him, but as he rose to go, Crabtree assuring him he would certainly attempt to help him all he could, Ambrose suddenly smiled, and the room appeared to be brighter, Caroline's sweet and charming smile brought back to life in the dusty office. As he watched the young man walk slowly and carefully across the street to be met by his sisters, Crabtree felt helpless; he could not think of anyone in the vicinity that would need a tutor, and he doubted whether Ambrose would do well in London as he was still too delicate.

Crabtree was more than happy, therefore, to be able to deliver the brief note to the White House to inform the family that Goshawk was in need of a tutor, and would consider Ambrose were he interested in filling the position. It might well be the answer to the family's difficulties, and God knew they needed it. As the family's solicitor, he knew exactly how straitened their means were, and if something were not done, and swiftly, they would be destitute in a year. He also knew that Maria Standish was aware of this, but she refused worry her siblings over it, most particularly Ambrose, for she was convinced that to have to move him from Standish Park would possibly bring on a relapse that might kill him.

The next morning, Ambrose was reading Crabtree's letter, a smile on his face despite the ambivalence of his feelings. "He says that Goshawk will call here this afternoon to interview me."

"Why can you not go there?" asked Sophy, her brow furrowing.

"He should have been here on his second day in the county," snapped Maria. "It is disgraceful that he has left it a week before deigning to grace us with his presence. With our history... The man should not be received. Mr Arnold told me that he went to buy horses yesterday! Horses! He..." Obviously bitter, she snatched the letter Ambrose was holding out.

"It is good news, though, Maria," he said, his words belying his thoughts. "I shall be able to remain here with the two of you and travel to the house daily. I know that I will not earn a great deal, but it will help, will it not? I will have meals there also, and that will put less strain on those famous purse strings." He grinned impishly at her, and she tousled his hair and kissed him as he smiled at her again, glad she was placated.

I will finally get to see inside the house, he thought. *I will be able to touch it, to feel it, to be inside it, have it encompass me.* Ambrose's thoughts of the house were almost sensual, so long had he dwelt on it. He had inherited his ancestors' lust for Standish. He could hardly believe that, pending the interview with Goshawk, he would be able to go...the word played treacherously on the edge of his mind, but he refused to let himself to think it...home.

The morning dragged past. Ambrose, being denied access to the library until the late afternoon, did what he normally did when pent up and frustrated — he caught Aries' enthusiastic stare and said the two words he knew the dog was longing to hear, "Rabbits, Aries!" At which direction, the great wolfhound leapt into action. Aries had never caught a rabbit and never would, but both of them enjoyed the dog's conviction that he might do, given the time. The weather was hot and sultry, and as they walked out of the garden, through the shrubbery, and into the small bay on the Standish lakeside, Ambrose felt more positive than he had in years. As he thought of the employment he might be offered, he reflected on his tutoring abilities. He was positive that he could teach the classical languages, as he was fluent in Greek, Latin, and Hebrew. He knew that the boy had lived abroad for most if not all of his life, and therefore possibly spoke French or some other tongue like a native. Ambrose spoke French well, but with an appalling English accent, as he had learned it, as he had done most subjects, from books.

In the Sciences, Ambrose was fully up to date, possibly too much so, as his beliefs were sacrilegious in the eyes of some scholars. He had read William Smith's two masterpieces regarding the fossil layer under the soil and believed, as did Smith, that most people's view that the creation of the Earth took place in October 4004 BC was patently ludicrous. He hoped that his prospective new employer was not mired in the Dark Ages. Although he loathed the thought of meeting the dread Goshawk, he realised that he was actually looking forward to the challenge of teaching. Unless one passed on what one knew, what was the point of knowing it?

Ambrose found himself gazing across the lake to the trees beyond, wishing, as he often did when he stood there that he could see the house from this spot. He sat on the bank, the sun beating down on his head, and watched Aries grub about for scent of the elusive rabbit. As he got hotter, the water looked more inviting. He unbuttoned his jacket and started to remove his shirt. He had often bathed from this little beach, although it had been a few years since his last swim. Technically the lake belonged to Goshawk, but as there had been no one but servants in residence for Ambrose's entire life, that seemed a moot point.

"Come on, Aries!" called Ambrose, as naked, he waded into the lake. The mud beneath his feet was pulpous and unpleasant, but he knew the lakebed became rocky underfoot once he got further out. When he reached waist deep water, he turned to Aries, who leapt into the water like an enormous shaggy bear, barking joyfully, the thought of rabbits apparently forgotten at the prospect of a romp. As the dog swam around him, barking, Ambrose splashed him. In spite of his worries, Ambrose began to laugh.

Across the lake, Rafe and an engineer discussed the possibility of siphoning water from the lake. The front of the mansion cried out for a majestic fountain, and although he had not decided on a theme, he had started on plans for its implementation.

"If we cut through from this point," said the engineer, "it is downhill all the way to the parkland you mentioned, and the pressure will build up nicely; you'd get quite a high flume. Then we simply run a pipe down to the stream by the house."

"When can you begin?" Rafe asked, slightly distracted by the sound of a dog barking.

"On Monday, if it pleases you, Sir. I'll bring a team of men and we can start on the foundations and pipe works."

"Fine, fine." Dismissing the man, he strode toward the lakeside to see what the commotion was. As he neared the pines by the lake's edge, he could see someone in the water. *Poachers?* He rather imagined that poachers were slightly more discreet than to steal during broad daylight, but then the house had been unattended for so long, perhaps they had grown bold. He walked swiftly around the lake, keeping to the dark of the pines so he could get a better view. Reaching a high bank above a tiny beachlet, he could see directly below him that there was one man in the water, and a dog. They did not appear to be poaching trout, but rather...playing! The man was tall and pale, with shoulder length blond hair, and Rafe found himself staring at the man's body with something akin to hunger. The stranger was slim, almost too much so, as Rafe could see every rib and every bone on his spine. The dog became tired and swam back to the bank, and the man stretched onto his back and floated like a sensuous, oblivious lily. Rafe's breath caught in his throat, and he stepped backwards lest he be spotted. He realised that he need not have worried: the young man in the water had his eyes closed, enjoying the sun on the water and on his body.

Rafe had not before seen anything so beautiful. The companions he had acquired in his sojourns abroad were usually dark and swarthy, and Rafe had ached for the English paleness of this sight before him. From his long slender legs to his perfect flat abdomen and hairless chest, to Rafe's eyes there was no fault in him. His face was marmoreally perfect, his features long and defined, with straight dark brows, and whether he was seen or not, Rafe wanted those eyes to open. Who was this man? Rafe felt he had to find out, but he could hardly stride down there while the bather was naked. While he stood there trying to decide what to do, the dog barked again from the bank. The man righted himself in the water and swam toward the shore, giving Rafe a vision of flattened white buttocks that made him hard in seconds.

The stranger swam out of sight, and Rafe realised that the only ways down were to jump into the water or to walk the whole way back around to the other side of the lake. Rafe realised with chagrin that he was going to lose his opportunity to follow the trespasser. *Stupid*, he thought, *stupid. I should have called out. But surely someone will know who he is. There cannot be many people in the village of such a description who owns a wolfhound.*

The clock in the stables at Standish struck one, and Rafe recalled with distaste that he had to be at the White House at two. Just time enough to get changed into something impressive and go and dazzle the neighbours.

Ambrose walked slowly back to the house as the village clock chimed the hour, carrying his waistcoat and jacket, his shirt damp on his skin. Aries bounded along in front of him as he entered the house. Sophy was there to meet him.

"Ambrose!" she cried out in horror, "you are soaking wet!" She cut short his explanation that he'd been in the lake. "You do not appreciate how dangerous that is, Ambrose! The lake is icy. You will be ill again, and then you will not be able to work, and we..."

When Sophy broke off, blushing furiously, Ambrose realised with a shock just how worried his sisters were about their finances. "Forgive me, Sophy." He took her hands in his, feeling the unlady-like hardness of her palms and knowing that it was due to the manual labour she'd had to do; they'd had to dismiss their only servant several years earlier. "I was thoughtless and, as usual, too carefree. I never think of you two, and you have done so much." His eyes filled with tears as he realised how hard they had worked through his long illness. "I will get this position, and all of the money will go to helping you and Maria to take life a little easier. You will see; things are going to change. I feel it, truly I do — something fine is going to happen."

Sophy smiled at him, but her expression was still slightly sour as she led him upstairs. Like a child, he allowed her to dry him and tidy his hair. By the time she had fussed over his appearance and had dressed him in his only truly presentable clothes — a black suit, which only had a little wear, as it was normally brought out only for funerals — there was a sound of hooves on the gravel of the drive. They both flew to the mullioned window to see two chestnuts pulling an enclosed carriage. Sophy shrieked and ran to her own room to make herself presentable.

Ambrose checked his appearance in the looking glass. He looked respectable, if slightly sombre, and thus satisfied, he clattered down the stairs and joined Maria where she stood by the front door. His elder sister turned to him and gave him a quick smile, and Ambrose opened the door to his future.

Chapter 5

His future stood at the door, his back to it, waiting. As it opened, Rafe turned suddenly, at first not seeing who was standing there, the light making the dimness of the hall obscure his vision.

He was greeted by a tall and slightly horse-faced woman, who stepped back as she spoke. "Mr Goshawk, please, will you come in? Forgive us for not being outside to meet you properly. I'm afraid that we have no servant to tend to your horses."

Rafe noticed her embarrassment and knew the reason for it but pretended he did not. "Kindly do not trouble yourself unnecessarily," he said smoothly. "My man can manage." He entered the dark hall, removing his hat with one graceful movement.

A younger woman rushed forward to take his hat and his cane. His eyes, properly fixed on the older woman, remained on her face as he held out a hand to her. She placed hers within it and he wondered at the lack of gloves. Her hand was marred by callouses, emphasising the lack of servants. He bent low and brushed the back of her hand with chaste lips, smiling unseen as she gasped at the courtesy.

"Miss Standish. Thank you for graciously allowing me to call. You must forgive me for not attending you sooner. You will understand that there has been much to arrange."

Miss Standish indicated the young lady beside her. "My sister, Sophy."

"Miss Sophy, delighted to make your acquaintance," Rafe said, finding this all too easy.

The younger sister giggled as he repeated the gallantry with her, and Miss Standish turned to the third figure in the hall. "And this is my brother, Ambrose."

For the first time Rafe's eyes moved squarely to the brother. He was so exquisitely disciplined that he did not allow himself to register the shock and joyful surprise he felt when he recognised Standish as the man from the lake. Rafe gracefully held out his hand, feeling a thrill of excitement shiver up his arm as their fingers met.

"Standish." His voice was acidly melodious. "At last. I cannot tell you how pleased I am to finally meet you. The intertwining of our families has long been of fascination to me."

Rafe saw Ambrose's facial expression change from a glare, to dismay, then back to anger. Then Rafe noticed Ambrose compose himself, and heard him say, "Good afternoon, Sir." Ambrose bowed almost infinitesimally, as if unwilling to look at Rafe's face again.

This was quickly followed by the older Miss Standish opening the drawing room door and leading the way through.

Rafe followed the women into the room whilst Ambrose closed the door behind them. Rafe took the chair that Ambrose indicated was the best in the room, then watched Ambrose take the chair opposite his.

Rafe examined the younger man and accurately gauged the feelings clearly showing in the young man's face. *How very delightful*, he thought. *He hates me!* He was thrilled to his core. He wouldn't have thought that the angelic-faced, bookish man would have had that emotion in him, and the hunter that Goshawk was rose to the challenge. Rafe had encountered many a shy virgin before, and they usually bored him. He hated the social niceties required to achieve the inevitable seduction. Usually the Goshawk money was such a powerful aphrodisiac that his quarry would demur for too short a span before falling into his bed. Usually they fell in love too quickly. Rafe felt that this time he might not have it all his own way; this young man would not be the easy target that he had been used to. Standish would have to be wooed, and his cock stirred a little simply thinking about it.

He will be mine, Rafe thought, *but time enough to plan for that*. He turned his attention to Miss Standish's brittle gossip. Small talk bored him. After five or so minutes the women must have seen the impatience in his face, and they made their excuses and left the men alone to talk.

The two of them stood as the ladies left, and instead of resuming his seat, Rafe moved about the room, examining the books and ornaments. He stopped beside a large volume that lay open on a side table. "*Systema Naturae?* You are interested in Linnaeus' work?"

Ambrose remained standing by his chair, but his eyes lit up at the man's words. "Well, yes. It's one of my passions, botany. You've read it too, Sir?"

"Mm," Rafe said. "Although I do think that the tenth edition is far superior." Seeing Standish's face light up at the mention of the latest volume, he pressed on. "I have it at Standish, of course. If you decide to teach my son, perhaps you would like to see it. The book collection is well known, I believe, but that particular work is my own. I studied botany and chemistry briefly at Oxford, but came down early." He looked up from the volume and saw with great pleasure that Ambrose's scowl had finally lifted, and, although not actually smiling, his face was brighter. "He was very...inventive in his descriptions, I feel." Rafe riffled through the pages and found what he was looking for. "'*The flowers' leaves serve as bridal beds which the Creator has so gloriously arranged, adorned with such noble bed curtains, and perfumed with so many soft scents that the*

bridegroom with his bride might there celebrate their nuptials
with so much the greater solemnity.'" He looked up at Ambrose
and was delighted to see he was blushing. "Very...carnal, for plants,
do you not agree?" As he gazed at Ambrose, he could not help but
marvel at him. *He is so very beautiful*, he thought. *And he has no
idea of it. I warrant even his own sisters are unaware of it. He's
Ganymede.* And then he laughed out loud.

"Sir?" said Ambrose in a worried tone.

"Forgive me, Standish. It was impolite of me. You probably
will not be in the slightest bit interested, but I am planning a fountain for the front of the house, and you have assisted me in deciding
its theme." He saw Ambrose wince. *So, that's how it is*, Rafe realised. *He hates me because of the house.* "So, what do you say? Will
you come and teach my son? Any lover of Linnaeus is welcome at
Standish." Viciously, he said the word again to check that his guess
was correct, and was rewarded by seeing the anger cloud Ambrose's
eyes as the young man paused, then bowed awkwardly as if unwilling to grant any ground.

"I would be honoured, Sir." He knew that his acceptance
sounded too stiff but unable to warm to this arrogant and dangerous
man.

Rafe removed a folded piece of paper from his pocket and held
it out to Ambrose. He dropped his voice so it was now gentle and
soothing. "Read this after I've gone. I know that this meeting has
not been easy for you and that I should have handled the matter
with more finesse, but I am an impatient man. I always have been.
If I want something done, I get it done." He stopped and gave a rue-
ful half smile. "Forgive me. We should not be blamed for the faults
of our ancestors." Ambrose swallowed, stepped forward and took
the note. "If you still wish the post, it is yours. The conditions are
in there. They are not negotiable. If you accept, I will see you
tomorrow morning at ten. Please don't show me out, Standish. I
have wasted enough of your day." He swept from the room and was
escorted to his carriage by a much-flustered Maria and Sophy.

The gravel flew as Rafe's carriage thundered down the drive-
way, and the women hurried back into the drawing room to find
Ambrose pale and shaking, slumped in the chair by the fire.
"Ambrose? What happened? Are you ill?"

The meeting had been too much for Ambrose, and his legs had
gone from beneath him. The emotions of his entire life, everything
he felt and longed for in regards to Standish, had surfaced in a
heartbeat, only to be torn from him.

Sophy clucked over him, while Maria raved. "That man!
Shoves his wealth, *our* wealth into our faces like that. Intolerable
man. We should not have received him. You cannot work for him,
that's more than plain. You are obviously not strong enough and

he's beyond the pale. He's...he's..."

"Our only hope," said Ambrose helplessly. It was paid employment, which he had to have. He would simply have to bear it. The only light in the darkness for Ambrose was the anticipation of finally going to Standish. He realised he was still clutching the piece of paper Goshawk had given him. He opened it, looked at it for a long moment, then handed it to Maria. His face was impassive, but his eyes showed his resignation.

"What does this mean, Ambrose?" Maria's voice sounded almost frightened. "Four hundred pounds! You wouldn't be paid that by a college in Oxford!"

"It means, Maria," Ambrose said in a dead voice, "that I am bought and sold. He has Standish, the fortune, and now he owns me. He owns us all."

Chapter 6

Light crept slowly into the room, and the small windows showed the glimmer of the coming dawn. Ambrose was awake. He had slept but fitfully, finally succumbing to unconsciousness at around three a.m. As the sun lit up the sky, he woke again, and it was not for five seconds or so that the heavy weight of the day to come dragged at his heart and he closed his eyes again, preferring the blackness to the encroaching dawn. The euphoria of finally entering Standish had been completely eradicated by Goshawk's visit. There was a taste of bile in his mouth, which had been omnipresent since yesterday afternoon. His sisters had helped him up to bed, as he was feverish and weak. They had fussed over him until he ordered them from the room, his anger finally resurfacing and making him lash out at the only people he could, before collapsing onto the bed. Then he wept as he had never wept before, his hope ebbing from him like a life force. The night had been endless, and he had been violently sick again and again, but still he refused to allow his sisters into the room.

Now with the morning came a form of peace. A heavy, bleak and empty peace it seemed, but he had a starting point; he had to move on from it. His dreams were lost to him, his ambitions thwarted, but he had a purpose at least. If he were indeed sold to Goshawk, then he would do the best work under the yoke he could; his pupil was deserving of no less. As the light in the sky increased, he slowly got up and made ready for the day.

After dressing, he tied his hair back, and with his shoes in hand, made his way down to the library as silently as he could. He was still very pale, but his mind was clear. In the library he selected a few favourite volumes — Aesop's fables, a Latin primer and a Greek, not sure what books were available at the house. The House. He called it that in his mind now. Never Standish, not ever again. He sat down at the desk, unrolled the top, and wrote down a plan for a weekly timetable, using as a guide his experiences with his own tutor who had given morning lessons in the house, and then afternoons, weather permitting, outside. Thence had his love for botany grown. His tutor had been an obsessive plant collector and had transferred some of his fanaticism to Ambrose. Whilst picking up on his tutor's love of the subject, Ambrose had been extremely catholic in his study, and had found most subjects fascinating. This pattern of lessons he planned to copy with the Goshawk boy, if it was agreeable with the father. As he thought once more of the black-eyed man, mocking him with that rapacious smile, the bile rose again into his throat and he gripped his quill so hard it bent in half and he had to prepare another, finding perverse pleasure in the slicing of the nib. *Perhaps*, he thought, *the man improves on further acquaintance, although I severely doubt it.* Goshawk's Parthian shot about sins of the fathers was true, but Ambrose could not see that Goshawk was any different from the man who had taken it all from them — callous and unfeeling.

There were sounds of movement in the house, and Ambrose went to join his sisters for breakfast. He could see they were concerned after his feverish bout of the night before, but his unusual burst of anger had obviously persuaded them to keep silent. He had heard them whispering late into the night, and he was ashamed for having lost his temper, having shouted at them, but could not trust himself to speak further of it, as his nerves were so tightly coiled. At half past nine, Ambrose rose to leave. Accompanied by the women, he put on his coat and hat and started up the drive, only to be met half way by a black curate cart driven by a young boy in ebony livery with silver frogging.

"Mr Standish, Sir?" The boy had a strong Dorset accent and sounded terrified. "The name's Trent, Sir. The master sends his compliments and says that you are to have the use of this carriage every day. He has given me instructions that I am to collect you and bring you home, Sir." He rattled off his announcement parrot fashion, and looked straight ahead while he said it. Then he jumped from the front seat and waited for Ambrose to mount into the cart.

Ambrose hesitated, frowning. He was more than glad for the ride, as it would have been a long and weary walk, but his heart rebelled at the gall of the man who had simply taken for granted that Ambrose would accept. He hated himself, and he hated Goshawk more than he believed possible, but with his lips in a thin line, he pulled himself onto the little seat and let the boy wheel them about. When the cart turned out into the main lane, and then sharply through the enormous gates by the lodge, Ambrose found that his hands were shaking. When finally the cart turned to the left, revealing the house at last laid bare before his gaze, Ambrose felt the tears rise to his eyes. Close to, the house was startling; he had never before seen the North Wing, as it was set back from the main building and could not be seen from the southerly vista Ambrose had always used. The portico was taller and wider than it appeared from a distance, the columns elaborate with carvings of snakes and reptiles. Its sheer magnificence and beauty made him dizzy.

Rafe was with Sebastien, watching the new horses being delivered. As instructed, the little chestnut had been brought with the first delivery, and as he trotted down the ramp of the horsebox, Sebastien cried out in a babble of excitement, "*Papa! Merci! Il fait trés beaux! Je l'appellerai Marron!"* at which Rafe smiled, at the unoriginality. He watched the boy go and introduce himself to the little horse in true horseman's style by approaching the shoulder and allowing Marron to sniff him, and when the pony touched the boy's face with his muzzle, Sebastien breathed out softly through his nose to indicate to the animal he was a friend. The pride swelled in Rafe as he watched his son, then his teeth clenched and his eyes hardened as he wondered how his own father had thought of him. Had he ever known a moment's love or pride? Had he always been disappointed, revolted?

"Come, Sebastien," he called to his son, and the boy's face fell. "You can ride him tomorrow. Your tutor will be here at any moment." Together they walked back to the house, Sebastien skipping around Rafe, chattering about the hunts they would have and the rides together, father and son. As they cornered the house and walked past the conservatory, Rafe could see the curate's cart in the distance. There were two figures in it, and as his heart soared with triumph, his stomach turned over in a way he hadn't felt since... Refusing to finish the thought, he strode to the portico, climbed the stairs, and stood waiting, his eyes narrow and his expression victorious. *Non-negotiable, I said*, he thought. *I am almost surprised that he's here. Maybe he is not as proud as he appeared.*

Sebastien ran to stand beside his father, and as Rafe put an arm around him proprietarily, the boy looked up at Rafe in a quizzical fashion. *"Mon nouveau professeur?"* he asked, his voice pathetic.

"Oui," replied Rafe abstractedly. The succession of tutors he had managed to find in France had been worse than useless, and it was as much for this reason as for the boy's physical health that he had finally decided to come back to England.

The cart stopped in front of the steps, and Rafe waited for Ambrose to come up the stairs to meet him. As if in a bizarre game of king of the castle, he was challenging the younger man to mount the steps, which of course Ambrose had to do.

The symbolism was not lost on Ambrose. He stood for hesitant seconds at the base of the steps, pretending to re-arrange the books he carried. He had seen the man at the top, and he had not missed the significance of what his climbing the stairs would mean. It was a bitter re-enactment of some ancient tribal rite: the vanquished nation's king climbing to the throne of the new insurgent to kiss his hand and lay his sword before him. Ambrose breathed out. *This is madness,* he thought. *They are just steps, nothing more.* The house overwhelmed him, now he was so close to it, and the thought of finally touching it almost frightened him.

Trent approached. "Can I assist you, Sir?" he asked.

Ambrose did not take his eyes off the dark figure at the top. "I am fine. Thank you," he said politely, thinking inwardly that no one could help him. Taking a deep breath, he climbed the stairs to his conqueror. With the shock of the house, the sleepless night, and such raw emotions, his legs felt weak, and his head was swimming.

Rafe noticed how unwell Ambrose looked, and with a sudden shock of compassion for the beautiful man, he descended and reached him as Ambrose was half way up the steps. Rafe grabbed him by the elbow and waist. He gestured to Trent, who swiftly ran up and caught Ambrose by the other arm. Together they supported Ambrose up the steps, through the hall, and into Rafe's study. Settling the tutor on the chesterfield, Rafe dismissed Trent and poured Ambrose some brandy, thankful to turn away from the young man for a moment. Holding him in his arms, feeling him compliant and fainting against his body had taken his own breath away.

Sebastien was standing by the door, a look of concern on his young face. As both men recovered their composure, the boy crept forward. Liking the look of his new tutor, feeling encouraged as Ambrose gave him a gentle smile, he came to stand next to his father. Ambrose made as if to stand, but Rafe motioned him to remain seated. Ambrose looked up at Goshawk and was amazed to see a look of genuine concern in the black eyes. He accepted the proffered brandy, and sipped it gratefully.

"Forgive me," he said. "I did not sleep well, and..." He was unable to admit to either his illness or the emotions raised by entering the house.

"Nothing to forgive, Standish," Rafe said, his voice resuming its supercilious tone, "I understand perfectly."

Ambrose's eyes flew to Goshawk's and saw that he meant exactly that. *Damn him,* he thought, hating the man for enjoying his discomfiture and hating himself more for his weakness. His strength returned slowly and with it, the dull anger.

"Sebastien, I would like you to meet Mr Standish." The boy's eyes widened in innocent surprise. "Standish, my son." Ambrose heard the unmistakable sound of love and pride in Goshawk's voice.

"*Bonjour, professeur.*" Sebastian said, and Rafe chided him gently.

"English ,Sebastien."

"Sorry, Papa." Sebastien gave the tall man a quick look and a smile and moved to Ambrose and shook his hand solemnly. "I am pleased to meet you, Sir. I forget myself. I am having to learn to think in English."

His accent was a strange mixture of continental overtones, whereas his father's was purely English, with no trace of accent whatsoever. Ambrose was charmed by the boy's frankness and pretty smile. "I am happy to meet you, Sebastien. I hope we can be friends."

The boy smiled at him again and asked innocently, "Your name is the same as our house, Sir. Is that a coincidence?"

Seeing Ambrose's eyes flicker, Rafe opened his mouth to silence the boy, but Ambrose surprised him by replying first.

"No. It is no coincidence, Sebastien." His voice was cool, but even. "My family used to own the house, but it was a long time ago, and it is not a pretty tale. Perhaps you will learn it one day, but not today."

"What happened?" Sebastien asked.

"That's enough, Sebastien," said Rafe sharply. "Go to your school room, and we will join you later. *Maintenant, vite.*"

The boy grinned at Ambrose and ran from the room. He clearly adored his father, and was not at all fazed by his apparent ire.

Rafe turned his attention back to Ambrose. "How are you feeling? I had heard you had been unwell, but I thought you were convalesced. Perhaps you should wait a week to recover more strength? Another week without lessons won't hurt the boy."

"No, I am quite well," said Ambrose, flushing. "As I said, I did not sleep well, but I am more than fit to take up my duties."

Rafe heard the pride in his voice and admired the man for still having some after all he had been through. He longed to caress the blond hair, to see those eyes look at him in passion rather than loathing. It was going to be a satisfying seduction; Rafe had no doubt at all of its conclusion. "Would you like to see around the house?" Rafe asked, and watched in fascination as a complicated gamut of emotions showed plainly on the man's exquisite features. "I would understand if you did not wish to, of course."

"No," Ambrose said sharply. "I would like that very much." Then he added as if an afterthought, "Thank you."

Rafe moved to him to help him to his feet. Eager to touch him again, his fingers tightened around the black sleeve, loving the same thrill that seemed to start in his groin and radiate outwards.

The young man looke dup sharply as Rafe's fingers gripped his arm and Rafe caught a look of confusion flicker across the handsome face. Realising he was showing his hand far too soon, he schooled his features to a carefully blank expression and opened the study door. "Shall we?"

Chapter 7

As they entered the schoolroom, Ambrose's thoughts were in a whirl. He thought he had known the house from his father's repeated descriptions of it, but he had found it far more intoxicating that he could have believed possible. It had him totally under its spell. Not in his wildest imagination had he envisioned just how beautiful the house would be. The stunning decorations, although of an earlier era, were fresh and opulent. Even the entrance hall, of which Ambrose had thought he had the clearest picture, surprised him. The paintings of mythical beasts on the grey slate slabs were vivid in colour — the gryphons pure scarlet, the unicorns gold and white — and they were set around the edge of the hallway. He had imagined them to be black and white and in the centre of the hall's floor.

On their tour, Goshawk was affable and engaging. Although he had only been in residence for a short time, his knowledge of the house was encyclopaedic. Ambrose realised that he must have studied the history of the house with as much detail as ever he had done himself, and that made him warm to the other man slightly. Surely it was better that the house was adored and cherished than left to disuse and decay. The very fact that although the owner had never lived in it, but had kept it in such good repair all of his life, suddenly made Ambrose realise that perhaps, the house meant almost as much to Goshawk as it did to him.

As they entered to the schoolroom, Ambrose had a lump in his throat as he imagined the fictitious history of himself and his sisters here as children. It was a long, sunny room, with a golden floor covered here and there in soft rugs, like coloured islands. Toys spilled everywhere in an untidy profusion, and a small desk and blackboard were prominent at the far end. Sebastien himself rode a large wooden rocking horse in the centre of the room, wearing a tricorn hat and waving a small wooden sword.

"Look!" he shouted happily. "I am Napoleon!"

Ambrose couldn't help but smile, and he watched as Goshawk, laughing, pulled his son from the horse.

"Be careful, Sebastien," he said. "The English do not hold Napoleon in the same high regard as you." He turned to Ambrose. "In defiance of recent history, my son unfortunately thinks the man can do no wrong. I will leave you two alone; luncheon will be served in here at one. Good day, Standish." He left without another word.

Down in his study, Rafe sat at his desk, letting his breathing slow, waiting for his loins to cool. *Madness to feel this aroused over the man*, he thought, furious at his own weakness and lust. *To restrain myself from taking him forcibly may be the hardest thing I have ever had to do.* He didn't know if he had the patience to convince Standish to allow him to strip him bare in every sense of the word. With the image of the naked Ambrose in his mind, he pulled his crested notepaper toward him and wrote in an elegant, sloping hand.

> *Standish*
> *August 12, 1820*
> *Sirs,*
>
> *I have decided on a theme for the fountain outside the house. It will be classical in style and will depict the abduction of Ganymede. I do not want the usual imagery of the Eagle and the flight itself, but rather Ganymede serving Zeus wine in Olympus. I am coming to town next week, and will expect some designs by then.*
> *Goshawk*

He sat there for a while, allowing the lust to flow through him, unable to block the image of Ambrose, face up in the water like Icarus drowning. He was damned if he was going to resort to boyish masturbation over this — not now, and not here. He needed some fulcrum, some way to turn the man's feelings toward him into friendship, and then he could move on. It needed some thought; he needed to know more about Standish. Perhaps the sisters could help him there. Finally, as his ardour cooled a little, he left the house to return to the stables.

As he moved down the steps, he saw a figure in the trees across the parkland. When the man spotted Rafe, he vanished, and this time Rafe was convinced it *was* a poacher. As he entered the stable courtyard, he found Mizen, the head groom, in the harness room. The Dalmatians sat up expectantly at seeing their master.

"Saddle the black they delivered this morning, and send someone to fetch the gamekeeper." He turned to head back to the house without another word.

"Sir," said Mizen, "are you sure you want to ride him yet? He's too fiery. He should be gelded without delay."

"Saddle the black," Rafe repeated. "I'll judge my own horseflesh."

Still thinking of Ambrose and trying to invent some plausible excuse to interrupt his son's studies, he strode back up the steps of the portico. There was a small cough, and Rafe turned to see Rockley, the gamekeeper, at the base of the steps. He descended to meet him as the black horse rounded the drive, towing Mizen along.

"There was someone in the park this afternoon — over there, by the stand of oaks. Find out who it was, and bring him to me."

In the schoolroom, Ambrose sat on the floor, getting to know Sebastien. The boy was lively company, and was, as Ambrose had suspected, fluent in French and Italian. However, his Latin and Greek were almost non-existent, his mathematics were woefully inadequate, and although he had a smattering of modern history, he seemed to know not much else.

Following their very long conversation, there was a knock at the door, and Ambrose shot to his feet, expecting Goshawk to sweep into the room. So did Sebastien, his eager young eyes flying to the door. However, it was simply two liveried servants carrying trays of food. Ambrose realised that it was lunchtime, and he comprehended with a start that since he was now a paid, or rather, over-paid servant, he would be expected to eat in the school room with Sebastien. His own tutor had always been part of the family, the house being too small for school rooms and separate dining rooms, and he thought fondly back to happy meals with all of them laughing.

As they ate, Ambrose took every opportunity to learn more about his enslaver. He was ashamed to do it, but Sebastien was guileless, and he innocently answered every question Ambrose asked him.

"I was born in Italy," Sebastien told him, his table manners exquisite. "I never knew my mama. She died when I was born. I don't even have a picture of her." The boy's voice sounded more puzzled than sad. "We lived in Venice until I was five, and then we went to France after the war ended. I had a pony in France, but we couldn't bring him with us."

Ambrose found that he was learning nothing at all about Goshawk. The boy adored his father, considered him to be a great rider, but couldn't give any details of what he did when they were not together. It appeared that he was away "on business" for long periods, but then he also spent a great deal of time with his son. There seemed to be no women in Goshawk's life, and very few friends, although the boy had mentioned a dashing officer who had taught him how to execute a cavalry charge. Ambrose wondered for a second if Sophy's giggling charm might attract the man after all; he had been a widower for a long time.

He had a very conflicted picture of Goshawk now. On one side, a loving father, a man who loved his wife so much that he still wore black eight years after her death and had removed every trace of her image from his home. On the other, a mocking sarcastic man, with a total disregard for the sensibility owed to a ruined family, his source of income shrouded in clouded rumours of nefarious misdeeds. A man heartless enough to think that money bought anything, but caring enough to send a carriage for a convalescing employee. Ambrose was very confused. After years of hating the name and the very thought of the man, it was becoming hard to keep up the loathing when confronted by the real person.

After lunch they went out into the park, and Ambrose taught Sebastien the names of the trees, the plants and the shrubs they encountered. It was the perfect opportunity to look around the grounds for the first time. Sebastien was more than happy to show him around the near environs of the house, chattering happily and taking notes on a small slate to be written up later in a school book. They reached the river to the west of the house, and they sat on the warm grass while Ambrose told the boy the names of the birds and trees around them.

"There, Sebastien, do you see that flash of blue?" He directed his pupil's eyes to a small bush on the opposite side. "That's a kingfisher." They watched the bird for a while, then he ordered the boy to go and find ten different wild flowers, while he sat reflecting on the day. This at least was the best part of it. He realised that if he could minimise his interaction with the boy's father, he might actually enjoy coming to the house and teaching. It was Goshawk himself who was the cause of his acute discomfort, the physical reminder of why the house was not his own. He hoped that he would vanish on one of his business trips, and the sooner the better.

As he watched the kingfisher, he saw a movement on the far side of the bank. There was a shadowy figure there in the darkness of the overgrown trees. Ambrose could just make out that it appeared to be a man, and that he was staring across the river, but whether he was looking at Ambrose or past him to the house, he couldn't tell. Ambrose realised it was probably one of the grounds staff tidying the copse. There was a lot to do, he supposed, but he felt awkward under the immobile stare, so he stood up and went to find Sebastien.

Rafe was far away to the east of the estate, galloping across the parkland, his hair loose, whipping out behind him. His face was set in a grim line, attempting with the fury of the mad gallop to rid himself of the lust for Ambrose. *Fury*, he thought. *That's this horse named at least.* The feeling of the powerful animal between his legs, the rush of the wind on his body and face tearing the breath from his throat, exhilarated him as the horse thundered across the landscape. The lust receded, as the great beast slowed, gradually tiring, and Rafe returned to something like normal, his black eyes alive and sparkling and a small smile of the contentment that horses always brought him on his face. Fury dropped to a walk, and Rafe let the reins slip through his fingers, allowing the horse to stretch its neck, which was white with sweat. He pointed the animal toward the small box house in the distance.

As he neared the house the sisters emerged and the look of concern on their faces made it clear that they expected bad news.

Miss Standish approached as Rafe swung down easily and stood by the horse's head, holding the reins. "I must apologise for the informality of this intrusion," he said, seeing Miss Standish's unwelcoming expression.

"Is Ambrose well?" asked Maria, her concern was obvious through her barely concealed distaste.

"Quite well, and forgive me for causing you concern. I called merely because I would like to aid him in his tuition and ensure he that has the tools to teach his favourite subjects. I thought you might enlighten me as to what those are?" He politely declined an invitation to enter the house, citing the horse as his excuse.

Miss Standish, seeming flustered by the the sudden visitation, told him exactly what he needed to know. Ambrose, she told him, did favour botany, but it was not his first love; that position was held by biology and palaeontology. Maria then began a lengthy description of how Ambrose's studies on those subjects had made him ill.

"I can assure you, Miss Standish, that whilst your brother is in my employ, I will make every effort to ensure that he does not over-exert himself." Forcing the image of Ambrose's beautiful eyes from his mind, he was pleased to see a look of grateful relief in Maria's face. Finally, he thanked the ladies, apologised again for disturbing them, and rode swiftly down the drive, smiling.

Chapter 8

The days gradually settled into a routine. Every morning, Trent appeared with the little trap and took Ambrose to the house. Sebastien would meet him, either on the steps or in the hall, and together they would go to the schoolroom. For three hours they would study languages, literature, and mathematics, then stop to eat luncheon. In the afternoon they would explore the grounds, concentrating on botany, geology, and natural history.

The other thing that swiftly became a routine was letters from Goshawk. After the first day at the house, Goshawk was absent. When questioned, Sebastien simply shrugged in his pretty Gallic way and said, "Papa is away."

Ambrose assumed he was in London, and a few days later this was proven to be true when he received a parcel and a letter from the man himself.

Tavistock Square
August 20, 1820

Sir,
Forgive me for not advising you of my departure. Business matters have made my presence here unavoidable, and I cannot anticipate a return date. Please accept these books with my compliments. I am certain my son will appreciate you the more, when you have digested them, as will I.
I am yours etc,
Goshawk

He opened the package to discover two books: William Smith's *Strata Identified by Organised Fossils* and Cuvier's *Discourse on the Revolutions of the Surface of the Globe*. Ambrose's eyes filled with amazement. He had read the first, but it was a copy lent to him by friends of Crabtree. He had not read Cuvier's masterpiece at all, although he had devoured every review about it. His emotions collided violently: he was grateful for the gift, thrilled to own the books, but he was well aware that they would have cost as much as the meagre allowance his family existed on in possibly two years. His sensibilities longed to return them with a stiff note, but the scholar in him turned the pages with something like avarice. He justified his keeping them by referring to Goshawk's letter that they would be useful in his tutoring.

Goshawk wrote every day, usually no more than a line or two, always enclosing something for him, or for Sebastien, or for the entire Standish family — boxes of bonbons (asking him to share them with his son), unusual fruits, parasols for the women. Each gift was unreturnable, due to its perishability (like a small case of just ripened apricots), its usefulness, or because it was to be shared with Sebastien.

Rafe was experiencing enormous enjoyment over choosing gifts he knew Ambrose would be unable to refuse or return. The only personal gift that he had sent to Ambrose was an exquisite orrery. Ambrose was rapturous about it, and would sit and watch its movement for hours. However, he had determined that he would return it when Goshawk came back to Dorset. It was too fragile to post, and would be a costly thing to arrange.

Goshawk's letters became more imperceptibly familiar each day.

> *Tavistock Square*
> *August 30, 1820*
> *Standish,*
> *I trust you enjoyed the tonic wine I sent. My physician here tells me that it has no equal in helping one regain strength after the ague. I am fretful and bored here in town, and would appreciate it greatly if you would be kind enough to write and tell me news of my son's studies. I miss his daily chatter, and the recalcitrant youth forgets me as soon as I leave until the day I return, laden with presents to assuage my guilt for leaving him for so long. It is only that he is settled and being taught so well that makes me easy in my mind to leave him behind.*
> *Yours,*
> *R Goshawk*

Ambrose was troubled, and his clear brow furrowed. Seeing he was reading the daily message from Goshawk, Sophy quizzed him, and he looked up at her and said, "It is Goshawk. He wants me to write to him."

"Whatever for?" asked his sister.

"He says he misses his son."

Sophy clucked sympathetically. "I dare say he must do, and it shows a true depth of feeling that he should require news of him. Of course you must write. You are under a duty as the boy's tutor to report on his progress."

Ambrose realised that as the truth, bitterly acknowledging that he had no choice. At the great house, while Sebastien stumbled over the *Iliad*, he wrote.

September 3
Sir,
We are most sensible of the favour you do us by your contin-
ued patronage.
Please be advised that your son is well and happy. He seems
well adjusted to your continuing absence, and speaks of you often.
After our lessons, he has been riding Marron under Mizen's watch-
ful eye, and he looks forward to the hunting season. We are work-
ing on Homer this morning, and with his usual talent for
distraction, he begs me tell you to return for the first meet on 1
October. I have told him I have relayed his request.
I am much recovered, thanks to your thoughtfulness.
Etc.
Standish

Rafe brought the parchment to his lips and held it against his
mouth. He imagined that he could smell the scent of Ambrose on it,
and he rolled his tongue around the edges of the paper where the
tutor had surely touched it as he folded it for the envelope. The act
was so erotic his member surged and became lancewood. A voice
from waist height said, "I am glad I am finally having an effect,
Rafe," and Rafe's eyes closed as he felt warm lips encompass his
hardness. In his mind, instead of the white blond head of Francis,
he saw the long, soft hair of Ambrose falling over each side of his
member, the wide expressive mouth, the beautiful dark blue eyes
closed.

Within a day of his return to London, Francis had appeared on
his doorstep. He was hostile and angry; Rafe was simply bored.
Not wanting an argument for the Square to hear, he'd invited the
officer upstairs, preparing himself for the inevitable jealous tan-
trum. "No, Francis," he had said quietly for the fourth time,
"there's no one else in my bed. I can assure you of that."

"Why then? God, Rafe, we were good together!" He moved to
him and put his arms around him. "Surely you must admit you
enjoyed it?"

Rafe's temper snapped, fuelled by the suppressed lust he had
been feeling for so many days. He seized Francis by the back of the
hair with one hand and kissed him violently. Francis struggled, but
Rafe held him tight, then broke away and said spitefully, "This is
what you wanted, Francis, isn't it? This is what you have been begging for? I seem to remember you like it rough." He started to tear
the uniform from Francis' body, the gold frogging ripping under his
hands, the embroidery shredding and falling to the floor. The
jacket off, he ripped the linen shirt in two without bothering to
untie it.

Rafe pulled the man toward him and bit his neck hard. Francis cried out, but Rafe — with his hand still tangled in the blond hair — threw him backwards onto the chaise. Francis landed awkwardly and was winded, unable to stop Rafe from forcing his breeches down over his hips. Before Francis could react, Rafe bent down and grabbed hold of the officer's waist. He was not gentle; the lust boiled within him, and the release he sought could not be achieved in any gentle way. His fingers bruised the pink flesh as he yanked the younger man round onto his front and forced him to his knees, bent him across the chaise. He put his hand over Francis' mouth, then knelt behind him and released his weeping cock from his breeches, forcing it into the man beneath him, feeling the tight muscles tear open. Francis whimpered, but Rafe's hand muffled the sound. Dry, tight flesh around his cock squeezed him, milking the semen from him, as he plunged again and again, the sweat dropping from his forehead on to the other man's back. Francis' resistance and struggling only served to inflame him, and before long he felt the familiar surge, almost painful in its release, and with Ambrose's face in his mind, he ejaculated violently with a wordless sough.

Rafe was still for a long moment, feeling the lust ebb and drain from him into Francis, who had stopped struggling. He took his hand from Francis' mouth, expecting a tirade, and was almost but not quite surprised to hear whispered endearments.

"God, Rafe, that was wonderful, exquisite. Why have you never done that before now? It was like the first time again."

Rafe smiled, pulled out, and slapped the pink fleshy cheeks.

Since then Francis had all but moved into the house. Rafe at least didn't have to sleep alone. He found the officer a convenient vessel into which to slake the lust he felt for Ambrose, and the lust was constant.

Francis was surprised and most gratified at how often Rafe needed his attentions. Sometimes he hardly had time to remove his coat when Rafe dragged him upstairs; they were hardly inside the bedroom door before Rafe tore the clothes from the Francis' body, or forced him to his knees to take him in his mouth. Francis never knew that every time his mouth swallowed Rafe's hardness, and every time Rafe penetrated his fundament, it was another man he was seeing — a pale, slim man with long hair.

The anger Rafe felt that the body beneath him was the wrong one, made him violent in his penetrations, but Francis, eager and submissive, seemed to revel in whatever attentions were bestowed on him.

Swallowing at last, Francis asked, "Who was the letter from?" He moved up the bed and put his head on Rafe's shoulder and stroked his bare chest with warm hands.

Rafe could feel the calluses on his palms, rough from years of holding two sets of reins. "My son's tutor," he answered tersely.

"Is this the one you send all the gifts to? This is why you are in such a hurry to get back to your beloved Standish? What about me? What about us?"

Rafe felt too tired to have the same argument yet again. "There is no 'us', Francis. You wanted me to bed you, so I have been bedding you. Please do not try and make this more than it is." He swung his legs out of the bed and walked over the washstand. "I thought you understood that. My business here is done. I am returning to Standish tomorrow."

Francis' brows contracted, but he knew better than to protest further. *At least I have one more night. Rafe will be back in London soon enough, and I'll have him to myself again.*

By the time that Rafe returned to Standish, five clippers had docked at West India, all with bursting hulls; Goshawk was considerably richer. Happy to be going home, he looked forward to seeing the progress on the fountain, which had been commissioned. It would raise some eyebrows in the neighbourhood, but he had never cared much for other people's opinions. Very early in the morning, his coach stopped before the front door, and Rafe got out. He was wide awake, anticipating seeing Sebastien and Ambrose again. It was too early to wake his son, and he didn't feel like sleep, so he followed the coach by foot around to the stables.

Fury was awake and looking over the stall door, his eyes wide and intelligent as he saw the lone figure enter the yard. He nickered softly, and Rafe moved to the beautiful black head and stroked it, feeling the velvet muzzle beneath his hands. *Horses*, he thought. *They ask for nothing, and they take it all and love you still.* He kissed the horse tenderly, like a child being put to sleep, and the beast nudged him in the stomach, winding him.

"All right," he laughed. "Let's go." He grabbed the saddle and bridle from the harness room and saddled the horse swiftly, then mounted and cantered out of the yard.

An hour later, Mizen saw the empty stall and the coach that had been parked in the yard. He walked over to the stalls that housed the coach horses and found the coachmen still grooming the last two Cleveland Bays, all the while whistling through their teeth. He realised that Goshawk had taken Fury out, and he frowned. The horse had a bad bot infection on the off side of his withers and shouldn't have been ridden at all. He wondered if he was being overly dramatic, but decided that even if he was, Goshawk would not blame him. With Goshawk, as for Mizen, the horses came first.

He saddled a dappled grey mare and followed Fury's deep hoof prints as he set out after them. He travelled for a mile or more at a hand gallop, keeping his eyes on the soft turf below him, following the trail of fresh prints. The mare neighed suddenly, and Mizen raised his eyes to the horizon. Fury stood about half a mile away, riderless. Hating himself for being right and fearing the worst, he spurred the mare on and found Goshawk face up on the ground and deathly pale, with Fury standing over him. The reins were broken, the horse's knees, flanks, and hindquarters muddy. The master was also coated in mud. It looked as if the saddle had caused the horse such pain that he had reared and then fallen, crushing Goshawk beneath him.

Mizen leapt from the mare, tethered her to a tree, and ran to his master. He was breathing. With experienced hands, he checked Goshawk for broken limbs. His arm was at an awkward angle, but his legs seemed intact, and there were no marks elsewhere except for a vivid blow to the forehead. It seemed the horse had only rolled on his legs, perhaps breaking the arm when he stood up.

As gently as he could, he lifted the man, who was heavier than he appeared for all his leanness, and managed to get him over the saddle of the mare. He unsaddled Fury and vaulted onto the animal's back, carefully avoiding the raw bite on the off side. Grabbing the mare's reins, he started the long walk back to Standish.

Chapter 9

They were met first by the stable staff and then, as word spread through the house, by the butler and the footmen. Four of them gently lifted Goshawk from the horse and carried him through the house. Inbetween maids sobbed softly as he passed. The butler sent for the local doctor, and word was sent to Trent to go early to fetch Ambrose.

Trent dropped the reins outside the White House and pounded on the door. The family had just begun breakfast when they heard the cart arrive and the subsequent knocking. Ambrose opened the door and stared with alarm at Trent's pale face.

"You've got to come to the 'ouse now, Sir," the boy managed, swallowing his panic. "It's the master, Sir. 'e's fallen off that devil 'orse of 'is. I don't know..."

Ambrose paled, and without a word to the women who were standing in the hall, he grabbed his coat and hat, hardly listening to Trent's further explanation.

"'Ee looked half-dead to me when they brought 'im in. Took four of them to carry 'im in. The doctor's been sent for, Sir, but Mr Copeland said I was to come for you, to look after the young master."

By this time they were moving down the drive, and Ambrose tore the reins from Trent's hands and urged the little horse into a canter. His mind was whirling. Surely that man couldn't be dead? He could hardly believe that something as innocent as a fall from a horse could snuff out the enormous personality of Goshawk. His mind was on Sebastien; had they told him yet? The boy would be devastated, and he prayed that they had not, that they would wait until he arrived.

Like a small chariot, the cart careered down the drive to the house. For the first time, Ambrose didn't watch the house come into view as he concentrated on getting them there speedily and safely.

Trent gripped the sides of the cart in concentration, frightened by Ambrose's uncharacteristic grimness. Reaching the base of the stairs, Trent was almost convinced Ambrose was taking the cart up them, but the tutor yanked the horse round in time, and gravel flew up in a wave, scattering the steps.

Sebastien came tearing down the stairs and flew into Ambrose's arms. *"Professeur! C'est Papa, je pense qu'il est mort! Les domestiques ne me dirai pas ce que s'est produit."* He clung to Ambrose desperately, sobbing.

Ambrose picked him up, and they ascended into the house. The nursery maid attempted to disentangle the boy from Ambrose, but backed away at the thunderous look on the tutor's face. The butler, Copeland, came into hall. Ambrose's manorial instincts were now fully in control, and he took command without a thought.

"Where is Goshawk? Has the doctor arrived? What fool took it into his head to tell the boy before I got here?"

Copeland, who had been the *force majeure* in the house until Goshawk's arrival, was caught unawares by the tutor's sudden dominance. He took a step backwards, submitting to Ambrose's anger. "The doctor has arrived sir," he said. His voice was almost insolent, but his manner was subservient. "The master is still unconscious, as far as I know. I apologise for the boy, Sir, but he saw the men bringing his father in."

"Then someone should have reassured him at least," Ambrose snarled, sensing the man's antipathy, but not in any mood to appease it. "The boy was convinced his father is dead." He turned to Sebastien and said gently, "He is not dead, *petit*, I am going up to see him now. You will wait for me in the schoolroom, please." The boy sobbed but allowed a maid to pluck him from Ambrose and carry him up the stairs. Copeland led the way up the other staircase and down long, carpeted corridors to Goshawk's room.

The curtains were drawn back, and there were several servants clustered around the bed, most of whom retreated when Ambrose entered. They acted as if he were part of the house itself, and they treated him with the same deference they displayed for Goshawk, recognising his poise and obvious breeding. The doctor had set Goshawk's arm and fingers with splints and was just replacing the covers. There was a large red bruise on the wide forehead. Goshawk was deathly pale, and for the first time, Ambrose saw the face in complete repose without its sardonic mask. It was a long face, a rounded chin with pronounced dimple, high cheekbones and hollow cheeks. The nose had been broken at some point, but that added to his masculinity. The mouth, normally sneering or mocking, in sleep was completely different. The top lip slim and curved, the bottom full and broody. Ambrose realised just how very handsome Goshawk was, and was amazed that he had not been snapped up by some fortune hunter.

"How is he?" he asked of the physician.

The doctor wiped his hands on a cloth and started to pack his bag. "He's very lucky. His arm is badly broken, as are several of the fingers, and he has taken a blow to the head, which has caused his unconsciousness. Luckily, there is no fever. As to his recovery, we can only wait."

With a sense of some relief, Ambrose listened to the doctor's orders concerning the patient's care. After giving Copeland instructions to ensure someone sat with Goshawk at all times, Ambrose strode from the room and ran down the hallway until he reached the schoolroom. Sebastien sat crouched against the wall, his face dirty with tears. Ambrose smiled at him, and it was enough for the boy as he launched himself at his tutor, who went down on his knees to meet him. They held each other as Sebastien wept with relief.

From that moment, Ambrose took charge of the house. It seemed second nature to him. He had word sent to his sisters and he had had the room next to Goshawk's prepared and moved into it. There was a connecting door, which he left open day and night. He could not have said why he took over in such a manner. If he had been asked outright, he would have said it was a duty he owed to his employer and to the innocent boy who had such trust in him, but there was a dark recess in his mind which he had not examined, a Pandora's box which he had not opened.

Seeing Goshawk, usually so virile and strong, lying weak and helpless with no friends, no relatives, no valet, no one in fact, except the house staff and a dependent boy, touched Ambrose's heart. He understood about sickness and being reliant on others. In his long illness, he would have preferred a father or a brother to have tended to him. He had found it acutely embarrassing to be dressed, fed, and bathed by his sisters. It was not an experience he would wish on anyone, not even this, his worst enemy. So he became Goshawk's nurse.

For many days, the man was comatose, and in typical Goshawk defiance of the doctor's diagnosis, developed a fever on the fifth day. Ambrose sat by his bed every minute he could, cooling his forehead, dropping water into the man's mouth, changing his clothes and sheets when they became soaked in sweat. Every morning, Sebastien tiptoed into the room and sat on Ambrose's lap, and these were the times when Ambrose could sleep, holding the boy close to him like a comforter, while Sebastien watched his father as Ambrose rested.

On the tenth day, the fever finally broke, and Ambrose ordered the staff to change the linen and the mattress and bring a new nightshirt for the master. He ordered hot water, soap, and soft towels. Copeland offered the footmen to help, but Ambrose declined with a short shake of his head; Goshawk's dignity deserved more than being washed by his house servants whilst unconscious. Locking the door, he took a deep breath.

He opened the curtains wide to give him light enough to work by, then pulled the unconscious man to a sitting position, propping him up with the many pillows, and with some difficulty pulled the nightshirt from his body. Laying the man back down, he steeled himself as he pulled back the covers completely and tried to concentrate on the task. Wetting a sponge and soaping it well, he began to wash Goshawk's neck and shoulders, over the pronounced clavicle, then working down, the sponge travelling over Goshawk's chest. His chest was broad and muscled and much more tanned than Ambrose's own, each breast defined and slightly rounded, the nipples erect, hard and pointed. Ambrose swallowed hard as the sponge grazed them.

The sponge swept on, almost by its own volition, and Ambrose tried to think about what he was doing without actually seeing, but he found it impossible. He had never seen another man naked, except in books of anatomy — the skin and bone cut away to show the organs and skeleton beneath. He knew what his own feeble body looked like, but compared to this magnificent torso, Ambrose was as undeveloped as Sebastien.

Unable to resist, Ambrose's fingers traced the line of the muscles on the man's abdomen, marvelling at the texture beneath the soft skin. The sponge continued downwards, Ambrose growing bolder and strangely anticipatory. Goshawk's manhood was flaccid on one thigh, but Ambrose could see it was thicker than his own. Nervously, feeling almost ashamed to be doing it, he took it into his hand and swiftly soaped it and the sacs beneath. As he wiped it dry, he felt it move in his hand, and he dropped it in shock, watching. It rose slowly and magnificently away from the golden thighs and black curls, and Ambrose felt a thrill of panic. His feelings were such as he had never experienced before in his entire life. The sight of this engorged thing revolted him, fascinated him, drew his eyes to it, made his eyes sting, made his breath short and fast. What did this mean? Why was he himself becoming hard looking at it?

Ambrose was not uneducated; he had read of unnatural lusts but had always placed them amongst the *hoi polloi*, the Mollies in the east end of London. It never occurred to him that 'gentlemen' could feel any attraction to one another, but he realised with mounting horror that what he wanted to do more than anything else was to reach out again and touch that desperate piece of muscle.

He stood abruptly, his breath coming in soft, short gasps. He couldn't take his eyes off the glory of Goshawk uncovered. Blinking back tears and shaking his head, he knew he had to finish what he'd started. He took hold of Goshawk hesitantly on one side, his fingers digging into the flesh, and rolled the man over on to his front, away from the direction of his damaged arm. The sunlight fell on Goshawk's prone form, and Ambrose felt the bile rise into his throat. His eyes filled with tears of pity, and water dropped through his long eyelashes. The broad back was a mass of white scars: some long and whip-like, some thick as a thumb; some rounded like burns, and some with jagged edges. The story plain for anyone to see of long years of abuse and beatings, some much older than others, but none of them new.

His legs failing him, Ambrose sat on the bed and put a hand on the flesh, tracing the line of one long threadlike scar from the shoulders down into the small of the back. Who had done this? He could not imagine the man, as he was now, succumbing to such treatment.

It was a Damascene moment.

Whatever privations Ambrose had had in his poverty, he had encountered nothing but kindness and gentleness from his fellow man, and the thought of someone violating Goshawk systematically for years, with all of his wealth and privilege unable to protect him, made his blood surge with anger. Business-like once more, but feeling more protective toward the man than he ever would have believed possible, he washed the ravaged back gently, even though he knew that there would be no pain, then sponged the buttock cheeks and the backs of his long legs.

After drying his patient, Ambrose pulled him back into a supine position, and found that his eyes were drawn to the place where the dark curls met the thighs, to see if Rafe was still erect. Blushing furiously to find he was, he turned away, fetched a clean nightshirt, and robed him as quickly as he could. As he pulled the shirt down over the torso, he reached the hard, jutting pole beneath the navel. Ambrose reached out hesitantly to move it, so the shirt would slip over. As his fingers touched it, his own loins tingled with a fire he had never before felt, and his stomach, diaphragm, and chest felt as if they had dissolved. Unable to stop himself, his fingers curled tightly around the alien rod, and he ran his palm down it, loving the feel of the silken rigidity under his hand, although revolted by what he was allowing himself to do. Goshawk cried out, and for the first time since being carried in, he showed signs of life. His hips convulsed, the tip of the cock glistening with a bead of moisture. Ambrose backed away, frightened, suddenly realising what scandal might ensue were Goshawk to wake and find the tutor investigating his privities in such an intimate manner.

He quickly covered the man with the bedclothes and turned away to tidy the washing things. There was another moan from the bed, and Ambrose turned back. Goshawk's eyelids flickered, and he thrashed in the bed as if in the throes of a nightmare. The pale lips parted, and Goshawk muttered, "Standish."

Ambrose sat down and gripped the man's good forearm. He spoke softly and urgently. "Goshawk, wake up. You are home. You are at Standish; your son is waiting for you."

The black eyes opened, for a second unfocussed and confused. The head turned, and Rafe saw Ambrose sitting by the bed. He smiled at Ambrose with a true smile for the first time. "It was you. I was calling you, and you were here. You called me, and I came home."

Ambrose did not like the sound of what appeared to be ramblings; the man seemed delirious, his mind obviously confused. He stood hurriedly and unlocked the hall door, calling down the hall for servants, for Sebastien.

The man in the bed called him back, using his Christian name for the first time. "Ambrose, please, come back."

Ambrose went to the bed and watched him. He was still smiling, a smile Ambrose could not have imagined the autocratic man could have possessed. It was a smile that started in Goshawk's eyes, then pierced his own and travelled straight into his soul, as if he was being possessed. He sat down and Goshawk reached out and took his hand, his eyes drooping again as he slipped into a natural sleep, murmuring, "Rafe. My name is Rafe."

Chapter 10

The gloom of the last week lifted as Rafe recovered, but it was a slow process. Even for a man so healthy and virile, his body had taken such a shock that it simply refused to obey his commands. He was characteristically impatient about this, and it galled him that his legs would not yet work. The physicians, in whom he had no faith, assured him there was no problem with his legs and that the use of them would return in time, whether it be true or an attempt to appease him.

Ambrose had stayed on at the house in the adjoining room, and he spent every spare waking moment with Rafe. Something indefinable had happened to the relationship between the two men; the roles were blurred, the lines of defence and attack scuffed, and both sides were confused in the ensuing retrenchment. Ambrose read to Rafe, as the words hurt his eyes, read to him from the papers, and from books. They read Shelley's *Frankenstein* and, between chapters, the men discussed the morality of science over nature. They read Byron and disagreed completely over his style and meaning. Sebastien joined them for the early evenings, until his bedtime or until Rafe became fretful and tired. When this happened, he allowed only Ambrose to sit with him.

At night, with the communicating door open, Rafe slept fitfully, as was his norm with re-occurring nightmares of claustrophobia and fire, dreams he had had all of his life. Now however, when jolted awake, when the lid of the ice-house was removed, Ambrose was always there, soothing him and mopping his soaking brow.

Ambrose slowly realised that he was coming to love the man, and had no idea what this actually meant. He loved his strength and passion, and he loved the sweet dependence and trust he displayed to himself. Ambrose had thought Rafe had despised him, and soon found out that he had been mistaken in that belief. Under the lethal charm and sarcasm, Ambrose had discovered a vulnerable, desperate, lonely man. He had no idea what path the pair of them were on, but it was not a path from which he felt he would ever be able to step aside.

Rafe, in turn, had forgotten all thoughts of a black seduction. The feelings pouring out of him toward the object of his desire were, he realised, the same love he had felt for Quinn all those years ago. He was terrified lest he frighten Ambrose away, and so he could not act on the impulses he felt. He longed to pull the man onto the bed with him, frightened that if he did, he would never see him again, and the thought of that he could not bear. As the weeks passed and he became stronger, his legs started to respond to his brain's commands.

Ambrose entered the room one evening to find Rafe sitting on the edge of the bed, attempting to get to his feet. Ambrose strode to his side, worried. "Rafe! What the hell do you think you are doing, man?"

Rafe rose triumphantly, something of the old Goshawk returning as he conquered his infirmity. "Standing, Standish, or rather, not!" he said, laughing as he slipped and Ambrose caught him. Falling across the bed with Ambrose beneath him, Rafe grinned disarmingly. "Forgive me, Ambrose." His eyes narrowed as he watched the man so wonderfully close to him, saw the bright blond hair disarrayed on the coverlet. Rafe raised a hand and finally did what he had long wanted to do — he gently touched one soft lock, his eyes on the man's hair, then the finger trailed to Ambrose's cheek and their eyes met. "Forgive me," he repeated.

Ambrose's mind was a blank; he had no idea what he was being asked forgiveness for. Rafe stroked his cheek, and Ambrose's eyes closed as his loins lit with heat. The arousal happened every time he was alone with Rafe, and so he'd dubbed it Rafe's Fire.

Seeing Ambrose submit to his caress, Rafe smiled and leaned down and kissed him softly on the mouth, chastely and dryly. Instead of reacting violently, as he had expected, Ambrose's arms surged sinuously around Rafe's body and his slender shape pressed against him. He opened his lips and moaned softly into Rafe's mouth.

Rafe's eyes closed in ecstasy, and tears seeped beneath his lids. He had never experienced anything as sweet as this tender moment. With trepidation, he let his tongue lick the top lip of his love's mouth, and Ambrose's tongue came to meet his. The sparks that ignited between them as they touched made Rafe dizzy. Then the splint slipped beneath his arm and he cried out in pain. The moment broke, and Ambrose was immediately solicitous. Although Rafe attempted to hold him, he wriggled free and helped Rafe back into bed.

"By the gods, Rafe, don't try that again," he said roughly, meaning the attempt to stand and then realised what it sounded like. He grinned impishly, seeing the look of worry on Rafe's face, then leaned forward and bussed him quickly. "Standing. The other thing, let's try that again, often."

Rafe's heart swelled. The triumph of the seduction he had been planning was replaced by love and tenderness that was greater and more real than any devious success. To have Ambrose come to him so eagerly was more than he expected, more than he deserved. As tiredness took him, he watched the other man potter about the room, putting out candles and drawing the curtains. The last sight

Rafe saw before lapsing into sleep was Ambrose framed by the communicating doors.

He was freezing, and there was the feeling of the lash on his back and legs. Someone was laughing. It was not him, he was certain of that. His legs and side were numb with cold, and there was a trickle of liquid running down his back and buttocks. He screamed as the pain came again, and the fire he saw in front of him was a ship with sailors, ignited and leaping from the burning deck into the sea. As he landed in the water, his hands flailed to reach a rope in front of him, but it was snatched away. He grabbed hold of the man in front to find it was only a torso, and he screamed aloud as the whip bit into his back again and again.

The sweetest voice in the world was saying his name, and he surfaced from the sea. The fire went out, and everything was blackness; he could not see where the voice was coming from. He was freezing.

"Rafe."

Rafe called out in the night, "Where are you? I cannot find you." He could not move his arms. He was in the box again, but the voice persisted.

"I'm here, Rafe. Open your eyes."

Terrified, knowing he would see the rats, he obeyed the trusted voice. Ambrose was there, holding a candle. Rafe gasped, the breath coming back to him in huge gulps. He turned to Ambrose, pulled himself to a sitting position, and held out his good arm. No words were needed. Ambrose got onto the bed with him, holding the older man to him as a mother would hold a child, as he had held Sebastien when he had learned his father was alive. He kissed Rafe's head and stroked his hair, and waited for the man to calm, then moved to rise.

"No," Rafe said in a broken tone. "Don't go, Ambrose. Please. Don't ever leave me again."

Ambrose looked at him for a long time, then answered, "Where are we heading, Rafe?"

"I don't care. As long it is 'us', does it matter?"

"It won't be easy," Ambrose said simply.

"Damn being easy! Anything easy is not worth having. Just stay with me. I love you so much; you make me insane. Every night, knowing you are ten steps away from me and I cannot even stand to make those ten small steps to you... I love you, Ambrose, totally and completely." He looked at Ambrose, his brow furrowed.

"I love you too, Rafe," Ambrose said, his mind clear of doubt at last. "If I had been more worldly, I would have realised that the first day I met you, but I was too busy obsessing over the house."

Rafe winced. "I have never loved before, and did not recognise it when it came knocking at my door." He stood up, and Rafe looked desolate, then watched in wonderment as Ambrose pulled the night-shirt over his head, leaving him pale and naked in the golden light. "I'm yours, Rafe, body and soul, and I have been since we met," and he climbed onto the bed.

Another morning dawned, and Rafe slowly awoke in heaven, feeling the warmth of Ambrose spooned in front of him, their legs tangled. They had talked together softly long into the night, entwined around each other, kissing and touching. Nothing else, and Rafe found that amazing in itself. He had never had a man in his bed that he did not perform with. Rafe told Ambrose about his life in Paris, about the Terror, about his father, Mauvaise, the ice-house, and Ambrose had kissed his face and hands, had curled his thin body around Rafe as if to shield him from the horrors of his past. They were both erect, but there was no urgency to release the tension. When Rafe finally took Ambrose, he wanted it to be wonderful for both of them, and he knew his body was not yet capable of loving Ambrose the way he deserved to be loved. He bent forward and kissed the alabaster back and shoulders, and Ambrose stirred in his arms.

"Wake up, Eromenos," Rafe said softly. Ambrose's eyes flickered open, and he wriggled around to face Rafe, putting his face up to be kissed, which Rafe was more than glad to do. Rafe's pulse increased and his hardness grew, tickling Ambrose's navel.

"Mmm," he said. "Good morning, Sir."

"Just for that piece of impudence," Rafe smiled, watching the beautiful eyes open and gaze at him limpidly, "you can organise breakfast. Someone made me talk to him all night, and I am ravenous." He crushed Ambrose to him with his good arm, unbelieving that he was there, that it wasn't just another dream.

Ambrose's voice was muffled. "If you want my body to be broken, Rafe, I'll get a horse to roll on me. It might be less painful."

Laughing, Rafe released him and kissed him. "Unlikely." But he let him go, and Ambrose got up. Certain proprieties had to be maintained, and the servants finding Ambrose in bed with the master was less than wise. "But Ambrose?" Rafe pulled himself up the bed and Ambrose paused in the doorway. "I have to get out of this room. Get me a bath chair so at least I can get out of the house." Ambrose frowned, but knowing Rafe's impatience with his confinement, nodded, and promised to speak to the doctor when next he came.

"I will have one sent from town. A chair will be ideal for him," the doctor said. "But the English winter will not. I suggest you get him to a warmer place as soon as possible. He is making good progress and will be on his feet soon, but any return of the fever may incapacitate him for life."

Ambrose's blood ran cold at the thought of the vibrant physical man reduced to a chair for life. He fancied that Rafe would be rather under the ground than wheeled around on it. He resolved to speak to Rafe about it as soon as he could.

After the morning lessons, he had some instructions for the grounds staff, as the fountain was arriving that day. He strode across the park toward some of them who were milling about watching the fountain engineers at work. When they had their orders, Ambrose saw a dark figure by the river, and recognised it as the man he had seen in August. He was staring up at the house again, and as Ambrose got closer, he could see the man was clearly a vagrant, dressed in rags, a filthy cap on his head, fingers wrapped against the early autumn air. He didn't see Ambrose until he was almost on top of him, and when he did, he turned away.

Ambrose called to him gently. "Please, wait. I have seen you here before. Is there something you need?"

The man looked with surprise at Ambrose, seeming to discern that he was no threat like the gamekeeper, and relaxed, but his eyes were constantly darting to the house, to the grounds staff, and back to Ambrose. "Nothing," he said. "Unless you are a great alchemist."

To Ambrose's amazement, the voice was cultured and deep. "What is it that makes you stare so at the house?" Ambrose asked, wondering who this man could be. He looked old — his long hair grey and wispy, his face lined — but under the grime he could have been any age, from forty to seventy.

"This is the Goshawk house, isn't it?" the man asked. "You don't look like a Goshawk. You cannot be...his son? So, who are you then? He is here now is he not? Rafe?"

Ambrose started in surprise at the man's familiarity, and his tone became superior, annoyed at being questioned. "What is Mr Goshawk to you? How do you know him?"

"I?" The man was suddenly sly, and Ambrose began to think he was not in his full mind. "No, not me, I could never know Mr Goshawk, not me. Not suitable. Never knew him."

The man trailed off, and Ambrose was convinced the man was mad. "If you have no business here, I think you should be on your way."

The man moved to obey, but suddenly turned. "Ask him," he said, his voice cultured and normal again. "Ask him if he remembers the *Song of Solomon*," and he disappeared into the trees.

Ambrose walked slowly back to the house, and ran up the stairs to Rafe's room. The doctor was there, removing the splints from his arm, and Rafe was in a joyful mood. His bones had mended well, and the doctor had brought him some crutches to use until the chair arrived. He beamed as Ambrose entered the room and, all thoughts of the tramp forgotten, he crossed to Rafe's side, longing to kiss him but unable to do so in front of the doctor.

"Fitzpatrick here says I should get out of country for my health. Dashed physicians, they tell me to bring my son to England for the climate, and now I have to leave it for a sunnier one. It gives me an idea, though, and I would be appreciative of your opinion, Standish." Ambrose smiled at the sudden formality in front of strangers. "What do you say to a Grand Tour? I know the lad is far too young, but we don't have to do the whole round. I thought Paris, Versailles, Rome and Venice to start with."

He looked at Ambrose with an eager expression, and Ambrose realised that Rafe was wooing him, attempting to wrap up the world and give it to him as a present. The beneficent heart, so loving and giving with his son, had found another outlet for its boundless generosity. Ambrose politely showed the doctor out, then raced back to Rafe, threw himself onto the bed, and kissed him furiously and hard.

Rafe laughed. "Careful, you make Fury seem delicate!" They composed themselves quickly as Sebastien entered, and lunch was served around the bed. Rafe told Sebastien of the plans for a Grand Tour. Sebastien was only mildly interested and worried about leaving Marron alone. But when Ambrose described the Venetian Carnival and the Palio horse race at Sienna, he perked up and seemed enthusiastic. After they had eaten, the boy returned to the school room, and the men had half an hour to themselves.

Ambrose locked the door and was gathered into Rafe's waiting arms. Rafe kissed him with such tenderness and such unmistakable love that tears welled up in his eyes. He had not analysed his feelings for Rafe as right or wrong. They felt perfectly right, perfectly natural; he did not see how could anyone say they were wrong. Rafe groaned and rolled over so that he was propped up over Ambrose.

Ambrose opened his eyes and kissed the end of Rafe's beautiful broken nose. "Rafe, something strange happened just before lunch," he said, frowning. He recounted his meeting with the man in the park.

Rafe looked puzzled. "He said he knew me? That's odd. I have very few acquaintances here, and certainly none that fit that description." He kissed Ambrose's neck and bit it with teasing teeth, licking up from the neck to the small ears.

Ambrose closed his eyes at the blissful feelings this invoked, and continued. "He said something else strange, too. He was obviously educated, or perhaps he was just trying to be clever. Mmmm, that is nice. He said, 'Ask him if he remembers the *Song of Solomon.*'"

It was as well that Ambrose had his eyes shut, for if he had seen the look in his lover's eyes, the sheer blank horror, he would have realised that Rafe knew exactly who it was out there in the park, watching.

Chapter 11

They were dangerously close to their first argument. It was in bed, so they could not even shout.

"Don't be impossible, Rafe," said Ambrose evenly. "You can't go up to London."

"And I can only tell you that I must. There are certain matters that only I can deal with, and besides I need to go to organise the tour."

"You are not strong enough. You can't walk yet."

"I hardly need to. I have a bath chair, I have crutches, I have three carriages in London, and I have staff sitting around eating me out of house and home. I promise you faithfully that I will not even attempt to stand." Seeing Ambrose weaken, he kissed him.

"At least take me with you," Ambrose whispered.

"I need you here, my love," Rafe murmured into his neck. "God, do I need you." He groaned and his hands flew over the slender frame as he pulled him close to press skin against skin. "You need to oversee the closing of the house, which I am not fit to do, the packing, and the boy's education. Oh, and..."

"What else?" asked Ambrose, still smarting from the imminent desertion.

"You will need to write me every day," Rafe said, his black eyes passionate. He hadn't changed so very drastically; he was more than capable of manipulating people to his own ends. He smiled as he saw Ambrose relax. "My Icarus," he muttered, kissing his forehead, his nose, his eyelids. The room was lit by many candles and the men lay on top of the coverlet. Rafe was propped up on his elbows looking down with longing into Ambrose's eyes.

"Icarus?" murmured Ambrose, his head tipping back as Rafe kissed his neck and shoulders.

"Icarus drowning," Rafe whispered, as Ambrose's gentle hands went around him and stroked his back. He went on to describe the time when he had first seen him, naked in the lake.

Ambrose's member, already hard, throbbed wildly as he remembered that day, floating peacefully in the cool dark water, and all the time, Rafe had been above him on the cliff. "My God, Rafe, you...make me...you know?" Ambrose put his hand on his own hardness, and gripped it.

Rafe saw what he was doing and said gently, "Let me." The younger man looked nervous, but when he felt another's hand on his hardness for the first time he cried aloud, making Rafe kiss him quickly to stifle the noise. As he kissed him, his tongue dancing between his teeth, his hand pumped the slender organ.

Ambrose's head was on fire. He couldn't concentrate on the kiss; all he could feel was divine inguinal pressure. He thrust against Rafe's stroking hand, and small cries of pleasure came from him in rhythm to the action of the practised fingers.

As the sound changed, Rafe realised Ambrose was close to release, and he held the man as close to him as he could. Ambrose sobbed his name, the semen shooting from him into Rafe's hand and over his own stomach. Rafe kissed his face again and again, as Ambrose fell back to the bed, his mouth open, his pale cheeks aflame. His breathing was so shallow it could hardly be detected, and for a moment Rafe was frightened he had hurt his lover in some way. He called him softly, and Ambrose opened his supernal blue eyes.

The look in them made Rafe ejaculate without any further stimulation. The love radiating from Ambrose was almost a holy reverence, nearly frightening in its intensity, like an inner light.

"I adore you," Rafe whispered. "What we have is nothing that anyone has had before. Divine. Eternal." He held Ambrose to him, fiercely and protectively. "Nothing," he murmured into Ambrose's ear, "nothing shall part us, I swear it to you."

The next morning, as the sun climbed past the horizon, Rafe lay on his back, staring at the canopy of the ornate bed; Ambrose slept sweetly in the crook of his arm. Rafe's mind raced. He had formulated a plan, but he needed to manipulate his love, to lie to him, and Rafe realised just how dangerous this might be.

Ambrose opened his eyes without stirring, saw his lover awake and thinking. "Rafe?" he said softly, "what's wrong?"

Rafe's expression immediately softened as he turned to Ambrose and saw him worried, his eyes wide and his hair dishevelled. Rafe ran a finger down Ambrose's nose and rested it on his lips, allowing Ambrose to kiss the tip. "You look no more than fifteen years of age lying there. Makes me feel old to look at you."

"You aren't old, my love," Ambrose said, taking the finger into his mouth and sucking it. "Maybe too old for such fiery horses perhaps. I will ask Mizen to see about finding you something broad backed, with feet like soup dishes."

"Presumptuous youth," laughed Rafe. "You should show more respect to your elders. Tell me, would you like to take the boy on a trip to Lyme?"

"I can think of nothing I would like more," Ambrose said eagerly, then seeing the mocking expression on Rafe's face, he blushed and added, "Almost nothing! While you were in London before, I was tempted to write to you and ask you then, but..." He trailed off, thinking back those few short weeks. The Ambrose of August seemed a different person than the Ambrose of October.

"But you did not want to ask me for anything back then, my stiff necked Standish." Rafe stroked his hair tenderly. "I think it would be the ideal time. Take him tomorrow. I won't be leaving for London for a few days in any event, and the hills and cliffs of Lyme are not conducive to a bath chair. When you return, I'll set off for town. You can close the house and meet me in Tavistock Square in two weeks. Does that sound agreeable?"

Ambrose agreed readily, sighing as Rafe's hands slid down his flanks and between his legs, and it was not until much later that he realised that Rafe had changed the subject so dextrously he hadn't noticed his doing so.

The rest of the day passed in a blur. Ambrose had never actually been away to stay anywhere, and had little or no idea what he was doing. Rafe, however, chairbound though he was, managed the whole affair of packing by bellowing at everyone in turn, and although Ambrose should have been embarrassed for the staff, he revelled in seeing the animation returning and the supreme confidence rising in Goshawk.

Once, when he was berating a footman for taking the wrong books from a shelf, Rafe saw Ambrose looking at him, and he grinned, his eyes alight with mischief. "Hope you are taking notes, Standish," he shouted. "Next week you will have to pack for all of us for at least six months!" Ambrose paled slightly and did not reply. Rafe, seeing the fright flicker across his beloved's face, wheeled himself closer to Ambrose and whispered, "Take no notice of me. Copeland will do it all. I know that, and he knows that; I just like to make them all run around." Wheeling back to the chaos and confusion, he frightened a parlour maid who flew out of the room, her apron covering her mouth. Ambrose didn't have the heart to scold him, as Rafe was having such a wonderful time simply being Goshawk again.

By noon they were ready to go, and Ambrose sat in the barouche with Sebastien and two liveried grooms. Ambrose had told Rafe that he was not happy travelling in such style and would be happier to go in the curate cart with Trent. He loathed the idea of travelling in such extravagance, and was terrified of the attention he would attract in the small town, arriving in such ostentation. But Rafe would not listen. He pressed money on Ambrose, more money than he had ever held or indeed seen in his entire life; Ambrose tried to refuse it. Finally he acquiesced, not wanting to make a scene in front of the staff. He realised that Rafe was not trying to buy him, but was simply attempting to make Ambrose as comfortable as possible, to pamper him, give him everything he thought he deserved. It had been the same with clothes, when Rafe suggested as discreetly as Rafe ever could, that he would like to buy Ambrose some new clothes. He had taken some days to convince, and when he had finally succumbed to Rafe's constant entreaties, more clothes had been ordered for the tutor than he had ever owned in his life. It was, Ambrose realised, Rafe's way of proving his love, and he did it only with the people he truly adored and trusted — Sebastien — and now Ambrose.

The public farewell was subdued and formal, both men playing the part of master and tutor. The private farewell had been passionate and agonising, although they realised it was unnecessary. It would only be for three days, but suddenly it seemed a lifetime. Ambrose could not bear to think how he would live without Rafe there holding him when he woke, or without himself holding Rafe while the nightmares wracked him for two whole weeks when Rafe went to London.

Rafe's eyes were black fires, banked fires, damped down and smoking with longing. He stared at Ambrose, all the while giving him instructions on how to find the better place to stay in Lyme, whose company to avoid, how to ensure the staff looked after the horses, as if branding the man's face into his mind. As Rafe finally let the carriage go, it took every ounce of Ambrose's willpower not to hang out of the back of the barouche, waving and shouting as Sebastien did, but keep his eyes firmly on the road in front.

Rafe sat in the driveway until the carriage disappeared from view; his cheek twitching as he felt the loss of Ambrose, his arms suddenly bereft. Then he wheeled round and ordered a staring footman to summon Rockley to his study, and only then allowed himself to be carried up the steps.

Rockley knocked on the door of the inner sanctum and entered, cap in hand. Rafe was behind the desk, his bath chair hidden by the huge piece of furniture. "You failed me, Rockley," Goshawk said. "I asked you to obey a simple order, and you failed me. How difficult is it to bring a simple vagrant to me?"

"Sir," Rockley started, "he's harmless..."

"And your *opinion* gave you the right to disobey me, did it?" His voice was lethal.

"No, Sir," the gamekeeper replied, now frightened. He knew the man was incapacitated, but it did not make him less dangerous.

"Find him, Rockley, and I don't mean this month or this week. Find him today, right now, and bring him to me."

Rockley backed from the room. He hated to have to bring the old tramp to Goshawk, fearing what the master might do to him, but he had no choice. It was either the vagrant or his position. He owed the tramp nothing, and his family everything.

Rafe was still sitting silently in his office an hour later when there was a commotion from outside — sounds of men shouting, an animalistic roaring, and women shrieking. The door flew open, and Rockley and two grounds staff crashed in, holding a filthy, ragged figure. He was very tall and dressed, or perhaps almost wrapped, in rags, no item of clothing recognisable. His face was black with dirt and tanned a deep brown from an outside existence, his hair, grey, long, and matted. Rafe waited impassively as they dragged the man into the room. Upon seeing Rafe — his eyes dead, his elbows on the desk, his fingers templed before him — the beggar ceased struggling. Rafe motioned for the staff to unhand him, and they stepped back, leaving the vagrant panting.

The man stared at Rafe, a look of curiosity and venal cunning on his face. Rafe's voice was autocratic, demanding. "Do I know you?" The man's eyes closed, and his head fell to one side, his fingers picking at a piece of cloth. His mouth worked and he seemed to be saying something to himself, but he didn't speak aloud. "I asked you a question!" Rafe's voice rose; it was not a shout, but steely and commanding. "Tell me who you are, what you are doing on my land, and how you know me."

"N-n-no one and nothing," said the man. "No one." It was almost a gibber.

One of the staff kicked him. "You will call the master 'Sir'!"

Rafe turned on the footman, angry at last. "Leave him!" He turned again to the beggar and said in a quieter tone, "Come now, you must have a name."

The man's eyes closed and he looked down at the floor. "If I ever had a name," he said, suddenly lucid, "it was Patroclus."

Although he was half expecting it, Rafe's blood froze and his head spun. "Get out," he said to the staff. "Leave him with me and get out." The staff looked worried and confused, but they left hurriedly.

The man's arms were hanging by his side now and there was a look of peace on his filthy face. "Don't you know me, Rafe?"

Rafe's face was a mask, his lips thin. "Quinn." It was a statement, a final admission, something he realised he had known since seeing the man in the park in the summer. He looked at him keenly. There was nothing there, not in the face or the voice that he could have recognised. If the man had been placed next to five men of the same height and colouring, Rafe would not have been able to pick his first love from the line. But his eyes, open and softly staring with a hazel hunger, were unmistakable and looked at him across twenty-four long years.

Not knowing what else to say, Rafe said, "Sit down, Quinn." His mind was in a torment, and he had no idea what to do next. "Tell me what it is that you want, why you are here, and why you've been haunting the house."

"I had been waiting, for a long time, to see Rafe. Now we finally meet, I find that he no longer exists, and all that lives here is the son of the man who destroyed me. I want nothing from the mighty

Goshawk. I have had all I can stomach from the name." Quinn sat down, as if suddenly fatigued. Without further prompting, he began to talk, as if he had been rehearsing what he would say on this day for many years, as was probably the case. He started with that day in the rain, lying unconscious in the gutter, and told his sorry tale through to the day, several years ago, when he had arrived on the Standish estate and had started his long vigil.

The tale was pathetic in its degradation. He had gone first to cousins in Suffolk, his only family, walking the distance. He had had nothing except the clothes on his back to sell. The cousins were shocked but kindly and allowed him sanctuary until word arrived from Rafe's father, a letter describing what had happened at the house with an additional account of things that had not happened but were simply in Goshawk's imagination. The cousins were horrified and asked him to leave, being kind enough at least to give him food, a little money, and clothes.

And so the persecution began. It seemed that Goshawk Senior knew where Quinn was at all times, as if he were having him followed. If he managed to get work in a town or a village, lowly work — such as on the fields or in a public house — after a short time, there would be a letter, and dismissal with no reasons given. Finally, in an attempt to disappear, Quinn had returned to London. His voice broke when he spoke of the things he did to stay alive, a sorry tale of theft and prostitution, which had ended in prison on more than one occasion. The last term of incarceration had been five years, and after he was released, he had made the long trek to Standish.

The irony of it, Rafe realised, was that when Quinn had given up and had sunk so low, his father was dead and the man could have returned to a decent trade. He listened to the tale without allowing his emotions to the surface. The spectre of Ambrose floated between Rafe and Quinn like an ethereal wall. Ambrose must never know; he was certain that if he found out about Quinn, the young man's sensibilities would be shocked beyond imagining, and he would never look at Rafe with those innocent eyes again.

Quinn finished at last and sat in the chair, his head bowed, like a condemned man awaiting judgment. Rafe realised there was nothing he could offer the man to make up for the mistreatment he had suffered, but he could do one thing and one thing only. He rang a bell behind him and two of the men who had dragged Quinn in reappeared.

"I would like you to give our guest a bath, and let him have one of the rooms in the north wing." Every eye in the room looked shocked, including Quinn's. "Clean clothes, and a haircut. After that, you are to prepare the North Lodge. I wish Mr Quinn to live there from now on. You may go." He had not looked again at

Quinn. The footmen moved to either side of the ravaged man and helped him to his feet gently, sensible of his now elevated status.

Quinn caught Rafe's eyes, but all he saw there were the dead black eyes of his father. The small spark of hope that was in Quinn's eyes faded, and he allowed himself to be led away.

The door closed on them at last, and Rafe's head sank to the desk, a terrible presentiment overwhelming him.

Chapter 12

The barouche descended the long, steep hill into Lyme, one coachman carefully applying the brakes and one holding the horses' heads as they walked, slipping slightly on the cobbled street. Sebastien was overexcited and babbling happily in French, Ambrose not feeling at all like curbing him. He ached with missing Rafe and having the animated child with him, chattering away, was some solace. He looked so much like his father, the same straight brows, wolfish slanted eyes — but blue, not black, the same shape face, but a straight, childish nose and a cupid's bow of a mouth. His mother must have been very beautiful, and Ambrose felt a chill of jealousy thinking of Rafe with her. Never having loved before, Ambrose was discovering just how jealous he could be. He now found it almost impossible to imagine Rafe married, and the very thought revolted him.

Eventually, they made it down to the Royal Lion at the heart of the town. Ambrose became painfully aware of the attention the barouche and liveried servants attracted. The Goshawk crest was well known, and fashionable men and women in the street pointed out the coat of arms on the barouche door, with its gold and silver birds of prey. He blushed furiously as officers riding by saluted, assuming him to be more than he was. He wished at least that they could have folded up the hood. They stopped in front of the hotel, and Ambrose had to check himself to keep from getting out on his own, to remember that he had to have the door opened for him. He thought of Rafe and how he would be if he were there, and, finding strength in the man's overwhelming confidence, he strode into the hotel with a fair show of borrowed arrogance.

Recognising the unmistakable signs of breeding and money, the innkeeper ushered Ambrose to his best suite of rooms. The light was starting to fade in the sky, and Sebastien's clamours to get to the beach and start hunting for fossils had to be silenced. Instead they had a quiet, private dinner, and he put the excited child to bed, which was no easy task. He read for a while, and then found himself reading the same page over and over, his thoughts on Rafe and what he was doing now, worrying about his love not being able to sleep or worse, waking screaming in the night, without him there to hold him. Finally, he went to bed himself and curled himself around the bolster cushion, his heart aching.

The next day, both dressed in old clothes, they were on the beach with a book on what to look for, a pail each, and a small trowel. Ambrose had more luck than Sebastien, as the child was more impatient and clumsier, wanting to dig up everything he found immediately and breaking his finds before they were uncovered. By lunchtime they were ravenous, so they went back to the inn to eat. As they entered, the innkeeper accosted him.

"Mr Standish, Sir, these gentlemen here would like to make your acquaintance." Three officers were there in the hallway, resplendent in red coats and white breeches. Sebastien's face lit up at the beautiful uniforms and shining swords. He wanted to race forward, but Ambrose held on to the boy's shoulders to prevent him. They waited for the innkeeper to make the correct introductions.

"Mr Standish, allow me to introduce Captains Ashurst, Halton, and Trenberry. Sirs, this is Mr Standish."

Assuming it was the manner of his conveyance to Lyme that had piqued the officers' interest, Ambrose inclined his head and greeted them. The three men looked at him curiously, and Ambrose did not like their expressions at all. The blond one of the trio spoke.

"Standish, eh? Would you be connected in any way to the great house? Surely that was Goshawk's carriage you arrived in yesterday."

His mouth was smiling, but his eyes, Ambrose noticed, were piggy and suspicious. They raked over Ambrose's old clothes, dirty and soaked at the knees and hem due to their morning on the beach. Ambrose stood his ground. If he was not cowed by Rafe's arrogance, he was not going to be ground down by this foppish boor. "I am tutor to Goshawk's son," he said, and was surprised to see a look of pure anger and hate cross Trenberry's face.

Trenberry spoke again, this time directly to the child. "How are you, Sebastien? How's your scruffy little pony?" The boy responded politely, but Trenberry wasn't listening to him. He was staring at Ambrose with a venal expression. "The orrery, that was for you?"

Ambrose was confused. How would this man even know of the orrery, unless... He flushed, and his hands started to shake where they rested on Sebastien's shoulders. He took a deep breath. "I am sure that Mister Goshawk sent many items for his son's education. Now if you will excuse us, gentlemen, I must get some lunch for this young man." He managed his escape with dignity. When he reached the safety of their rooms, he sat on the bed with his head in his hands. He realised that the jealousy raging through him was stupid and pointless, but he could not help himself.

He had realised that Rafe was an experienced lover, that he must have had many others before himself, but meeting the sneering, pompous officer had shocked him. Putting the facts together, he deduced that the cavalry officer Sebastien had spoken of as being "Papa's friend" was none other than that obnoxious man he had just met. Somehow he had imagined that Rafe had always sought out the aesthetes — the poets and the romantics, not some coarse, pretty boy with pink skin and no manners.

With rising dizziness, he suddenly realised that the only way Trenberry could have known of his existence and the gifts he'd been sent, was if he had been in London with Rafe before the accident. *Just* before the accident. *He left his bed in London, with the officer in it, and had me in his at Standish in no time at all,* he thought. He felt nauseated, and the room dimmed.

Seeing his tutor pale and shivering, Sebastien shook his arm worriedly. "Are you all right, *m'sieur?* Should I call for help?"

Recollecting his responsibility, Ambrose calmed and smiled at the boy. "Don't worry, it is all right. I was just fatigued. I believe I am not as recovered as I thought I was." The child seemed placated by this, and they went down to luncheon. Ambrose dreaded seeing red coats, but there were none.

At Standish, Rafe was overseeing the installation of the fountain. He had been pleased and impressed that it had all been done so swiftly, but as he had learned over the years, money oiled many wheels. He had particularly wanted it installed when Ambrose was absent and before they went abroad. With Quinn on the estate, Rafe was also extremely happy that they were getting away from Standish. He was planning to ensure that Quinn stayed away from Ambrose at all costs.

"Still a lover of Greek, I see," came a voice, and Rafe turned in his chair. Quinn was standing behind him, the noise of the installation having masked the sound of the approach. His grey hair dressed and tied behind him, he was clean, and dressed in a dark brown jacket and breeches. Rafe's heart missed the smallest of beats as he finally saw in this man, who looked twenty years older than he should, the vestiges of the tutor he had once loved so much.

"A very touching tribute," he said acidly, looking up at the marble figures. "For that boy, is it? I met him, you know — over there. He seems an innocent, so very trusting. I can see how he would appeal to you." Quinn looked down at Rafe, and the golden eyes, still the only feature true to the Quinn of old, looked at the chair with curiosity, but with no pity or feeling.

He was almost miraculously lucid, and Rafe realised that the beggar act was simply that, an act, and Quinn, too, had learned a lot about manipulation over the years.

"I thank you for your 'sincere' patronage, Goshawk, and the clothes. I only wish I could accept your offer of the house on your estate; it sounds simply wonderful. The very Greek-ness of it all almost tempts me. What a happy little trio we would make." The voice now was sarcastic and bitter. "But I realise in the cold light of dawn that it is simply a sop to the Goshawk guilt, and not out of any concern for your old tutor. I will therefore leave you with your new one. I dare say you will destroy his life soon enough."

"At least take some money with you, Quinn," said Rafe, feeling the most enormous relief.

"Oh, don't worry about that, Goshawk," Quinn went on, his eyes cunning. "I believe your father owed me six month's salary. Over twenty-four years, the...interest on that must be considerable. What is an invisible man worth to you?"

Anger surged in Rafe, and he utterly regretted being bound in the chair. He had killed men for fewer reasons than Quinn had given him, but behind it all was Ambrose and protecting him from the truth at any cost. "Name your price, Quinn," he said, and Quinn did.

On their final morning in Lyme, Ambrose and Sebastien were walking around the town shopping for small gifts for Rafe and for Ambrose's sisters. Ambrose was getting used to greeting all the people who acknowledged him. The gossipmongers had been busy, and everyone seemed to know about the young heir to Standish and his handsome tutor. Sebastien had become quite famous in the three days they were there. Ladies asked his forgiveness in the street for talking to him un-introduced, everyone took every opportunity to make their acquaintance, possibly thinking that as Ambrose was a tutor and the child so young, certain niceties need not be observed. Ambrose was not worried about protocol, and was starting to enjoy meeting new people, recognising them and being able to greet them in the street. He had lived such a sheltered life, he had never before experienced all the small happinesses a wide range of acquaintances could bring. However, they were due back in Standish that afternoon, so Ambrose turned Sebastien around, and they returned to the inn.

As they approached the hotel, Rafe recognised the blond officer from the day before waiting between them and the front door, and his blood ran cold. Fearing the worst and unwilling to put Sebastien in a position of embarrassment, he told the boy to run to the desk and ask the porter to start packing their belongings and the grooms to get the barouche ready. The boy skipped off happily, waving at Trenberry as he passed, casting a longing look at the sabre. Trenberry was lounging against a wall, and Ambrose went to pass him without comment. However the captain put out a booted leg to prevent him.

"So," he sneered, "this is what Rafe has left me for, is it?"

To his annoyance, Ambrose found himself blushing.

"An impoverished and ruined tutor. Oh yes," he continued,

seeing Ambrose's eyes flash, "Rafe has told me all about the Standish family decline. You still live on the estate, I understand? You would have thought that your father would have had more sensibility."

Somehow the name of Standish sounded like an insult in the man's mouth. Ambrose's heart turned to ice. He refused to react, but the officer was not finished with him.

"I was with Rafe this morning, you know," he continued smoothly. "Do you know, he never mentioned you once. But then," his smile twisted into a sneer, "pillow talk was never Rafe's strong point. Surely you have noticed that? He probably never mentioned me, either. Does he still have nightmares? Has he told you what they mean?"

Tears sprang to Ambrose's eyes, and he walked past the man as if he were not there, praying the captain could not see his face.

Francis had indeed been with Rafe that very morning, and Rafe had not been at all pleased about it. He had been in his study, and was not in the bath chair, so Francis had not seen his incapacity. The meeting had been brief and violent. Francis, as usual, had gone too far, and had smashed several valuable antiques. The more he failed to get a reaction from Rafe, who simply sat, dark and brooding behind his desk, the angrier he had become.

"Tell me it is not true then, Rafe!" he'd shouted. "Just tell me! Your son's tutor? Surely you could have done better than that? Who's next, the stable boy, the gamekeeper?"

Finally, feeling murderous for the second time in two days, Rafe rang the bell and had Francis escorted from the house. His last words had been threats against Rafe, and worse, threats against Ambrose. Rafe was now decided, it was too dangerous to leave Ambrose in Dorset. He would have to take him to London with him.

As they neared the drive that led to Standish, Ambrose still felt numb with shock. He'd hardly spoken on the long drive home, and Sebastien finally gave up his questions. The boy was now asleep, stretched out on the cushion on the other side of the carriage, leaving Ambrose to thoughts blacker than he had ever experienced. He tried to think of some way to face Rafe, to question him without seeming weak and jealous, but he could think of none. He was suddenly alert as the barouche went past the main gates, and he called out to the driver, "Where are you going?"

"Master's orders, Sir. He said to me, 'On your way back, take the North entrance and come around the back of the house.'"

"But why?" asked Ambrose.

"Not my place to question, Sir," answered the man. "When the Master gives an order, I obey it."

That seemed to be the end of the matter, and Ambrose waited patiently as they went the long way around through the North lodge gates, Sebastien now awake and excited. Rafe waited for them on his crutches, his face alight with happiness, and Ambrose, in spite of every dark thought he'd had in the last two days, found himself absurdly happy to see him. All thoughts of Lyme pushed to one side, he longed to throw himself into Rafe's arms, but had to restrain himself for propriety's sake.

A footman helped Rafe into the carriage. He sat next to Ambrose and gave his arm a quick squeeze as Sebastien clambered onto his lap. "Welcome home," he whispered, his eyes hungry. "I have a present for you." The barouche set off again around the front of the house as Rafe, laughing, took a silk neckerchief from his pocket and tied it over Ambrose's eyes. "It's a surprise, no looking!" he said. Sebastien, joining in the game, insisted that he wanted the surprise too, so Rafe put his hands over the boy's eyes. When the carriage came to a stop, Rafe said quietly, "Ready?"

Ambrose felt the scarf come away, and his eyes focussed. He had guessed that the fountain was the surprise, but he couldn't help but gasp. It was tall, majestic, and very beautiful. At the top was Zeus — in human form but with huge wings, a thunderbolt in one hand — looking down and reaching to take a cup from Ganymede's fingers. Ganymede was kneeling at the god's feet and looking up at him; in the youth's other hand was a cockerel. Water gushed from somewhere behind Zeus, fluming high into the air, and also from the cup Ganymede held, which spilled over the feet of the god and into the basin beneath. There was a simple, one word inscription on the front of the fountain. "Standish." Rafe wasn't looking at the statue, but at Ambrose's face, which was alight with wonder.

"Rafe," he whispered, forgetting momentarily they had an audience, "it's beautiful."

"It's for you," breathed Rafe, looking only at Ambrose's rapt face. "It *is* you."

"It's us," replied Ambrose. It was a simple statement of fact; Ambrose had been abducted by a god-like creature to serve him, and love had blossomed between them.

Rafe ordered the carriage back to the house, and when they were alone in their room he pulled Ambrose onto his chair, kissing him at long, long last, hungrily, fiercely. "Ambrose, I never want to be away from your side again, not for one minute, not for one second. If I am ever more than one room away from you, I shall surely die." He started to peel the man's clothes from him, but Ambrose stopped him.

"Rafe?" he said, and Rafe, lust searing within, caught the serious look in the youth's face and stopped short.

"What is it, Ambrose? Tell me!"

"I met a young officer in Lyme." The memory was bitter in his mouth, but he had to discuss it with Rafe or he could not continue.

"He told me...he said...that he'd been here, with you, just this morning."

Ambrose's eyes filled with tears and Rafe's insides melted in horror at the anguish on his love's face.

"It was Trenberry, wasn't it?" Rafe's voice was cold and Ambrose nodded, tears falling onto his cheeks. Rafe kissed them swiftly away, and then held Ambrose's head in his hands and looked him straight in his eyes. "It's a lie, Ambrose. He came here, granted, but he came to shout at me about you." Ambrose tried to break away, but Rafe held him fast. "Listen to me! Listen! I should have told you about Francis, but when you were suddenly in my arms, our pasts meant nothing to me, nothing. I never loved him. He was a moment, five years ago; that is all. Since then he has been impossible to shake off. The man is desperate, needy, jealous beyond imagining, self-obsessed, and boring. He was, I admit, a convenience when I was in London. I was so desperate for you, I would have bedded anyone to assuage the feelings of unrequited lust I had. I do not and cannot expect you to believe me, but you are the only person I have ever truly loved. Just give me every opportunity to prove it to you!"

Chapter 13

As Rafe slipped back into sleep, a small smile on his face, Ambrose wriggled out of his arms, pulled a sheet around himself, and padded across the room. He picked up his jacket, which was tangled on the floor, took out a piece of paper from the pocket and walked to the huge bay windows. He slipped between the heavy drapes and sat on the window seat, his legs tucked up, hugging his knees, gazing out on the scene below him.

Paris spread out from his window like a magic carpet. Rafe's house was on the Champs-Élysées, and from where Ambrose sat, he could see the construction of the Emperor's Arch at the top of the majestic road. He hardly registered the magnificence of it all, as his pulse was racing; his loins were still aflame from what he had just experienced in Rafe's loving arms.

They had awakened early, which was surprising due to the lateness of the hour they had arrived at the Paris mansion. As usual, both men were hard as iron. They had kissed, Rafe's hands exploring every inch of his lover's body, encouraging Ambrose to do the same. He had, timidly at first, but when he saw the looks of pleasure and desire he caused on Rafe's face, he became bolder. He straddled the man at the hips and ran the flat of his palms over the muscled chest, touching the hard nipples and seeing Rafe's eyes close. Encouraged, he leaned forward and kissed them, and Rafe clasped his head, groaning with the feel of the beloved mouth on his skin, his hardness grinding against Ambrose's behind. Ambrose took the lead, and manipulated Rafe's prick for the first time, as had been done to him so many times now, feeling unutterable joy when Rafe came violently, calling his name.

Unable to restrain himself, Rafe had grabbed the younger man and pulled him to him, then rolled over and started to kiss him, his hands touching his penis, lightly teasing. Then he left his mouth and trailed his tongue down, over the chin and down the neck, kissing Ambrose's nipples and continuing lower, over the pale skin, lingering over the navel, and finally stopping at the nest of golden curls where Ambrose's manhood was thrusting to the ceiling.

Ambrose had been in ecstasy, the mouth on his skin was cool as it blazed its way across his body, leaving a fiery comet trail behind it. Every touch caused an inferno, and he was consumed with the now familiar Rafe's Fire. He thrashed upon the bed and grasped the covers and sheets, trying to stop himself floating from the bed toward the ceiling. Rafe paused and Ambrose cried out in desperation, "Don't stop. Rafe! Please. You will kill me." Then he found he was near to fainting as the blood surged from his head as he felt the softest, warmest wetness encompass him, and he couldn't speak thereafter, he could only whimper with pleasure.

That tender sound made Rafe smile inwardly, knowing that he was so virgin. It was a cry from the heart, and Rafe knew he would never hear anything so sweet again. He pushed his mouth over the entire length of the shaft and then rose up again, feeling Ambrose thrust toward him. He held it in his hand and gently pulled back the skin, exposing the pink head. He let his tongue encircle it, flicking the delicate slit. There was dew seeping from it, and Rafe licked it lightly, feeling Ambrose flinch with every tonguing, gasping for breath. Enjoying himself immensely, he fondled the youth's thigh, feeling it flinch beneath his hand, and ran his palm up until he had his fingers on his scrotum, brushing it with butterfly strokes. Then as he took Ambrose into his mouth again, his fingers slid behind his ball sac and massaged his perineum and teased his dark, puckered opening with a gentle fingertip. It was like a magic touch; Ambrose ejaculated immediately, thrusting up into Rafe's eager mouth with a low guttural sigh. Rafe swallowed slowly, his eyes closed in delight as he made sure he was there for every last drop. He remained holding Ambrose in his mouth, allowing him to throb and shrink, sucking and licking him softly, knowing that the post ejaculatory mouthing was a mixture of pleasure and pain, but so unwilling to leave the haven of Ambrose's groin. There was a whispered call, and Rafe looked up to see the man holding his arms out, his eyes pleading. He swarmed back up the bed, and they held each other tightly for a long, sweet time, until Rafe finally fell asleep.

Now sitting alone in the morning light, Ambrose held the paper in his hands. He had found it on the day they were due to leave Standish. It had been on his pillow in his own room, which he had found strange. He could not understand why Rafe had left him a note in that place, as he had not slept there since their first night together. He was holding it now. He had kept it with him for weeks, in London and all through the journey to Dover and to Paris. At times it seemed as if it was burning a hole in his side, and he would take it out in the rare moments when he was alone and read it.

It was not from Rafe. It was not even to Ambrose. It was just a few stanzas of a poem, written in an unknown hand on an old piece of parchment, the ink faded. Ambrose knew the poem, of course, and had long loved it, but now the sight of it sickened him. Jealousy had entered every line of the love song of Solomon and had eaten it away like canker worm. He knew now that the paper had been placed there by the tramp in the park, and the implications behind that were almost too monstrous to contemplate, but he had done nothing but think of them ever since. The only time he could forget his jealousy was when Rafe was touching him, kissing him. As soon as they were apart for seconds, the doubts began again.

Ambrose hated himself for this. He remembered how disdainful Rafe had been over Trenberry's jealous neediness, and he had tried so hard to push the accusations he longed to throw at Rafe to one side, but he wanted to know the truth. How had the tramp entered his bedroom? What was his relationship to Rafe? Why had Rafe denied knowing him? Why did Rafe keep so much from him? Hot, jealous tears fell onto the parchment, and the writing, elegant and upright, smudged and ran.

"Ambrose?" Rafe's voice was tinged with worry.

"I'm here, Rafe." He emerged from the curtains, tucking the parchment in the bed sheet he wore and dropping them both on the floor.

Rafe looked keenly at him and his face clouded. "What has happened, Love? You have been crying."

Ambrose's heart was breaking, but he refused to show Rafe his jealousy, afraid of driving him away. Instead, he smiled and clambered back onto the enormous wooden bed. He wrapped his arms around Rafe's waist, feeling the fears drop away from him as he held him fiercely, his head in his lap. "Nothing, my love," he lied, his stomach churning with the first falsehood he had ever told Rafe. "I'm just so happy."

Rafe laughed and pulled him up to kiss him. "Strange child," he said. He wriggled to the edge of the bed and used the huge headboard as support to pull himself to his feet. "You should be crying real tears now, then," he laughed. "Look!" With his hands on the bed, he took a few stumbling steps around toward Ambrose. "Another few weeks and I will be chasing you around the bedroom."

"You've already caught me, Rafe," said Ambrose, his heart feeling the weight of the poem.

"So solemn!" Rafe said. "Pull the curtains, Ambrose. It's Paris, and I want to show you all of it!"

Much later, Ambrose had almost forgotten his worries again; he was dazzled by Paris. Rafe had been spending far too much money as usual, and he had bought and bought. No one had been forgotten. Ambrose had more books, and a beautiful cane with a silver wolf's head; Sebastien had candies and toys, and parcels were dispatched daily to Standish. Gifts for his sisters — an exquisite pear wood escritoire for Maria, bonnets, gloves and ribbons for Sophy, even Aries had not been forgotten. They had watched and waited while a craftsman had fashioned a magnificent leather collar and engraved it with rabbits.

Rafe had shown him all the sights of his terrible childhood, and they had treated it like a history lesson for Sebastien: the Place de Concorde, where the huge Guillotine had stood menacing in the centre; the site, now cleared, where the infamous Bastille had been, now torn to pieces by the mob, the prisoners released.

"Only seven prisoners in the entire castle," Rafe told the fascinated child. "Le Marquis de Sade was one, and he'd been there for eleven years. He boasted to me once that it was he who started the revolution, by shouting from the windows that all the prisoners were being executed. It was so typical of him."

Ambrose's eyes widened at this admission, and his heart grew heavier. He knew so little about Rafe's life before he had come to England, the people he had known, the legendary and historic places that had been familiar to him. Over the weeks, they explored Paris and the environs thoroughly. Sebastien was now more in love with Napoleon than ever, being in the city upon which the little general had impressed so much of his personality. Ambrose had spent hours in the six hundred-year-old university, poring over as many books as he could in the limited time, while Rafe and Sebastien had watched the soldiers drilling on the Champs de Mars. They had marvelled at the Tuileries and the fountains at Versailles, but Ambrose had touched Rafe's hand and said that their fountain was better than any.

Ambrose's doubts began to fade from him as Rafe showed no sign of diminishing love or interest in any other person. Indeed their social life was very solitary. Goshawk's presence in Paris had been noted by society, however, and every time they returned to the house there were cards inviting him to soirées, balls, and concerts.

"You should really go to some of these," Ambrose said, leafing through the latest batch. "People will be thinking that you are snubbing them."

"I am," said Rafe. "Society bores me." He looked at the young man with sudden alertness. He gestured for Ambrose to come to him and pulled him onto his lap, taking the cards from him and scanning them. Ambrose kissed his hair gently, and Rafe said, "I'm selfish, as usual. Though I am bored by these functions, you would probably enjoy them. After all, you've never been to a ball, have you?" Ambrose shook his head. Rafe selected a pair and handed them back to Ambrose. "There, those are the best of them. Tell them we will be delighted, honoured, although it galls me to have to go in a chair. And even if I were well, I could hardly dance with you, now could I?" He laughed sharply, imagining it.

Ambrose kissed him, suddenly excited, "By the time we get to Venice," he said, "you'll be fit enough to dance all night. Have you decided how you want to get there?"

"By sea, most definitely. I've been over the Alps more than once, and it is not an experience I wish to repeat, or put you and Sebastien through. Not only are the roads appalling, but they are not safe from brigands. We can sail from Marseilles. I prefer braving the risk of corsairs to the mountains. Now, talking of brigands..." His eyes gleamed and he began unbuttoning Ambrose's waistcoat.

So they began to socialise. Rafe refused to be carried to these events, and would use his crutches, but was happy to sit comfortably when they arrived. Ambrose had been terrified; dressed in unaccustomed finery, with the finest silk embroidered clothes Rafe could buy for him. Thoroughly uncomfortable and glad his sisters couldn't see him looking such a popinjay, he had managed it only as Rafe's urbane confidence supported him. He was introduced to the highest level of French and English society, simply as Standish. Rafe never once mentioned that he was ostensibly his son's tutor. Ambrose caught several glances from other men directed at him and realised that some people had likely guessed the relationship between them. He recognised several of his acquaintances from Lyme, too, and they looked surprised to see the shabby tutor in such resplendent surroundings. The highlight of these otherwise disappointingly tedious gatherings was for Ambrose to be introduced to a very handsome and debonair man with a beautiful blonde female companion — Lord Byron and Countess Teresa Guiccioli. The brief meeting had made his head swim.

If the ubiquitous mammas knew, guessed or even cared about Rafe's relationship with Ambrose, they did not show it. Rafe was always the centre of attention, and women flocked to him like bees around a hive, arranging introductions from their own acquaintances and sitting around him like hens around a rooster, each mamma in turn introducing daughter after endless line of daughters. Ambrose was staggered by how many unmarried women there appeared to be in Paris. Ambrose's ethereal beauty, the Standish name, and his obvious prosperity attracted a fair amount of attention also, and he found himself in great demand. Rafe's dark eyes watched him constantly as he was introduced to all and sundry by the Master of Ceremonies and whisked onto the dance floor time and time again by yet another predatory female. Not having the excuse of feeble limbs, he was helpless to prevent it, and several of the young ladies were making it very obvious that he fascinated them. The more aloof and remote he attempted to be, the more they were drawn to him.

Rafe teased him about it at night. "You are a challenge, my love," he said, spooning Ambrose's body to his, thrusting his prick between the top of the youth's thighs and kissing the white shoulders. "Women cannot resist such a beautiful, mysterious man, a man with no past, who tells them nothing, who will not play the game with them."

"I don't understand their games!" retorted Ambrose. "Simpering quizzes, the whole bunch of them — rolling their eyes, and shak-

ing their ridiculous heads and tapping me with their fans! 'La, Sir!'"
he imitated, "'I meant no such thing!' I now know what you mean
about society boring you. Let's not bother with any more of it." He
pressed his back against the hard, warm body and wrapped his arms
around Rafe's.

"The flirting does seem to go over your head, I must admit.
However, we are engaged for one more, so we will have to grin and
bear it."

As Rafe turned him round to face him, monopolised his mouth,
and took hold of his hardness in his hands, Ambrose was finally
happy. He was glad that he had not brought the parchment up
between them. Their honeymoon was sweet, the love between them
strong and becoming stronger each day. Why ruin it with accusations of a relationship which must have been over many years ago?
He hoped that one day Rafe would tell him everything, but for now
he was happy to wait.

The next day Ambrose had a chill, and although he was well
enough to sit up and be pampered horribly by the servants, Rafe,
and Sebastien, he was too unwell to go to the party in St Germain.
Rafe wanted to stay with him, but Ambrose would not hear of it.

"I am fine. Truly. You go; you know you wanted to finish the
deal with Rolandson about the racehorses, so go. I am only planning to read for a while and then sleep." Rafe needed much more
persuasion and would only leave on the strict understanding that
Ambrose was to send word if he felt at all worse, and that he would
close the deal with Rolandson and leave as soon as it was polite.

When Rafe had gone, Ambrose slept for a while. When he woke
some time later, he felt strangely fretful and couldn't fall to sleep
again. He missed the book he was reading and remembered with
annoyance he had left it downstairs in the library. He was still
unaccustomed to ringing for servants for the slightest thing and
decided to get it himself. He got out of the bed, but felt weak as the
blood rushed to his head, so he waited for it to clear. Then he
pulled the heavy brocade of Rafe's dressing gown around him,
which was comforting as it smelled deliciously of his lover, and
went down the stone stairs to the library. As he entered the room,
he heard voices outside. Picking up the book, he walked back out to
the hall, his blood turning to ice when he saw Trenberry and the two
officers from Lyme enter the house. They pushed past the footman,
who was attempting to tell them there was no one at home.

Spotting Ambrose, Francis advanced, all smiles and charm.
"Standish!" he said jovially. "Good man! We were hoping you
would be in, were we not Ashurst, Halton?" The other two men
smiled in the same manner they had at Lyme.

Ambrose noticed that although they were all in dress uniform,
none of the men were wearing great coats, in spite of the chill of the

November air. Ambrose summoned a welcoming smile and dismissed the footman, who looked relieved that he was not in trouble, gestured to the officers, and invited them into the upstairs drawing room, apologising for his dishabille and pulling the bell rope for drinks.

When they were all seated and brandy had been provided, Francis, who was doing a fair show of friendliness, asked where Rafe was.

"I believe he has retired for the night," said Ambrose after the slightest of hesitations.

"That's most odd," said Halton, sneering. "You obviously do not have the hold over him that you think you do, as we were certain we just saw him in St Germain."

Ambrose blushed to be caught out in such an obvious lie, and Francis stood up and walked around the room. "Perhaps," Francis said, his voice now soft, "Standish did not wish us to think he was all alone here in the house." He stopped behind Ambrose's chair and touched the collar of the dressing gown lightly with pale fingers. "Do you often wear your employer's night things when he is out of the house?" With a whip like movement, he grabbed both of Ambrose's arms and pulled him to his feet. The other two men stood sharply, Halton's pale eyes gleaming and his mouth agape. "Shall we see if you are wearing any other garments that do not belong to you?" Francis hissed, and dragged him over to the large couch in the centre of the room.

Ambrose panicked, trying to struggle against Francis, but years of cavalry training had given his upper body strength that was twice that of Ambrose, and he held him as easily as he would a child, his hands bruising the slender arms. Ambrose considered shouting out, but the child's room was on this floor, and being a light sleeper it would be likely that Sebastien would come into the room before any servants could be roused, and with despair, Ambrose realised that he couldn't inflict that on the innocent boy.

Francis forced Ambrose down onto the couch and with rough hands, tore the dressing gown from him and used the silken tie to fasten Ambrose's hands behind his back, leaving his own hands free. Seeing Francis' intentions, Ashurst backed away. "Come now, Francis, you said we were only going to frighten him! This isn't necessary." Francis hardly seemed to hear him, and Ashurst said, "Sorry, Francis, but I am not with you in this," and he left the room.

Ambrose prayed that he would go one step further and summon help, but as he heard the front door slam, that hope faded, and his soul darkened. Halton got onto the couch and knelt before Ambrose, and with a horror that rose from the pit of his stomach, Standish watched the man start to undo his breeches. He felt Francis lift the nightshirt from his body, exposing his nakedness.

The blond officer ordered, "Halton, stop him from shouting out."

Ambrose wondered for a second what he meant and then nearly screamed in terror as Halton straddled in front of him, his prick released, thick, dark, and engorged. Halton forced his cock into Ambrose's mouth. Holding one fist tightly to the hair at the back of his head so he couldn't move, he began to thrust slowly, each movement accompanied with animal-like grunts, Ambrose did the only thing he could think of to prevent this violation, he bit down. Immediately Halton started to beat him around the head with his fist, punching him over and over and swearing violently. Under the torrent of blows, Ambrose's vision dimmed. As his senses slipped from him, a black veil fell around his eyes. He felt hands on his behind and a warm rigid something pressing against his anus. He screamed at last, but no sound came, as his world tore apart and he slipped from consciousness.

Chapter 14

Rafe sat by the bed, his eyes on Ambrose, his face a mask of black fire. Ambrose was asleep, finally, but it had taken several hours, and eventually Rafe had to dose him with laudanum to calm him. It was three in the morning. Rafe had not wept, but had held Ambrose while he had. All the man kept saying was that he had not subjected Sebastien to the scene, and he seemed to hold it to himself like a comfort while Rafe stroked his hair and rocked him as he sobbed. Ambrose seemed to be blaming himself in some way, and that tore Rafe apart.

Entering the house, some four hours earlier, he had been met by the footman who said that there had been uninvited guests and he hadn't seen the gentlemen leave, having not been summonsed to escort them out. On questioning, Rafe guessed by their descriptions who the visitors were and feared for Ambrose's safety. Grabbing the crutches from the terrified servant, he hastened up the stairs as quickly as he could. Seeing the drawing room door slightly ajar, Rafe threw it open, then stopped dead. Gagging, he was violently sick. It was worse than he could have had imagined. Ambrose was still bound, but thankfully unconscious. The nightshirt was covered in splattered blood from the terrible damage to his face, and further down, a deep red stain was spreading.

The doctor had been called and Ambrose had been tended gently. "He'll survive," the doctor said. "The bleeding has stopped, and his cuts will heal, but what this will do to his mind, Goshawk, I cannot say. Have you any idea who could have done such a terrible thing?" Rafe denied any knowledge, shaking his head and escorting the doctor from the room. Turning back to the bed, he found Ambrose waking to the horror of his reality.

Now, hours later, he knew what he had to do. Summoning the carriage, he left instructions that Ambrose was not to leave the room and made his way across Paris. He entered the officer's club and sat in the hall while the night watchman summoned Trenberrry. At first the man had refused, but a handful of gold had made him suddenly compliant. After keeping Rafe waiting for an hour, Trenberry finally arrived, face flushed, jacket open. He was accompanied arm in arm by the officer Rafe recognised as Halton, and he assumed they had been in bed together.

"Leave us," Rafe snarled to the watchman, who scurried out. On his crutches, he propelled himself toward Francis, and with as much strength as he could muster, smashed the glove he was holding across Francis' face, gratified to see that it left a vivid cut on his cheek.

Francis' sneering demeanour hardly flickered. "Because of him, Rafe? I can assure you he is hardly worth the effort, was he, Halton?"

Realising what Francis meant, Goshawk turned to the second officer and struck him in the same manner. Halton at least had the good grace to look nervous.

"And anyway, Rafe, honour forbids us to duel with cripples."

Rafe dropped the crutches, summoned his strength to hold him upright, stepped forward and grabbed Francis around the throat. His voice held the promise of death. "If you were not in uniform, Francis, I would kill you here and now like the diseased dog you are, but my honour prevents that, whatever yours dictates. You will be at the Bois at dawn, and you will need a third because your second will be dying with you."

He had several hours to pass, and after a brief stop at the military academy, he went back to the house. Ambrose was sleeping, but he was so pale Rafe's heart was pierced. Slipping off his shoes, he climbed into the bed, lay next to his love, and folded him to his breast. Ambrose rolled against him in his sleep, clinging to him desperately. Then, in the quiet of the pre-dawn, Rafe allowed himself to weep, sobbing with each breath, wept as he had not done for twenty-four years.

The light in the sky changed, and Rafe was still wide-awake. He gently freed himself from Ambrose's tangled embrace and got up. He removed his evening things and donned a warm black suit and cape. When Ambrose stirred, Rafe was beside him in a second, the glass of laudanum in his hand.

Ambrose was drugged and confused. When he saw Rafe dressed, he frowned and struggled to his elbows, "Rafe? You are going out?"

Rafe soothed him, making him sip slowly and stroked his hair. "Not for long, *amour*. I will be back in an hour, I promise you." Ambrose slipped back into slumber without recalling the night's events. Rafe looked at him for a long while, then kissed him tenderly, tears falling onto the man's bruised face. He moved to his bureau and took a parchment from the drawer, folded it and put it in his pocket. He would need his will if his plan didn't succeed.

On the way back to the Bois de Boulogne, they collected Rafe's second from the military academy. Captain Rees Howell Gronow was a veteran duellist and had seconded for Rafe many times, in many countries. This time, however, he attempted to dissuade Rafe from the challenge.

"You can hardly walk, Goshawk! Time enough for this to wait, surely? Trenberry will be in Paris for many months, same as myself. Finish your tour, man, and come back and do this when you are yourself."

Rafe did not listen. As they entered the forest, the November mist hung about like smoke, dew dripping from the trees, and Rafe could see three horses in the distance, their coats steamed, their hot breath puffing in the chill of the morning.

"He's here then," said Gronow unnecessarily.

"I had no doubt of it," Rafe muttered. "He may be a fool, but he's no coward." The carriage stopped, and the men got out. Rafe used the crutches to reach the waiting officers and stood patiently while Gronow talked to Ashurst, who was as white as a sheet and shaking. The necessary formalities were observed. Rafe was asked if he would retract the challenge, and his reply was that he would, but only if he had written confessions from both men. The other side declined, and pistols were chosen in deference to Rafe's incapacity.

Gronow whispered aside to Rafe, "I can ask Trenberry to take twenty paces, if you wish."

"I'm capable of walking ten paces," Rafe snarled.

As he looked across at Francis with hate in his heart, he remembered that he had said something so similar to Ambrose. Only then, it was ten paces toward his love; here, he was aware that those ten paces might remove him from Ambrose's life forever. Forcing his muscles to obey, he started the long walk across the wet grass, the only sound being the slow counting of Gronow, and the sound of horses' harnesses jingling. They reached their marks and turned. Rafe did not raise his pistol but waited for Francis to fire, his face impassive, his breathing slow and measured.

Francis looked across the grass at the man in black, and he knew he couldn't kill him. He wished he could make him love him, the way he wanted him to, the way he loved the tutor. He did the only thing he could do, fired over Rafe's head and waited with clear eyes for the response. Rafe's expression did not change, and Gronow watched in horror as Rafe levelled the pistol and calmly shot Francis through the chest.

There was a strangled roar from Halton as he surged forward, drawing his sabre. Rafe reached into his overcoat and produced a longbladed knife. Gronow shouted, "Rafe! No!" and started running toward the man, but he was too far away. He watched in horror as Rafe's arm lashed out and Halton fell across Francis' body, the throwing knife in his heart. Rafe fell to the ground on his hands and knees, and Gronow spun round to Ashurst, who was retching violently. Gronow shook the trembling officer and said, "I will get Goshawk out of the city. You *must* give me a few hours."

Ashurst looked up at his fellow officer. "You would protect him? A killer like that?"

"It was self defence," said Gronow deliberately. "The man

attacked him with a sabre!"

"And Francis?" Ashhurst stood straight, wiping his mouth. "Francis complied with all of the rules; Goshawk murdered him."

"Trenberry missed," Gronow said swiftly. "Goshawk was perfectly within his rights to do what he did." He paused, then continued. "The scandal that will ensue if the truth of this matter gets out will cause repercussions through society and the army on both sides of the Channel. Trenberry's name will be disgraced, as will Halton's; the regiment will suffer as a result; and you and I will be the ones who are blamed. Who else knows of this?"

Ashurst considered. "No one," he said quietly, his mind racing as he realised the truth of the older man's reasoning. "We went to the ball at St Germain last night, and Francis saw Goshawk there on his own. He realised that the tutor would be unprotected, and he told us it would be fun to frighten him. I honestly had no idea what he meant to do and took no part in it. Francis loved Goshawk very much. He would have done anything to get him back."

"Raping his rival was hardly likely to achieve that," snapped Gronow, and the other man flinched.

"Get him out of here," spat Ashurst, glaring at Rafe, still crouched on the grass.

"I'll do what I can." Gronow strode to Rafe and supported him back to the carriage.

For the third time, Rafe returned to Ambrose's side and was relieved to find him still asleep, with a little colour in his face. Desperately tired, the very marrow in his bones aching and cold, he longed to slip in with Ambrose and sleep until they had both forgotten today, but he had promised Gronow. He packed a small bag with clothes for Ambrose; anything else they needed immediately could be bought, and he told the servants to send Sebastien and their luggage after them to a hotel in Melun, out of the city. Then he let the servants in, Ambrose was scooped from the bed, and they descended to the carriage.

The next weeks were some of the hardest Rafe had ever known. At first, Ambrose teetered between lucidity and madness. He slept for long, long times, begging Rafe to drug him until Rafe, unable to ignore the pleading in his eyes, gave in. Then afterwards, when he was not sleeping, he was silent. There was a terrible wall in front of his eyes, a terrifying lack of expression. Rafe could see it when Ambrose looked at him — the blankness, the clamped jaw, an emptiness that frightened Rafe. The innocent blue eyes that had looked at him firstly with hate, then curiosity, and finally with longing and love, were now closed shutters, and Rafe was excluded.

Ambrose would not allow Rafe to touch him and asked for a separate room in each hotel where they stayed, locking any communicating doors between them. Rafe, unable to argue with his love, granted him this, thinking he was helping but feeling impotent and lost. The intimacy between them was frozen. Ambrose would only discuss the landscape, the journey, or the hotel, and Rafe was powerless; he had tried every avenue of conversation, to no avail. Wherever Ambrose was, he was unreachable. The only person who could touch him physically was Sebastien, and although he would not talk, even to the boy, he would sit staring from the window with the boy held tightly in his arms. Forced back to sleeping alone, Rafe became insomniac again, and when he did sleep, the nightmares returned. This time, there was no soft white hand to pull him from the box, no loving voice to guide him through the dark, fiery water. This time he was alone and damned.

Finally they reached Marseilles, and Rafe chartered a ship that would take them to Venice. His original plan had been to visit Elba, for Sebastien's sake, disembark at Pisa, and then travel overland via Florence. Now, it seemed simpler to remain in the ship and sail around the boot of Italy for Venice. Ambrose would not need to be disturbed again, and they could visit the sights of Florence and Rome when Ambrose was recovered. Rafe had a palazzo in Venice, and he felt that he needed to get Ambrose there without delay to recover. He had to believe, every day, that Ambrose would recover. Any other thought was too terrible to contemplate.

On the ship, Rafe's nightmares troubled him less, as he slept with Sebastien clutched to him. He found that when he had someone to hold as possessively as he had Ambrose, the terror did not penetrate his mind, and the fire, the drowning men and the rats did not disturb his slumber. Ambrose did not leave his cabin during the day, but unbeknown to Rafe, he crept out of his bed at night and sat on the deck in the dark, sobbing. He could not bear Rafe to look at him, to touch him, to speak to him. He could not meet Rafe's eyes. He could not stand to see the face that had once looked at him with such tenderness, love and passion show any flicker of disgust and horror. He knew that beneath the fine clothes, he was defiled and filthy, unfit to be a companion to Sebastien, too tainted to ever touch Rafe again. The wounds on his face healed, but the damage to his mind seemed irreparable. There was only one option for him: he knew that he had to ask Rafe to release him, let him return to England.

One morning, as Venice came into view, he left his cabin and saw Rafe standing at the ship's prow. The winter sunshine glittered off the Adriatic, and Venice, pink and white, nestled in the vast lagoon. The wind buffeted the little ship, the sails flapping as they tacked across, so Rafe didn't hear Ambrose approach. Rafe was like some carved idol, immobile, his black eyes focussed on the entrance to the lagoon. Ambrose reached out but withdrew his hand slowly, unable to touch him with polluted hands. He suddenly saw that

Rafe's cheeks were wet with tears, and he choked. Rafe spun round at the noise and for the first time since Ambrose had withdrawn into himself, their eyes met. Ambrose's walls melted at the sight of his magnificent love, the tower of strength that was Rafe, openly weeping, no sign of disgust in his face, nothing but agony, loneliness, and despair.

Rafe grabbed him, and Ambrose felt his knees buckle as he was swept into those great arms. Uncaring about the curious crew, Rafe picked him up and carried him to his cabin, all of his strength returning as he held Ambrose tightly to him.

Ambrose said nothing as Rafe placed him on the edge of the bed, but he was trembling, and his eyes were anxious. Rafe knelt by the bed between his legs and started to undo Ambrose's clothes, gently and slowly, as he did when preparing Sebastien for bed.

"Don't Rafe. I can't bear you to..." Ambrose said.

"...Can't bear me to touch you..." Rafe's voice was hollow and he got up and turned away. "I can't say that I blame you. I would not blame you if you could not let anyone touch you again."

"No, Rafe, no...no!" Ambrose was desperate, realising how hurt Rafe was. "That's not what I meant. Rafe." His voice was so desperate that Rafe turned back toward him. "I can't bear you to touch me, because...well, how could you? After what happened, why would you ever want to again?"

Rafe surged back to him, kneeling before him again and looked up into his eyes, which had life in them at last, desperate, tortured life, but better than the blue ice of the last weeks. Rafe's voice was husky with emotion. "I want to, and I will always want to. I love you more than my life, and I discovered that in Paris, because of you. You are my heart. When you bleed, I bleed. When you laugh, I laugh. We are entwined, now and irrevocably. I could no more put you from my life than I could cut out my heart. Both would kill me, and neither will happen.

"Your body is precious to me, and nothing that you could do could stop me from wanting to hold you and love you. What happened," Ambrose's eyes flinched, "was something I could have prevented, and I will blame myself till the day I die. If you never allow me the precious boon of your body, I will respect that and cleave to you in spite of it, but it will not make my love for you any less."

Ambrose was shaking so hard, the tears fell from his eyes without his needing to blink them away. He kissed Rafe at last, the kiss salty and wet. "I cannot say it as well as you," he whispered. "I love you too much. I was going to ask you to let me go today." Rafe's heart chilled. "But when I saw you, and how unhappy I had made you, I couldn't. I belong to you, Rafe. Body and soul I said, and body and soul I meant. I only ask that you wait a while longer. Can you?"

Rafe nodded. "Yes," he murmured over and over, "yes." There was nothing else he could have said, he knew. His mouth was dry with a feeling something akin to panic, as he knew, even as he said the words that Ambrose wanted to hear, that he was lying.

Chapter 15

Rafe had said yes. After his impassioned declaration of love, there was nothing else he could have said. At that delicate moment, any other response would have destroyed them both, and he had already as good as said that he would wait forever. He had had few regrets in his life, taking what life had thrown at him and making of it what he could, but he almost regretted saying the things to Ambrose that he had.

That morning as the ship docked in the port, they had lain naked in each other's arms, and Rafe had passed his hands over every inch of the beautiful pale flesh. Ambrose had lain submissive and trembling. It was as if he imagined that Rafe's hands were washing the taint of the rape from him. Rafe did what he could, but Ambrose was strangely passive, and although he would kiss his lover and hold him, he couldn't bring himself to fondle Rafe's manhood as he once had, and Rafe had to satiate his own desires himself later and in private. It was a procedure he loathed, as the memories associated with it, belonged to the time when Mauvaise had found him masturbating and had been so violent for so many days, Rafe had been in a semi-coma for a week afterwards.

He found himself longing to beg Ambrose to touch him, but could not bring himself to make the man do anything he was not willing to do.

Ensconced in the Palazzo Veneziano, overlooking the Grand Canal, Ambrose had not shown much improvement. He had lost much of the joy he had in the world around him. He had always been more serious and sombre than Rafe, but he seemed now to prefer to be solitary and would sit for hours reading, not even seeming to see the marvellous vista outside the windows. Whereas once he would throw himself into Rafe's arms after a separation of even an hour, now he would not initiate even the smallest of physical contact. He would come home from a gallery or St Mark's, and more often than not, Rafe would not even know he had returned, and would have to seek him out.

Christmas and the New Year arrived, and although Ambrose made some effort for Sebastien's sake — smiling as he helped Sebastien wrap presents, and participating in the celebrations — Rafe hadn't once seen him laugh. He missed the gaiety and light-heartedness almost as much as the sexual contact. It was driving Rafe frantic, and the longer it went on, the less able he seemed to be able to address it. He knew that he should talk to Ambrose, but he did not have a notion of how to begin such a conversation. Instead, he pretended he was content with matters as they were, and Ambrose, being unused to guile, took this for the truth, thinking that Rafe was content to wait to allow him to come to terms with the rape in his own time.

The only intimacy they shared was in bed, or in the huge black Felze gondola Rafe owned. The covered canopy allowed them to be private, and Rafe would kiss Ambrose so passionately he thought his heart would burst, all the while railing inwardly against his lover's almost inert body, wanting to shake him, to release the impetuous, impish, sensual Ambrose he knew was hiding in there somewhere. Rafe would not allow himself to believe that the man he loved had gone forever.

They were still invited to many social functions, but Ambrose refused to go to any of them. At first Rafe stayed in too, fearing that Ambrose would need him and unwilling to leave the man alone in the palazzo. It soon became apparent that Ambrose was not frightened of staying at home alone; he just refused to socialise, and seeing that Rafe was caged and impatient, Ambrose told him to go out, to see his acquaintances — he had no intention of spoiling Rafe's enjoyment of their time in the city. The carnival season was upon them, and Ambrose was happy to sit and watch the masked figures float past the palace, but he steadfastly declined to join the happy throng.

Rafe eventually realised that it was pointless for him to sit in the palazzo each night, drinking and morose, while Ambrose was tucked away God knew where. He started going out at night, sometimes to invited functions and other times simply pacing the streets crowded with masked revellers, glad to be wearing a mask so the world could not see the torment in his face.

As he strode through the freezing night, down the narrow alleys and over bridges, he thought, *Maybe I should let him return to Standish.* His heart ached at the very thought of it. He knew he could not do it; the separation would be too hard. He needed Ambrose close for selfish reasons, if only for the brief hours of darkness when he allowed him to hold him close and whisper words of love into his ear. Recalling the night before, Ambrose held tightly to him, grinding his swollen erection against the unresponsive thigh in a desperate attempt to relieve his lust, Rafe's member hardened once more. *Wine,* he thought. *I need to drink, and forget, at least for now.*

Glad to escape from the cold and the senseless, endless walking, Rafe entered an inn where revellers were drinking and singing. He ordered a bottle of wine, changed his mind and bought brandy instead. Like a wounded fox retreating to its den to lick its wounds, he took the bottle to a table in the furthest dark corner. He threw the fiery liquid down his throat, hardly tasting it. Glass after glass followed until he could think of Ambrose without his stomach churning.

A shadow fell over the table and a lilting voice said in accented English, "Tell me, where is fancy bred, in the heart, or in the head?"

Rafe looked up, glaring at the tall, slim man in a skin tight Harlequin costume and mask. "Go away," Rafe snarled.

The man smiled, his mouth not covered by the mask which only hid his eyes and nose. "All things that are, are with more spirit chased than enjoy'd."

Rafe surmised he was a prostitute, but was nonetheless intrigued by his eloquence. "Sit then, if you must, but no more Shakespeare if you want to live. Sit, drink, and keep silent, and you may earn your money." He called to the landlord for another bottle. The Harlequin did as he was told, leaning against the wall and putting his feet up on the long bench. He sipped the brandy with a contemplative demeanour, watching Rafe with half closed eyes. Eventually Rafe tired of the silence. His black mood numbed by the alcohol, he turned to the Harlequin and inspected him. Firstly he noted the amused expression on his face, the full mouth, and under the tight suit, wide shoulders and long slim legs. "What's your name?" Rafe asked.

"Achille," said the Harlequin. "And now you have me at a disadvantage, Sir. I rarely drink with those to whom I have not been introduced."

"If you're paid," Rafe slurred, throwing coins onto the table, "I expect you would drink with anyone." Instead of taking offence, the Harlequin laughed, and the sound was a bright light piercing Rafe's depression.

"You think I'm a gigolo? *Come divertendo!* He stood up and bowed deeply, taking off the mask. "Let us be formal. *Il Conte Achille Alfredo Bonetti de Alvisi*, Sir, at your service." Unmasking, Rafe got to his feet, for once in his life completely disconcerted, and apologised profusely. Alvisi swept away his apologies with a slim hand, then held it out to Rafe saying, "And whom do I have the pleasure of meeting?"

Rafe introduced himself, and as they sat again, Rafe saw the man's face properly. It was a triangular, puckish face, with wide green eyes topped by short black hair in tight curls. Rafe's member, hard from lust for Ambrose, twitched treacherously as he noted that the tight costume left *nothing* to the imagination.

The Harlequin resumed his position on the bench, his mocking eyes not leaving Rafe's. "Goshawk, yes, I've heard of you my friend. Your life has been an adventure, has it not?"

He was still smiling, and Rafe didn't like it; he mistrusted people who smiled too much. But he was captivated by his guest's arrogant manner.

"What brings you to this suppressed and beaten corner of the Austrian Empire? By your reputation and the look of you tonight, I'd say you were perhaps on the run from some diplomatic scandal, or just drowning your sorrows over a pair of sparkling eyes that will not look your way."

Rafe started and flushed. The man's bantering guesses were too close to the truth, so he changed the subject. "Not at all. I am merely recovering from an over indulgence of culture. I am taking my son on a small Tour: Paris, Italy; perhaps we might travel as far as Greece if I haven't died of boredom by then."

"I heard you had married — as much as I could hardly believe it," Alvisi said with a dangerous smile. "We have some mutual acquaintance in Venice — my family knew the Venezianos well." He raised an eyebrow as Rafe showed no reaction to the mention of his wife's family and continued, "I live in Florence for most of the year, of course, a beautiful city which does not suffer with the excesses of climate as this plague ridden hole." He dipped a hand into his stocking, pulled out his card and held it out to Rafe.

As Rafe reached to take it, Alvisi grabbed his hand and kissed the palm, his tongue flicking over Rafe's skin, never taking his taunting eyes from Rafe's.

Rafe's breathing became more rapid, but he didn't pull away. The tongue was warm, sharp, probing, and he savoured the active touch of another man.

Alvisi slid toward him on the bench, and with one slippered foot, rubbed between Rafe's thighs. Then as suddenly as it had begun, he swung his legs onto the floor and stood up. He bowed theatrically and replaced the mask, concealing all but his own lips with their sly, twisted grin. "I am often in here," he said simply, and left.

Rafe sat there in stunned silence, then he shot to his feet and strode to the door. It was snowing hard, and the visibility was extremely limited. Alvisi had vanished.

So it began. Rafe returned to the inn every night for a week, but Alvisi did not reappear. He asked people about the Conte, but everyone said he was not currently in Venice, and for once Rafe was out of his depth, not the master of his own destiny. On the one hand, there was his beloved, broken Ambrose, whom no amount of care and love seemed to rouse; on the other, a smiling, elusive man who had called himself Achille. Neither of them seemed quite real to Rafe, and he would have thought he had imagined the incident in the inn, were it not for the card, which he kept in his desk.

The weather was the coldest Rafe had ever known it on the Adriatic. Venice was beautiful at any time of year, but Venice in the snow was spectacular. Rafe took Sebastien on his daily trip to St Mark's to watch the famous clock chime ten. Covered in snow, the church looked like an enormous cake. Sebastien ran happily around in the snow, feeding the pigeons, and Rafe stood outside Florian's watching him, waiting for him to tire so they could go inside and get a warm drink. Suddenly there was a butterfly touch on his buttocks, then a warm squeeze, and Rafe spun round to meet laughing green eyes.

"Mmm," said Alvisi. "So very firm. A black Angel, an Angel of happy meetings. I shall call you Raphael." Whereupon he walked away, leaving Rafe furious, wanting to race after him, to question him, to find out who he really was, but unable to do so with Sebastien in his charge.

His night time ramblings became hunts. He would go first to the inn where he had met the stranger, and then he would search the city like a man possessed. It infuriated him that twice he had let the man disappear without a trace, without explaining himself. One dawn he returned home, wet and exhausted, and stood watching Ambrose sleep. The look in Rafe's eyes was tender as he saw him so peaceful, and he could not wake him; it would do neither of them any good. He walked softly to the door and went to sleep in another room.

But Ambrose was not sleeping. When Rafe started staying out late, he waited awake in the dark, unable to relax until Rafe returned, curling around his chilled body, finally able to sleep. This night when Rafe left the room became the first of many, and Ambrose was alone in the night with every black thought returning. Like Rafe, he wanted to talk about the divide between them, he wanted to talk about the vagrant at Standish, the poem, about Francis, about the rape, and where Rafe had gone the next morning, but he did not have the words.

The city wasn't large, but it was proving impossible to find someone who did not wish to be found. After another night of searching the entire Rialto district to no avail, Rafe was back in the same bar where he had first seen the elusive Alvisi. He was drinking hard, but he had a lust that alcohol wouldn't dent. The door opened, and in the doorway was the fox-faced stranger in a high collared cape. He did not enter the inn, but with one finger on his lips, he beckoned to Rafe. Intrigued, Rafe stood and walked to the door.

Alvisi grabbed his hand and led him, child-like through the dark streets. He led him down a snow-filled alley and pushed him against a wall. He was tall as Rafe, but slight. His lips were open, and his eyes were alight with triumph. He slipped his cold fingers into Rafe's breeches, and Rafe cried out, silenced as Alvisi kissed him, that pointed tongue dancing in his mouth. He broke away and stared at Rafe, his hand working Rafe's member swiftly. "Raphael," he hissed, "were you looking for me? Were you waiting for me? Have you been thinking of me?"

Rafe groaned and thrust into his hand; the cold, the alley, Ambrose, everything else forgotten but the feeling of skin on his prick. Blood roaring in his head; the lust overtook him. "Gods, yes. Who *are* you?"

"Incognito," whispered the tantalising man, dropping his other hand to cup Rafe's scrotum, flicking the sacs with his thumb, causing Rafe to whimper with pleasure. "Tobias, Legion, Achilles, you choose, my angel. You name me, my black Raphael." He kissed him deeply again, his hands busy at their work.

Rafe felt as if the tensions of the past two months were in his loins and groaning in time to Alvisi's pumping. His seed flew from him in a torrent of relief, explosive and violent, the name Achilles on his lips.

He leaned against the wall, panting. He was out of control; this demon had done something to his mind, and he had no idea as to what he was doing. Ambrose...he thought of Ambrose, sleeping sweetly and alone, and he pushed the devil from his arms, or tried to. Achille was tangled round him like an octopus, kissing him, his arms everywhere at once and in trying to disentangle him, he simply managed to attach him more thoroughly.

"Raphael," Achille breathed, "do you not want me? Do you not want to plunge yourself into me, feel me beneath you, hot and tight and quivering?"

"God..." Rafe groaned. "What are you? You are not a man; you are an incubus."

"Mmm," sighed Achille, his mouth on Rafe's neck. "That describes me very well." He straightened and kissed Rafe on the nose, letting him go. "I'll let you get back to your sweet love now, for I wager he is a sweet love, vanilla and strawberry." He walked to end of the alley, and stopped at the opening, lost in the murk, only his eyes gleaming in the darkness. "I wonder if you will think of your incubus next time you are in his arms? I think perhaps you will."

He was gone again, and this time, disgusted with himself, Rafe did not run after him. *A dark alleyway, with a man I do not know — how low have I fallen?* A long way from the perfect love with Ambrose, he realised, but he was obsessed with this dark creature, and he knew he had to see him again.

Chapter 16

He returned to the palazzo earlier than usual and found Ambrose sitting in the study, a book on his lap. He looked up at Rafe and smiled, which made Rafe's stomach flutter with love for him and revulsion for what he had just done and longed yet to do with Achille, *to* Achille. Rafe strode across to Ambrose and dropped to his knees. He buried his face in Ambrose's lap in an agony of penitence. *I should tell Ambrose now. Confess it, after all it was not such a bad thing. I did not fuck the man, did not touch him; Ambrose might forgive me, he might.*

His eyes soft, Ambrose stroked the wet, black hair. "Rafe? Are you all right? I was..." He wanted to say, *'missing you, longing for you,'* wanted to shout at him, accuse him, but could not speak the words, frightened again by his own jealousy. Instead he said, "...just going to bed."

Rafe swallowed. *No, I can't tell him. How can I? How can I explain that I was driven to another man, all because of a promise I myself made and should not have done? It is impossible.* All he could do was to resolve to himself not to seek out the intoxicating Alvisi. He stood, helping Ambrose to his feet, and kissed him chastely. "Good night, *amore*," he said, holding his love gently in his arms, feeling him soft and pliant, his heart tearing in his chest as Ambrose went to the door and left him alone without a backward glance.

As Ambrose sat on the bed alone, his worst fears returned to him. He suspected that Rafe was seeing someone else. What else would explain the fact that he went out night after night? If it was simply to parties, then why did he come home soaked to the skin? They had hardly spoken for days, and Ambrose knew that it was partly his own fault. He had been reflecting on the past few weeks, slowly coming to the realisation that it was Rafe that was the best, strongest part of himself, Rafe who made him the person he was, able to get through the horror of Paris. *I made him wait too long,* Ambrose thought unhappily, remembering Rafe's words after he had met Francis in Lyme. *'I would have bedded anyone to satiate the lust I had for you.'*

The next day, Ambrose surprised Rafe by seeking him out in the breakfast room. "I wanted to go to the Redentore today. May I take the gondola?"

Rafe's heart leapt at this change in his lover, however slight, and feeling caged and restless, called the servants to prepare the Felze for the journey. "I'll come with you," he said. "Sebastien is spending the day with cousins."

Once in the Felze, Rafe took Ambrose's hands and kissed them, then held him close as they made their way up the Giudecca, clutching him like a shield as if to ward off temptation. His thoughts were black, contaminated with an obsession to feel cold thin hands on his cock again. Possessed and driven mad by the whispered, '*I wonder if you will think of me,*' Rafe had hardly been unable to think of anything else.

Ambrose was pleased that Rafe had accompanied him, and squeezed his hands gratefully, longing for Rafe to kiss him. When he did not, Ambrose was too unsure of the state of their relationship to take the initiative, watching Rafe's abstraction with worried eyes. As they entered the great church, built in thanks to the Redeemer who had saved the city from the plague, Ambrose's head spun. He was still in awe of the opulence of Venice, and he walked down the church towards the sacristy to examine the paintings by Veronese and Tintoretto.

Rafe, who had been there many times, sat down and watched Ambrose until he was out of sight in the huge place. He was restless and fretful. Hating churches, he walked out into the cold air, to the massive steps overlooking the canal. There were many gondole in front of the stairs, and Rafe, his eyes empty and bored, watched them come and go for a long while. A second Felze pulled up to the church, its windows completely curtained. No one got out, and Rafe's heart beat faster as he stood and stared at it. The front door of the compartment opened, but still no one exited. Without hesitation and without thought, his erection growing, he strode to the bottom of the stairs and stepped into the Felze, not even considering his actions. He knew, without knowing how he knew, exactly who was waiting in it.

Cool hands pulled him into the darkened space. The door closed, and it was black, pitch black, the velvet curtains shutting out all of the weak winter light. A viper's voice whispered in his ear, slim fingers feeling his clothes and undoing buckles and buttons by touch alone. "Raphael."

It was the voice of Rafe's doom, and he knew it, even as he kissed the treacherous mouth as hard as he could. There was a scent of musk and civet, as the man coiled himself around Rafe like a python. "You are following me, Achilles," he groaned. "Why can you not leave me be?"

"But my angel," said the husky voice that crept through his soul like a clinging vine, like a parasitic lust, "you *want* me to pursue you. Do you not realise that yet? You named me yourself. I am your weakness, your Achilles' heel."

Hands pushed him gently against what felt like a bed of large velvet cushions. Rafe's chest was naked, and he could feel a mouth biting and kissing every inch of his flesh. His arms went to hold the other man, but Alvisi, surprisingly strong, pushed him back.

The disembodied voice said, "No. I want you to lie there and feel, my black hearted love, feel what I do to you, the better to remember later."

The agile tongue flickered down his torso like a snake's, fingers fluttering along either side of it. In spite of the cold, Rafe was on fire, and his loins were bursting. Achille divested him of his shoes and breeches with practised ease. Then he seemed to melt away, and Rafe could not tell where he was, although he could just hear him breathing softly. Then, oh joy, hands again, on the top of his thighs, rubbing them gently, hot breath on his cock, then a tongue, lapping at his scrotum, making him gasp as each sac was licked and nipped, and taken into a hot mouth, rolled around and then left in the cold, while the mouth moved on, never still. One finger explored his fundament and pushed into his orifice, making Rafe whimper with ecstasy as it slid in and out over that spot that set fireworks off in his brain.

Rafe was lost. When he opened his eyes, he could see nothing. When he closed them, all he saw was Ambrose, so he kept his eyes open. He felt the man moving up his body again and straddling his hips. He raised himself up, and unfamiliar hands positioned his prick. Rafe could feel it pressing against the man's fundament, and he gave a cry of anguish.

"Ready?" the devil whispered to him, bringing tears to his eyes. "Tell me that you do not want this, my Raphael, and I will stop. You can go back to your sweet life, and I swear to you that I will never bother you again."

Rafe was shaking; partly with cold but mainly with a passion he could not contain, as his soul was torn from its moorings.

"Tell me," came the voice again. "Or are you joining with me in the dark that you know you deserve?"

"I...cannot." Rafe's voice was forced from him. "For pity's sake..." His breath came in huge gasps, "please...do it." There was that silvery insane laugh again which chilled him, incensed him, and Rafe felt himself impaling tight hotness like a fleshy vice. Tears flowed from him then — for the betrayal it was too late to retract, and for the lust that consumed him. All he could do was thrust savagely into the dark, warm grip while Achille — or as he had so rightly said, his Achilles — hissed in pleasure with every movement, goading him, wanting more, demanding more.

Rafe's release came swiftly, the semen shooting hot and exquisitely painful, filling his tormentor, trickling back down onto his body and down his thighs. As he lay there, his cock throbbing, dazed and guilty, Achille lay over him and kissed him again, praising him.

"You took a step into Gehenna today, my angel," he said, "but what a long road it is. Will you stay the distance, I wonder?"

Rafe had no idea what he was talking about, and pushed him off, shaking. He made a chink in the curtains so he could see to dress. "No more of this!" he said, dismayed to see how far they were from shore. His heart sank. How long had he been away? It might only have been ten minutes, but it could have been an hour; Ambrose surely would be looking for him. "Leave me alone, Alvisi. No more, for the love of God."

"Too late, sweet blackness, too late," said the corrupter, entwining himself around Rafe's back, his long legs encircling him. "You had the choice back there — between the light on the steps and the hell in the water. You chose the dark."

The voice in his ear was honeyed poison, and Rafe felt his insides melt and his erection return.

"But I will let you discover that for yourself." Alvisi lay back against the cushions, his hands behind his head watching Rafe looking back at him with hunger at the long, slim body, bronzed and lean, the cock huge, hard, and unfulfilled.

With a shudder, Rafe forced his eyes away and finished dressing. The Felze bumped against the steps, and Rafe tore back up the snowy steps to the church, fear paralysing his mind. His heart was sitting quietly on one of the seats. Rafe slid in beside him, his soul bleeding at the lost look on Ambrose's face.

"Forgive me," Rafe said quietly. "I was bored, and chilled. I went for a walk to warm up." He quietly took Ambrose's hand, which was deathly cold, and was immediately solicitous. "God, Ambrose, you are freezing to death!" He removed his cloak and threw it over the younger man, rubbing his hands. Ambrose hardly seemed to be aware of him, and Rafe was terrified that his mind was slipping away again. He raised him to his feet and supported him down the steps to the gondola, trying desperately not to notice that Alvisi's was still there, knowing that he was watching through the curtains, loathing the fact that Alvisi had seen Ambrose, feeling that just the Conte's glance would pollute him.

Promising the gondolier gold if he could get them back quickly, he tried to warm Ambrose, wrapping his cloak and his arms around him, rubbing his cheeks and holding him tight. Although Ambrose's hands regained a little warmth, he was still as pale as milk, and Rafe hated himself. *Twice I have deserted him*, he thought savagely, *and twice he has suffered. I swear to heaven I shall never desert him again.*

Back at the Palazzo, Ambrose appeared to come to his senses somewhat and looked at Rafe for the first time. His eyes were soft and gentle, and Rafe gulped in relief and guilt. Ambrose allowed Rafe to fuss over him, giving him brandy and drying his feet, putting on warm slippers. Then with a quiet, formal tone he said "I'm tired. You will excuse me, Rafe."

Ambrose's hands were shaking and he barely made it to the bedroom without collapsing. He had wandered around the church at length, aware all the time of Rafe's powerful presence in the chair, and then next time he looked around, he had missed Rafe. Somehow he always knew where Rafe was. His essence called to Ambrose like a beacon, so that when he had gone, Ambrose was puzzled. He walked down to the main doors and saw Rafe standing hunched and hawk-like on the steps, gazing out at the horizon, stamping in the cold. Ambrose started down the steps to him, to tell him he was frozen and wanted to go home, but Rafe suddenly set off down the remaining few stairs and got into a covered gondola. His mind in torment, Ambrose watched as the door closed behind him and the gondola was poled out into the wide channel. *Who was he meeting? He must have been on the steps waiting for whoever it was, no wonder he agreed to come with me*, he thought bitterly. He had stood on the steps in the frozen wind for what seemed eternity, until the gondola started to head back to the church.

He picked up Rafe's cloak, which was lying beside him, and brought it up to his face and inhaled deeply. There were scents unfamiliar to Ambrose on it, scents he could not name, mingled with the distinct smell of his own love. He fell back onto the bed, clutching the cape to him and whispering Rafe's name, and cried himself to sleep.

In his own chamber, Rafe lay awake. He'd tried drinking, and he'd tried walking, and neither had tired him. The moon was out over the city, the night cloudless for a change; it would be cold, but there would be no more snow. The large fireplace was ablaze, but the huge room was chill, for all that. He knew what he had to do — he had to rid himself of the infection that was Alvisi and concentrate on Ambrose. He could not understand how Alvisi had addicted him so quickly — to his mouth, his skin, his perfume, his hands. Rafe groaned and reached down and stroked his cock, which had been hard ever since leaving the man. He thrust gently up from the bed in counterpoint to the silken strokes, then froze when he heard an unexpected noise. There was a figure by the door in the dark. "Ambrose?" he whispered, hardly daring to believe it. The figure laughed, a manic, soft, silvery laugh, and flew across to the bed and took possession of Rafe's soul.

Ambrose woke in the late evening and sat by the fire, thinking. He used his logic for once, something he had been lacking in recently. Rafe was still with him. He knew Rafe still loved him. He had no proof that Rafe was seeing another man. *Or woman*, his jealous heart said venomously. He could think of only one way to ensure that Rafe was no longer tempted. It frightened him, having known it only in violence and pain, but it was something he could freely give to Rafe, who had given him so very much without any demand for recompense.

It's mine to give, he thought, *and it's something I want to give him, finally, to make us one. He'll forgive me, I know he will.* He did not bother to wrap up on the walk down the corridors to Rafe's room; he anticipated being cold when he got there, and being warmed in the best way possible. Tears of happiness sprang to his eyes when he realised how much he'd missed Rafe's arms, and he hurried his pace. He opened the door silently and stepped across the large room. The fire had nearly burned out, and it was almost dark. As he neared the bed, his heart stopped. Rafe was asleep, but uncovered, naked, and wrapped around him at waist height, a slim beautiful man with black curly hair, his eyes wide open and gleaming, gently kissing Rafe's hip bone and caressing his half erect penis.

Seeing Ambrose standing there, his fist to his mouth to stop himself crying out, the stranger stopped kissing Rafe and smiled. His eyes still locked with Ambrose's, he continued his work, harder and more insistently, as Ambrose backed up toward the door.

Under the assault of the man's lips and hands, Rafe awoke. Seeing Alvisi was looking at something, a triumphant smile on his lips, he followed his gaze and saw Ambrose flattened against the doors, shaking and pale, fighting with the door handle. Rafe's erection vanished in a heartbeat, and he threw an arm out to Ambrose, screaming his name, but his love had gone.

Chapter 17

Rafe threw Alvisi savagely onto the bed as he tried to restrain him. The Conte said, "It is too late, lover, he is gone. I know it." He paused and then said with a gleam in his eye, "Ambrose," rolling the name around his mouth sensually, then continuing with mock drama, "The blond tragedian. His life is blighted forever, and you are renounced!"

Rafe rounded on him viciously. "Don't you dare to speak his name! You foul...depraved..." He broke off as he pulled his breeches and shirt on, and then ran for the door.

Alvisi smiled and lay back on the bed. "Mmm. All my fault, I dare say. You can blame me, if you like. I don't mind. He may even believe you."

Rafe ran from the room, and Alvisi called after him, with a manic laugh, "Check the canals, Raphael!" which piece of callousness made cold sweat break out on Rafe's forehead. He reached their bedroom — Ambrose's bedroom — and found it locked. He knocked quietly, every fibre of his being longing to kick it open, but unwilling to cause a scene, to rouse the servants and frighten the sleeping Sebastien.

"Ambrose." Silence. "Ambrose." Rafe's voice grew louder and more desperate. "Ambrose, my love, my own, let me in, please." There was no response, and he kept knocking softly, repeating his entreaty. After a few minutes there was a click, and Rafe fell into the room, Ambrose was fully dressed and packing a small bag. He didn't turn to look at Rafe, standing there in just breeches and a white shirt, pale beneath his tanned face. When he spoke, Rafe could hear his voice was tightly controlled.

"I have taken some clothes, but only a few. I have been in your employ for seven months, and I have taken that amount of salary only. I will repay you for the clothes upon my return to England and when I gain another position. I trust..." his voice nearly broke, but he continued, summoning the last reserves of his strength, "that any future employers can apply to you for a character."

"Ambrose," Rafe's voice was ragged, "don't say such things. Don't go. There must be something we can do, I can do. I did not mean this to happen, I was swept away, blinded. He's nothing, nothing to me." Rafe broke off, unable to explain, even to himself.

"And Francis was nothing, and the ragged man at Standish was nothing."

Ambrose's back was still to Rafe, but his voice was stronger, and Rafe's blood ran cold as he heard Ambrose's words... *He knows, he knows about Quinn.*

"You've lied to me or concealed things from me since the day we first met, Rafe. Maybe you will be able to tell your next conquest that *I* was nothing, too. After all, that is how you have made me feel." Rafe rushed to him, tried to turn him around, but Ambrose shook his arm off violently. "Don't touch me!" The words went through Rafe like a knife.

Ambrose shut the bag and turned to him finally, and Rafe saw a new expression in those blue eyes he loved so. They were hard and betrayed, and his voice — never less than kind — was bitter and sarcastic. "I was coming to you tonight. To give myself to you, finally, completely, to meld us together into one indivisible soul, and I find that your words are ashes in your mouth, your promises worthless, and your soul corrupt and weak.

"I only wish I had had the strength to see you for what you were in England. You are a true Goshawk after all, like your father and your grandfather before you. You pervert and destroy everything you come into contact with."

He picked up the bag and went to the door without another word, leaving Rafe helpless and speechless. All he could do was follow. Leaning over the banister, Rafe watched his heart leave him forever.

He walked dazedly back into Ambrose's room, closed the door, and sat on the bed, picking up one piece of clothing at a time and touching it as if it were a small animal, then putting it back tenderly, tears in his eyes that he did not dare let fall. If he opened the floodgates he felt he would cry until he died. His eyes moved blankly around the room, coming to rest on the bedside cabinet. There, lined up in a neat row, as if by someone who was being so very careful of them, were all of the personal presents he had given Ambrose — rings, watches, books, pins, the cane. The fact that Ambrose had really taken nothing but a few clothes broke Rafe finally, and he raged against his broken heart. Picking up the cane, he began to smash the room, breaking mirrors, small tables, and pounding the pile of clothes on the bed with savagery, his breath sobbing in his throat. He didn't hear the door open, didn't hear anyone enter, just felt strong arms restrain him. Realising it was his nemesis, he struck out wildly with his fists, punching and shouting incoherently.

Alvisi took the beating calmly, without retaliation, standing back and letting the blows rain on him, simply defending himself with his arms where he could. At last the attack abated, and Rafe went limp, falling to the floor sobbing; and Alvisi held his black angel until the dawn.

Rafe had found the true meaning of the word Gehenna. It was the final abode of the damned. He was trapped with a demon he did not want, that he hated but could not keep away from. Alvisi had been right when he had said that he would leave Rafe to discover it for himself. It was a craving worse than any for alcohol or opium. He had awakened that first dreadful morning to feel his arms around someone. In the sweet, brief moment of waking, he had forgotten everything and thought it was Ambrose, and then the events of the night before had returned like a tidal wave of grief. Realising whose arms he was in, he sat up in horror.

Alvisi's beautiful, feral face was bruised and battered, and for all his loathing for the man who had maliciously destroyed his life, Rafe was sickened that he had been responsible, and Ambrose's words cut him through again, *'You destroy everything you come in contact with.'*

He had bathed and bandaged Alvisi, although he could not bring himself to speak to him, and left him while he went to Sebastien, who had to be told. Sebastien had been truly inconsolable; he had loved Ambrose deeply. Rafe had to lie to his son and say that the tutor had had to go because one of his sisters was ill, and that they would all be together again when they went home. Sebastien could not understand why they had not all gone to Standish together, and Rafe said that Ambrose did not want to spoil his trip, trying to console the boy with the places they had yet to go — Pompeii, Rome, Athens. "Surely," he had said to the child, "you are looking forward to the Coliseum?" But Sebastien just wept, and Rafe longed to join him, feeling wretched that he had been the cause of yet more suffering, that even his own son had not been immune from his curse.

He tried to find Ambrose in Venice, but there were too many inns and boarding houses, and he never discovered where Ambrose had gone. Sickened by the Pearl of the Adriatic and all it entailed, and feeling beaten and helpless, Rafe allowed Alvisi to arrange to move them all to his villa in Florence, justifying his actions by the fact that it had been the next stop on their journey. Deep in his soul he knew that, even if he hadn't been invited, he would have followed the Conte like a whipped dog. Worst of all, he knew that the Conte knew it too. Thus he was consigned to his private purgatory: his days spent in morose and aggressive activity, and his nights filled with familiar nightmares that Alvisi's presence did not banish.

He kept away from Alvisi as much as he could, taking Sebastien around the city, day after day, dragging the poor child from gallery to library to museum, but inevitably having to return. Alvisi's villa was huge and magnificent, and Rafe had been given a suite to himself, but he soon realised that this was just another torment his captor had for him. He always returned to his rooms directly after the day's sightseeing, and then the hell began. He and Sebastien ate together, and after he had put the child to bed, he fought the demons of temptation. He sat on his bed, or paced the floor, forcing his mind on the sweetness of Ambrose, but his mind found it more and more difficult to summon up his face, his expression, except the last he had seen, with the fire of accusatory betrayal in his eyes.

The craving for Achille was tangible. His hands itched, his skin felt too tight and irritating, his mouth became dry, and his manhood was always burning for relief. He had never experienced anything like it, wanting someone physically, all of the time, while being revolted and disgusted by their innate depravity. He would suffer in his room, sometimes for hours, before he did what he knew he would do, and sought out Alvisi in a twisted echo of those times he had sought out Ambrose. Alvisi was always expecting him, and was smugly triumphant and mocking, as Rafe threw himself on him like a man who has been desperate in the desert throws himself into an oasis pool.

What he experienced with his tormentor, however, was no quenching of desire, no release or satisfaction, but a bottomless well of subverted pleasure. The more he drew from it, the more he craved and the more Alvisi laughed. Alvisi, he was learning, was completely amoral in true Roman style. He would take Rafe through the city at night, and find the most dissolute of taverns; he seemed to know them all intimately. There he would find some Apollonian youth, or better, two or even more, fill them with drink, and take them back to the villa for his entertainment. Alvisi always found it easy to get the youths to accede to his every request, bribing them with opium or money. The boys would be stripped of their clothes for Alvisi's delectation and the inevitable bacchanalia. He would press them on Rafe time and again, and indeed several times the boys made active advances toward him, but he always refused, even though he was always boiling to sink his cock deep into his Achilles, he couldn't do it to those Alvisi called his pets. So he would leave them, Alvisi's eyes on Rafe, his hands stroking the firm naked skin of his latest find.

Nor was the Conte content to confine himself to youths; he also stalked and seduced young women. Rafe took no part in that but retired to his suite, unable to sleep, waiting for the morning, when he knew the girl would be gone and he could burst into Alvisi's room and take out his frustrations on the slim frame.

In the midst of this nightmare of sex and avoidance, he wrote letters, reams of letters, to Ambrose, knowing he would not get them for weeks. He did not know where Ambrose would go first, so he wrote to Tavistock Square, to the White House, and to Standish, consigning them all to his bank in London for onward transmission. Letters of contrition, sorrow, repentance, love, lust, and longing.

Words splattered with tears, begging Ambrose to save him from his torment. At times he reminisced over the tender memories, finding it harder and harder to remember those sweet, innocent moments when he taught Ambrose the pleasures of his own body. The memories had begun to fade, smothered by the blackness of Alvisi's incarceration. His letters told Ambrose everything — about the duel, about Quinn, knowing it was too late, but finding that the torrent of confessions rushing from his quill was cathartic, and his soul was eased by it.

He explained the nightmares, about the rats, and the night in 1813, when the ship he was running to New Orleans — loaded to the gunwales with gunpowder, arms and ammunition — caught fire. He told Ambrose how he could have saved the lives of twenty men trapped in the hold, but not thinking he had the time, chose to fling himself into the sea. When the ship finally exploded, the water itself was alight, and there were bodies everywhere.

"All this," he wrote, *"is too much too late, and will only reinforce your opinion of my curse, that I destroy all I touch. You were right to say it, but remember, my heart, that I have destroyed myself first and foremost, by letting go the one who would have been my redeemer, the most precious soul that passed my way and one whom I was honoured to have love me, if only for too short a time.*

"The torture I now endure, you will not understand, and although I do not conceal it from you, would tell you of it, if you were to ask me, I will not write of it willingly. Forfend that I should cause one more look of misery on those perfect features, which I kiss in my mind every day.

"Would that I could be certain that I would ever be welcome back at Standish (read into that how you may) I would leave this Tartarus and crawl home."

And

"It is only the memory of your perfect body that keeps me sane in these dark times. He parades his lasciviousness before me and taunts me with your sweet memory, attempts to corrupt even that. He saw us together at the Redentore, and the sight enrages him. He knows my heart is in your keeping, no matter how he thinks my body is his. I think that the touch of your pale hands would bring me back to reality, instead of as it is, locked in a vortex of sin and madness."

And

"Ambrose, the first time you entered my bed, you entered my soul and heart so completely I shall never be free of you, unless you release me. Write and tell me your judgment: either I am lost to darkness and despair, or I can turn again to your light and be saved. Write, and I will take my sentence, whatever you decide.

The greater justice is with you, and I deserve none of it."

He groaned as his incubus slid onto the chair behind him and wrapped his naked body around him as he sat writing, late into the night.

"Why do you waste your efforts?" Achille said, dreamily one hand rubbing a hard nipple, the other running down Rafe's chest and into his breeches. "If he gets them, he will burn them, unopened." He undid Rafe breeches and released his cock, which was, as always hard and angry as soon as Achille touched him.

Rafe ignored his words and continued to write, even as his body betrayed him and the mood changed with the devil tangled round him.

"If I had the strength of character I once believed myself to have, I would stab him now, or wrap my hands around his throat and watch the vicious creature die, but you are right, you knew me better in those few short months than I knew myself. Where I am is where I deserve to be; there will be no redemption and no dawn. If you can never forgive me, write and tell me so, but keep my heart, for I am dying little by little every day without it, and that perhaps is the best end for us all."

Achille read the words dispassionately. "How very poetic, my sweet. Would you really kill me? For love? How wonderful."

His hands and voice drove Rafe insane, and the blood lust rose along with the disgust and bile he always felt. Standing, he grabbed the naked man and threw him onto the bed, smiling as ever. Rafe stripped and flung himself on the fiend, hooked his elbows under the man's knees, forced his legs apart wide and plunged his cock into his fundament without pausing. Alvisi opened to Rafe easily. His eyes stayed open, green and dreamy, half closed like a cat's as he watched Rafe desperately plunging, groaning brokenly in abhorrence of his own actions, his own eyes tightly closed.

"God," whispered Rafe, "I loathe you, and I despise myself." The words came out of him like endearments, and moisture beaded at the corners of his eyes.

"Mmm..." said Alvisi softly, "I know you do, *bel ami*. I know. Did your Ambrose let you take him like this? Or was he less 'fundamental' in his tastes?"

Alvisi laughed again, chilling Rafe to the marrow as he plunged his soul into hell again and again, seeking salvation. Alvisi had taunted him for days about Ambrose and always when they were conjoined.

"Or did you come to me because he would not let you at all?" Seeing Rafe's brow furrow, Alvisi guessed the truth triumphantly. "So," he whispered, panting slightly under Rafe's pounding onslaught and wrapping his slim fingers around his own cock, "your precious 'heart' refused you. Now I realise why you were so easy."

Rafe's eyes snapped open as he felt his seed rise within him and his mind, driven mad, lost control. His hands flew to Alvisi's throat and gripped him, tightening with every thrust into the foul body. Alvisi did not react, but gazed at Rafe with those green mocking eyes and smiled as Rafe strangled him, his own hand still bringing himself to his own explosion. As Rafe came, with a cry of despair, his hands dropping from Alvisi's neck, he was disgusted and horrified to find that Alvisi had ejaculated too, and was still smiling.

"Raphael," he breathed, his voice distorted and his neck bruised, "how did you know? That is an art form worthy of de Sade himself. What you did simply accentuates the pleasure."

Rafe leapt from the bed as if he had been scalded, retching with the conflicting emotions. De Sade had indeed taught him that very technique, but he had not meant it to be an erotic tool with Achille. He had actually meant to kill him. He realised, his black eyes falling on to the dissolute man, that sooner or later, he *was* going to have to kill him.

Chapter 18

The wind blew freshly off the Mediterranean, and Ambrose noticed that there was a warmer feel to it today. He leaned on the sea wall, enjoying the feel of the sun on his face and wind in his hair. Standing there in the light, staring into the distance, he looked like a young Siegfried, his handsome face and elegant figure attracting much attention, although he was unaware of it. His face was leaner than a year ago, and had lost some of its angelic softness, replaced by a look of the inner strength he was only just beginning to discover. His eyes had lost that innocent wonderment at the world and now had previously unknown depths.

After leaving Rafe's palazzo, he had walked and walked. Finally exhausted and nearly frozen to death, he had found lodgings and had collapsed into his bed where he had stayed for two days, neither eating nor sleeping. Finally, having cried every tear he had, he had two options: to return to Rafe, or to get as far away from him as he could. There was no choice. So he had travelled overland to Genoa and was waiting there for a ship to England. He thought it would be easier and less expensive than to try and arrange to go over the Alps and then all through France. Besides which, the last place he wanted to visit again in his life was Paris. He did not anticipate any difficulty finding a ship, hopefully one that would be calling at Plymouth, Southampton or Poole, which would cut days from his journey.

Although the thought of Rafe was with him constantly, it was now a dull ache rather than a raw open wound. He had spent so long suspecting him of infidelity that the discovery had been less of a shock than anticipated, although he did wonder who Rafe's new love was, how long it it had been since they'd met and where, and whether Rafe was still with him. The vision of the beautiful, mysterious man wrapped around Rafe rose yet again before his eyes, and the jealousy surged through him like a sickness.

Travelling alone, he felt strangely free and independent. Having to arrange his own methods of transportation, to arrange where to eat, where to stay had been a liberating experience; he had left all of that to Rafe before, but now it kept him occupied, and his mind clearer than it would have been if he'd had time to brood. He had also thought seriously about his future. There was no point in staying on the Standish estate, as he was sure that Rafe would follow him at some point. He needed to get away, and as fast as possible. A swift visit with his sisters to collect his belongings from there and from the great house, then on to London to attempt to secure a position, either as a clerk or a tutor, perhaps even a teacher in a school somewhere. He had enough money to last for a while, and he knew that his having been tutor to Goshawk's son would open many more doors than his being Ambrose Standish would. He had thought that he might be better to make straight for London, but he could not face that. He wanted to see his sisters, although they would want some sort of explanation, and he had no idea what he was going to say to them. There were goodbyes to be said, too — to the house he had lived in all his life, to Aries, and...to Standish. He doubted he would ever return again to Dorset.

A cough sounded behind him, and he turned to see a plump man with a flustered face.

"*Perdonimi, il signore*," the man said in an appalling Italian accent.

Ambrose interrupted him with a swift wave of his hand. "Sir, do not trouble yourself, I am English."

"Ah, I am so pleased. I was hoping you might be, Sir. I appear to be having trouble making myself understood. My sister and I are returning to London. Would you happen to know if there is a ship to England in all this throng? I assume you are here on the same errand?"

Ambrose saw the man inspecting his elegant, expensive clothes bought in London and Paris, and flushed at his own misrepresentation. "I am making investigations on that very matter myself, yes. That sailor there," he said, pointing toward the dock, "has promised to find out for me." The sailor was in negotiation with a swarthy man in brown leather, who, concluding his discussion, made his way toward Ambrose and the newcomer. Speaking volubly in Italian, the sailor said that the captain of the *Athenodorous* would take passengers, and was stopping at Southampton and then London. Ambrose turned to the stranger and explained.

"You are most kind," said the man. "Allow me to introduce myself — Dunstan, Christopher Dunstan. I am the rector of the Parish of St Olaf's. It's a small and quite depressing parish in the East End of London, but one has to do good works where one may."

"Standish," Ambrose said, "Ambrose Standish." He was relieved to see no glimmer of recognition in the man's face at the name, merely a welcoming smile. "If I can be of any assistance, I would be happy to. If you will allow me, I can arrange passage for you and your sister."

"Most kind, most kind. I would most obliged. I have a smattering of the language, but I am afraid that it is woefully inadequate for detailed negotiation. We will want to go to London, naturally. I hope..." he faltered and blushed, "that the passage will not be too dear?"

Ambrose was embarrassed for the man, who was probably just

as badly off as himself, for all his own borrowed finery, and assured him that the price was far less than the overland journey, as he had already made inquiries.

"My mother died quite recently," Dunstan said, "and we came out here to settle her affairs, bit of a waste of time." Dunstan flushed, as if he'd said to much, and it seemed to Ambrose that the mother had obviously not left her son and daughter enough even to warrant the journey.

"I am sorry for your loss," he said, and then turned to the sailor and concluded the negotiations swiftly and to the satisfaction of all.

The ship was due to sail at eight the next morning, and as he had talked to the little man, Ambrose was pleased that he would have company on the boat. He had been too solitary for too long, wrapped up in Rafe as he had been. It would make a pleasant change to talk of normal matters once more.

As he carried his bag up the gangplank the next morning, Ambrose could feel curious eyes on him, probably wondering why such an obviously prosperous gentleman would be travelling in such a manner and without servants. He hated the very clothes he wore. Not only did they give the wrong impression of his status, but every item reminded him forcibly of Rafe. Getting dressed, earlier that morning, he could not help but think, *and this, we got at Westons in Bond Street and the day he bought this was the morning he made us all laugh with his impersonation of Wellington.* It had become a painfully sweet torture, and Ambrose resolved to burn every item when he returned home.

Dunstan met him at the top of the gangplank and introduced his sister, who was blonde and very pretty and, Ambrose was pleased to see, displayed none of the false coquettishness of the young ladies who had flirted with him in Paris. Instead, she seemed serious and full of sensibility. Like her brother, she evinced no awareness of the name of Standish, and Ambrose was grateful for it. He had lived under the shadow of the name for too long.

As Italy fell further and further behind, Ambrose's mood lifted. His heart was broken, but he was young, and spring in the Mediterranean was a tonic for his senses. The ship called at Gibraltar and anchored there for three days. The diversity of ships in the harbour was staggering, not the least among them, mighty British ships of the line.

Ambrose took the opportunity to visit the Ifach, exploring the tunnels used in the great sieges, wishing that Sebastien were with him. The boy would have adored it all: the naval officers everywhere, the obvious signs of Napoleon's futile battering on the fort, the apes on The Rock, and the dolphins swimming in the bright blue water. He missed Sebastien almost as much as he missed Rafe, and leaning on the harbour wall, he allowed himself a moment of grief, his eyes closed.

"Mr Standish," came a feminine voice. Ambrose started, his reverie shattered. Miss Dunstan beside him, a parasol blocking the sun. "Forgive me for disturbing you," she said. "You were lost in thought."

"You need no forgiveness, Miss Dunstan," he said, as a flush suffused his face. "I was thinking...of home."

The woman turned and walked, and Ambrose fell in step beside her. As they walked along the quayside, she asked him with simple candour about his home, and he found himself happy to tell her about the White House and his sisters, Aries, and his studies. He did not mention Standish or the Goshawks. She then went on to ask him of his travels, and Ambrose found this harder to respond to. Apart from a brief time in Paris, when he had been truly happy, the remainder of his travels had been blighted. He glossed over them, deftly changing the subject.

"I found that I missed England more than I ever imagined I would, and I look forward to seeing Dorset more than I looked forward to seeing Rome and all her marvels."

"Your sisters must have missed you," Miss Dunstan said.

He managed to smile, in spite of the pain of the mention of his family. "I'm afraid they will miss me again. I plan to move to London, because there really are no opportunities for teaching in the county." He found it surprisingly easy to converse with her, and hated to so dissemble, so he changed the subject. "Tell me of your brother's parish."

Her face lit up, at the mention of her brother. It was clear from her expression that she was devoted to Dunstan, and had decided to keep house for him when their mother moved abroad a few years earlier. After being laid low with consumption, Mrs Dunstan wanted her last years to be in a sunny land where she could see the sea every day.

"We were never very close to mother," she went on to say, "and so we have always been closer to each other. Christopher works hard, but truly he deserves a better Parish. He would, I fear, be disappointed to hear me tell you of that, but St Olaf's *is* a dark and dismal place, and there is always more to do than can be done, more money needed than there is available."

"Could he not ask to be moved?" Ambrose asked.

"He refuses to," she said. "The Bishop offered him a living outside the city, but he did not accept it. He feels he is doing more good with the poor than he would ever be able to do with the rich."

"He prefers to be busy, then."

"He does." She smiled with her mouth, but her eyes were sad. "He is always too busy; the overcrowding and disease are dreadful. We do what we can, but it is never enough."

Ambrose delivered Miss Dunstan to her brother at the ship and, unwilling to be incarcerated again within the wooden hull, he continued to walk along the quay and then turned north toward the Garrison Library, which had been recommended to him by Dunstan. Considering that it housed a celebrated collection of books, it was surprisingly empty, and Ambrose welcomed the musty stillness like an old friend. Books were a refuge for him, a solace and a temporary escape. The library was not completely deserted, however; there was a lieutenant studying in one corner. As Ambrose sat down, the young man looked up and smiled hesitantly. Ambrose smiled back at the disarming greeting, unable to help noticing how very handsome he was, and a pang shot through him. Was this to be his lot in life: to see men and to find them attractive? What about the mind, and the soul? Surely there was a way to disassociate oneself from the pleasures of the flesh and to rise above them. In spite of this disquiet, he was unable to prevent himself from stealing looks at the lieutenant, admiring the golden blond curls, the small nose and rosy lips. Before he could stop himself, Ambrose wondered what they would feel like on his skin.

The young officer stood to return a book to the shelves, and Ambrose watched, hypnotised at the sight of perfect rounded buttocks. With an audible groan, his head fell into his hands. How could he return to his "normal" life? He felt he was infected with some sort of satyrism. Was this how Rafe felt? Was his lust so intense that he truly could not restrain himself? If that lieutenant came to him now, sat on his lap, kissed him, touched him, felt him in his private places, would he be like Rafe, be unable to stop? Would he be sucked into the temptation, or would he be able to pluck the boy from his lap and deny his urges? *God help me*, he thought, as he felt his manhood harden. The lieutenant looked up frowning, and said, "Sir? Are you quite well?" The sound of his voice forced Ambrose to his feet muttering words of assurance before he fled.

Back aboard the ship as it sailed along the coast of Spain, Ambrose's mind, in its half-healed state, began to assail him again, setting his recovery back by several weeks. Sitting on deck, he watched the coastline as it slipped by, whilst sailors around him busied at their work. Fascinated by the teamwork needed to negotiate the waters, Ambrose watched the crew for hours at a time as they worked like ants with a hive mind, seeming to know what the ship needed without the shouted instructions from the Quarterdeck. Suddenly his eyes fell on one particular sailor, and his breath caught in his throat. The man wore just a pair of ragged trousers, his torso naked and glistening with sweat. Tears sprang to Ambrose's eyes, for the body was Rafe's remodelled, but perfect with no scarring: tall, brown, and lean, with every muscle defined.

His hair was long and black like Rafe's, but tied into a pigtail. Ambrose remembered with agony the first time he had put a hand on Rafe's taut flesh and closed his eyes, finding the man there in his mind also, smiling with his arms outstretched. When he opened his eyes, the sailor had turned toward him, and the face was so different from Rafe's that the spell was partially broken. A very Italian face, rounded and laughing, with hooped earrings and wide eyes. His Rafe-like body, however, was a torment to Ambrose, and he found that he was not strong enough to deny himself the daily torture of sitting and watching him, wondering with disgust in his heart, whether, if he touched the man, his flesh would feel the same as Rafe's.

This and the incident in the Garrison Library haunted Ambrose. Previously, on the journey from Genoa to Gibraltar, he had sought out the Dunstans. Both Christopher Dunstan and his sister were excellent company, intelligent and discerning. To Ambrose, tormented by dark thoughts, they appeared pure and shining, like salvation. Ambrose was drawn to that goodness, hoping it would wash over him, purge him of what he now felt were unnatural thoughts. But it did not work, and little by little he slipped away from his new friends, spending more and more time closeted away. His love for Rafe had been a gradual awakening, and he had never thought of it as anything but real and true, but now he felt that the thoughts he had about strangers were lustful and perverse. Eventually he stayed in his cabin, now unable to face the deck at all, neither the half-naked sailors, nor the Dunstans.

The Dunstans had no idea of the torment Ambrose suffered, but they could tell that the young man was burdened with some secret. They missed his company, and discussed him often. After a week of Ambrose's absence from their trio, Dunstan inquired of his health from the captain and reported back to Constance.

"The captain says he has not been well, and does not wish us to catch his malaise."

"You should see if there is anything we can do," she answered. "I like him, but his eyes are so sad."

"Perhaps he has lost someone too?" Christopher ventured.

Constance shook her head. "I don't think so, for we spoke at length of his family. His father died when he was young and his sisters await him in Dorset. He's never said. What was he doing in Genoa?"

"He was tutoring," Christopher said, re-reading the newspaper they had collected from Gibraltar.

"Oh," said Constance with a small gasp.

Christopher looked up. "What is it?"

Constance looked at her brother with a pitying glance. "Sometimes, Chris dear, you are rather unimaginative."

Christopher threw the paper down onto the table and stood up, narrowly missing cracking his head on the ships low beam. "Constance, I don't know what I would do without you." He dashed from the cabin, even forgetting his hat.

He knocked on Ambrose's cabin door less than a minute later. "Standish?" The door opened and Dunstan was almost shocked at Ambrose's appearance. He was half dressed and pale, his hands shaking. "Can I be of assistance, Sir? Are you not well?"

Ambrose gestured him into the cabin, falling back into his chair. "I am grateful for your solicitation, Dunstan, but there is nothing you can do. I was ill a long time last year, and I suffer for it occasionally and become weak and giddy." The lies fell easily from his mouth, and he hated himself, yet another talent he had learned since meeting Rafe.

"My sister advised me of your plans for finding a new position," Dunstan said. "We feel that we have got to know you quite well on the voyage." A shadow clouded Ambrose's face at the erroneous assumption. "You may not know, but our small church has a school attached to it." Ambrose's eyes flickered to Dunstan with a faint ray of hope. "It is within my remit to appoint a tutor, and the post has not yet been filled. I understand that you wish to return to Dorset, but would you be at all interested? It is poorly paid, and very much below you..." Seeing Ambrose's eyes close, Dunstan thought him offended. "However, I realise that it may not be something you would ever consider."

Ambrose's mind cleared; it was like the sunlight had broken into the windowless cabin. It was a prayer answered, a way out of the dark. He was being offered a chance of redemption, and he grasped it with both hands and pulled himself to shore. His eyes flew open, and he clasped Dunstan's hands, unable to speak, but his face showed the other man the heartfelt gratitude and relief he felt at his prospective salvation.

Chapter 19

Ambrose allowed himself to be talked out of his cabin by a persistent Christopher and sat with his back to the crew, resisting the temptation to watch them. He talked, but mostly listened to the Dunstans, learning more about their life, the little school, their work, and their faith. Not having any himself, he found it fascinating, the way they clung to the belief of a higher power in the face of the immense suffering and degradation they encountered daily. His sisters both believed, but in a different way. With them it was a belief that God was in his Heaven and all was right with the world. Theirs was a God who was as remote from them as was the Emperor of China, who conducted His business and did not involve them in it. With the Dunstans, it was a pathetically sweet love, giving everything and receiving nothing in return, in the simple trust that the meek would inherit the earth as a reward for their suffering. Ambrose longed for the gift of belief, but found both points of view impossible to reconcile with his own knowledge, both of science and of humanity.

They gently quizzed him for his religious standpoint, and when he changed the subject for fear of getting into a theological argument with them, they backed away and did not force theirs onto him. He was simply grateful to be among gentlepeople again. His life until the previous summer had been peaceful, and although filled with a longing for Standish and all that it entailed, had had few peaks and troughs. With Rafe, he had found himself out of control, run away with passions of which he was hitherto unaware, like a rider on a horse that has the bit firmly between its teeth. There had been no peace with Rafe, not in the joy or in the despair, although, and his heart jolted to remember it, there had been tenderness, such tenderness that only such a truly powerful man had it in his gift to bestow.

So his days improved, but alone in the dark, his nights remained a trial and a torment. His traitorous hands skimmed his own flesh as he imagined they were Rafe's roughened palms, learning every bump and curve of his own skin, perceiving his body through Rafe's touch, and attempting to remember how Rafe's had felt beneath his own senses. He doubted he would ever forget that first touch of Rafe's abdomen, the silken tautness of his muscles, the warm adamantine of his manhood. The feeling he had had when Rafe first kissed him, Rafe's tongue trailing down his stomach.

Every night Ambrose grasped his own hardness, feeling the familiar burning pressure at his groin. It was not Rafe's Fire, as that was sweeter. This was a heat that even when doused was dormant and smoking, having no vent to it but his own manipulation. Wrapping his fingers around his length, he caressed himself softly, remembering a rainy afternoon in Paris, Sebastien in his nursery playing with a huge new set of lead soldiers, with which he was avenging himself on his arch rival, the Duke of Wellington. Rafe had softly shut the door on the boy and looked at Ambrose with unmistakable love in his eyes. No words were spoken as Ambrose helped Rafe climb the second flight of stairs and they closed the door on the rest of the house. Rafe had taken him to paradise that afternoon, and the recollection of Rafe's eager but patient ministrations caused Ambrose's seed to fly from him there, while Rafe held him close, and also here, in the cold, alone and so far from that tender touch.

At long last the ship docked in London, and Ambrose entered a world quite unknown to him. He had been to London before, but that had been in the cosseted privilege of the Goshawk carriage and the Tavistock Square house. The London he'd seen before had tree-lined avenues, and a good many of the shops and streets were lit up at night with the new gas lamps. Rafe had shown him only the beauty of London: the parks, the bridges, Regents Street, Bloomsbury. The dark squalor of the East End was a shock to his system.

They arrived late at night. Dunstan hired a hackney from the docks, and they rode the short distance from West India to St Olaf's. Even as late as it was, the traffic on the roads was constant. St Olaf's was in a dark part of the East End, and even in the unlit streets, Ambrose could see the signs of human misery. Prostitutes lined the street, and the violent preyed on the weak. It was a world beyond his experience, and for a second he felt genuinely frightened and wondered if he had made a terrible mistake. But as he looked across at Miss Dunstan sitting quietly in the corner of the hackney, her eyes closed, he remembered that she had lived and worked here for three years, and his spirit rallied. Eventually they pulled up at the rectory, a small square building set back from a dingy looking church. Ambrose was shown to his room, Miss Dunstan, who was now 'Constance' to Ambrose, at her insistence, fussed about airing the bed for him and making sure he had all he needed. It took him a while to assure her that the reoccurring tremors in his hands were simple exhaustion, not illness, and eventually placated, she left him to collapse onto the bed. For the first time in the weeks since the flight from Venice, he slept a deep and dreamless sleep.

Over the next few days and weeks he was busier than he had been in his life, helping the Dunstans settle back in to life in the Parish, and getting matters ready for the opening of the little school. As soon as he could, he had written to his sisters and told them of his new situation. He had lied to them, hating himself for every black word he put onto the page. He told them that he had been homesick for England, that he had met the Dunstans in Italy (true, he thought, attempting to vindicate himself) and they had offered him the teaching position.

"I understand how disappointed you will be that I have taken a lesser salaried post, but I know you will understand when you realise how much I am needed here. I intend to live a quiet life, and my expenses will be few. The majority of my salary will be yours, and it will help you, I know.

"My love to both of you, I strive daily to become the brother you deserve.

Ambrose"

As he wrote this at Christopher's small desk, his attention wandered, and he found himself remembering the tambour shutter on his father's desk and its beautiful silver inkwell. Each thought led to another like a story book, his eyes filling with tears when he realised he could never again go home.

Watching him quietly from the other side of the room, her needlework on her lap, Constance exchanged a glance with Christopher, and he gently touched her hand. Both brother and sister felt that whatever secret sorrow Ambrose was holding, it would be revealed to them when he was ready, and perhaps together they would be able to bring him to Christ in good time. The revelation of his sorrow and the exposure of it when it came, was something that none of them expected.

Months had passed since Ambrose's flight, and Rafe was a changed and broken man. They were in Rome, for Sebastien's sake, and Rafe felt he was no longer on the same planet as his love. He no longer resisted Achille and was, for a man of his strength and violence, blankly compliant. It was as if he had given up all hope, for despite the torrent of letters, Ambrose had ignored every entreaty he had sent.   Rafe knew then that it was hopeless, that his Ganymede had indeed fled Olympus and returned to earth with a crash and that it was entirely his own fault. So he wrote no more letters to Ambrose, but he had written to his bank with directives to set investigative agents in action to find the man. Rafe felt that if he could only find out that Ambrose was safe, well, and settled somewhere, he could breathe again. The thought of his love living a Quinn-like nightmare chilled his blood. He would move heaven and earth to prevent that from happening.

Achille was still a drug to him, although he felt that now Achille had what he set out to achieve, the Conte was becoming bored. Rafe realised, finally and far too late, that it was the challenge of the

chase that drove Achille, and not any sort of emotion, bitterly realising that it reflected his own life too clearly. From his absences,
Rafe was certain that Achille had another quarry in his sights, and
he was glad of it. He realised that he could leave Rome at any time
but did not bother to do so. He could not bear to return to Standish
if Ambrose was not there, and he hated Tavistock Square for the
memories it held. He showed Rome to Sebastien in a leisurely fashion, but the child was disappointed with the Eternal City. Apart
from the Coliseum and the Pantheon, Sebastien could not picture
any of the buildings as they should look and was most angry with
the Circus Maximus, a flat barren field, and the Forum, which con-
sisted of a few columns. The boy was fretful, missing Ambrose terribly, and Rafe wondered, despite his loathing of London, whether
or not they should go back, and began to think of excuses to do so.

He received the excuse he needed that same week. Gronow had
written to him in care of his bank, and the letter eventually reached
him. His heart drained of blood at the news Rees imparted: Francis
was alive. Rafe had killed before, more times than people knew —
sometimes in self defence, sometimes out of necessity. He realised
that it was better to kill a mad dog than to allow it to bite even a
first time. But in the past he had always made sure that when a man
looked dead, he was dead. The one time he forgot to verify this simple fact was the one time it needed checking more than any other.

*"It would seem that the bullet missed his heart and pierced a
lung, a wound that would carry off most, but Ashurst tells me he
has fought like a lion against death, after more than one doctor
had given up hope. Ashurst has tried his best to disguise the full
details, but the manner of Halton's death has caused repercussions
at the highest level. It has been assumed that Trenberry and
Halton duelled, and that Francis failed to shoot Halton and
stabbed him through the heart. Ashurst knows the real truth will
cause even more damage and is silent for his friend's sake. Francis
was court-martialled and has been dishonourably discharged. His
father has disowned him, and his engagement is over.*

*"I urge you to return to England as soon as is practicable, my
friend. You are not implicated in the death of Halton, but with
Trenberry's recovery I am concerned at any mischief he may find
it in his heart to do. As he is released from the regiment, what
small honour he once had no longer binds him. The man is penniless, I understand, and although it galls me to even suggest such a
thing, you are in a position to perhaps provide him with some sort
of allowance. This might at least secure his silence."*

Rafe wrote back immediately.

"I am indebted to you for this information.

*"Once more you prove yourself to be a greater friend than I
deserve. I am leaving for London as soon as I can prepare the*

journey, and I will collect any further mail at the Poste Restante at Calais. Either send to me there, or to my bank in London, who have instructions for its forwarding to me.

"I do not know if silence can be achieved by the method you purport, but your suggestion seems to be one of the two options available to me, and the one I shall attempt first. God forgive me if I have to resort to the other."

Rafe told Alvisi that same night, as the slim man was curled around him, head to toe, kissing his instep gently. It seemed to renew a spark with the Conte, and the green eyes gleamed. He whispered, "Raphael, you would not abandon me?" Tongue and mouth busy, he ran a finger from behind Rafe's knee to his heel, gently rotating his finger around the heel itself.

Rafe groaned as the man aroused him, and muttered, "You do not need me, Achilles. What of your latest prey?"

Achille slid up Rafe's body, slowly, taking his time, kissing where his hands touched, his eyes fixed on Rafe's erect member. "Mmm," he said as his mouth slid over it and then off. "He is not worthy of the game. It took one kiss and he forgot about his milk white fiancée, and has broken with her for good."

Rafe arched to the wetness as Alvisi engorged him again. "Achilles," he said in an undertone, "why do you do these things? Destroy all these lives?"

"Because I can, my sweet, and because they deserve me; they live such dull lives. You deserve me, don't you, my darkness?"

"Yessss," hissed Rafe, knowing that he deserved no better.

"And," whispered the viper, his tongue flicking out like the serpent he was, "you want me to come with you, don't you?"

There was only one true answer to that question, but Rafe gave the lie.

Chapter 20

"Ambrose?" Constance called as she searched the upper floor. "Are you up here?"

"I'm in the attic, Constance," Ambrose called back, and carefully dropped back into the main house.

He was carrying some books under his arm and looking triumphant as well as extremely dirty, dust on his hair, his hands and face black. "Christopher was right. There are many old books up there, and most of them will be useful."

Seeing Constance staring at him, he looked down at his hands and the pile of books he held in his arms, everything filthy, and laughed out loud. It was an unaffected and unrestrained laugh, the first time he had really laughed since Paris, and Constance could not help but be infected by it. Joining in, she took a tiny lace handkerchief, woefully inadequate for the task, and attempted to wipe some of the grime from his face. They both continued giggling helplessly, without either of them really being aware of what the joke was. Ambrose's grip slipped on the books, and they crashed to the floor, making the both of them laugh all the more.

She stepped toward him, and they both knelt to pick up the books. As they reached for the same one, Ambrose's hand touched hers, and he retracted it sharply as if he had been burned, his brows furrowed. The moment shattered, and the laughter stopped. Seeing the look in his eyes, Constance assumed that he thought he had offended her. She gave him a reassuring smile and, to Ambrose's embarrassment, took both his hands in hers.

"Ambrose?" She spoke softly and stepped a little closer to him. "Will you not...can you not...trust me?" She saw a look in his face that puzzled her. It was worry, and something almost like panic. She went on, feeling the need to make her meaning plain to him. "I know that something has been troubling you deeply since the day I met you. Can you not trust me enough to tell me of it? I always find that sharing my burdens makes them lighter. Can you not be like Christian and learn to put down your own?" she quoted from Bunyan. "'I saw a man clothed with rags, standing in a certain place, with his face from his own home, a book in his hand, and a great burden upon his back.'"

Ambrose could not think of what to do or what to say. She was so close to him, her face tilted up, her eyes moist. He could not understand how someone so very tiny as she was could hold him trapped in her small white hands. His instinct was to tear his hands from hers and fly into his room, but that would upset and frighten her. He was suddenly aware that she was half expecting him to kiss her, and his eyes widened in panic.

Seeing the expression on his face change, she misinterpreted it and said, "I am sorry, Ambrose." She let go of his hands and stepped back, still smiling. "I should not press you. Just realise that I...we...both of us only wish you to be happy with us, and it pains us to realise that you are not."

Ambrose flushed and stammered in acute discomfiture, "I did not wish to give the impression that I am not happy here. I understand what you say, but..." He was unable to think of the right words. How could he tell her that Christian's sins had been forgiven him as he lived in the same world as Christopher and Constance? Christian had had a wife, and children. The Dunstans' God could forgive Bunyan's protagonist but could never forgive Ambrose, and neither would the brother and sister themselves. The Bible was more than clear on the fate of Sodom. He longed to escape from her bright blue eyes, and his hands shook at just the thought of kissing her rosebud mouth. He was amazed at how revolted he felt. He felt enormous sympathy for her, sorrow that he could not make her happy by returning her affection, and ashamed at himself all at once. "I have been more content here in the past few weeks than I have been..." he faltered, "...for many months."

Constance's keen intuition made her realise that the guesses she had made about his secrets were right. Whatever sadness haunted this beautiful, sensitive man, she was certain now that it had happened in Italy. It was an elusive puzzle. What was such a poor man doing alone in Europe dressed in expensive clothes? Why was he catching a tramp merchant vessel home? Why, when his trunk arrived from Dorset, did he burn every scrap of clothing he had with him on the journey from Italy? Why did he burn the letters he received forwarded from his sisters, never opened, never read, never mentioned?

Constance had her suspicions. She imagined a liaison with a beautiful Contessa. She imagined that Ambrose must have been with her, but in what capacity her mind refused to speculate, then for some reason their ways had parted. She put Ambrose in the role of romantic hero, involving intrigue, high exotic castles, and romance, like the novels she read secretly. Looking at Ambrose's pure, shining face, she could not imagine him in an illicit liaison. Perhaps he had loved his Contessa unrequitedly. He must still love her very much to be in so much pain. She wondered if the woman had died, or whether they had simply quarrelled, or perhaps he had renounced her.

Ambrose excused himself, went to his room and sat on the bed. He was not insensible to Constance. He realised that she was good and kind, as well as being very pretty. His very limited experience of interaction with the opposite sex had helped him to recognise the signs — he realised that she was becoming more and more interested in him, and he felt trapped. How could he reject her without making his life here intolerable? It seemed an impossible situation. He was just beginning to feel settled; he was truly fond of the Dunstans and his work was just beginning to show fruit.

The little charity school was doing very well. It had a mix of boys from ages five to fourteen. They were woefully ignorant, of course. None of them had been able to read, and Ambrose had thought seriously about why he was bothering to teach them. When they went to work in the docks, or in the black factories which sucked the life from them so that they died much earlier than their allotted time, they would not need to be able to read. There was something that drove him on, however. If he could make a difference to one life, to raise one out of the darkness of this terrible existence where there was only a lifetime's drudgery, then he could at least feel he had achieved something worthwhile.

The majority of the boys were unwilling or unable to learn, but there were one or two who actually had a thirst for the unknown. The unknown to them was the written word, mere marks on the page, which meant numbers, or stories out of the heads of men long dead. Ambrose felt responsible for those lives. Did he have the right to fill their heads with battles, adventures, and an unrealistic view of the world, when their own future was so bleak? Christopher, however, had such plans. He intended to petition the Bishop in the attempt to create a college scholarship fund for the best pupils. Ambrose doubted the merits of such a scheme, but Christopher was an irrepressible dynamo of optimism. Christopher believed that everyone's life needed improving.

He was loath to leave Christopher's brave experiment, but if he could not think of some way of deflecting Constance's affection for him, he was beginning to think he must.

Over the next few days he avoided Constance as best he could, always making sure he was not alone in a room with her. It was simple enough to manage during the day, as he was teaching, but in the evening it was becoming obvious that every time Christopher left the room, Ambrose would leap to his feet and make an excuse that he was tired. He need not have worried.

Although Constance found him beautiful and was very attracted to him, longed his gaze to look on her in a loving manner, she was thrilled by his faithful heart and simply hoped that their friendship might turn to something greater when Ambrose had recovered from his Great Love.

One morning Ambrose entered the little school hall early and found Christopher in discussion with a short, stocky dark man he did not know. Ambrose had been almost hermit-like in his habits since arriving in London, and, apart from the boys and occasionally one of their relatives, had seen no one apart from the Dunstans. He hesitated to enter, considering flight, not wanting to see strangers.

Christopher spotted Ambrose paused in the doorway, smiled at him and turned again to the man. "Ah here he is," he said amiably. "Ambrose, I would like you to meet Mr William Archer. Mr Archer, this is Ambrose Standish, the teacher of our happy band of whom I have just been speaking."

Ambrose reached them and held out his hand for Archer to shake. The stranger gave him the most contemplative look. He greeted the man, but he felt as if a cloud had gone over the sun. He felt that this stranger knew him, even though he himself had never seen the fellow before. His mouth seemed dry, but he managed to say, "Sir, at your service." Archer did not smile, but gave a curious look and Ambrose's heart sank, as with a flash of intuition, he knew what the man was going to say.

"Standish? That's an unusual name. You are not by any chance related to the Standishes in Dorset?" When Ambrose did not reply, he added, "I have relatives in Charmouth and know something of the Standish history."

Ambrose answered monosyllabically, saying as little as he could but unable to deny his own identity.

Christopher looked amazed at this sudden revelation of Ambrose's past, but to Ambrose's relief he did not belabour the point. He said, "The Bishop has asked Archer here to write a report on our work in the school. It is as I have always said, Ambrose, if more people knew about the dreadful conditions in the East End, reform would be forthcoming." Archer nodded to Ambrose and Christopher, and he left them to start the day's tuition. Boys had begun to file in to the school hall and Archer was forgotten in the morning activities.

At luncheon, Christopher was quiet and thoughtful, not his usual effusive, enthusiastic self. Constance looked across the table at him. "Brother? Are you quite well? You seem somewhat preoccupied."

Christopher's eyes cleared, and he looked up with a smile. "It is nothing much. I suppose I have been a little surprised today. Ambrose?" Ambrose looked across the table with the smallest presentiment of fate showing in his eyes. "Why did you not tell us about your relationship with Goshawk?"

Ambrose paled, and his reflexes urged him to rise from the table, but found himself unable to do so in terror. He could not believe what Christopher was saying, and the blood roared in his ears. Then he realised that Christopher was still talking amiably to his sister.

"It would seem that the secretive Ambrose has been hiding his

light under a bushel, Constance. His family used to own an enormous estate in Dorset, of which I have never heard, but sadly the
family lost it many years ago. Archer was telling me all about it.
Ambrose and his sisters still live on the edge of the estate. But the
most interesting thing is that the man that owns it now is none
other than Rafe Goshawk. Can you believe such a thing?"

"Is this true, Ambrose?" asked Constance, her eyes alight.

The waves of fear that had swept through Ambrose's heart and
mind gradually ebbed away, and he relaxed. They had not discovered his shame. He was only linked to the house; he was safe. He
nodded dumbly, not trusting himself to speak, not ever wanting to
speak the name of his love again.

"This is wonderful!" said Constance. Seeing the look of
stunned surprise on Ambrose's face, she went on. "Don't you see,
Ambrose? Not only is he one of the richest men in England, but he
owns much of the misery you see around us. He owns factories,
housing, and shipyards. If we really want to make a difference to
conditions here, we need to start with people like Goshawk. How
well do you know him? Do you think you could write to him, appeal
to him on behalf of the Parish? Perhaps if you asked him, he would
be willing to come and see what it is really like here." Not waiting
for an answer, she turned back to her brother, her eyes shining, and
hope and light spilling from her face. She bubbled over with enthusiasm and excitement, and Christopher reflected that in a similar
joyous expression.

Ambrose felt nauseated. They would both assume that there
could be no possible reason to keep Ambrose from writing to Goshawk. There was only one route he could take. He managed to
stand and kept his face completely blank, his voice more cold than
anything they had heard from him before. "The Goshawks," he said,
"cheated my family and robbed us of everything we had. I feel it
more for my poor sisters than I do for myself, as at least I can earn
my living. The name brings nothing but misery, and I would be
grateful if it were not mentioned in my presence again." Leaving
them at the table, he departed the room, unable to endure the disappointment in Constance's eyes.

Two days later, Ambrose was clearing away the books from the
morning lessons with the aid of Lang, one of the more promising
students. The side door opened and, to Ambrose's surprise, Archer
entered unescorted. Ambrose frowned. "Dunstan is in the rectory if
you need him, Sir." He turned back to the blackboard. Undeterred,
Archer walked straight up to Ambrose, two other men behind him.
Turning, Ambrose suddenly saw that Archer was carrying a small
wooden staff with a crown carved on it, and he murmured quickly to
Lang, "Go and get Dunstan, *just* Mr Dunstan, you understand?
Quickly." He turned to the man who was tapping him on the shoul-

der with the tipstaff.

"Ambrose Alexander Standish," he said, his eyes cold, "I have a warrant for your arrest." He unscrewed the top of the tipstaff and removed a piece of parchment, which he unrolled and read out.

The blood draining from his face, Ambrose saw the two men come and stand on either side of him and catch him by his arms. Everything seemed slowed down, unreal. As he watched Christopher race into the room, he heard someone's voice reading, "Ambrose Alexander Standish, you are under arrest, for unlawfully and wickedly permitting and suffering one Rafe Francois D'Alphonse Goshawk to commit that horrible and detestable Sin known as Buggery, and did, against Nature, carnally know the said Rafe Francois D'Alphonse Goshawk in the same manner. This warrant issued on this day of our Lord, 15th May, 1821." Rough hands pulled him toward the door and he heard Christopher shouting at Archer.

"You lied to me, Sir! Where are you taking him? Ambrose! Be strong, you are not deserted! I asked you, Sir, where are you taking him?"

Lang and Christopher followed Ambrose, who was quietly passive in the arresting officers' hands, watching as he was shoved into the back of a barred carriage. Archer turned to Christopher. "I cannot believe that you would care about such dirt. He's going where he deserves to be — Newgate. They'll have him hanged before the month is out."

Chapter 21

Sebastien was thrilled to be returning to England and, so he thought, Ambrose and Marron. Rafe did not have the heart to disillusion the child. The boy skipped around the villa, happier than he had been for weeks, babbling about all the things that Ambrose had promised to teach him and had not yet had the time to do. As Rafe sat at his desk organising his paperwork into a small case, Sebastien begged Rafe to buy Ambrose a horse of his own, "*Pour aller chasse avec moi!*" he yelled excitedly, clinging to his father's arm. Rafe had to turn his head away and not let Sebastien see the pain on his face. Unseen by Rafe, Achille was half-hidden by the doorway, had seen Rafe's look of anguish, and his catlike eyes gleamed.

The little Parish of St Olaf's was in disarray. Christopher immediately closed the doors of the school and the church and went straight from there to visit the Ordinary of Newgate, telling him he was Ambrose's spiritual advisor. He was given special permission to visit Ambrose freely in the cells and not in the dreaded yard cage; however any visit would not be possible until the next day, as inmates had to be processed. Christopher returned to the Parish and broke the full news to a terrified Constance, who had heard the gist of the story from an overly excited Lang. She had taken it quietly, as was her wont, but had retired to her bedroom and stayed there for hours, finally emerging just after dawn the next day, pale but strengthened. She sought out Christopher in the study, and he looked up and held a hand out to her as she came toward him and fell into his arms.

"Can this be true, brother?" she whispered.

Christopher tried to reassure her. "I believe it to be some kind of terrible misunderstanding," he said. In his heart of hearts, however, he thought the opposite. The evidence, whatever it was, and from whatever source, would have been sifted by a Grand Jury, and they would have decided whether there was a case to be answered. "I am going to see if they will let me see him today," he added quietly.

"And I will come with you!" Constance implored.

Her brother shook his head and spoke as firmly as he could. "I know that you think you are inured to suffering, Constance, but I have been there before, and you have not. I know that you would not be able to stay strong in the face of such horrific conditions, and Ambrose needs us to be strong for him now."

Constance looked up at him, her eyes filled with tears. "Chris," she whispered, "if it is true, what shall we do?"

"Do?" Christopher said, "It will still be Ambrose, will it not? I am surprised, Constance. He has been with us for so long now, yet you cannot trust in him? Is he a good man?"

"Yes. Yes, of course he is," said Constance.

"And has that changed, just because he has been accused, and imprisoned?"

Constance shook her head numbly. She thought back to all the odd things that had not made sense in Ambrose's life, and one by one they clicked together like a perfect jigsaw puzzle; everything slotted. The clothes, the letters, his disinclination to speak of his travels, his reaction to Goshawk's name. "It is true," she breathed, and her eyes flew wide open to Christopher's face. "If they find him guilty, then he will hang! Chris, there must be something we can do! Goshawk must be told. His sisters must be told. We have to do something!"

Christopher held her at arm's length and spoke firmly. "We write to no one, do you understand me? No one, not until I have met with Ambrose, ensured his safety, and had his instructions. Pack me up some bedding and food, Constance. That is something we can do for him." He knew that not even the smallest amenity was free at that detestable place, and imagined the first night would be a terrible ordeal. If he could make the second night more bearable, it would be a blessing.

Half an hour later, Christopher made his way through the maze-like corridors of the jail's entrance. The stench stung his eyes as he was led along a long passageway, the turnkey opened and closed interminable doors until they reached the ward where Ambrose had been assigned. He told the jailer he would not be needed and dropped coins into the man's hand so that he disappeared. Christopher's eyes scanned the filthy room. There were perhaps twenty or so men locked away in one ward, and Christopher was struck with the absolute stillness of their tableaux: some leaning against the walls, others lying on small mats, three men playing cards in a prime position by a meagre fire. Most of them looked at him but seeing his dog collar, lost interest. The men's ages ranged from impossibly young to men with long, grey beards, all filthy and bereft of hope. He was just beginning to think that the turnkey had directed him to the wrong place when he spotted Ambrose in a far corner, sitting crouched against the wall, his arms around his knees, his coat and hair ribbon missing, a purple bruise on his cheek. He seemed not to be aware of his surroundings, and seeing the slim, elegant man in such squalor, Christopher's heart went out to him. This was an environment so alien to the man's innate sensibility. He strode across and crouched down in front of him. To his amazement, Ambrose looked up and smiled, but with a sweet troubled frown in his eyes.

"I knew you would come." He reached out a hand and grasped Christopher's with a firm grip. "But your God will not be pleased with you, for these are the cities of the plains."

Christopher could think of several ways of answering that, but could not see any of the responses being appropriate. He simply placed the bundle before Ambrose, feeling horribly inadequate. "Here, take this. It is not much, but I was not sure what you would need straight away. How are you?"

"I have a mattress," Ambrose said in a dazed manner, "however I fancy I managed the worse end of the deal, as my coat appeared to be the price for that, as well as the price of admission."

"Have you eaten?"

"Some women came yesterday, and so I had a little bread. I do not think I will ever have an appetite again." He looked around the filthy straw-strewn room, and his eyes closed briefly. There was a long pause.

"Is it true, Ambrose?" asked Christopher softly. Ambrose's eyes flew open, and Christopher was surprised how gentle they were.

He spoke softly, as if to himself. "Truth? What is truth? Do you think that the thought implies the deed, Chris? For surely the law will think so. If so, then I am guilty, yes." His eyes dropped to the floor, and there was a sigh, almost like a small laugh. "Does it matter?" he said in a tired voice.

Christopher thought quickly, thought about the Clap Houses, the Mollies, St Paul's Churchyard, notorious for sodomites — he had encountered all of this in his work — then thought about this beautiful young man and all he knew about him. "No," he said honestly, then swallowed and asked the question he had to ask. "Ambrose, let me write to..." He was amazed at the violence of Ambrose's reply, as he shot to his feet, a look of such fierceness on his face that with his hair loose he was suddenly a Nordic prince before battle.

"NO!" he shouted, and in the quietness of the room, his voice echoed around the wall and all the men looked around curiously. Ambrose apologised swiftly. "I'm sorry, I did not mean to shout, but no. No one. Not to my sisters and not...ever...to...*him*. They must never know, Christopher, none of them. They must never know." Ambrose became agitated and clasped Christopher's hand again. "Swear to me, Chris. Promise me you will not tell him, not if he were to come to you and beg you."

"I will swear," the man replied, "if you force me to, but surely he would be able to help you. He could pay for Counsel, install you in better accommodation than this open ward." He looked into Ambrose's eyes and realised that he was wasting his breath. "All I can afford to bring you is food."

"I'm sorry, Chris. You cannot understand, and I cannot, will not, explain. We are parted, and I will take no help from him, even if it means this...place. How can I expect you to comprehend it? But you are more of a friend than you realise," he said gently. "If at least I have your friendship, I can bear this, I think. I have been in a prison of my own making for such a long time, this will not be so very hard. I would like a book, however, if you will lend me one."

The simple request tore at Christopher, as he had not thought to bring one. He promised he would, tomorrow without fail. The turnkey hulked back into the ward and told Dunstan that he had to leave. Ambrose shook Christopher's hand and thanked him, but he could not help but notice that for all the strength of mind Ambrose showed, his hands were like ice and his body shuddered. He took off his own coat and gave it over, and Ambrose smiled again.

"If I manage to keep it with me, you shall have it back. Bring me one of mine when you come again." As Dunstan left the room, Ambrose sank back down to the floor, unrolled the blankets, pulled them around himself, and resumed his vigil in the corner.

Christopher walked slowly back through the endless claustrophobia to the front gate, deep in thought. He understood why Ambrose did not want his sisters to know of his fall, but Goshawk should be told. Then he realised with a sudden flash of clarity that both sides would be accused, both perpetrator and victim. Was it pride that made Ambrose so vehement in his refusal of Goshawk's help, was it shame? Or was it, Christopher now suspected, fear that Goshawk would be arrested, too? He only had a week before the next Old Bailey Proceedings, and if Goshawk were still in Italy, there was no way that he could be back in England in time. He had not had the courage to tell Ambrose of the possibility of the capital sentence.

Ambrose knew the danger. As he sat quietly on the floor of the jail, he was actually more at peace than anyone who knew him would have expected. It was as if the Sword of Damocles had fallen, and it was not until it had struck him that he realised it had been held over him for such a long time. Now that he was impaled upon it like a butterfly on a pin, there seemed to be no point in struggling. His new found strength kept him calm, but he could see no end to the tunnel, and a dark depression crept inexorably upon him.

As good as his word, Christopher visited every day, and whether it was Ambrose's reluctance to speak to anyone around him or the rector's daily visits, he seemed to be ignored by the other men in the ward. On the third day of his confinement, he felt numb in mind and in body. Christopher had gone, having stayed as long as he could, bringing him fresh clothes and a basket of food, but he had hardly been able to drag a word from Ambrose. Christopher imagined that his mind was attempting to escape its reality, but this was far from true. Ambrose stared straight at his situation, and the brain processes were beginning to shut down. It all seemed to all be happening to someone else.

"'Aint yer eatin' that?" a cockney voice said, and Ambrose roused, looked up and saw the child who normally slept close by the fire. The boy was skeletal, the rags he wore just covering his frame. He stared at the basket of bread and chicken Christopher had left. Ambrose gestured to the boy to help himself, his own appetite negligible. As the child took handfuls of meat, a voice came from above his head.

"Get away with yerself, Tam. You should know better than to try your starving orphan tricks on the newcomers. T'aint polite." The man, whose lilting brogue it was, leant against the wall and slid down it, hunkered next to Ambrose, leant in conspiratorially and said, "Don't you go takin' no notice of these amusers and anglers. Tam looks like he's half starved, but believe me or believe me not, he's had more to eat today than you have. He makes a good living from it too. It only amazes me how he stays so thin. He'll do well in Botany Bay, I'll warrant. You need to be more careful with your possessions, man. You've lost one coat already, and I am beginning to suspect that the place is full of robbers. It's a scandal." The man looked at Ambrose and his blue eyes crinkled at the corners, the edges of his mouth turning up in an irrepressible grin. "Fleury," he said, pointing at his chest, "Padraig Fleury. Everyone calls me Fleury." He looked inquiringly at Ambrose with his head tilted to one side.

Ambrose was taken aback by the man, who seemed entirely unconcerned with the horror of their surroundings. It was as if he were introducing himself at the theatre, or in a coffee house. He wore a long caped surcoat over a cut away frockcoat, Hessian boots with heart shaped tops, worn, but unmistakably well made, and an extravagant neckcloth, tied in a manner Ambrose had not seen before and suspected was the man's own invention. There were also shirts and waistcoats to be seen under the coats. Ambrose had never seen quite so many clothes on one person before. He suddenly realised he was staring and stumbled an introduction.

As Ambrose inspected him he was looking inquisitively back, and continued his chatty ramble. "Now, looking at you now, I'd say you were not used to such insalubrious accommodation, and to be frank," he leant toward Ambrose again and whispered, as if imparting the most treasured secret, "this room is not one of the best in the house, if you get my meaning." He stood up suddenly and held out a hand to help Ambrose up. "There are much better accommodations to be found on the other side of the yard."

There was a rumbling from one of the filthy inmates sprawled in front of the fire, and a sudden guffaw broke out from the three men who were playing cards. Fleury looked down at Ambrose and smiled disarmingly, his mouth mobile and expressive. "If you will be so good as to excuse me for just one moment." Ambrose watched him walk toward the group at the fire, and crouch down.

The child Tam who was still sitting close to Ambrose said, "That'll teach 'em to mind their manners. Fleury's a great one for nice manners."

Ambrose had the feeling he was missing something, but watched Fleury as he spoke quietly to the three men. He did not stop smiling once, and made all three of the three men laugh with whatever he was saying, although the laugh cut off sharply. Tam continued, "It's all words with Mr Fleury, has a way with 'em, if you know what I mean. Saved 'imself from an 'anging 'e did. Cor, I wish I'd bin there. They say that 'e stood there, with the noose round 'is neck and talked the crowd up somethin' proper. At the end of it, ladies was weepin', and the men was shoutin', so they 'adn't the 'eart to 'ang 'im, and 'e comes back 'ere. The 'ole prison was cheerin' that day, they tell me."

"What is he here for?" asked Ambrose, still watching Fleury, who was glancing back at Ambrose as he spoke quietly to the men, who now looked serious.

"Ah, Sir, that's a question yer don't generally asks in 'ere. Not to a man's face if yer want ter live, anyway. Jes' a word of warning, like. But Mr Fleury, 'e wouldn't mind — 'e's a gentleman of the road — 'e's famous! I thought everyone knew about 'im."

As Fleury walked back, Ambrose had the time to see the Irishman was about his own height, but stocky, with a little extra flesh here and there, and straight brown hair to his jawline.

The Irishman glanced down at Tam and ruffled his hair. "Now, Tam, not spreading lies about me, are ye?"

Tam looked up at Fleury with a startled expression, then seeing that his attention was on Ambrose rather than him, he grabbed his chicken and retreated to the fire and the now silent group around it.

Fleury's eyes met Ambrose's again, and they twinkled in mischievous delight as if sharing a secret joke with only him. "Now," he said shortly, "let me give you the full tour of the facilities," and without allowing Ambrose to affirm or deny any interest in being shown around the fearful place, Fleury grabbed the bundle from the floor, gripped Ambrose's arm, and lugged him to the door. "Open up," he shouted, and to Ambrose's astonishment, the door swung open, and Fleury towed him out.

He led him down the corridor, past other rooms like the one he had been in. Men seemed to be everywhere, and when he commented on this, Fleury said, "It's near to the Proceedings, we are, and they'll shove a lot more in here yet. The old girl is not full by a long chalk. Lucky for you you met me." They came to the exercise yard, empty at present, the visitor's cage in one corner. As they reached the far side of the yard, Fleury opened a black door on the opposite side from where they had come out, and they traversed another dark corridor, at the end of which stood a locked door.

Fleury turned and grinned, then in the manner of a great magician, produced a key from somewhere within the layers of clothing and unlocked the door, waving him into a small room. Ambrose gave a gasp of amazement. Apart from a bed, the little room was bare, but cleaner than he had seen anywhere else in the entire dank place. "How?" was all Ambrose could manage.

"Ah now, we've just met, and that would be telling. What I would be suggesting is that you make use of the room. I don't sleep here myself, not often anyway." He gave an impish grin. "You can shut yourself away here, read or whatever, and the others won't bother you. You can even lock your own door. What do you say?" Ambrose frowned at Fleury, which was obviously not the reaction he expected, judging by the look of surprise on his face.

"Why? Why would you do this?" Ambrose asked, his voice dangerously unstable, anger and frustration finally surfacing.

Fleury cocked his head at him speculatively, his eyes thoughtful. "Well, I could say that it is out o' the kindness of me heart. Or I could say, that I was hypnotised by your baby blue eyes." Ambrose turned to leave sharply. "Or I COULD say," Fleury continued, thrusting an arm across the doorway and looking serious at last, "that two years ago, someone did a similar act of kindness to me. Ambrose Standish," he said, his brogue soft and cajoling, "don't let your pride kill you. You know nothing of the horrors of Newgate. I've seen novices die in here for looking at someone in the wrong way. You wouldn't last another week on the Master's ward, holy friends or no, I've heard the talk in the yard; you are too pretty for your own good. Now, do you want this key, or am I going to have to lock you in until you decide?"

Chapter 22

It was not that Fleury did not find Ambrose devastatingly attractive; he did, but Ambrose had misjudged him. He had seen the panic and the mistrust in Ambrose's eyes and had acted partially as he had said — to protect him from the other inmates and partially out of an unvoiced fear that Ambrose might harm himself. Fleury had seen that blank expression on prisoners many times before, just before they disappeared somewhere and were found later with their veins opened, or hanging from the bars of a window. Trouble was, the length of the incarceration had no bearing on it — it could happen the first day, or eight months in, but once they started getting that look of despair, Fleury found they were not around for long.

He didn't make a habit of intervening, but he knew Ambrose's indictment, as he knew every man's in the place. He was the only one under that particular charge in the prison at present, and that in itself had caused a great deal of the wrong kind of interest. So he'd sought him out to see what all the gossips were talking about and was startled to see how very beautiful the newcomer was. That was when he decided to act and to act fast, Tam having reported faithfully that morning on some of the men's plans.

Putting Ambrose out of the reach of the others solved one problem, but not the other. Fleury guessed that nothing would happen until after the hearing, and so, to build Ambrose's trust, he kept away from the little cell except to escort Christopher to it the next day. Ambrose had asked him to join them, but he grinned and made a joke about having several vital appointments which he could not defer or delegate.

"Sure and wouldn't the place go to rack and ruin if I wasn't around to organise things?" Ambrose rewarded him with a smile that made Fleury's insides squirm, and with an effort he shut the door on the pair of them. "Well, that's handy, Fleury, my boy," he said out loud to himself as he sauntered down the corridor. "You normally have trouble getting hard on a Thursday." At the end of the passageway he knocked on a door, entered without waiting for a response and said to the man on the bed, "Ready for me, Milord?"

He'd been in Newgate for two years and the story of his escape from the gallows was partially true. His reprieve and lesser sentence had been bought for him by a wealthy and grateful customer, but the fact that it had come so late, and Fleury himself had given up and was giving his farewell speech, had worked perfectly. On his return to the prison, he found himself a hero and a legend. The Ordinary had added his tale, suitably embellished, to the Newgate

Calendar, and Fleury was content. The Newgate Calendar had the reputation of publishing the biographies of the most notorious criminals. It had been his reading of the Calendar as a young boy, devouring the daring tales of Dick Turpin and Jack Sheppard, that had piqued his interest in crime, and to be immortalised within the Calendar had long been his fondest wish.

"Damn ye, Fleury," the disgraced peer muttered, panting slightly. "You could be a little gentler!"

Fleury realised he had not been concentrating and slowed to his normal, slow thrusting, the peer's hairy back and buttocks before him. His own erection softened slightly as he examined the man's flabby body, and he closed his eyes again and tried to imagine what Ambrose would be like naked, under which excellent stimulation his member rose gallantly to the occasion, causing the lord to ejaculate loudly and at last. Doing up his breeches, Fleury took the generous tip on the side table and sauntered out onto the exercise yard. There were a few catcalls, and many people turned to look at him. At a glance from him, most turned away. Only one man was bold enough to fall into step with him.

"Henry," Fleury greeted him.

Henry Stark, coiner and counterfeiter, gave Fleury a quick glance, noticing that his friend, who would normally be dealing with the sniggerers in his own inimitable style, was instead deep in thought. He handed Stark one of his newest guineas.

"Milord asked me to thank you for making the appointment." He put one of the coins into Stark's hand. "Rhino for you, Rhino for me. Milord is good for a lot more yet, I think. I'll see him again, if he wants it." He looked around the yard at the groups of men. "Sounds like the chickens are clucking as usual; what's the buzz?"

"Your latest act of chivalry, Fleury, and you well know it. They are saying you are wasting your efforts, and he will dance at Beilby's ball."

"I am not so sure," Fleury replied, carefully. "My informant tells me that the evidence is just in letters. They haven't had a hanging on that evidence for a while. Ah well, we'll know on Monday, and if I hear ONE WORD," he turned and addressed the entire yard, which was instantly silent, "about anyone having been less than a perfect gentleman to Mr Standish, well now, I can't say that I'll be a perfect gentleman meself." He grinned his V shaped grin at Stark. "Now, you are my social calendar; where am I due this afternoon?"

Christopher had been pleased about Ambrose's safe lodging, but was suspicious of the reasons behind it. However, he believed Ambrose's assurance that Fleury had not demanded any reward for his protection. Since Christopher's gentle questioning and Ambrose's admission of his relationship with Goshawk, they had been able to discuss the matter hesitantly, both finding the matter distasteful. Finding a common language proved difficult, Ambrose only really being able to discuss love.

"If you loved a woman, Chris," Ambrose said, his eyes on the floor, "and had been hurt by her, would that make you profligate? Would you run into the first pair of arms that were offered?"

"No, of course not," Christopher answered.

"Then try and believe it is the same for me. I know you are still struggling with the concept of this unnaturalness... Oh yes, you are," he added, seeing Christopher attempt to disavow it, "but loving the way I do does not make me more uncontrolled or promiscuous than you, nor does it make me attracted to every man I meet." Ambrose caught Christopher's eyes and the rector blushed. "I knew what you were thinking. I don't blame you, and I am more grateful that you still continue to come here thinking as you do." He paused and changed the subject. "How is Constance?"

"Worried."

"Have you told her?"

"Yes. She had heard the charge and worked the rest out for herself. We have no secrets from each other, and she is my rock. Daily she begs me to be allowed to come here, but she cannot. She beseeches that she may come to the hearing. What can I tell her?"

Ambrose ran both hands through his hair and rested his palms on his forehead, his elbows on his knees. "No. There will be things said there that I could not bear her to hear. God knows they will report them in the newspapers, but we can protect her from the hearing, at least. Please tell her to stay away. My sisters..." His voice was hopeless. "If there were only some way to keep this from them, but there is not. If I hang..." He grasped Christopher's arm as the man looked up sharply and opened his mouth, "If I hang, it will at least be an end to it, and they can deny they ever had a brother."

All too soon it was Sunday evening. Ambrose was alone, pacing his cell, trying to walk away the sick, dull panic rising through him. Stifled by claustrophobia, not having been outside the tiny room since Fleury gave it to him, he yearned for the openness of the yard, but could not face seeing other people.

Fleury peered in through the small, barred window in the door and watched him quietly, admiring the way he moved, gracefully like a young horse. His jacket and waistcoat were thrown over a chair, his torso clad only in a simple shirt, undone at the neck, and Fleury could not take his eyes off him. He'd found out about Goshawk's stupidity of putting evidence into writing. The bastard deserved hanging himself for landing this angel in here and then leaving him to rot. Fleury had heard that the coward was hiding his head on the Continent, although how the incriminating letters had ended up at Bow Street was still a mystery. Notwithstanding that, Fleury cursed Goshawk for his crass stupidity; it was tantamount to madness to write letters that could have such dire consequences. He suddenly wondered if Ambrose even knew that those letters were the basis for the charges against him. As he watched the man's anguish, he knew exactly what was going through Ambrose's mind, having been through the same and worse. Perhaps Ambrose was sick of spiritual support; something a little worldlier was called for.

He backed away from the door and went to the room that served as the prison tavern. It was smoky, dark, and crowded. Those who could afford the exorbitant prices frequented it as a temporary escape, and those who could not afford it hung around those who could — women and men pressed together, the flatterers and flattered. Finding that private assignations were far more rewarding, it was not somewhere Fleury usually visited except to obtain alcohol, as he was doing tonight. He slipped behind the bar, and as he took two bottles of gin with him, he touched the barman suggestively on his back and dropped him a wink. The barman leered at him in an anticipatory manner, and Fleury ran his hand down the man's spine, grasped his buttocks hard.

"Ah, Sam, I'll see you right for this, you know that, I'll be around to see you tomorrow morning." *I'll just have to find the time.* Having poured some of the gin away and some down his coat, he arrived at Ambrose's room as if it were a spur of the moment thing. Before he reached the open door, he started talking loudly, to give Ambrose a second to compose himself. "Well, now, I always say that when you are feeling depressed, there's nothing like gin to make you feel worse." He stuck his head around the door, and said, "Are ye decent? Oh no, I forgot, you are not," and he snorted in a manner which suggested to Ambrose he had already had a few drinks already, "but then, now, neither am I, or I wouldn't be here."

"I apologise, Fleury," Ambrose said distractedly, "but I am not a suitable companion tonight, so if you don't mind?"

"Ah, but you wouldn't be throwing me out?" Fleury fell onto the bed in a heap and took his first gulp of gin from the bottle. "There's no one about upstairs and poor Fleury is unwanted by all his friends. We haven't had a proper chat since you arrived. I should be jealous of your fat friar for monopolising ye, but I'm not sure he's your type." Ambrose spun to him, his face livid. Fleury held his hands in front of him apologetically. "Ah now, now I've made you angry and I wish I was sorry for it. But, tell me this — you've forgotten to be depressed, now haven't you? That's another favour you owe me."

The sight of Fleury's manic smile stopped Ambrose in his tracks and reminded him of the debt he owed the man. "The trouble is, Fleury, that I am beginning to owe everyone favours." He sat down abruptly on the bed and ran fingers through his hair, giving Fleury the tantalising glimpse of beautiful ears. "I cannot repay you, any of you." Fleury produced an almost clean glass from his inexhaustible pockets, poured a large tot and pressed it into Ambrose's hands. Ambrose drank it without thinking and choked. "Gods, Fleury, that's vile."

"The only cure for the taste is another mouthful, believe me." Fleury laughed, taking a pull from the bottle. Ambrose screwed up his face and drank again. Seeing him starting to relax, Fleury refilled his glass. "Now, what were you saying?" He shuffled to the far end of the bed, not to disturb Ambrose's mood by getting too close. Fleury wanted him to talk about himself. He was dying to know this man, inside and out. "Ah yes, how you intend to repay us all for our immense bounty."

"People help me, and I have no way of repaying them. Take Dunstan for example."

"No thank you." Fleury shuddered. "Protestant priests? I may have sunk low, but even Fleury has standards." Infected at last by Fleury's irreverence, Ambrose gave a short laugh and drained his glass. After topping him up again, Fleury continued. "Catholic priests, ah, now you're talking. That's a different story altogether. Ambrose, you would *not* believe what some of them like to do!"

Ambrose, not used to strong drink of any description, felt the spirit warm his legs and stomach. He found his brain numbing and his face smiling for no particular reason as he let Fleury ramble on. As he listened to the man telling him a debauched tale of the priest who could only ejaculate when being ridden like a horse and beaten with a cane, he suddenly realised he had never listened to another person talking the way Fleury did. Here was a man who understood, a man who lay with other men and could talk about it.

Fleury was so open, he didn't find the subject embarrassing, or distasteful, or unnatural. He seemed to take immense amusement in recounting each adventure. Ambrose realised that he had never actually spoken of it openly to another man, other than his tentative discussions on love with Dunstan. Even Rafe and he had never talked about it. *Maybe if we had*, Ambrose thought, absently taking another mouthful of gin, *there wouldn't have been the secrets between us.*

He turned and faced Fleury, who was lounging at the foot of the bed, still expounding the vices of the Catholics. "Fleury, have you ever been in love?"

Fleury stopped in mid-flow, and the omnipresent grin slowly faded from his face. "Love is it?" he said softly. "You touch a nerve there, boy." Ambrose watched his eyes, so mischievous and dancing, fog over slightly. "I don't know if we know each other well enough yet for such a baring of our souls. Why do ye want to know?" He filled his glass again and allowed his hand to touch Ambrose's fingers as he pretended to be more inebriated than he was.

"It's just..." he stumbled, not knowing how to start, "I have never talked about...him."

"You don't have to now, ye know."

"I want to. I feel that I need to. Especially tonight, if you can understand me. I feel that if I can tell one person the truth of it, then the lies told tomorrow will not matter so much."

"Well now, looks like I'm the lucky one, then. Drink up, lean back, and tell me all about it."

Ambrose finally let go. Starting slowly, and telling the tale exactly as it had happened, he told Fleury everything, held nothing back — the jealousy, the fear, the love.

Fleury sat fascinated as Ambrose told him, with obvious innocence, about the blossoming of his sexuality, describing every nuance he had felt with such gentle honesty that Fleury became dreadfully aroused and had to work hard to maintain his concentration. By the time he reached the rape, Ambrose was in tears and Fleury was visibly moved. Ambrose, thinking he had disgusted him, attempted to gloss over it quickly, but Fleury stopped him, reached over and gripped his knee.

"No," he said firmly. "All of it. Get it all out. You were going to tell me, so tell me." He moved closer, reassuring Ambrose, whose breath caught in his throat. Fleury put his arm round the man and pulled him onto his shoulder, and Ambrose, grateful he did not have to watch Fleury's face any longer, talked on and on, the words spilling from him in a cathartic torrent. Fleury was touched by Ambrose's account of the love story. He could not understand, would never understand, how Goshawk had been so outstandingly stupid as to let this man escape him. He could not believe that the man Ambrose had found in Goshawk's bed could have been anything of this man's quality. Fleury himself, with all of his high (and low) connections, had never seen anything like him. In this dark place, Ambrose shone like a golden torch, and Fleury was drawn like a hypnotised moth. Whatever type of fool Goshawk undoubtedly was, Fleury was grateful to him for ensuring their paths had met, and he raised his bottle in a silent toast.

Ambrose was finally silent, and Fleury looked down at his companion's face. There was peace in Ambrose's expression. His eyes were open and full of moisture, but the tears had stopped. He was gazing into some middle distance. Fleury gave him some more gin, and after watching the man's beautiful face for a selfish moment longer, he broke the silence in a low voice. "So, do you know why they arrested you?" Ambrose didn't stir, but simply shook his head, his hair tickling Fleury's face. He reached over and pushed back the recalcitrant lock.

"That is the question that has been torturing me since Monday. I can only assume that it was Rafe's doing, in an act of vengeance for my abandonment."

For a second, Fleury thought he might allow Ambrose to continue to think this way, knowing he could use it to his advantage, as a fulcrum to turn Ambrose against his first love. He realised that the letters would come out in the Proceedings, though, so he quietly told Ambrose the truth. "I doubt," Fleury said, "that Goshawk would have sent the letters to Bow Street himself; they would implicate him as much as you. It must be someone else with a grudge, although my sources don't help me there. They were dropped off anonymously, or so I have been told. Anyone you know hate you and him so much?"

"Only Francis Trenberry," said Ambrose sleepily, his eyes closing, "but Rafe killed him." He started to talk quietly about Rafe's dawn disappearance, and then his voice suddenly stilled.

Fleury realised he was finally, peacefully asleep. He kissed the man's head softly and let him sleep, silently resolving he would make some investigation into whether or not there had been a duel. The light was changing in the sky, and Fleury estimated that there were at least a few hours before the guards would come for him. *Until then,* he thought, *let him be at peace. He will return today to me,* he thought, *and whether it is for a month, or a lifetime, is in the lap of the gods.*

Chapter 23

Fleury blinked, finally realising with a jolt that he had been staring at nowhere for too long. The bells of St Sepulchre-without-Newgate chimed eight, and he was still awake, unwilling to lose one second of the feeling of Ambrose in his arms. But now the dream had to be broken. Fleury heard a cough outside, a clinking of chains, and a sudden rap on the door. He gently shook Ambrose awake. "Ambrose," he said, "wake up. They're here."

As Ambrose surfaced slowly from the dreamless sleep, his eyes opened, and his head attacked him with vicious revenge for the abuse it had suffered under a pint of gin. He groaned, and his head fell forward into his hands. As Fleury helped him to his feet, the pressure in his head increased, blinding him temporarily. He managed to get to the bucket and was violently sick into it.

"Gin virgin," Fleury said deprecatingly, and without further words he sat Ambrose back on the bed and tidied him, washing his face and hands swiftly and tying his hair back, giving him a semblance of respectability. Ambrose managed to get to his feet again, and Fleury helped him on with his waistcoat and jacket. As he tied his neck cloth for him, Ambrose simply closed his eys and allowed him to, feeling too ill to lift his arms to do it himself.

"Well, you smell like you were bathing in the stuff, but I dare say you won't be the only one. You're horribly pale, but that might go in your favour, as you look like you're too ill to be hanged." Fleury did not like to tell him he was more green than pale. He pulled an unresisting Ambrose into his arms and held him to him, tenderly nuzzling his soft hair. He kissed the skin under his ear and whispered, "Come back to me, boy. Promise me that." He released him and opened the door.

Out of deference to Fleury, the turnkeys waited outside, but when Ambrose stepped over the threshold, they grabbed him, an arm each, and propelled him down the corridor. Fleury leaned on the door frame, watching him go, longing for his return and dreading it. Then he remembered he had debts to pay, and with a strengthening breath, assumed the Fleury persona.

Ambrose was almost grateful for the support of the guards, as he did not feel he could have walked across the yard. His forehead was clammy, and he had to clamp down to avoid spewing used gin down himself. However, at the entrance to the graveyard tunnel the stench overwhelmed him, and he vomited again, this time incurring the anger of the turnkeys. They dropped him in disgust and kicked him hard as he lay on the floor. Ambrose lay in his own vomit, thinking that hanging would actually be welcome. After picking Ambrose back up, they went down into the bowels of the earth, along the passageway which connected the court with the gaol. It was where interred the hanged men, and the paving slabs felt loose underfoot. At the end of the tunnel, they climbed up what seemed to Ambrose, endless stairs. First stone and then wood, finally to emerge blinking into a huge, light courtroom, the dock in the centre, the ceiling moulded and gold, to join the other prisoners on the bare benches.

Ambrose took in next to nothing of this. He had never felt so wretched in his life and resolved that if he lived, although he rather hoped that he wouldn't, he would never touch gin again. He sat numbly, not hearing or seeing anything as the machinations of the court rumbled around him. He was aware of being yanked to his feet, at one point, and someone repeatedly asking him what was his plea. Clenching his jaw down to prevent sickness overwhelming him again, he managed to mutter, "Not guilty," at which there appeared to be a general laugh, and he was sat back down again while the other cases proceeded. He heard the church bells ring out twice, and he gradually started to feel better. Although his mouth was dry and foul and his head hurt with every heartbeat, the nausea had passed and he could open his eyes without retribution from his brain. He resolved to kill Fleury for putting him through this nightmare if he ever saw him again, and then as his brain slowly reasserted itself, he realised that Fleury had done it deliberately — the terror of the anticipation of the trial had been completely forgotten in the wretchedness of his hangover. The noises of the law processing around him slowly pieced themselves together, and he found himself finally listening to the cases, sad pathetic stories of stolen goods and counterfeiting. He was surprised how short they were, some lasted no more than five minutes.

Finally, after some time which felt like months later, someone thumped his back, and he stood and listened again to the charge against him. Again he was asked for his plea, and again he responded, now clearer eyed and with his head held high. His presence in the dock caused much interest in the crowded courtroom. To the women, he seemed fragile, vulnerable, pale and defenceless, obviously a victim, but to the men, he seemed debauched and effeminate, an obvious catamite, and by the look of him, pale and shaking, addicted to drink or opium.

It began. The prosecutor stood and addressed the jury. "I apologise to you all," he declaimed, "because this crime is one that will be unfit for publication within the Proceedings, so vile are the practices within it. This man is accused of a grossly indecent unnatural act, even an unnatural crime. He let another man use his body in the way that a man would use a woman's. Not just once, as we often see in this courtroom, where innocent men are accosted in inns or in the street by sodomites such as this one, but he lived with this man, slept in his bed, as if they were husband and wife together."

Ambrose listened, dully, hearing the lies, but also the truths in the words. Some of his nausea returned, his forehead breaking out again in gin-scented sweat. He gripped the bars of the dock to stop himself falling.

The prosecutor went on. "We have abundant proof of this man's guilt and that of his accomplice, who is hiding away in a foreign land, too ashamed to face his own guilt, content only that his 'wife' does." There was a lewd guffaw from the men in the court at this; the prosecutor waited in a practised manner for the laughter to die down and continued. "Gentlemen of the Jury, the proof is legion. From this man's accomplice himself we have letters, making clear to anyone what vile deeds were done. Not only that, we have witnesses to their unnatural relationship."

Ambrose frowned and his heart pounded. Witnesses? What on earth was this new torment?

"I call my first witness. Call John Copeland."

The name reverberated around the court, and for long seconds Ambrose did not even recognise the name, so long it was since he had heard it. It wasn't until the butler came swaggering into the court that he realised whom they had called. Copeland took the stand and swore the oath.

"Your name is John Copeland, and you have been the head butler at Standish House in Dorset under the employ of one Rafe Francois D'Alphonse Goshawk for five years?"

"Well, one year in Dorset, Your Honour," Copeland said. "Before that, I served Mr Goshawk in London, whenever he was in town, that is."

"And when did you first meet the defendant?"

"When he came to be tutor to Mr Goshawk's son, in August of last year."

"Tell the Court, Mr Copeland, in your own words, what the relationship between Mr Standish and Mr Goshawk was like."

"Well, at first, Sir, it was innocent, I think, but I've known Mr Goshawk a long time and I know his practices, if you get my meaning. Mr Standish is not the first man in his bed."

Ambrose longed to close his eyes and to sink insensible to the floor, but he forced himself to remain impassive. He must not show one glimpse of emotion, not now. He allowed himself to stare at Copeland with hate in his eyes, as the man continued.

"But after the Master had a bad fall out riding, the tutor took it upon himself to oust my authority and take over the running of the house. He moved into the Master's room, and though he maintained the pretence of sleeping in the adjoining room, I'm here to tell the Court today, that that bed was never slept in." There was a disturbance that rippled around the sides of the courtroom as people commented to each other on this.

Ambrose flushed, loathing the lies the man was telling.

"Did you ever see them in the bed together?" the prosecutor asked.

"No, Sir, I did not."

"But you know that the second bed was not used, so we can safely assume that we know where Mr Standish was sleeping?"

"Yes, Sir."

"Thank you, Mr Copeland." One of the judges turned to Ambrose. "If you wish, Mr Standish, you can cross examine this witness."

Ambrose shook his head, knowing that nothing he could ask Copeland would be of any use at all. The second witness was called. This time it was a woman whom Ambrose did not recognise. She told the Court she was a maid at Standish and affirmed the truth of what Copeland had said, and had gone further to say that she often went into Goshawk's room to open the curtains and had seen Goshawk and the defendant curled up in bed, naked and embracing in sleep. There was a general commotion at this, and the judges had to call for order.

At this lie, Ambrose started to get angry. He knew her testimony was blatantly untrue, as Goshawk's doors were always securely locked at night, to keep out Sebastien as well as the staff. In addition, he did not know the woman, and that led him to suspect that she was an invention of Copeland's. When asked if he would cross examine her, he accepted, and in a voice made clear by anger he asked, "Do you remember that I took Mr Goshawk's son on a trip away?" At this totally unexpected question, the girl blanched and looked confusedly around her. Ambrose noted that her eyes flew around the court looking for Copeland, but he was no longer present.

"Yes, Sir," she stammered.

"Where did I take him?" asked Ambrose, his eyes piercing.

"I'm sure I don't know, Sir. Mr Goshawk would not have made me privy to that."

"Come now, you say you don't remember it? It was quite an event. The entire staff was involved in packing up and dispatching us away."

"No, Sir, I do not remember."

"When did you start to work for Mr Goshawk?" Ambrose asked.

"September 17th of last year," the girl said glibly, far too glibly.

Ambrose understood then that his suspicions were right, that she had been coached. "Describe Mr Goshawk to me."

"He is tall, with dark hair and eyes."

"How tall, would you say? Taller than I, or the same height?"

"About the same height."

"And his accent? Seeing as he has been abroad for so long?"

"It's very Frenchified, I think."

"Thank you." Ambrose dismissed her. He turned to the Bench. "My Lords, it is obvious that the girl has never seen Goshawk, as he is quite a head taller than I, and has no trace of a foreign accent. She could not recall my taking the Goshawk child away, yet we took several staff with us to Lyme Regis for three days in October. I believe she is perjuring herself under instructions of a third party. If you need confirmation of Goshawk's appearance or of my trip to Lyme, recall Copeland."

This was duly done, and Copeland confirmed Goshawk's height, accent and the details of the trip. The judges told the jury to ignore the statement and testimony of the girl. Ambrose began to feel slightly more optimistic.

The prosecutor continued, unfazed. "Now, we come to the written testimonies we have from one of the perpetrators of this vile crime. I will have to read out certain passages and if there are any ladies of a particularly delicate constitution, although these practices would nauseate even the very strongest of men, they may be wise to leave."

Ambrose followed the prosecutor's eyes around the public galleries and froze to see two white, frightened faces, so dear to him, so missed, and so horrific to see them here — Maria and Sophy. His strength fell away from him. His only wish in the whole sorry mess had been that they would have been spared this. He had planned to get Christopher to write to them and tell them that he had died in the Parish of St Olaf's; now, his disgrace was theirs. He gazed at their beloved faces, and tears stung at his his eyes.

The tears that had started at seeing his family, fell upon hearing Rafe's impassioned pleas of love and loneliness. In the mouth of the prosecutor, they were violated and parodied, but Ambrose could see Rafe so very clearly, and he bled inwardly at hearing how desperate his defection had made him.

"*At night, when my nightmares return and there is no cool, calm Ganymede to pull me from the wreckage, I wake sweating and screaming, and he laughs at me, for I have been calling your name.*"

"It would appear that he has found a new wife." More guffaws from the court.

"*The cries of joy you made when first I touch'd your...*' I cannot say this word, Milords, but it begins with m and ends with r. '*...stay with me and the scent of your seed on your perfect skin will never be washed from the memory of my mind.*'"

There were gasps from the audience. One woman fainted, and

there was much commotion in the galleries. At this, the Judges ordained that it was better that the letters not be read out, as they were too inflammatory, and instead they were passed directly to the jury to read.

An eternity passed. Rafe's love letters read by a leering jury, sniggering, laughing, casting lewd glances at him as he looked sullenly at them, wishing he could jump from the dock and tear the letters from their defiling hands. Finally, they finished reading and the letters were handed back to the prosecutor, who simply handed one of them, marked at a certain passage to Ambrose to get him to identify Rafe's writing, which he had no choice but to do. The prosecutor sat down, having told the Bench that the case for the Prosecution was finished.

The judges turned to Ambrose. He was shaking with emotion, the shock of seeing Rafe's writing and catching the few words therein. *"I love and adore you, no matter what you may think of me — remember that. If you need me at any time I will tear down mountains in my efforts to get to you. You have left me, but I am with you always, and will never abandon you."* Ambrose realised that the prosecutor had, as a final taunt, saved that passage in particular to use as identification, laughing at him for the irony of the words.

"Is there anything you have to say in defence of the accusations laid against you here?" a tall judge said, his face solemn.

Ambrose looked into the man's grave face, then shook his head, unable to think of one thing that would negate anything that had been said, or assumed by all concerned.

The middle judge spoke again. "You don't think that it would be better to state your case?" Ambrose shook his head again. "Very well. Do you have any witnessess to call?"

"I have no-one," Ambrose said, fatalistically. An usher stepped up to the bench and spoke quietly to the judges. The centre judge listened, passed a note to the usher, then turned to speak to Ambrose.

"It seems, Mr Standish, that you have some friends, after all. A Mr Dunstan wishes to give a character. Does he have your permission to so do?"

He realised with a flash why he had not seen Christopher in the courtroom. He did not want Chris to do it, but he knew his future was hanging by a thread, and to deny the chance to be spoken well of would do him no good at all. "Of course."

Christopher was wide-eyed but professional. Apart from the briefest glance toward the dock, he kept his eyes on the jury.

The Court did not keep him waiting long, and after swearing him in, the prosecutor stood. Faced with a man of the cloth, he lost much of his sneering, insidious air. "How long have you known the prisoner?"

"Many months," said Christopher. "We met in Genoa, travelling home by ship from Italy."

"You employed a man with no references — a man you met on a sea voyage?"

"During the journey we became friends," Christopher answered, his honest face serious. "It was obvious to me and to my sister that Mr Standish was a gentleman."

"And in all the time since, did he give you no indication of his proclivities? Showed no sign of unnaturalness? Never approached any of your students in an unsuitable manner?"

"No, Sir, no. Mr Standish has behaved in a totally correct manner at all times."

"But he never mentioned his past?"

"No, he did not."

"And you didn't question him?"

"My business is one of forgiveness, Sir," Christopher said sternly. "If Mr Standish had something secret in his past, I trusted in God to help him. And to forgive him."

The Prosecutor rolled his eyes at the Jury, as if to indicate that God and his forgiveness of Sodomites had no place in the Courtroom, and released Christopher.

Christopher left the court, and as Ambrose's was the last case in the morning's proceedings, the jury huddled together and made a note of all of the verdicts from the morning session. This took a while, but Ambrose was mentally and physically exhausted. Now that it was all over, he could accept the fate he was now certain would be his. The letters, albeit so loving, had condemned him.

At last, the jury returned to their three tiered box and handed the usher their list of verdicts. They were read out to the accused — some guilty, some acquitted, which caused various reactions from his fellow prisoners and their friends and relatives. The court was quite raucous by the time they reached the last verdict, and the judges had to call for silence. Realising it was Ambrose's verdict, the court stilled instantly.

The head judge looked at Ambrose and said, "Ambrose Standish, you stand accused of unlawfully and wickedly permitting and suffering the said Rafe Goshawk to lay hands on you, and allowing him to commit the said sin of sodomy. The jury is in agreement that the evidence, intolerable and revolting as it is, is not sufficient to prove the actual crime of sodomy, and you are therefore found guilty of the lesser charge of a misdemeanour — that of allowing an assault with sodomitical intent. For this you will be fined forty pounds, imprisoned at Newgate for six months, and will have to provide sureties amounting to twenty pounds for your good behaviour before your release. Consider yourself a lucky man, and if you appear before this Bench again on a similar charge, the Court will not be so lenient. Take him down."

There was silence in the court as Ambrose was led back down the stairs, his mind trying to come to terms with the shock of his sentence. He had been certain that he would hang, could not understand how he had been saved. The guards took him to the end of the passageway and shoved him roughly into the yard. Fleury was leaning against one of the walls, one leg tucked up, smoking a small pipe. He wore a preposterous buckled hat, and sported a smug grin. Ambrose found that he was ridiculously pleased to see him. All his kindnesses over the past week, the cell, the companionship and a shoulder to lean on, especially on the night before when he really needed it, all meant much to him. He was grateful to Fleury, yes, but it was more than that. He'd met someone who was honest about his feelings, about his sexual needs. As he smiled a tired smile at his new friend, he realised that Fleury just was what he needed.

"See, me bucko?" Fleury said. "I told you they couldn't hang you. It's those bonny blue eyes." Ambrose was astounded that Fleury had had the news as fast as he had. Fleury took his hand, gently teasing his palm with his fingers and said gently, "Come on, let's get you home. You look like you are about to fall asleep where you stand."

With a bit of relief, Ambrose realised that his home, for the next six months, was indeed here, with Fleury by his side in spite of his desire to be elsewhere.

Chapter 24

"Wait," Ambrose said, seeing the visitor's building open. Visitors were filtering into the more distant of the two cages, waiting for the inner one to open so they could talk to their imprisoned friends and relations. "Five minutes, Fleury, and then I promise I'll sleep for a week."

He squeezed Fleury's hand, and walked toward the cage. Fleury followed him across the yard, stood a decent distance away, and watched heartbroken as Ambrose greeted two women, both in black, the younger one weeping uncontrollably and supported by a sterner looking older one. Ambrose reached through the bars of the inner cage, his fingers stretching as they held their hands out to him in turn. But the cage was an instrument of torture. Fleury knew from bitter experience that the distance was such that you could never touch the people on the other side. The most that could be done was to pass allowed items through, throwing them, like feeding animals in a zoo. The meeting was brief, and whatever Ambrose said to them made them kiss their fingers to him, both now openly weeping as they were led away.

Ambrose spotted Dunstan coming through the door, and shouted to him, "Christopher! My sisters, the two in black — look after them, please!"

"I'll return tomorrow," Dunstan assured him, as he spun on his heel and disappeared.

Dunstan caught up with the women as they waited to be let out of the visitors' exit. He removed his hat and clutched it nervously in his hands. "Forgive me for intruding on your distress, ladies, but do I have the pleasure of addressing the Misses Standish?"

"You do, Sir, and you have us at a disadvantage. Please let us pass; my sister is unwell." The taller lady, and obviously the elder moved to pass Dunstan, but he spoke again.

"I do apologise, but your brother asked me to ensure your well being. He was living with us and working as tutor to my parish church when he was..." He paused, not liking to dwell on painful matters.

"Mr Dunstan? Of course, I am sorry, Ambrose wrote and told us of your kindness to him, but I really must get my sister to our inn."

Dunstan accompanied the ladies into the street, opened his umbrella for them, and summoned a hackney from the waiting line.

"Allow me to offer you a resting place and some refreshment," he said as the carriage pulled up and the driver jumped down and opened the doors. "My rectory is not far, and I would be more than happy to facilitate your journey onward."

Miss Standish smiled gratefully, the lines of worry showing clearly on her face, and she allowed herself to be helped into the carriage. She patted Sophy's hands and applied sal volatile to restore her.

When the hackney pulled up at the rectory, Constance was at the door. She took in the situation in a glance. Realising in an instant who the ladies were, she helped them into the house and lead them all upstairs to the withdrawing room. Once they were all seated and Sophy was recovered enough to be handed tea, Constance saw Miss Standish visibly relax.

"You are too kind," she said. "I did not know if I could manage. Sophy was almost fainted away. That terrible, terrible place. I can't bear to think of him in there — the filth, those terrible men... Even if, as the law says, he deserves imprisonment, anywhere but there."

Dunstan was quick to reassure her as much as he could. "He is more fortunate than many of the poor souls in there, Miss Standish. He was in a communal ward on the Master's side, but he has managed to secure a private room, which I have seen, and although sparsely accoutred, it is as clean as it can be under the circumstances." He forbore to tell the ladies of Ambrose's protector. He had spoken at length to the Ordinary in the past week, and had learned some highly disturbing facts about Padraig Fleury.

The Ordinary had interviewed the highwayman for his chapter in the Newgate Calendar, which was a dark enough tale of robbery, but his behaviour at the prison worried Dunstan far more. He ruled the prison with a disreputable, dashing charm that the Ordinary feared masked a murderous violence. Desperate, dangerous men — murderers and rapists who were waiting execution — were submissive or avoided Fleury completely. The Ordinary had never seen him attack anyone, or indeed even threaten anyone, but there was an undercurrent wherever Fleury went, or so the man had said. *"Men stop talking when he talks. Men whom I would hesitate to be with in a room alone leave the yard when he enters it. There's something not right there, Dunstan, he is half the size of the last top man we had."*

So Dunstan did not mention Fleury to the ladies. He worried about Ambrose's association with the man. He dreaded having to do it, but he had to broach a subject just as distressing. It transpired that he did not need to do so.

Constance said to Maria, "However did you find out, Miss Standish? I trust you do not think we were being secretive. Ambrose...Mr Standish..." she blushed at using his name so familiarly to his sisters, "...was adamant that we were to tell no one."

"We found out even before he was arrested. The pageboy from the house learned that the butler was asked if he would testify as a witness. Trent had been fond of Ambrose."

Maria's eyes clouded over, and Dunstan knew what she was thinking.

Her voice had a broken quality to it as she continued. "So he came straight to us and broke the news. Our solicitor found the date of the next Proceedings, and we came up to town with all haste. No matter what, he is still our brother and he's...a good man, Miss Dunstan, truly." At this, she temporarily lost the power to speak, and produced a small handkerchief. Constance went to her side and offered comfort.

Tears pricked at Dunstan's eyes as he watched the three women, so affected in their united grief. "If there is anything I can do," he stumbled, "anything at all."

Maria raised her head, her expression proud, but her eyes tragic. "Perhaps there is, Sir, although to have to mention it at all is distasteful, but I feel that God must have brought about our meeting today. Ambrose will never be able to pay his fine, or find anyone in our acquaintance that will provide the twenty pounds surety. What I ask of you is something you may not be willing to do, given the circumstances, but will you write to *that man* and demand that he pay it all? He cannot refuse, must not refuse. If he does, our options are bleak. We will either have to sell our house and enter a workhouse, or Ambrose must stay in prison indefinitely."

It had started to rain heavily, and one by one the visitors and the inmates faded away, but Ambrose did not stir. He was still leaning on the bars, his hand reaching out to people who were no longer there. Fleury waited for Ambrose's shoulders to stop shaking and then stepped up behind him.

"Come away now, *luran*, come away," he said softly. "They've seen you, and by the looks of things, you are still in their hearts." The rain had drenched Ambrose, his blond hair soaked and in ribbons around his face. "Come home wi'd ye now, and sleep. It's no use, you are, escaping the gallows only to be dying of pneumonia." He put his arm around Ambrose's waist and led him across the yard. Once in their small room, Fleury put some more coal on the fire, sat Ambrose in a chair, and started peeling off wet clothes.

Slightly dazed, Ambrose helped him. "I don't know how I feel, Fleury. I should feel worse than I do. I don't understand it. Why did they reduce the charge?"

"Ah now, that's my fault, you see," Fleury said, rubbing Ambrose's hair with a cloth. "I would have told you about it before, but I assumed your spiritual advisor had some legal background. If the Court cannot prove actual sodomy has taken place and an...how can I say, let's call it an emission...has occurred, then the case cannot be proven. Of course, I didn't know what sort of evidence they had."

"You seem to know everything else."

"Ah well, that's my inquisitive nature, you see. It's my curse. I like to know what's going on, and I'm lucky enough to have people who like to tell me things. I do people small favours here and there, and I find that sooner or later they like to repay me." He pulled off Ambrose's shirt. The rain had soaked him to the skin, and seemingly casual, he put his hands on Ambrose's shoulders, becoming aroused at the feel of the cold, damp skin under his palms. He was disappointed but not surprised when Ambrose pulled forward and stood up, so he made a pretence of folding the cloth fussily. Ambrose turned around to face Fleury, his hair in damp waves to his shoulders, his naked torso pale, gleaming and softened by the fire's glow, his calves and feet bare. As Fleury looked at him, he stopped breathing for a second or two, drinking in his beauty.

Nearly a year of good food, exercise, sex, and travel had matured Ambrose's once slight frame. There were taut muscles to be seen beneath the skin, the chest was broader, filled out, which only accentuated the slim waist and slimmer hips.

Ambrose's eyes gleamed in the firelight as he reached out a hand to Fleury. "I know you say you want no repayment. But I would like to repay you, Fleury, if you would let me." He stepped around the chair to the stunned Irishman and pulled his head in for a kiss. Fleury dropped the cloth and snaked his arms around Ambrose's waist. Ambrose's mouth was active; he took control of the kiss, opened Fleury's expressive smile, his tongue exploring and Fleury's responding, one lashing itself around the other, encircling it.

Fleury's fingers dragged over the porcelain flesh. Groaning, he broke the kiss. "Ambrose, don't you go playing with this poor whore now. I don't want your charity, and I don't want repaying for some mythical debt you feel you owe. If you come to me, boy, it's for keeps. I want you to stay."

"I am here, Fleury, and I am not leaving." He smiled and looked Fleury straight in the eyes and mimicked, "Ah now, you wouldn't be throwing me out again, now would you?" His eyes teased as he removed his own breeches and kissed Fleury lightly. Fleury gave him the happiest of grins and started throwing off his wardrobe collection, trying to kiss Ambrose frantically at the same time, his arms getting tangled in the mass of waistcoats and shirts. Ambrose attempted to unbutton what he could, laughing softly at the pile of clothes that were coming off. "Fleury," he said, laughing in spite of, or perhaps because of, the rigours of the day. "I really thought that you were, well, portly. It's just all these damned clothes! Why, for heaven's sake?"

Fleury was down to one shirt and breeches, and grabbing Ambrose, he marched him backwards toward the bed, kissing him in impatient pecks on any part of him that he could reach. "When I first came here, I didn't have anywhere to put them, so I wore them." He pushed Ambrose back onto the bed. "Then, as the months went by, I gained more and it was easier to store them on me. Now, although I have my room or rather, your room, they have become part of my...character."

"*Our* room," muttered Ambrose, his eyes on Fleury as he stripped. The highwayman's frame was not dissimilar to his own, although more weatherbeaten, with some scars here and there, the arms more muscled from hard riding, the torso lean, the hips narrow, and an obvious bulge dead centre under the fabric of his last remaining pair of breeches. Feeling a lust he had not allowed himself since Gibraltar and an uncharacteristic impatience, he stood up and pulled Fleury to him, wanting to be close to him when his final glory was revealed, rather than supine, passive, and waiting. He knelt before Fleury to unbutton his breeches and was rewarded with a thick, shortish cock, eagerly springing forward for his attention.

Whether it was a remnant of the night before when his inhibitions had fallen from him, or whether it was pure lust, for once in his life Ambrose did not deliberate or cogitate. He was here, with a man he desired, his face was inches from his cock, and he thought no more. He engulfed it, pulling the breeches down in a swift movement, feeling Fleury step out of them. Gently pulling the velvet steel into his mouth, he taught himself the shape and feel of it with his lips and tongue, using the mouth's senses to map it forever in his mind. Fleury moaned something Ambrose could not understand, but it sounded like pleasure and, encouraged, Ambrose slid his hands up the back of Fleury's thighs, feeling them tremble under his touch until he reached hard, muscled buttocks, wider than his own but tighter, and much firmer. He grasped them and pulled Fleury hard into his mouth, the brown wiry hair brushing against his face, the musk of the man arousing him to further sensual delights. As he suckled, able to get the entire length into his mouth, he felt as he had been described that very morning: wanton, debauched, immoral. The feeling intoxicated him.

Fleury's knees were in danger of buckling, so he held on to the top of Ambrose's head for balance, and was crying out to every movement of the warm, wet embrace.

Ambrose had never felt so powerful, to be able to give another person that amount of pleasure from such a simple act. Remembering what had been done to him, what he had enjoyed, he explored

Fleury's scrotum with light strokes, feeling them lift and meld under his hand. Fleury was immobilised, gently thrusting, a soft groaning coming from him in rhythm, incomprehensible words in his native tongue which melted Ambrose and inflamed his own hardened phallus.

"Mar sin, aris, súigh é, go dian!"

Ambrose felt Fleury's cock begin to shudder; he sucked harder, desperately excited and wanting to taste the essence of the man, to swallow him, to take him into his body. He grazed his teeth gently along the flattened base of the length and, with another cry, Fleury's seed shot into Ambrose's eager mouth, salty, hot and bittersweet. Ambrose remained on his knees, nuzzling Fleury's thighs and privities, inhaling the sex-musk, his hands flat on the man's flanks, and they stood there for a long moment as Fleury recovered his mind. Then impatiently, Fleury pulled him to his feet and kissed him, sharing the taste of his own seed and joined, they lay on the bed.

Fleury's blue eyes were urgent, needful, desperate to thank Ambrose for the most beautifully intense ejaculation he had had since his incarceration, feeling awed to finally get his hands on the perfection of the graven image that was Ambrose. He kept his eyes open as they kissed so he could watch the handsome face twist in pleasure, as Fleury's hands ran over the chest, down the flanks, feeling the sensitive heat of the skin between thigh and scrotum, and finally claiming his prize as his fingers wrapped themselves around Ambrose's long, slim rod.

Inspired, he straddled Ambrose and buried his lips and teeth under his ear, murmuring words of love and encouragement in Gaelic, feeling Ambrose tremble beneath him, thrusting up into his hand. His thumb and fingers pulled back the skin from the tip and spread the dew escaping from it, lubricating the entire head. Then he placed his buttocks over it, resting it against his puckered entrance.

Ambrose's eyes opened with the sudden realisation of what Fleury was doing; his breath came in deep gusts, and his pupils were huge. "God, Fleury, what?" was all he could manage, but his reflexes took over and he thrust upwards, holding Fleury by the hips and pulling him down onto him. Ambrose cried out, a long keening cry as he experienced new sensations, hotter and tighter than he could have imagined, thrusting wildly, unable to stop himself, given over completely to the pressure of Fleury's body milking him. Fleury's head was tipped back, supporting himself on Ambrose's knees, moving gently in time, slowing the pace, controlling Ambrose's enthusiasm, letting the shaft filling him brush over and back, over and back, tantalising that secret place deep inside him which was somehow connected to his cock and balls. Ambrose grasped Fleury's member as it hardened again.

"Yes..." breathed Fleury. "Mmm...do that. Are you all right, *mo luran*, darlin' boy?"

"Never..." gasped Ambrose, "imagined anything so wonderful." Breathing raggedly in time with the thrusts, he sped up, his eyes closed, up and up and up into the heat. "I cannot hold on," he groaned, and with a final violent twisting movement, shot his seed into his new lover, whose cock responded in turn, spilling itself over Ambrose's gentle fingers.

Fleury tightened himself around Ambrose, sucking him dry and causing the man to whimper in post coital pleasure, then he fell forward onto his chest, slid up and nestled in Ambrose's arms. They lay in blissful silence for ages, the room darkening around them, Fleury gently running his mouth and fingers over Ambrose's chest and nipples, Ambrose stroking his hair, and kissing him from time to time. Fleury pulled the blankets up over them both. "Sleep, me boy," he said, his wicked grin returning. "Ah now, if anyone had been watching that little display, Mr Standish, you'd be back to Court in the morning, and there'd be no reprieve for you. There's plenty of proof of your guilt about ye now. Now sleep, *mo stor*; you've had a busy day. I'll be here when you wake." The pretty speech was wasted on Ambrose, who was already asleep, the edges of his mouth turned up.

Chapter 25

They had not stopped in Paris; to Sebastien's disappointment, they had driven straight through. Rafe had no desire to return to the house there, and was in fact determined to sell it. He suddenly had a loathing of the Continent, and Standish called to him like a siren across the waves. He had been adrift and rudderless too long. Now he had purpose, a goal: get to England, find Ambrose, find Francis. He was a driven man.

In his haste to get to Calais, he had fatigued Sebastien and Achille, hardly stopping, taking every available post connection, paying to have the entire coach for themselves and not resting even a day in any place. He was sorry for his son, who was pale and exhausted, but he he did not regret for even a moment the discomfort he caused the Conte. As they came nearer and nearer to England, Rafe became more himself, more focussed on his destination, like a pointer scenting its quarry. He set his face towards England and away from Italy. Achille was becoming bored with Rafe's indifference. Although he had tried every artifice he knew and every wile in his considerable arsenal to re-ensnare him, this time Goshawk was not conquered. Achille realised that Rafe was in control — using him, allowing himself to take pleasure from every little trick Achille knew with lips, hands, tongue, but the dependence was gone, the addiction broken.

If Achille were to leave him tomorrow, Rafe knew that he would simply continue northwards like a homing pigeon. There was something calling to him like a magnetic force, something more than Francis' destitution. What it was, he had no idea, but the nearer to England he came, the less Achille attracted him and the more he was pulled toward the Channel. Consequently, the Conte spent less time in Rafe's bed, scouring the streets at their overnight stops, searching for fresh prey. Sebastien frankly hated Achille. He had become sullen and rude, and retreated into silence while he was in the man's company. Rafe was concerned about his son's happiness, but was unable to do much about it, hoping that a return to Standish, and more particularly to Marron, would be enough to return some of the colour to Sebastien's cheeks.

At long last and late at night, their coach entered Calais, and Rafe settled them all in the inn. He was desperately tired — tired of travelling, tired of Achille, and most of all, tired of himself. Despite there being three of them on the road, Rafe found himself terribly lonely, missing the intellectual stimulation that Ambrose had offered. Once again he realised just how large a vacuum Ambrose's absence had left in his life.

The innkeeper, who knew Rafe quite well, had been very odd in his manner, distracted, almost rude. Rafe had the impression that he had nearly been refused accommodations. He settled Sebastien down for the night, and the child turned his dark blue eyes up to his father and said, "Papa, is Ambrose here in Calais?"

"No, *mon fils*, he's not here."

"Is he waiting for us at Standish? Is his sister quite well now?"

Rafe's heart skipped a beat as he prepared himself for the conversation he had been dreading. "I do not think we will see Ambrose again, Sebastien. He—"

"But why, Papa?" The boy's voice was shrill, and he sat up suddenly in the bed.

Rafe stroked his son's head and tucked him back down, loathing the lies he was having to tell. "He was offered another position, and it was too good for him to refuse. I am afraid it is a very long way away from Dorset."

"Will he not miss us? And his sisters?"

"Yes, of course he will. When we get home, you can write to him, I promise, tell him all about Florence and Rome. Would you like that?" Placated slightly, the child smiled and threw his arms around Rafe's neck. Rafe kissed him goodnight.

As he went to the door, a small voice came from the darkness, "Papa, when is Conte Alvisi going home?"

Rafe had no real answer for him, so he pretended impatience. "No more talk, Sebastien. Sleep." He walked back to his own room and locked his door. There would be no serpent in his bed this night.

Next morning he walked down to the Poste Restante, accompanied by Achille and Sebastien, who was far happier than he had been for a while, buoyed up by the smell of the sea and the sound of the gulls. On his way through the town, Rafe nodded to various acquaintances, and although slightly bemused that he was cut by most of them, he was too distracted by his impatience to collect his mail to give the snubs more than a passing thought. He collected his letters, an extraordinarily large number, and then led the way down to the quay to book a packet to Dover.

Achille attempted to take his arm, and Rafe shook him off, "Raphael," he said, "are you usually so unpopular?"

For a moment Rafe stopped flicking through his envelopes and looked up at Achille, frowning. "What do you mean?"

"Don't frown so, cherub," Achille said, smiling at the furious look Rafe gave him for the public sobriquet. "All I mean is, that not one person has spoken to you since we arrived. I would have thought that the mighty Goshawk's return would have produced a flurry of sycophantism." He pouted. "I was expecting to be quite shut out."

Rafe looked up at the promenade filled with people walking, waiting for their transport or simply enjoying the sunshine. Achille was right; not one person was showing the slightest interest in them. Rafe had been too distracted to notice. "I cannot say that I am troubled," he said icily. "Fawning bores me, as you well know. Whatever the gossips have found to cut me over, it will be forgotten in a week and they will be throwing their dull daughters at me again in a month." He strode into the shipping office and booked them passage on the next morning's mail packet. Once back in their hotel, he sat in his suite and sorted out his post. He had spotted several from Gronow, various reports concerning his businesses and other miscellany. He could not see anything from the bank or the investigative agency, so he began with the one letter he could not place, postmarked London, two weeks previously, hoping it was from the agency. Instead it was baffling and vague.

St Olaf's, London, 21st May 1821

Sir,
This letter is as distasteful to write as it will be to read, and if I were not on a commission of mercy, you and I would have no correspondence.
Miss Standish, with whom I understand you have an acquaintance, requests from you the sum of 60 pounds. She will not, nor will I, state what this sum is for; however I am certain that you will honour it.
I will give no further details here, Sir, and trust on you being more of a gentleman than I consider you to be.
Etc
Christopher Dunstan

As Rafe sat there puzzled, angry, and offended, the door opened and Achille slunk in.

"Raphael, I'm bored." The Conte assumed his favourite position — wrapped around Rafe where he sat on the bed.

Rafe ignored him and continued opening letters, vaguely aware that Achille was kissing his neck, merely commenting, "I hope you locked the door." He went next to the letters from Gronow, three in all. The first one described how he had met with Phillip Ashurst and was keeping himself apprised of Francis' recovery and plans. The regiment had moved, and he enclosed Francis' current address in Colchester and urged Rafe again to hurry his return.

"I am coming as fast as I can, Rees," he muttered.

"I can help you there," murmured Achille, licking his ear.

Rafe shrugged him off and opened the next, which hit him like a deathblow, a knife through the heart.

"*There is no easy way to impart this news to you, Rafe, and I am only surprised that it has not happened sooner. Your letters to young Standish were intercepted, but by whom, the authorities or your staff, I am unable to tell. However it happened, they have arrested him, and if found guilty, he will hang. He waits in Newgate, and I go there today.*"

The blood drained from Rafe's face, and he stood up sharply, dislodging Achille, who fell backwards with an unhappy hiss. As Rafe paced the floor the remaining words came into focus.

"*The charge implicates you as the perpetrator and accomplice of Ambrose's crime, so DO NOT, and I repeat DO NOT leave France, as there is a warrant for your apprehension also.*

"*I have written to your Paris address, so you may already know of this. If not, go back to Paris and wait for word from me there. Send me a letter of authority to deal with your bank, as I have contacts in Bow Street (from whence I heard about this) and a few favours are owed to me. I do not know how long it will take, but for God's sake, stay there. I know you will be desperate to act, Rafe, but trust one with a calmer head on his shoulders and leave it to me. If you return now, they are waiting for you, and you will be arrested in Dover.*"

Rafe gave a wordless cry of horror.

"Raphael?" Achille was concerned, never having seen Rafe so anxious.

Rafe ignored him again dropped the second letter onto the floor, and with trembling hands tore open the third, dated a week later, dreading what was within it. It was a few lines only, a quick reassurance.

"*SAFE. He is safe. Guilty, but of the lesser charge, a misdemeanour. Six months imprisonment. Not a light term in that black place, but he is alive. God keep him so. Send me the letter, Rafe, and return to Paris. I will send word when it is arranged, and you may cross.*"

Rafe sank back onto the bed, feeling faint with relief.

Achille sat up cross-legged, perusing the second letter, his eyes unfathomable. He looked over at Rafe at the desk with his head in his hands, and said in a bored and sarcastic drawl, "I cannot believe how exhilarating your life is, Raphael. What an adventure you have me on! How do you stand the excitement? Is it always like this? You should get someone to write it down — it would make a far more thrilling tale than *Udolpho*!"

Rafe threw him a long, slow look of pure venom, as if seeing him truly for the first time. Then he stood and, reaching his side, tore the letter from his hands and yanked him to his feet. His voice was cold, dark, and lethal. "My life is not your entertainment,

Alvisi. This is not a game. You treat people like playthings, and you have no right to destroy lives for sport. I blame myself for this, but we are both equally guilty." He pulled Achille to him and stared hard into his eyes, "We did this, you and I, and if he is harmed in any way, I promise that I will take such vengeance on you that you will beg me to let you die."

Achille felt genuine fear for the first time, realising that Rafe was deadly, and deadly serious, but his erection rose as he was also aroused by it, intoxicated by the hitherto unseen power Rafe had within him.

"Get out," Rafe growled. "Out of this hotel, out of France, and out of my life forever. Crawl back to the viper's nest from whence you came, and stay away from me, my son, and Ambrose, or I swear to God the next time I see you, I will kill you." He threw Achille from him, so he fell backwards and hit the door.

Achille stood there, contemplating Rafe for a long minute, a smile playing on his face, one hand on his crotch, his head tilted to one side, considering whether he should approach him to turn him again. *Oh what a challenge*, he thought. *What a magnificent challenge*. Then, deciding, he bowed deeply, as he had the night they had met. "So we are at Check, Raphael. I am forestalled at last by your white knight," he said, "and the laurels go to him. But I think perhaps that you are overly optimistic. Surely the milky whiteness has been soured by now. You may not find your Ambrosia quite as sweet to the taste after six long months in Newgate. Men without women...mmm. And how pretty he was, so very very pretty."

This hit Rafe exactly where it was aimed, and Achille had the sense to flee before Rafe was able to get his hands around his throat. Rafe leaned against the door, breathing heavily. He had missed his opportunity to kill Achille, but was almost glad of it. Calais was not the place to try and conceal a strangled Italian Count. Alvisi was gone, and Rafe was was free of him; that was the most important thing.

Remembering his letters, he returned to the pile and started opening them randomly, praying that one of them had more news. None did.

Gronow had known Rafe for years. He knew how impetuous Rafe was, and knew he would be in anguish at the impotence of his situation. Although Rafe realised that his friend was right, that the best place for him was Paris, he knew there were other ways into England other than Dover. If he had been alone, he would have chartered the most disreputable ship in the harbour and sailed directly for the Dorset coast. However, there was Sebastien to consider. The boy had no one but his father. Rafe could not countenance the shame the boy would be subject to if he were arrested, tried, and imprisoned. With a sinking heart, he realised that

Ambrose's family had gone through exactly that, and for all that he had said to Achille, the fault was his own. His jaw twitched in determination. At least there was something immediate he could do about that. He sat at the desk and wrote to his bank, telling them to send two hundred pounds directly to Dunstan, and giving Gronow the authority to draw from his accounts at his discretion. Then he penned a swift note to Gronow thanking him, but telling him he would not remove himself from Calais and would wait for word there. Finally, he wrote to Dunstan himself, finding it easier to write such a letter to a stranger than to Ambrose's sisters, who must consider him the very devil.

Calais 6th June 1821

Sir,
I deserve, and penitently accept, your censure for the harm I have caused a noble and innocent family. Please believe me that it was not done with any malice, and that no one, not his sisters or you yourself, can feel any worse for his suffering at my hands than do I.
What you have requested from me I have sent, and it will be with you at the same time as this letter. I must do more. Money cannot right the wrong I have caused, but I offer it nevertheless. Some scheme must be devised to ease their burdens. Whatever you need, Sir, ask it of me.
Goshawk

He sat, his head in his hands. Three weeks. Ambrose had been in Newgate for three weeks. He could only imagine the horrors the man was enduring. He spotted a copy of the Newgate Calendar on the desk, placed there, together with the Bible, for the guests, picked up up and threw it violently across the room.

The "sensitive man" was at that very moment sitting on the bed in his cell with Fleury, leaning against the wall. Ambrose was reading aloud, using Fleury's back as a book rest as Fleury nestled between his legs. For all his love of words and his gift of oratory, Fleury was woefully uneducated, and Ambrose was introducing him to worlds he had never imagined. They had recently finished Keats' *Odes* but Fleury had found them over-flowery and romanticised, frankly laughing at "Ode On a Grecian Urn".

"Ah, really now, Ambrose, not even an Irishman would write a poem to a pot!" They were a third of the way through Scott's *Bride of Lammenmoor* and Fleury was ensnared, every word of the book dropping from Ambrose's lips was like drugged honey.

Fleury kept turning back and demanding kisses, interrupting the reading, and Ambrose marvelled at how happy he was. Marvelled that in this, the darkest of places, with the stench, the lice, the death, and human despair, he had found someone who loved him.

Ambrose found that he was just as jealous of Fleury as he had been of Rafe, although at least with Fleury he could discuss it openly. They argued about Fleury's "work" about the prison. Ambrose demanded that Fleury give it up, and Fleury was infuriatingly frank about it. In the end, Ambrose locked him out of the cell in angry bitterness, releasing his demons, making accusations to a non-deserving Fleury that should have been said to Rafe. Finally, he had to relent when Fleury simply sat outside the cell door for two days and talked and talked. He told Ambrose the truth that he already knew: that it was Fleury's clients and the work he did that had led to his favoured position, kept them both alive, fed, and in this private room together. Beaten down by Fleury's unremitting words, Ambrose realised how selfish he was being, tore open the door and crushed Fleury to him, begging his forgiveness, trying to explain that while he understood what Fleury was sacrificing, he could not bear to think of him with other men.

Fleury had kissed him contemplatively. "Now, me boy," he had crooned, "I made no secret of my activities, did I? I have loved before, and so have you. Does that make what we have any less? No. I do not work for just anyone, Ambrose. If I fuck a man, it is for Rhino, granted, or we would have none of the freedoms we have in here, but I will never lie to you and tell you they are nothing to me, like he did. What you have to realise, my boy, is that love exists on many levels. I thought you'd know that, being the educated chap ye are." Fleury's hands moved to Ambrose's groin and fondled the burgeoning shape with a wicked grin.

Ambrose frowned. "You're talking of Eros, Philos, and Agape, a Greek ideal of love, but I am not sure they exist," he said, his heart beating faster as his need for Fleury rose.

"Ah now, there's my scholarly boy: desire, friendship, and affection," Fleury whispered, his eyes burning with a soft lust as he started to remove Ambrose's clothes. "They exist, all right, and I can prove it to you. Eros now, I can manage to show you that right now. The other two will take a little longer."

Chapter 26

After another long three weeks full of fear and anxiety, word came at last to Calais. Gronow had greased the appropriate palms, and it had cost Rafe a great deal of money, but his warrant had been conveniently lost. Suddenly the powers of the land considered a scandal involving Goshawk too enormous, the financial implications huge. The newspapers still printed scurrilous articles, some of them more than libellous, one of them stating, "That cowardly cat-amite, the bird of prey G------- who, having *entered* the noble house of S--------, now abandons it to moulder in ruins", which left nothing to the imagination. Rafe had never been afraid of publicity, his wealth and arrogance setting him above it, but he realised that innocents were being hurt with every printed accusation.

During the three weeks he had been waiting, he had not been idle. He had laid his hands on as much information on Ambrose's trial as he could. He had discovered Copeland's betrayal, and it was lucky for the butler that his employer had been delayed. Word came from Standish that Copeland had vanished, obviously fearing Goshawk's wrath, which was indeed raging incandescently, the more violent for its impotence.

He rebooked their passage to England and was in London within two days. The first thing Rafe did after arriving in London was situate Sebastien in Tavistock Square, then he drove immediately to the East End to make the visit he had been dreading. He had written to Dunstan beforehand, suggesting that they meet somewhere public, if he wished it, but Dunstan had replied saying that he preferred that Rafe should come to St Olaf's. The thought of them being seen together and of a newspaper linking his name to Goshawk's made Christopher's blood run cold.

Christopher opened the door, and as he let his visitor into the hallway, he thought back a few short weeks, recalling how he would have welcomed Goshawk before he knew what he knew now. He was surprised at the man's appearance. There was a power to him, a radiance of fury, no sign of contrition or sadness in his face, which Christopher noted was tightly controlled, his eyes black and angry. Christopher had banished Constance to her room; she would have been unable to keep her temper in check, and although he did not know exactly why Goshawk wanted to see him, whatever they were to discuss would only be facilitated by calm, rational speaking.

They entered the drawing room, and Goshawk began pacing. "I must see him," were the first words out of his mouth. "Is he well? What does he need? There is much I can do for him. Money will buy him any kind of comfort, I understand."

There was a sudden change in the man, and Dunstan watched in amazement as the face, which had been impassive and almost frightening when Goshawk entered the house, softened and now was almost desperate in its worry. Was it guilt? Or could it be that he really did love Ambrose? Christopher was still struggling with the very concept of male love. Whatever Goshawk really felt, Christopher dreaded having to tell him what he did.

"He will not see you, Sir. I have his explicit instructions on this. He could not be more clear on the matter, or in his mind. He said, and allow me to quote, 'I do not blame him for this, you may tell him that, but I do not want or need anything from him — not his pity, his mercy, or his charity.'"

Rafe's heart sank at Ambrose's words channelled through Dunstan, so similar to the last speech he had had from the man himself in Venice.

"'If he comes here, I will not see him. Rather he would think me dead and let me rest in peace. There are other people caught up in this, people who should never have been hurt. He knows who they are. Let him turn his beneficence onto them and leave me alone.' That is what I have been instructed to say. He had no other message for you." Christopher watched as Rafe sank into a chair, the blood draining from his face.

"It is truly over then," he whispered. He turned his face to Dunstan, now controlled once more, but his eyes were soft. "He sounds so strong. I am glad of it; his strength may carry him through." He stood and placed an envelope on the table. "This is for you. No, not for you, do not mistake my meaning, Sir," he added swiftly, seeing the Rector's discomfiture. "Use this how you will. It is not a sop to the Goshawk guilt, as another victim of my curse once called my money, but it is the only way that I have to ease the suffering my actions cause. If he will not take it, does not need it, then take it yourself and do what you may with it." He paused and looked out of the window into the squalid street. "You can do much good with it, I fancy. Strange that I never manage that." He turned to Dunstan again. "Thank you, Sir. You have been discreet, and kind beyond words. Let me give you a message for him, as he has given one for me. Tell him..." His eyes went back to the street. "No. Tell him nothing. Tell him I had no message. Let him think I am as black as he thinks I am. Let him have his peace, for God knows he deserves it." He shook Dunstan's hand. "I understand his words, and I will do as he says. If you are to say anything to him about this visit, tell him only that. I can see myself out." And with a sudden movement, he was gone; leaving Dunstan suddenly exhausted as if he had been running. The man's presence overwhelmed him.

Constance timidly opened the door and crossed to Christopher's side as he stood by the window.

"You were listening, weren't you?" he said as she took his hand.

She smiled at him. "You know me too well." There were tears on her cheeks. "He loves Ambrose terribly, you know. Every word he spoke gave that away. It must be beautiful, and terrifying, to love like that."

They watched Goshawk cross the street to his carriage and lean against it, as if dizzy. Christopher took the envelope and opened it. It contained a banker's draft, and a letter stating that an extraordinarily large sum of money was to be paid each quarter into a bank of Christopher's choosing. "Ambrose is right," Christopher said bitterly, "Goshawk really does think that money solves everything."

Constance took the letter and read it. "No, I do not believe he does. He may have thought that once, but now he knows that all the money in the world cannot buy him the one thing he wants above all else. He feels that money is the only way he can show his love. It is the only thing he has left; how empty his life must be."

"You are truly a better person than I, Constance," Christopher said. "You pity him." He walked to the far end of the room and put the envelope in his desk.

"I do," she whispered, watching Goshawk's carriage out of sight. "I know what it is to love hopelessly."

"Come out, Ambrose. When was the last time you were even in the sunshine? You're too pale, even for you. You read about Vampires, are you sure now you are not becoming one?" It was said with a laugh, but Fleury worried about his lover. Ambrose had not been outside the cell for two weeks, and although he seemed happy enough to live quietly in there, cleaning it the best he could, reading during the day and talking to and loving Fleury at night, it did not seem natural to Fleury, when Ambrose had the freedom to come and go, that he did not.

Ambrose finally acquiesced and allowed Fleury to drag him out of the room. Locking the door behind him, the Irishman hid the key in the depths of his layers of clothes. "Now you'll not be able to run away and hide like you did last time."

The truth was that Ambrose hated the yard. The dangerous looking men there frightened him. He was acutely aware of the glances he got from some of them; there was a lustful quality in their faces. Ambrose preferred to be in his room with the door safely locked. This morning however, there were not too many people about, and Ambrose quietly sank down against a sunny wall with a book as Fleury sought out Stark.

Stark was pleased to see him. In his new-found happiness,

Fleury had been neglectful of his clients and Stark was getting aggravation from them, and more importantly, a feeling of light pockets, as his own Rhino was completely dependant on Fleury's popularity and commission.

"I know, I know," Fleury's hands went up in their usual penitent posture, "I have been out of service for a while, but, well, you know how it is." He gave Stark a quick smile and shot a glance across the courtyard at Ambrose, whose hair was shining gold in the sun.

"Aye," said Stark. "And if I had a pretty piece like that to curl up with at night, I don't know if I would ever come out of my room." He stopped dead at the sudden shutting down of expression on Fleury's face. "Now, Fleury, I didn't mean anything by it. It was a compliment, really. Forgive me, eh? I was just annoyed that I haven't seen you for two weeks, that's all."

"Make sure it was," hissed Fleury. "And never talk about him like that again. I will have respect, even from you, Henry."

Stark swallowed and abruptly changed the subject, talking about the appointments Fleury could make that afternoon, if he was so minded. Fleury had a quick look in the small notebook Stark held and put ticks against three of the seven entries there. Stark noted they were his wealthiest clients, and was tempted to comment but did not. Although Fleury smiled with his mouth, his eyes were like flint, and Stark knew his friend better than to push his luck.

"I'll do that one now," Fleury said, pointing to a fourth entry. "You keep an eye on young Standish, and if he needs anything, you get it. Understand me, boy?"

His mouth dry, Stark nodded. Worried about the coldness he had so easily engendered in Fleury, Stark watched him as he walked to the far side of the yard and disappeared through a door. Stark went and sat down against a wall in the shady part of the yard and watched Ambrose between half closed eyes, lusting after him secretly, as did many a man in here, but more pleased that he was under Fleury's protection than the alternatives. The day was hot, and even in the shade, the bricks were warm against his back. He was asleep in minutes.

Ambrose did not realise he was being watched, not by Stark, or by anyone else; he was too engrossed in *Dracula*. It was ironically amusing — that he had done more reading and study since his incarceration than for a year previous to it. Fleury had been right. It was almost pleasant in the sunshine. After two months in this place, his nose had accustomed itself to the smells, and he did not pay any attention to the other prisoners. He glanced up, but the sun in his eyes prevented him from seeing across the yard, where he assumed Fleury still to be. There was a low sob, and Ambrose's attention was drawn to three children, for they could be no more than that, huddled together on the far right of the same wall against which he was resting. They did not look to be more than fourteen or fifteen, and Ambrose wondered, not for the first time, what sort of society would find boys like this so much of a threat that they could send them in here to suffer torments, as they would no doubt do, before transportation or worse. As he looked over to them, someone slid in next to him on his left.

"Interested in them are you?" came a growling whisper, and Ambrose turned to see a bearded man, with dark brown eyes and a fat, jowled face. "I'm not surprised, many are. You want to be quick, though. All three hang on Monday. So, you'd be Fleury's latest, then," he said, trying to put an arm around him.

Ambrose shot to his feet and attempted to walk away, but the man grabbed him by the arm. He was tall, taller than Rafe even, and very heavily built. "No need ter be rude, pretty boy," he said quietly. "Yer Master's not around, is he? 'Ow about we go to your cell, then? Fleury won't do me, but I'd pay you, 'andsome." He grabbed Ambrose's hand and held it against his own groin saying with a leer, "I'll show you what I've got, and you'll like it, I promise." He pushed Ambrose through the dark arch toward his and Fleury's cell, and Ambrose felt a rising panic. He could not believe that it was all going to happen again, but this time he was not going without a struggle.

"Fleury!" Ambrose shouted at the top of his voice. The man clapped an enormous bear-like hand over his mouth. As they got to the door, the man snapped an order at him.

"Open the door." He looked behind him once with a sly, nervous action.

"I can't," Ambrose muttered through the man's fingers, struggling vainly as his assailant's free hand slipped between his legs. "Fleury has the key."

"You lying to me?" Ambrose shook his head, and the man squinted at him. "Well, I reckon we'll have just enough time to enjoy ourselves right here then." Spinning Ambrose to face him, he grabbed him by the scrotum so hard that Ambrose cried out, his eyes closed in pain. "Take my yard out," the man muttered, pinning Ambrose against the wall, "and handle it just the way—" The man broke off in mid sentence, and Ambrose heard a soft voice behind them.

"And what I have sticking in your liver is nine and a half inches, and it's not my yard, Quested, so unless ye want another hole in you that's no use to man or beast, I would heartily recommend that you take one step backward." Quested's head yanked back and down as Fleury grabbed his hair and tugged him toward him. Fleury put out a foot and spun round as Quested fell heavily further up the corridor, leaving himself between the grunting, panting man and

Ambrose. Ambrose saw a vicious looking stiletto in Fleury's hand. "Perhaps you missed my bulletin regarding Mr Standish here. It may be," Fleury said, "although I am sure I saw you there. I think, in deference to Mr Standish, I'll give you the benefit of the doubt, as I don't want your filthy blood down this corridor."

Fleury stood his ground, Quested got slowly to his feet, fixed by Fleury's stare, terrifying and lacking in all humanity. He backed down the corridor, knowing he would be insane to turn his back, fearing a knife between the shoulder blades. Fleury watched him go, took two deep breaths as he let the violence ebb away from him, put the knife away, and turned to meet a furious Ambrose, which quite took him by surprise.

"THAT," he roared at Fleury, pointing up the corridor, "is why I need the key, and why I prefer to stay in here! You might be safe out there, but I am not! Even with three boys in the yard younger than I, I am prey to animals like that! And where did you get that blade?" Seeing Fleury's bemused expression, he stopped shouting. "What?"

Fleury started to laugh, retrieved the key, dropped to one knee and handed it to Ambrose in mock ceremony. "Here, take it, lad, and welcome." He stood up and kissed Ambrose. "Who would have guessed you had such a temper, Mr Standish? Perhaps you don't need quite so much protection as I thought, but I think a knife might be a good idea in future. Come on," he said, towing Ambrose back up the corridor. "Come back out there while the sun lasts. If anyone heard that outburst of yours, there's no way they would touch you, if you can say such things to me and live." Fleury roared with laughter. "No, I don't think you'll have any problems with protection from now on."

Chapter 27

The prison bell was ringing, and Ambrose, as was usual on a Monday morning, was in torment. Fleury held him, both curled up on the small bed. Ambrose shook in fear. "How do you ever get used to it, Fleury?" he whispered.

"You don't, lad, you don't. Not if you want to stay human, you don't. All you can ever do is thank the Lord it's not you."

"Every Monday. It is worse than any punishment. At least if it had been me, I would never have to hear it again. How can people bear to live near here where they can hear it every week?"

The noise of the crowd outside was unbearable; the public treated a hanging like a holiday. The sounds of laughter, street hawkers, shrieks and laughter agonised Ambrose into despair. This morning was worse than any preceding Monday, as Ambrose had made the mistake of approaching the three boys in the yard, much against Fleury's advice, had sat down with them, learned their names. It transpired they were older than they looked, malnourished and ragged as they were. The oldest one said that they were sixteen, seventeen, and nineteen, respectively, but he could not be certain, he said. They were condemned to hang for highway robbery.

"We was starvin'," the boy said, "and 'e was ill." He pointed to the youngest, who looked like he still was not well, leaning against the wall, almost insensible, his mouth lolling open, "I couldn't fink of what else to do. We was caught before we got to the next village. Should 'ave nicked 'orses first, I reckon. We din't even get much." He trailed off and looked up at the sky. "Still, looks like it'll be nice, and they say there'll be a big crowd."

The boy's intolerable fatalism and acceptance made Ambrose sick to his stomach, and he had insisted that the boys sleep in their room until their execution, only two days away, to at least keep them safe from the other men. Somehow Fleury had managed it, and the boys had two nights of relative peace, all curled up together under the barred window at the end of the bed. Ambrose knew that he would hear their weeping until the day he died.

Now Ambrose realised that Fleury was right. It would have been better not to have become involved. The boys were marched out of the room at dawn, and now the prison bell was tolling. Instead of faceless criminals being led across the yard and out of the Debtor's Door into the street in front of the waiting thousands, Ambrose saw in his mind's eye the three scared, pale faces that he had allowed himself to know. The youngest almost had to be carried, he was so weak. The oldest took responsibility for the two younger boys, his own head held high. Ambrose closed his eyes as the crowd went quiet. He felt Fleury's arms tighten around him, as if he could spare Ambrose this agony. Then the crowd started screaming again, and Ambrose retched, dragging himself off the bed and vomiting.

Fleury's brow contracted. That was only the first hanging, and Ambrose did not know whether it was the boys or not. This horror would continue all the morning. He watched his love, kneeling sobbing in the corner. "God forgive me," he whispered as he took a small cudgel from his pocket and expertly knocked Ambrose out, catching him as he fell. Fleury carried him back to the bed, tears on his own face for the hurt he had inflicted on one so precious to him. He lay and watched Ambrose all the morning, hearing each shout from the crowd, being fairly sure himself of when the boys were hanged. They would have been hanged together, and the time taken to string up all three gave the baying crowd the most entertainment and was noticeably longer. Quested also met his end that morning, but Fleury shed no tears for him. Eventually it was all over. The crowds grew quieter as they dispersed, and the noise in the street resumed its normal mixture of carriage wheels and the cries of street vendors.

An hour later, Ambrose awoke and clutched his head, his eyes creasing. "What the deuce happened? My head..."

"You fainted, don't you remember? You were vomiting, and you just keeled over. You knocked your head on the bedstead. I was worried about you, boy. I think next Monday, we'll just get so drunk so we can't hear the crowd, what d'ye say?"

Ambrose looked at him gratefully, and nodded. "You were right, Fleury, I shouldn't have—"

"Ah now, don't be regretting an act of kindness. It made you feel worse, but it made the boys feel better. Wherever they are now, *luran*, they aren't here, and that's a blessing." He did not expound on where their poor bodies were, either being buried in the graveyard, or worse, going to the hospitals for dissection. He hoped Ambrose would not think of it.

Another month dragged by. Dunstan visited every Tuesday, and each week Fleury left them to it, making himself scarce. They were still hiding their relationship from the rector, and this was now infuriating Fleury. He felt that Ambrose was ashamed of him in some way. Ambrose was a gentleman, Dunstan was a gentleman, Goshawk was a gentleman, but Fleury? Oh no, Fleury was just a ragamuffin from the back streets of Dublin. After Christopher left, Fleury stayed away and did not get back until dawn, having spent the day seeing all of his clients, getting drunk, and sitting up talking to Stark about Ambrose for hours. He staggered down the corridor, grateful for the walls, thrusting an arm out here and there to hold himself up. He pulled out his keys and glared at them. *Not much good, me boy,* he thought. *You've given this one to Ambrose.* He stood there for a long while, debating with himself, but the problem solved itself as Ambrose opened the door and let him in without a word. His lover sat on the edge of the bed and watched Fleury stumble about as he peeled off some of his clothes before giving up and flopping onto the bed with most of them on.

"Where have you been?"

"Me?" said Fleury, slurring, his voice unnaturally high. "And why should you care where I've been? I've been with my *friends*. Those people who are not so embarrassed to be seen with me, that is."

"You think that of me?" Ambrose was amazed, and shocked.

"What am I supposed to think? You hide in here all day and all night, and you have not even told your precious priest about us. He knows about Goshawk, but not me? Why is that, Ambrose? Is it because of the messages he brings you from Goshawk? You don't want Goshawk to know about me, so you don't tell your priest? Is that all it is? Six months here with Fleury to look after you, and then back to the landed gentry and the proper gentleman's life? Nice to know I've had my uses."

Ambrose was shocked at the bitterness in Fleury's voice. He had been ready to shout back, to turn all Fleury's words back on himself, accusing him of jealousy, when Ambrose was the one who had the right to be jealous, when he realised that Fleury wasn't jealous, he was simply hurt. He lay down next to the man and kissed his cheek, tears springing to his eyes.

"Fleury." Fleury turned to the wall. "Fleury...Padraig...please." Fleury spun back, sitting up as if he'd been scalded. "He's a *priest*. I gave him a big speech about how my loving men did not make me more promiscuous than someone who loved women, and I was in your bed within a week. He cannot cope with the fact that he is supposed to denounce me as the devil and send my soul to hell, rather than being one of my truest friends. It is only because he has told his Bishop that he is converting me from the paths of Sodom and bringing me to God that he is allowed to visit me at all." Ambrose swung a naked leg over Fleury's and sat on his lap, and kissed him so deeply that Fleury's erection was strangled by three pairs of breeches. "I have no communication with Rafe, I swear that to you. That chapter of my life is over; the rest of the book is yours. Forgive me, Padraig," Ambrose whispered into his neck, pushing his own fierce rod into Fleury's stomach and taking off layer after layer of his clothes. "I could never be ashamed of you. If you wish it, I will tell Dunstan next week. Better still, stay here and we'll tell him together."

No one, not even the mother that Fleury could hardly remember, had ever called him by his Christian name, and to hear it from Ambrose's mouth was like a prayer, a supplication. He groaned into Ambrose's mouth, crushing the kiss so hard and tight that he drew blood from Ambrose's lips, the metallic taste shared between them. Reluctantly, he struggled to his feet and tore off his clothes as if they tainted him.

Ambrose peeled off his shirt and sat on the edge of the bed, waiting. Fleury's eyes devoured Ambrose's form. After all this time with the man, when he was away from him he could never quite remember how Ambrose's body looked, and every time it was laid before him, it was like a revelation. He knelt on the floor between the man's knees and looked up at him in the dawn light. The blue eyes were loving, his face smiling. The chest and torso so perfect — not one nick or scar anywhere. Beautiful bony hips joined long lean legs, the thighs of which led irresistibly to Ambrose's glorious cock, which Fleury now knew so well, surrounded by gold curls. Ambrose was always scrupulously clean, even in this hellhole, soap and water being the cheapest of luxuries. Fleury threaded his fingers around Ambrose's shaft and watched as his love, always so very sensual, threw his head back and laughed softly, his hair falling behind him like a silken curtain.

"Fleury," he whispered, "kiss me." He was leaning back on the bed, propped up on his elbows, pushing his rod through Fleury's fingers. Fleury obeyed, lowering his head down onto the pale length, tasting soap and the indescribable scent of the man, as unmistakable to himself as any scent on earth. "Aaa," gasped Ambrose, in sudden rhythm, "not...what...I meant, but better."

Fleury closed his eyes and let his senses take over. This act he now shared with no one else was something that he had only discovered could be so mind encompassing with Ambrose. Sometimes he felt the slightest bit jealous when he thought of Rafe Goshawk enjoying the delights of what he had in his mouth, but then, Goshawk didn't have it now. As his speed increased Ambrose forced himself to a sitting position.

"Fleury, come here, please." And he dragged Fleury off his cock and onto his lap. "I need you more fully than that," he muttered, slipping into Fleury like coming home.

Fleury loved this way they fucked; he got to feel Ambrose straight inside him like a flagpole, and Ambrose, sitting upright, held him tight, as they rocked together. Ambrose's arms around him, Fleury's own cock was in friction between the two of them, and they could kiss the entire time. Ambrose grew ever more excited, his breathing fast and desperate, frantic for release. Fleury found Ambrose's sensuality arousing beyond measure, his expressions of desire and want having just as stimulating an effect on him as did the slender rod setting off fireworks inside him. Ambrose muttered urgently: "Padraig, Padraig," accompanied with hungry, violent kisses and he felt Ambrose's seed flying hot into his deepest recesses. Hearing his name called out in such passion had the same effect, his ejaculation needful, cathartic, and a healing communion between them. They clung together as Ambrose shrank within him. Ambrose kissed Fleury's neck and shoulders, still muttering his name. Fleury had never felt so loved, and he could hardly believe that such a seemingly quiet man was capable of such vehement passion. Falling back onto the bed, Fleury said, "Forgive me, *caraid,* ye don't have to tell him if ye don't want to."

Close to sleep, Ambrose murmured, "Yes, I do. There have been too many lies and silences in my life. If I could shout it from the roof of the gaol, I would."

Colchester's bustling streets were filled with red-coated soldiers. As Rafe drove up the hilly High Street, he thought of Francis. *Yet another life blighted*, he thought blackly. He realised that if he had not seduced the boy on that glittering night, the young man's life might have been so very different. He would be married, perhaps with children, a rising star in his regiment. Rafe knew that his own lust had destroyed Francis as utterly as it had destroyed Ambrose. At least he was fairly certain that Francis would not refuse money.

The lodgings Francis shared with Ashurst were shabby and smelled of excreta. Ashurst wordlessly opened the door to Rafe and led him up the narrow stairs to where Francis was waiting. Ashurst moved to Francis' side and whispered urgently to him, "I have to get back to barracks, but I do not like to leave you alone with him." He looked at Rafe with loathing. There was a terrible tension in the room; Rafe's and Francis' eyes were locked together — Francis' head was high, his eyes bright and challenging; Rafe's suspicious and hooded. "It's all right, Phil," Francis said without looking away. "It will all be all right, I promise."

Full of concern and very reluctantly, Ashurst backed out of the room. He had not wanted Francis to see Goshawk at all, and since the letter had come, asking for this meeting, he had tried every argument he knew to dissuade Francis from it. Francis was determined to see the man, had been almost jubilant and triumphant when he read the letter, but Ashurst could see no good coming from it.

Francis gestured to a chair. "Please, Rafe, sit."

Rafe obeyed and studied Francis, disgusted by the change in the man. He was a shadow of his former self, a wraith of the confident pretty boy he had been. If Rafe needed proof of Francis' disgrace and downfall, he only had to look at him. He was pale and gaunt, almost to a skeletal thinness, and his hands shook constantly. He was dressed only in breeches and a loose shirt, neither of which was clean; his feet were bare, his hair long, dirty, and unkempt. Along with the dissipation, there was a shine to Francis that Rafe did not like, a brittle excitement he had seen in the man once before, the night before Waterloo.

Francis produced a bottle of gin and two smeared glasses. Rafe waved a refusal, but Francis poured two glasses anyway. "Let us have a toast, Rafe, shall we, for old times' sake? What shall we drink to? James Halton, perhaps? Yes, absent friends would seem appropriate." He downed the gin in one, and poured himself another. "That not to your liking, Rafe? Well, you choose then." He flopped back into the other chair, laughing mirthlessly.

Rafe twirled the glass in his hands, the liquid untasted, and after a long silence, said, "I haven't come here for yet another argument, Francis. Our past is past, and the wrongs we have done each other should remain there. I am partially responsible for your current circumstances, and offer you the only thing I am able — decent lodgings in London and an allowance."

Francis stared at Rafe in silence, his mouth open. Then he started to laugh, a maniacal, sinister giggle. "Wonderful, Rafe," he choked hysterically. "So typical of you, and so very ironic. I have been reading all of the newspapers recently. You are quite the talk of the town. Perhaps you think that I can be bought, is that it? That's what you do best, after all, isn't it? Buy things? I see you bought the Grand Jury, too. Impressive, even by your standards. Perhaps you think that you can buy my silence? That I will not make a bad situation worse?" He reached down into the cupboard beside him and took out a small bottle and drank from it. "Well?" His laughter stopped as suddenly as it began, his breathing slowing, a look of peace overcoming him.

"Opium, Francis? I don't know if I am willing to finance that particular habit, but yes, to be honest with you, those were exactly my thoughts."

Rafe's eyes filled with a black loathing, but Francis was thrilled to have provoked any human reaction in them at all. "But don't you see, Rafe? I cannot make it any worse. I have already done my worst, although that wasn't good enough." He was giggling again, quietly to himself, with a small sly smile.

Rafe frowned across at him, random thoughts slotting together in his brain, but not yet making a coherent whole. When next he spoke it was a cold voice from hell, which held the horror of the discovery within it. He stood and moved to Francis, gripped him by the shoulders and shook him violently. "What are you saying?"

"Yesss," hissed Francis, his face mad, still with the same smile.

"I knew you would come, and I waited and waited. I wanted to tell you to your face that it was me. The letters, the trial — me, all me. Phil got the letters from Tavistock Square. Except it all went wrong. As poetic as your writing is, they just were not graphic enough, it seems. He should have hanged, of course. There is no justice."

Rafe dropped Francis as if the touch of him burned his hands. Francis sank back into the chair, panting hard, still laughing, froth appearing at the side of his mouth, his eyes too bright in his pale face. Rafe stared at him, his own breath fast and his head spinning. He could hardly believe what he had just heard. "You hate me so much," he said in a low whisper, "that you risked murdering an innocent just to hurt me?"

Yellow and bloodshot, Francis' eyes slowly raised to Rafe's face. "That's what you have never understood, Rafe," Francis said slowly, almost rationally. "I have never hated you; I have always loved you. Don't you see? I love you. They would never have hanged the mighty Goshawk. I knew that, but I wanted you to come to me, finally, when you had nothing left, like me. When *he* was out of the way. And you did, I knew you would." He clutched at Rafe's jacket and smiled up at him, "We could be so happy together. I used to make you happy, Rafe, don't you remember?"

Rafe shook off the clutching hands. As his temper finally snapped, he picked the man up by a wasted arm and threw him onto the floor, his eyes murderous. "Happy? You animal! How dare you talk to me of happiness? I have spent nearly five years regretting fucking you, nearly five years trying to fob you off, buy you off, shake you off. You deserved to die for what you did in Paris, and had I not been incapacitated, I would have finished the job then and there. I should kill you now, put you out of your misery." His voice lowered to a menacing growl, and he watched the man grovel on the floor, backing toward a corner as Rafe paced toward him. "And I could, but why should I? To know the depths of your degradation is almost pleasurable. As he suffers, so do you. Perhaps," he knelt down, very close to Francis, watching the fear grow in his eyes, "that is what you want — for me to kill you?" Seeing a sly expression flicker over Francis' face, he realised that he had struck the truth at last. "No, no more favours." He straightened up and turned away toward the door, turning as he reached it. "Be a man, Francis, for once." And he was gone.

He walked down the dingy stairs and stopped just inside the door, waiting. He stood there a long while, listening to the sounds coming from the upstairs room. First there was silence, then a soft sobbing. A sound like a body being dragged, three footsteps, and then another endless silence. Rafe held his breath, closed his eyes, and allowed his mind to go blank, resisting the temptation — small as it was — to run back up the stairs. Then suddenly there was a loud report, the sound of something hitting the floor, and Rafe breathed out, opened his eyes, and went to his carriage.

Chapter 28

"Fleury? Fleury!" Ambrose kissed him and shook him slightly. He had been lying awake, unable to believe that he had not asked his lover one simple question.

"I am asleep," grumbled Fleury. "And if you want a repeat performance, Mr Standish, then you will just have to wait. I am afraid some of us are not as young as you are."

Ambrose smiled, and his cock twitched at Fleury's words. "I will not drain you further, my love. I am just surprised we have not discussed this." He kissed Fleury's head as he cradled the man to him. "When is your sentence finished? I remember that you once mentioned that you had two years, and I have but six weeks to go, so, when do you get out?"

"Go to sleep, *luran*," murmured Fleury.

"No. I'm sorry, Fleury, but I want to know."

"Two weeks. Go to sleep. It's not important."

"Not important? I thought you might be slightly concerned as to how I might manage after you leave."

"Because," rumbled Fleury, from somewhere in the region of his chest, "it was two weeks *ago*."

"You should have been released two weeks ago?"

"Mmmm." Fleury was awake now and kissing a nipple gently, expertly.

Ambrose lay back thinking while enjoying Fleury's ministrations. He knew so little of Fleury's life outside the four walls of their cell. He tried to recall two weeks ago, but could not remember any hint that Fleury should have been released; one day was so like another. Granted, he had been closeted with Stark for long times, and his "appointments" seemed more frequent in the past few weeks than previously, but Ambrose had not noticed when the change had taken place.

The sacrifices that Fleury made for him had not been so clear before, as he had been servicing his clients even before Ambrose's arrival. But to stay on one second more in this hell hole, just to protect him, brought tears to his eyes, and he pushed Fleury over onto his back and looked deep into the blue eyes which looked back at him laughingly in the dim candlelight. He said nothing; there was no need. The kiss he gave Fleury then was deeper and more heartfelt than any he had ever given him.

Fleury had stayed on to protect Ambrose, but also to earn their release fees, necessary evils which must be paid at the end of a sentence, or they would rot in here forever. He had earned his once, but had spent much of it on ensuring Ambrose's relative safety. He had learned from Dunstan that Goshawk had paid Ambrose's fine and surety, and that Ambrose had attempted to refuse it. As much as Goshawk's interference galled Fleury, he had had to convince Ambrose to accept it. "Let's face facts, lad. I cannot earn that amount of money in the time we have left. Swallow your pride and take his money. We can pay him back when we get out." Neither Ambrose nor Dunstan was aware of the strictly unofficial release fee, and Fleury had not mentioned it to either of them, having had a word with the warders to say it was something he would be dealing with personally.

Things had changed in Newgate. Although Elizabeth Fry's reforms on the women's side were making life easier for the fairer sex, the conditions were harder in the men's prison than previously. There was a new warder and new regulations. The men's language was monitored, and any swearing was punishable by a fine or a flogging, and there were many other laws, all exceedingly petty and simple to break, all warranting fines between a penny and a shilling, or lashes of up to twelve strokes. Not many men had the spare cash, and floggings were now a daily occurrence.

Fleury had not told Ambrose, but the new warder was also attempting to curtail Fleury's prostitution, and he was now getting worried that he might not be able to pay their release fees on time at all. Within two days of the new warder's entering the prison, he had had Fleury dragged to his office, leaving Ambrose frantic with worry and the prison agog with the unaccustomed sight of Fleury being towed across the yard by two almost smug looking guards. Once he was before the warder, the man motioned the other guards out and sat looking at Fleury under veiled lids, as he stood there his face immobile, gauging the situation.

"Padraig Fleury," the warder had said, "self proclaimed living legend. The man who stole an entire servants' retinue away from Lord Larborough, the man who will not steal any hard goods except currency, the man who cheated James Foxley of the pleasure of hanging him, the man who I hear terrorises this prison so expertly that it has never been so peaceful."

Fleury bowed deeply, one foot in front of the other, holding out his coat tails. "Ah now, why should I bother to take pearls and rubies? Gold and silver are so much more useful, and sure ye can't spend rings and earbobs straight away, and the man himself had far too many servants who had expressed a preference they would rather not be working for him at all. But then," he said, smiling with only his mouth, "I would not be believing everything ye read in there." He pointed to the Newgate Calendar.

The warder stood up and walked toward Fleury. As he came out from behind his desk, Fleury saw he dressed severly, in plainest black. He was tall, hollow cheeked, his long grey hair receding, and his dark bright brown eyes alight with an expression of fervour.

"You are a dying breed, the last of your kind, Mr Fleury. The likes of Turpin and McLaine are long gone. You are clinging to a romantic past which died with the advent of the Bow Street Runners. You may have cheated death before, but you will end up dangling outside these windows, you may be sure of it. However, that is in the future, and it is the present that I am concerned with. I will tolerate no further unnatural practices in this prison, Mr Fleury. We have a convicted sodomite here right now. I know who he is, and I know who protects him. I also know what would happen to him if his protector were proved to be as guilty as he most undoubtedly is. I trust, therefore, that I can rely on you, as the self appointed guardian of the prison's manners, to make sure that such practices cease immediately? I trust I make myself plain?"

The man, for all his skeletal menace, was urbane and charming, but Fleury knew a killer when he saw one, and he found his words ambiguous and odd. However, he replied in the same civil manner, careful not to remove the defiant smile from his face, "You are clarity itself, Sir, and wicked as this place is, I will try my very best, Mr..." Fleury bowed infinitesimally, not taking his eyes off the other's.

"Mauvaise," said the man, "Warder Mauvaise."

Fleury had walked unaccompanied back to his cell, quelling the impertinent looks from the yarders with false ease. In his two-year stretch here, he had met corrupt warders, violent warders, honest warders (rare), sadistic warders. Most of them, whilst denouncing Fleury's activities, were happy for them to continue, with payment in kind or Rhino. Others could be intimidated, but all were malleable. Looking into the hellish eyes of Mauvaise, he could not see any avenue for him. He had not asked for money or hinted at any type of corruption or blackmail, and Fleury hoped he was not going to turn out to be the one thing he dreaded: an incorruptible zealot.

He had returned to a desperately worried Ambrose, who threw himself at him in relief while Fleury oozed an air of confidence he did not feel.

"Ah now, boy, it's only natural that the new man would want to meet the man in charge now. It happens every time a new warder comes."

The next meeting with Stark was difficult to arrange. Stark was exceedingly paranoid and had destroyed his appointment book, burning it in his cell. He avoided Fleury for a while by staying out of the yard, but he could not escape him forever, and one evening on the way back to the privy, Fleury ambushed him and dragged him into the shadows, his blade on his throat.

"Stark." Fleury whispered, "Are you playing me for a fool?

After all I have done for you in this place?"

"No, Fleury, truly. It's the new man. The word has gone round, and I can't...can't work for you. If I am caught, we'll all be hanged, and I've still got a year to do. Damn, Fleury, you've seen the regulations! Just leaving the lid off the privy merits twelve lashes!"

Fleury dropped him, his eyes cold. "If I do not work, then I do not get out; you know how that works. If we are still here one day after Standish's official release date, I will come looking for you. You ask yourself, Stark, what is more important to you — the possibility of being hanged, or the certainty of this in your throat? When you've decided, let me know. You know where I am."

He left Stark shaking and pale, knowing that Fleury's threats were not idle. Stark, through being frugal and not minding the communal wards and filth, had amassed enough for his own release fee, and now, in the light of this change in everyone's fortunes, he very much regretted letting Fleury know where he had hidden it.

Things did not improve; punishments came thick and fast every day. One man was heard to say to say "bugger" and was given twelve lashes, being unable to pay a simple penny fine. Another man was caught pissing in the yard during visiting hours and was fined sixpence. Ambrose had railed at the flogging and said that he would have been happy to pay the penny, and that was when Fleury had to tell him the truth. "We have no money to spare, lad. What I have saved is to get us out. I will not allow you to ask Goshawk again, not after you refused to let him visit you. Don't worry, I can do it. I just need to concentrate my efforts and not let a certain young man monopolise me. A few more weeks and then it's the open road for us, and a fair wind westwards."

Fleury had talked many times of travelling to the Americas, and Ambrose was beginning to see that it could be the new start both of them needed. He would love to be able to travel to Dorset, say a secret farewell to his sisters, and then sail away with Fleury to a new life, but here in this hopeless place, he could not see further than the next day. Green fields and blue oceans were as alien to him and just as hard to visualise as owning Standish once had been.

Rafe returned to Tavistock Square and tried to start his life again. He engaged tutors for the boy — elderly, fussy, scholarly men whom he interviewed thoroughly in advance to ascertain they would not mistreat his son. In deference to Ambrose's teachings, he only allowed the tutors to teach in the morning, and gave himself over to afternoons with Sebastien. They would drive to the country or a park, and Rafe would himself continue Sebastien's education on nature and botany. In this small way, he felt he kept a bond with Ambrose. He kept a bond with him another way, although no one except Dunstan knew of it. He set up a small pension for the sisters, and Dunstan disguised it as alms from the church, "For the relatives of prisoners," he called it. At first the ladies refused the benefi- cience, but Maria's sensibilities were worn down by necessity, and they were now at least out of the danger of destitution. Rafe would happily have made it more, but Dunstan tempered his generosity, explaining that while a smaller amount would be accepted, a larger one would be more suspicious, and would be refused.

"We can increase it in time," the sensible man said. "Blame the banks for an increase in the interest, perhaps."

In the meantime, Rafe's boundless wealth helped the poor of St Olaf's, too, although Dunstan never discussed the details of it with him. Rafe had paid for Francis' funeral, Gronow arranging it all through a numbed Ashurst who once again proved to be a better friend to Francis than Rafe felt he deserved. Francis had at least left a scribbled note, which exonerated anyone from the fault of his death. The note had been repressed, Ashurst had given evidence to protect his friend. The death was confirmed by the coroner's court as a firearms accident. The funeral had been attended by Ashurst and Gronow only, and when this was reported back to Rafe, he could only feel sorrow for the poor demented man whose obsession had prevented him from being all that he could have been.

In the grip of his own obsession, and at least once a week, Rafe travelled across London to Newgate Street and sat outside in his carriage looking at the forbidding walls, trying to imagine what Ambrose was suffering within. As he kept in touch with Dunstan, he knew that Ambrose was alive and was as well as could be expected. He also knew that Dunstan was keeping something from him, but what it was, he could not imagine. The little man had assured him on many occasions that if anything were wrong, he would inform Goshawk without fail. Twice, Rafe had bribed the gatekeeper to allow him to visit in the cage in the hope of seeing Ambrose's face, knowing that he should not risk such a venture, that it would cause more harm than good, but being unable to stop himself. It was in vain. He had not seen Ambrose, and he did not dare to speak to any other prisoner to ask where he was. The second time he ventured inside the walls, Dunstan had found him out and lectured him unmercifully. Rafe had not tried it again, as Dunstan threatened to tell Ambrose of his visits. Rafe knew if that happened he would never again come out of his cell on a Tuesday.

His staying in Tavistock Square was a penance. He could very easily have sold the house, but something made him stay. If he was unhappy there, then at least he shared something with Ambrose. If he could have fitted in the icehouse, he would have forced himself into it.

As September turned to October the weather worsened; every

day was wet and cold. Prisoners caught colds and influenza, and Fleury had to spend money he could not spare on coal, hot gin, and more blankets. Another week slipped by, and Fleury was failing in his task to pay their release fees. Mauvaise's spies appeared to be everywhere, so he could not blame Stark for failing in his pimping duties. His usual clients were becoming as frustrated in their sexual tension as Fleury was becoming in his inability to earn Rhino. He found that his freedoms became fewer. He could not move from yard to yard and from ward to ward as he previously could. Trapped in one area, the opportunities for earning were limited. The richer pickings were on the far side of the prison. The only day Fleury had a free rein was Friday when Mauvaise had a day off, and he bucketed around the prison like a one man sexual frenzy, attempting to see as many clients as he could. It was not enough. There were four weeks to go, and he was still short of the fees. Then one day, at the beginning of the last month, Mauvaise had him brought to him again.

"Mr Fleury," he said, standing before him, "I thought you and I had an understanding."

Mauvaise was taller than Fleury, and Fleury found himself having to look up at the warder as he stood so close to him. "I'm sure that I don't know what you mean, Sir," Fleury said carefully.

Mauvaise shot out a hand and grabbed Fleury by the hair, then with the other, swiftly divested him of his stiletto. "Would you say that the unnatural practices in this prison have lessened?"

"I could not say, Sir."

"I think, Mr Fleury, that that is my point exactly," Mauvaise said, dropping Fleury and turning the stiletto over in his hands. "You are supposed to be able to say. You should be able to say that they have, whereas I *know*," he said sharply, bringing the stiletto down on the table, "that they have not. The only resolution for this, I feel, is to separate the worst elements, starting with the convicted sodomite in 12c." Fleury looked up sharply, and Mauvaise smiled at him. "Yes. I think the men will be safer if Mr Goshawk's wife is in the ward he is supposed to be in, don't you? And you, I believe," he moved to his desk and consulted a pile of papers, "were originally billeted for the Chapel Ward, so what you are doing over on this side, I could not tell you. Some administrative error, I would imagine."

"Sir," Fleury managed, trying to think of something fast, feeling that the man must be hinting about some bribe Fleury could offer him. "Surely there must be something I can do? For you?" He tried to smile roguishly in spite of his panic.

Mauvaise moved nearer and nearer to him, and looked deep into his eyes. "Are you suggesting what I assume you are suggesting, whore?" The voice was almost dreamy and utterly terrifying.

"Do you think that I would want your filthy hands on this?" He grabbed Fleury's hand and directed it to a sizeable erection.

Fleury realised then that there was no hope; the kind of arousal Mauvaise enjoyed had nothing whatever to do with pleasure.

"Get out," Mauvaise said, opening the door to let the two guards in. "Get back to the ward you belong in, and let me deal with Mr Standish."

Ambrose looked up from his book as the warders crashed in the door. He stood in terror, as no one except Fleury and Christopher had been through that door in the months they had been together. One warder ripped the book from his hands, and they both grabbed hold of his arms and marched him out of the room. Ambrose questioned them, attempted to get them to tell them where they were taking him, but they ignored him and pulled him, resisting, down the dark corridor. They entered the yard, and Fleury was standing there in the rain, a look of helplessness on his face such as Ambrose had never seen.

"Fleury?" he called uncertainly, but Fleury was unable, or unwilling to reply. They crashed through several more doors until finally Ambrose was shoved unceremoniously into the ward into which he had been thrust five months before, the door clanging shut behind him. He was back in the same state, or mildly worse, that he had been at the start of his incarceration — coatless, penniless, and without even a bed to his name.

Chapter 29

Fleury was desperate for news of Ambrose, but none of his lines of communication was open. Three days had passed; Friday came and he was finally able to perform several favours to allow him to travel across the yards, back to the communal ward where he had found Ambrose five months earlier. He was gratified to find Ambrose alive, though pale, cold, dirty and defiant. Fleury had brought him a mattress, one of his beloved books, some blankets and Rhino, so at least he could buy extra food.

"I am not the soft option they once thought I was," Ambrose said, smiling as Fleury held both his chilled hands and stared at him, a worried look on his face. "Either that, or there are a different set of men in here. Tam's gone, of course. He must be in Australia by now. They made a move on me on the second night, thinking I had more than I had. They didn't think I'd have a knife, and they weren't expecting that I'd know how to use it."

"You want me to—" Fleury began, but Ambrose cut him off.

"No. If I'm here, I stand on my own. I don't think they'll try anything again." He smiled, aware that it wasn't purely his own self defence that would keep the predators off. "If they think you will be here on Fridays and Christopher on Tuesdays, I think they may leave me alone."

"They will, by God, or they *will* answer to me," Fleury said fiercely. "Look, Ambrose, I cannot hide it from you. We are in trouble. With the prison shut down the way it is, I cannot earn what we need to get out of here. At best, I can earn your fee. So this is what I suggest: we get you out, and you wait at Dunstan's..."

"No. NO. Fleury!" Ambrose's anger burst through like a flood, drowning Fleury's words, "I will not leave you in here, not when you could have left me weeks ago."

"You are not listening to me, lad. I cannot afford to keep us both, or I can, but I cannot keep us both and save as I did before. I can have enough for you, in time, and if you go, I can save enough to get me out later. I want you out of here, and safe, *luran*, that's all."

He softly stroked Ambrose's cheek, and Ambrose's eyes darkened and once again he was reminded just how much Fleury had done for him, without any request for repayment or gratitude. How he longed for a private moment so he could kiss that impish mouth, those pleading eyes. Instead, he had to be content with squeezing his hands and nodding in silent agreement. "When I get out, I'll be earning again. Christopher will give me an advance. We will get you out as soon as we can, my love."

"Ah now," Fleury's old self returned with the mention of Dunstan, "he considers you to be redeemable, me boy, but he knows that this Catholic soul is doomed for Purgatory if I'm lucky, and no mistake. He may not welcome me in his house."

"He will, for he is a good man, and no matter if he doesn't. A fair wind westwards, remember?" Ambrose coughed violently. "Damn this straw dust."

"Aye, lad, a fair wind," said Fleury, but his eyes were worried.

As they passed the day together, Ambrose kept saying that Fleury probably had better things to do, but Fleury would not budge from his side. Fleury held him all night until he finally fell asleep, coughing intermittently. It was clear Ambrose was sickening and was trying his best to hide it. Regretting having to leave at dawn the next day, he passed around the room and spoke to the two or three men he could trust there to send word if anything happened he needed to know about.

"And by that," he said grimly and softly, not to wake Ambrose who had been a long time getting to sleep, "I mean *anything*. Don't let the rumour that I'm toothless make you think I am." He was gratified to see that at least most people were still convinced who was top man around there. Mauvaise might be able to flog them, but men were more frightened of Fleury's certain retribution than Mauvaise's possible punishments. When it came to direct violence, Fleury had a proven record, and while he mourned the loss of his stiletto, it wasn't the only blade he had, and the inmates knew it.

On Tuesday morning, Christopher entered Fleury's ward and listened as the Irishman explained what had happened and his concerns for Ambrose. "He's not well, Dunstan," he said. "He caught a chill the first night there, and now I'm told he's feverish and light headed. I cannot get to see him, not before Friday, and what can I do anyway? It may be the ague back again, but I am afraid that it may be the gaol fever. By all that's holy," he shouted, "has the boy not suffered enough? He's come too far to die now." Fleury's eyes were frantic as he said to Dunstan what he loathed to have to say. "You have to contact *him*. Get Ambrose out by whatever means it takes. You know what I am saying, man." Fleury's cheek twitched with the violence of his emotion. "Get him out, Dunstan, I beg of you."

Christopher went straight to the Master's ward where he knew Ambrose would be and found him much as Fleury had described — feverish, shaking, and not quite aware of his surroundings, his eyes rolling back into his head. One of Fleury's "trusties" was sitting by him when Dunstan came in and jumped back when Dunstan knelt down to assess his friend's state. It took a few seconds only, and he left Ambrose in the convict's care, walking back through the entrance to the Ordinary's lodge. He was reluctant to acquiesce to

Fleury's demands and hoped that he could arrange matters himself.

The Ordinary was sitting down to an enormous breakfast, and Dunstan apologised profusely for disturbing him. Accepting only a cup of coffee, he sat opposite the Ordinary at the large mahogany table and waited for him to finish eating.

"I suppose this is about your 'lost cause' again Dunstan?" said the Ordinary at last, dabbing his mouth with a large napkin.

"Yes, Sir. He is most unwell. He is not strong, and I fear for his safety. If at least he could be isolated for now?"

"Out of the question, although of course it is not up to me. If we had to isolate every case of ague and La Grippe, we would have no individual cells. The doctor will see him, I dare say, when next he comes."

"May I, in that case, at least make an appointment to see the Governor, to put my case to him?" asked Dunstan, feeling angrier than he allowed himself to sound.

"My dear man," the Ordinary said patronisingly, "I cannot run to the Board every time one of the prisoners is taken ill! Why, if I did that, the Board would refuse to see me when there was a case that warranted my urgent assistance!"

Dunstan's blood boiled and, in unaccustomed anger, he drew himself up, and with both hands on the table, he said, "Of course, your apparent lack of Christian concern would have nothing to do with the man's crime, would it?"

The Ordinary rose to his feet with extreme dignity, throwing his napkin onto his plate. "Mr Dunstan, I have tolerated your interference in the normal routine of this prison because you were a fellow cleric on a mission from our Bishop, but I will brook no insinuations against my charity and compassion from you, Sir. I would be grateful if you would remove yourself from my house forthwith, and ask yourself, Sir, if you would, is *your* deep interest in this case as impartial as *you* claim it to be?"

Dunstan glared at the Ordinary with loathing, nauseated by the leer on the fat face. Without another word he strode from the house. Outside, he did what he did not wish to have to do and summoned a hackney.

"Tavistock Square," he muttered to the driver. His anger abating, he wondered whether he was doing the right thing after all. Drawing up at the house in the airy green square, a thousand miles from what he had left behind, he very nearly turned away. He sat a long while in the hackney, debating with himself and asking for God's guidance. If only he had Constance with him; she saw things so much more clearly than he did. He was still smarting from the Ordinary's slur, and was regretting his outburst. It would make matters difficult with his Bishop, he knew that.

As he sat there, confused, a door slammed and Goshawk was

there, tearing open the hackney door, paying the driver, and not so much inviting as dragging Dunstan into the house.

Rafe could see by the rector's face that something was deeply troubling him, and he guessed correctly without being told. They hardly entered the the hallway when he said in a low, urgent voice, "He's ill again?"

Dunstan nodded, unable to look into Goshawk's eyes after the first glance. He had never seen such fire in anyone's expression. "I spoke to the Ordinary this morning, but he refuses to listen. I wanted him isolated, but I failed." He was aware that Rafe was arranging things, servants were being dispatched, baskets of provisions were being ordered, and a doctor was being summoned.

A slim boy came downstairs during all the commotion, and Rafe took him into his arms and held him tight. "I am going to help Ambrose," he said gently to the boy. "He is unwell. I may be gone for a while, so please do not worry. Stay here, and pray for him."

He clasped the lad close and Dunstan had to look away, so obvious was the love that the man had for his son. What a different man this was from the man portrayed by the newspapers, a man they represented as callous and obdurate in his wealth and power. He was nothing like that to those he trusted; he was so very capable of the deepest human love. Dunstan realised that he was privileged to see this secret side to the Goshawk persona.

Faster than he would have believed possible, they were in the Goshawk carriage and flying back through London as fast as the horses could go. As he risked a sideways glance at Goshawk, to Dunstan's eyes he looked like some king of ancient days, setting forth with every man in his country arrayed with him on a forlorn hope, praying for glory but seeing nothing but death.

As they reached the prison, Goshawk finally spoke again. "Go to him. Take him what I have here; the doctor will be with you soon. Do what you can for him, as will I."

Dunstan watched him stride to the dread portal and disappear inside. The coachman picked up the various bundles, and followed Dunstan as he returned to Ambrose's side.

Rafe was ardent and aggressive. He swarmed into the foul place as if entering a foreign court, like a nobleman who knows he will be granted an audience and certain that his credentials are so impeccable, his bidding will be done. His unbounded arrogance and sense of superiority swept all before him. Once he said he wished to see the head warder, it was so. Turnkeys grovelled before him; lesser warders rushed to ensure doors were opened before his arrival to save him waiting in front of them. Each man was ostentatiously rewarded with coinage, ensuring his immediate loyalty. Nothing like Goshawk had been seen in the prison for a very long while.

He was shown into a small, well appointed but depressing office, and he waited impatiently, slightly irritated that after his flamboyant entrance there was not already someone there to meet him. The door clicked, and he spun round.

"Master Rafe," said a voice from a place in Rafe's mind that had been locked for so long the padlocks were rusted through. With no expression on his face, Rafe stared at Mauvaise, feeling as if his life were imploding around him, the rusted locks flying apart and creating an explosion that tore through his mind and ripped holes in the shuttered past — red, bloody, and full of rats. "I was hoping that you would pay us a visit. I have often wondered what you would be like after all this time."

"You." Rafe's voice was not a whisper, but a dark syllable of his youth, like a drop of blood onto a snow covered lawn. "What in hell are you doing here?"

"I am doing what I do best," Mauvaise said. "Teaching." He sat behind his desk and steepled his long grey fingers together under his chin as he looked speculatively at Rafe across the long years. "I could ask you the exact same question, but of course I already know the answer."

"Teaching? Is that what you still call it?" Rafe raged.

"Ah, still the fire, Master Rafe," Mauvaise said gently. "I could never quench that fire in you. You have too much of your father in you, I fear."

Rafe spun away from the loathsome creature and faced the door, taking a tight rein on his shattered memories. He controlled his breathing, knowing that Mauvaise was capable of saying anything to produce a reaction, but that was the only power he had left. He had no physical control; there was nothing he could really do. "Too little, too late, Mauvaise," he said. "If taunting could destroy me, the newspapers would have done it twenty times over. You know why I am here. Either release Standish early, or allow me to give him every comfort this miserable place can offer him."

"But why are you so strong, Master Rafe, answer me that?" the hated voice continued, ignoring his demand. "Because of your sickly mother? Your huff of a bullying father? That molly Quinn?"

Rafe took a step forward and stopped again, furious with himself to have broken covert. Mauvaise's gentle smile broadened.

"I made you the man you are, and you know it. I took a romantic boy with a black soul and forged steel into his being. You are my finest creation, Rafe, my ablest pupil and a credit to me."

"Do what I ask," Rafe said in a dangerous monotone.

"Release him? Allow you to pamper him? What would the inmates learn from that? What would the sodomite learn from that? No, it would not fit the *lesson*, Master Rafe. You are wasting your time, and you knew that from the second you saw me."

"I repeat myself, Mauvaise. You will do what I ask."

"And why, for purely theoretical reasons would I be likely to do that? You forget who has the power in *here*."

"Because," Rafe hissed, in control at last, "how would your precious Board react to knowing they had a sodomite as their chief warder?"

Mauvaise's eyebrows rose slowly into his hair, and his smile was quizzical. "I would imagine they would be as surprised as I would be. What is this, Master Rafe? Blackmail? You know you have no such leverage on me. I am virgin to man and woman."

"If there is something I have learned, Mr Tutor, it is that public opinion is swayed by scandal." Rafe was beginning to enjoy himself. "You taught me for three years. I am a known sodomite, although sadly for you, not a convicted one. Where did I learn such evil practices? People might say — from my tutors. Who else was so influential in my formative years? Quinn and you."

Mauvaise's eyes narrowed as he listened to Rafe. "Nonsense, and you know it. Impossible for you to prove such a lie after all this time."

"I have found," said Rafe slowly, "that the older a lie is, the easier it is to prove. I agree, of course, that my word against yours would possibly not have the effect I require." He leant forward and rammed every word home as if he were raping the man. "But what if I were to produce sworn affidavits from every house boy and every housemaid working for my father at that time to the effect that you practised your unnatural practices on them at the same time as you were buggering your employer's only son and then beating him to keep him quiet? The court can be shown ample proof of the beatings, Mauvaise, and as you know, as *everyone...really... knows...*there is no smoke without fire." He paused, triumphantly, seeing the man finally crumble, back down, and as Rafe conquered his past, it fell from him like broken chains.

The warder looked up at Rafe and nodded, his eyes furious but beaten. "I cannot allow you to take him early, but he can have his old cell back, and everything you wish." He stood up and left without another word.

Rafe stood there for a moment marshalling his strength, then set out to find Ambrose. The squalor and filth of the prison were worse than he had imagined. As the turnkey took him along the dark corridor, the stench, detectable from the street, bearable from the warder's office, caused him almost to gag by the time the ward door was thrown open.

Dunstan stood and exchanged glances with Rafe, and Rafe spoke quickly. "Not release, but isolation, his old cell. Do you know where that is?" He knelt down by the figure on the floor, hardly believing his eyes.

Ambrose lay on a dirty straw pallet, insensible and shuddering, and so very pale. Rafe's eyes stung with tears as he gently touched the beloved face, so much changed, so much thinner, but still his Ganymede beneath the dirt and the new look of strength. Unmindful, he let a tear drop onto Ambrose's face, trailing the dirt into streaks behind it.

The doctor leant down and whispered, "If we can get him out of this dankness, Goshawk, he may be saved. It is not Gaol Fever; there are no spots or lesions. I believe it to be Influenza."

Rafe continued to stroke Ambrose's face, the soft well-remembered hair, unwilling to drag his eyes from the vision until Dunstan spoke.

"Goshawk, please."

Rafe stood and picked Ambrose up as easily as he would Sebastien, remembering bitterly the last time he had picked him up like this, on the boat, as they neared Venice. "Lead the way," he said shortly.

As he laid Ambrose down on the cot in the tiny cell, he determined that this cell was not much better than the previous. Dunstan and the doctor did the work for him — ordering food, wine, bedding, clean blankets, water, lye, soap, fires to be lit, and candles to be brought. All the while, Rafe sat and held Ambrose's hand as tightly as he dared, hardly believing that he was finally with his love again. He tried to pour some of his own strength into Ambrose, willed him to fight, to wake up. If only he could look once more into his eyes and not have them look at him with hate.

The day wore on, the doctor bleeding Ambrose and blistering his flesh, much to Rafe's disgust. Rafe could only drip wine-and-water into his mouth and wash the filth from his body, while Dunstan and the maid he had procured scoured the small cell with lye and water. Darkness fell, and finally Dunstan pulled at Rafe's arm.

"We must *go*, Goshawk." Rafe nodded, not taking his eyes from Ambrose's face, burning it onto his mind. "Come, now," Dunstan repeated and Rafe allowed himself to be pulled up, the doctor taking Rafe's place by the bed. As he backed away, Rafe turned as the door flew open and a scruffy, wild-looking figure raced to the unconscious man and tumbled to his knees on the opposite side of the bed, clutching at his hand.

"*Luran*," the man muttered. "Ambrose, *caraid*, Fleury's here, your Padraig. Come back, *luran*, my own. Come back to me."

Rafe made to step forward at this invasion, but Dunstan held his arm vice-like in his hand, caught his eye and shook his head fiercely. "No. Not now," he whispered.

At the noise, the man by the bed looked up, dazed, and saw the others in the room for the first time. His face paled visibly beneath the dirt when his eyes fell on the unmistakable form of Goshawk, but his expression strengthened as he stood up and walked toward him. He did not offer his hand, but he looked his rival straight in the eye with a look that pierced Rafe through, as if he was reading his very soul. Then he spoke in a soft lilting brogue. "I have you to thank for saving the man's life, and I'm grateful, Sir, more than I can say." He looked long at Rafe, his eyes soft and slightly questioning, then he smiled, but the searching burrowing into Rafe's soul continued. "When he wakes, do ye want me to tell him, tell him you were here?"

Rafe realised there were tears in both their eyes as each understood what they were asking of one another. There was a slight noise from the bed; a sigh and then the sweetest voice in the world said the one word that killed Rafe where he stood.

"Padraig?"

Rafe stiffened, and swallowed, forcing himself to stay impassive. He gave a stiff bow to the Irishman and shook his head once, then watched the man return to the bed to take possession of his heart.

Chapter 30

"You knew about him." Rafe and Dunstan sat in the carriage outside the gaol.

"I knew he was protecting Ambrose, yes, but I did not know of their...friendship until recently. I suppose I am too naïve."

"He called him. He was insensible and he called for *him*." For the first time in his life, Rafe was learning what jealousy tasted like, bitter and bilious. His Icarus, in love with a man like that — a criminal, a guttersnipe. In love? Were they in love? It did not bear thinking about. Rafe's eyes closed. Now, as he felt the first pangs of bitter envy for whatever relationship that man had with Ambrose, suddenly the realisation hit him of what Ambrose, such an innocent in love, had suffered when he learned about Francis, Quinn, and Achille. Rafe's stomach churned. He felt could not bear it, not the jealousy or the renewed guilt.

Dunstan instructed the coachman to remove to St Olaf's, or they would have been sitting outside the prison all night, and it was already icy. For the second time, Rafe entered the rectory in a highly emotional state, pacing the room like a caged panther while Dunstan poured him a large brandy. He came to his senses as Constance entered the room, and he bowed gallantly as she was introduced.

"Constance, dear," Christopher said as diplomatically as he was able, "I think what we discuss is not suitable for mixed company."

"If it concerns Ambrose, it concerns all of us, I believe," she said firmly. "I am as fond of him as you are, brother. I know his crime, and you may not have noticed it, but I am a grown woman."

Rafe smiled slightly at her show of temper and said softly, "Miss Dunstan is a lady who knows her own mind. I for one will not be indelicate, Dunstan, and I would enjoy her company, if she will grace us with it." He sat down at last, relaxing slightly for the first time in that endless day. "What can you tell me of this Fleury?"

Constance moved to the bookshelf and pulled out the Newgate Calendar, opened it to a marked page, and handed it to Rafe. They sat in silence as he read it, his cheek twitching with suppressed emotion. Then he handed it back to Constance with quiet thanks. He sat immersed in thought, his eyes velvety soft as he recalled the sweet face he had missed for so very long, trying to recall the feeling of Ambrose's hair beneath his fingers.

Mistaking Rafe's thoughts, Dunstan broke the silence. "He has been very good to Standish, Goshawk. I do not deny that he is a dangerous man. I've heard stories of his violence, although nothing has ever been proven against him, but he may have saved Ambrose by simply removing him from that dreadful ward five months ago. You saw it today. Do you think Ambrose would still be alive today if he had stayed in there?"

Rafe shook his head. Snapping out of his reverie, he mobilised his thoughts and rearranged his features. Finishing his drink, he stood up. "Keep me apprised of his health, Dunstan. He is to have anything he needs, anything. He can complain about it afterwards and, knowing him, he will." A true smile came to his face finally; it seemed to light up the room. "It is about time that he realised that he can accept help when it is offered." He shook Dunstan's hand and kissed Constance's. "Will you have him here when he is released, or would you prefer not? He will never accept my hospitality."

"We will have him here, of course, and Mr Fleury, too," Constance said firmly, glaring at Dunstan as if challenging him to contradict her. "They will be in need of somewhere to gather their thoughts before they do whatever they plan to do."

Rafe shot a quick glance at Dunstan, who was looking decidedly worried. As Rafe turned to Constance, his eyes iced over, and his features shut down. "Can you see Ambrose as a gentleman of the road, Miss Dunstan?"

Constance blushed. "I do not think so, Sir," she answered, looking him in the eye.

"If he chooses that path," Rafe sneered, "he will be wasting all of our efforts to keep him alive."

"You are assuming, Sir, that Mr Fleury has a greater influence for bad than Ambrose has an influence for good. I feel, and indeed he has proved as much, that Ambrose is capable of engendering love and tolerance in all whom he befriends."

Rafe was impressed and slightly amused at this tiny blonde woman bristling with indignation in Ambrose's defence. He bowed from the waist. "I am chastised, and suitably so." His eyes were clear, and he met her challenging ones with some penitence, intrigued by the joust. "And you are right, Ambrose has no evil within him. But the other has, if what I have heard and read about him. And evil is not so easily transmuted as good. I do not truly think that Ambrose would turn to a life of crime, but he may be caught up in it and implicated along with the highwayman. I cannot see that man allowing Ambrose to support them both by tutoring, and let us face honest facts, who would now employ him to tutor their children?"

"Goshawk." Christopher's voice was a rebuke.

"Forgive me." Rafe bowed slightly once more, "I am tired and should not allow myself to speak my mind at times. I will take my leave. Accept my gratitude for coming to me this morning. If, or rather, when Ambrose tries to blame you for what I have done for him in his illness, tell him I did it all against your will. He will readily believe that."

Released at last from his ward by a surly turnkey on Mauvaise's orders, Fleury had fled back to their old room in some panic, fearing the diagnosis. Seeing Ambrose unconscious and deathly pale made his heart stop in his chest, and he had held the thin hands as tightly as he dared. Suddenly he had been aware of the two men standing against the far wall, and finally he had come face to face with the one man he had hoped he would never meet. With a sinking heart, he saw just how very handsome his rival was, taller than both he and Ambrose and with such a dark brooding attraction. In spite of hating the thought of Goshawk, Fleury could see the magnetism the man emanated. It seemed to him as if Goshawk were holding himself so tightly reined in that the only outlet for his emotions was his eyes. Fleury never thought that eyes of such a dark colour could hold such an inferno. They were terrifying in their passion. As their eyes met, Fleury was touched beyond measure with the silent exchange — the clear inference that Ambrose's happiness was important above all, and that he, Padraig Fleury, had been entrusted with it, but he was to keep it safe, or Goshawk would call him to account. The man had said a great deal without uttering a word.

After they had gone, Fleury talked to the doctor and learned that Goshawk had retained his services. He was under instructions to come first thing in the morning and daily thereafter. When the doctor left, Fleury looked around the little cell with a sense of wonder. For six months he had been working hard to keep the two of them with the simple essentials in life, and in a few short hours, unlimited money had almost transformed the place: clean white sheets and soft blankets; clean night clothes, pillows; fruit and wine, bread, milk, meat, and coal. Money, it must be wonderful to have that sort of money. The relief Fleury felt was palpable. This largesse would mean that they could both get out in two weeks, together. *And I was wrong*, he thought speculatively. *Mauvaise obviously had a price.* His eyes returned to Ambrose, still unconscious, his face flushed with fever. He knew how angry his love would be at this apparent betrayal.

He whispered to the sleeping man, "But we just all want you to get well. All of us, it seems."

Rafe came again the next day and each day thereafter, telling himself that it was only to ensure that Ambrose was not deteriorating, but secretly knowing that he could not keep away. It was a perverse and masochistic pleasure watching the man with Fleury present, knowing that if Ambrose were in a conscious state he would be ordering Rafe from the room. Ambrose was not much improved, but the fever had not yet turned to pneumonia, and the doctor was optimistic. Rafe sat unmoving for hours at a time in a hard chair at the end of the bed, his eyes never flickering. He made no further move to touch Ambrose in any way, and his face was completely impassive while Fleury tended him.

Fleury was beginning to resent the man's presence but could hardly ask him to leave while the evidence of his generosity was all around them and more poured in daily. They both knew that Rafe would go when he had no other choice, and so, in this way, the men reached an unspoken and bitter compromise.

On the evening of the fourth day, Ambrose stirred. Fleury was dozing, his arms on the bed as he sat on the floor. He woke instantly and felt Ambrose's face; it was cool and dry. Fleury turned to Rafe. "The fever has broken. He is waking up." Rafe stood and left the room without a word. Fleury felt suddenly weak. It was as if he had been poised and tensed up for days, but for flight or fight, he could not tell. He watched as Ambrose's eyes slowly opened and focussed immediately on him. He gave him such a smile that Fleury fell in love all over again, leaned forward and kissed him chastely. "And about time too, *falsòir*. If you'd slept any longer, I would have paid me own release fee and left you to it. I cannot wait in this place forever you know."

"*Falsòir*?" murmured Ambrose.

"Lazybones, in your heathen tongue. How do you feel?"

"Like Lord Ruthven has drained every drop of blood from my body. Deathly tired."

"You and your Vampyres," Fleury joked, but he was pleased that Ambrose sounded so alert. "Sleep then, lad." Kissing his hands, he watched as Ambrose went back to sleep. From the corridor, there were the sounds of footsteps that faded into the distance.

As everyone had predicted, Ambrose was furious when he had discovered that Rafe had been so instrumental in his recovery. His temper, rarely seen, was childish, irrational and uncontrolled. Fleury listened to every word, then ignored him, Ambrose already having been told by Dunstan and the doctor that there had been no option, and he would have been dead without Rafe's intercession.

"Your pride," Fleury would say, "will be the death of you, and that is a fact." He refused utterly to discuss with Ambrose whether he had met Rafe, what his impressions were, or how many times Rafe had been to the jail. He knew that when his temper cooled, Ambrose's logic would prevail and he would see the sense in it all. Complaining to Stark later, his friend had given him a sly sideways glance and said enigmatically, "Do you not think the lad protests too much?" and when Fleury had asked him what he meant by that, he had denied meaning anything.

Fleury knew exactly what Stark had meant. If Goshawk meant nothing to Ambrose, he should not be obsessing over taking help from him. Fleury had not thought twice about it and would do it again if Ambrose needed it. It worried him, but there was nothing he could do. Fleury was a practical man. He decided that Stark should be repaid for the insult, however.

Finally the long night ended. Ambrose, still not well enough to walk unaided, was assisted by Fleury, who would allow no one else to do it, out through the corridor, out through the long gated tunnels, and to the outside door. Fleury had sold nearly everything they had, including most of his clothes and the remaining items brought by Rafe, and it had been enough, barely. Fleury's remaining savings and Stark's poached nest egg nestled warmly in his waistcoat pocket. Fleury gave Ambrose a quick grin. "Ready for the real world, lad?" he said as the main door was unlocked.

"Fair wind," said Ambrose firmly as they made their way out to the hackney that Dunstan had waiting. Fleury smiled, but his eyes were contemplative. If he had anything to do with it, they would not be staying at Dunstan's for longer than he could help. The men were so involved in each other that they did not notice that there were two private carriages on the far side of Newgate Street. As the hackney drove off towards St Olaf's, one carriage followed them toward the east, the other went west.

Dunstan provided them with separate rooms and, without any discussion, all parties understood why this was necessary. But it shored up Fleury's resolve, and he explained his plans to Ambrose later that evening as he sat by Ambrose's bed.

"We need to move on, me darlin', be independent, make our own way in the world. You cannot teach, at least not where you are known, and your shining example has made an honest man of me, so I'll be refraining from the Standin' and Deliverin'." He grinned at Ambrose, who pulled him down for a kiss, if that was all he could have. "I'll be gone as long as it takes, maybe two days, perhaps longer. I have people I can see and favours I can call in for repayment. I will find us work, I promise you that." He left the remainder of their money with Ambrose, and in the morning he was gone before the house was awake.

A week later, he was in an alehouse in Cheapside, not far from Ambrose but unwilling to return without definite success. He was re-evaluating his plans quietly over a pint of ale when someone touched his arm. It looked like he had a client.

Ambrose was really worried. Not only did he have to live without Fleury, who had been his rock for so long, but he had to live with the Dunstans, who were so kind he could hardly believe it. Constance could not look him in the eyes, and Christopher was his normal bluff self. Ambrose was not yet a drain on their limited resources, but he knew that his money would not last forever. He had told the brother and sister that Fleury was looking for work for them, but as the days went by and a week had passed, he knew that they were both thinking the same as he — Fleury wasn't coming back.

Fleury was not, in many meanings of the word, an honest man, nor had Ambrose made him so, no matter what Fleury said. He had been raised in abject poverty and his ethos, for as long as he could remember, had been that finders were most definitely keepers. And if he had to look in a man's purse to find something, well then that was no different than finding it on the street. He had spent a few days getting reacquainted with the city and relieving a few burdened men of their coinage.

Now, his fortunes were definitely on the rise. He had seen the man in this inn before during the week and wondered at his presence there. By the look of his beautiful clothes, he was obviously extremely wealthy. Now, he simply put money in front of Fleury and then made it clear he wished Fleury to follow him in the time honoured tradition — the handkerchief between the coat tails. Fleury followed him warily, but instead of an alleyway or a secluded doorway as he had expected, the stranger led him to a carriage. Fleury hesitated, unsure whether this was an elaborate trap by the thief takers. The man had stopped by the carriage door in the dark and had held a hand out to Fleury. When Fleury reached him, he gathered him into slim arms, bent down and kissed him deeply. Then, with another bewitching smile, slipped a great deal of money into Fleury's hand and stepped into the carriage.

Fleury was intrigued by the silent man who exuded money as if from every pore, and determined to milk him for all he was worth. The man took him to a house in a part of Mayfair Fleury knew quite well. They were let in by a silent footman, and the man led him up the stairs into a large, opulent bedroom lit only by a roaring fire. Fleury began to speak, but the elegant stranger put slim fingers on his lips, handed him a perfect crystal glass filled with a deep red wine. Emerald eyes shining in the firelight, he watched as Fleury, suddenly feeling untidy and provincial in the face of such sophistication, drank it too fast.

The man moved to him, tall, slim and smiling, and started to remove Fleury's clothing deftly, without words. Fleury's hand moved to the buttons of the man's jacket but was restrained by a slight shake of his customer's head. When Fleury was naked, the man stepped back and simply looked at him appreciatively. Fleury felt suddenly vulnerable. This was not how things were supposed to go. Usually his patrons lay back while Fleury pleasured them, and he had never been in this situation before. He liked to feel in control when whoring and he did not feel that he was. He felt wrong footed, somehow; the game was all out of kilter, and he was unsure whether he would be wise to stay, or make his escape. If it had not been for the fact that the pre-payment from the man had been enough for their passage, he would have fled, but if the man was such a high tipper as he seemed to be, then their future was assured. One fuck, maybe two was all it would take; Fleury could hardly believe his good fortune.

Still dressed, the man fell to his knees and sucked Fleury's member into his teasing mouth. This was something he had never encountered with a client before; they had never pleasured him. Fleury was aroused but discomfited, feeling that he should be participating far more in this. When the man judged, perfectly accurately, that Fleury was on the brink, he led him to the bed, stripped himself, and arranged Fleury on his side. Then he had spooned behind him, draping one of Fleury's legs over his, and entered him gently and expertly, inching in with a huge cock that left Fleury gasping. The man paused, still smiling, and allowed Fleury to catch his breath, running slim fingers over Fleury's torso and hips causing him to groan quietly in pleasure. Then he pulled his mouth to his and kissed him as he pushed forward until his organ finally reached that sweet spot where Fleury melted. As he moved the tip of his cock over it, massaging it with every small thrust, he watched Fleury's face with a cat-like gleam. One hand cupped Fleury's scrotum and massaged it gently as the other wrapped around Fleury's cock and shafted it in rhythm, slowing down every time he felt his balls contract or felt the thrumming of a pending orgasm until Fleury felt that he would never climax and he never wanted to; he just wanted this to go on forever.

Then the man spoke in an elegant accent. "Yes, you feel that...deep inside, how I delay you. Exquisite torture, is it not? You will earn your money this night, little whore." He expertly manipulated Fleury's cock, and it leaked profusely. The pleasure went on and on. His seed spilled as he was milked, but there was no conclusion. "Tell me," the man whispered in Fleury's ear, "does your lover do it to you like this?"

Fleury could not answer, as he was attempting to get one step ahead of the man, to speed up, to force an ejaculation, but the man was too practised, and he played Fleury like a clarinet, bringing him to the brink but always slowing down just in time.

"Answer me, little whore, and I will end it all for you, and it will be like nothing you have had before, I promise."

All control gone, Fleury was at the point where he was considering begging, so he shook his head. His brain felt numb and clouded, and the colours of the room had changed. When the man spoke again it was like he was at the end of a long tunnel, and Fleury could hardly make out the words.

"He told you about me, I know it, for I ruined his life, or so he thinks. How could it have been me alone? Raphael was just as guilty, but poor Achille gets the blame. Now I have had you both, but the dilemma is the same: Will *you* tell the blond Ambrosia? Raphael did not, and look what happened to them." Finally the punishment stopped, but the pleasure continued. The man thrust savagely into Fleury, while pumping him hard.

Fleury was too drugged to care; his orgasm ripped through him without his being aware of it. A soft quiet laugh was the last thing he heard.

Morning came and Fleury awoke with a headache he could not remember deserving. His fundament was sore, and his mouth had the stale taste of semen he did not remember tasting. He lay quietly assessing his surroundings and allowing the mistakes of the night before to filter back to him before he disentangled himself from Achille. He stood up shakily and dressed, then moved back to the bed and sat on the edge of it. The movement aroused Achille, who woke with a sybaritic stretch.

"Mmm...so eager to go, my little whore? You did well." He reached to the side of the bed and took many golden coins from a purse and handed them to Fleury, who pocketed them without a word. "Why so stony this morning? You have no morning smile?" complained the man in the bed, looking into the deadest eyes he had ever seen.

Without a thought, a word, or seemingly, even a movement that could be discerned, Fleury plunged a long pointed knife straight into Achille's shoulder, pinning him to the bed while his other hand choked him, making him unable to cry out. "One strike from me...oh, not to kill you, but to make you realise you are going to die for the humiliation you caused me. And one strike from Ambrose, a blow to your heart to repay you for the one you made to his." Fleury fixed the man with his eyes, seeing the fear grow as the blood flowed from him, then he removed the knife and plunged it into the creature's heart.

When the man's struggles ceased and the light had gone from the green eyes, Fleury took the purse from the side table and swiftly searched the rooms for the money that he knew must be there. He had quite a large amount here and there, and Fleury searched until he was certain that he had found it all. Then he stood over the dead man and spat on him.

"A better death than you deserved," he said. He threw one

guinea back onto the bed. It landed in the pool of blood on Achille's chest. "That's for the fuck." He made sure the bedroom door was locked from the inside, then opened the window and jumped down to the street, sauntering away amongst the milkmaids and street vendors with a tuneless whistle.

Chapter 31

"Mr Fleury!" Constance looked genuinely pleased to see him.

"Guilty, as charged, Ma'am," he said, bowing low and kissing her hand with his most infectious grin. "May I come in?"

Constance blushed and moved aside to allow the rake into the house. He was, she noted, dressed head to foot in new and quite garish clothes — a green and white cutaway coat, pantalon trousers, and a tall hat.

He smiled again at Constance. "So, I suppose you were all missing me madly? Or perhaps you all thought I was dead?"

"I will not say we were not concerned," Constance said honestly, taking his hat and realising it was quite expensive. "I will say this, as we can speak frankly, I feel, and have the same sensibilities: you should have sent word to let us know that you were not dead. It was not only myself that worried."

A look of contrition shot over Fleury's face. "Ah now, I should have thought of that. How is he? He is not unwell again?"

"No, Mr Fleury," Constance reassured, seeing the genuine panic flicker across his face. "He is quite recovered." She opened the door to their sitting room and ushered him in where Ambrose was seated by the fire. "Well enough to upbraid you more thoroughly than I, I dare say." Smiling at the sight of Fleury striding to Ambrose, whose face was alight, she closed the door on them.

"Ambrose," he muttered, sinking to his knees between Ambrose's legs, "truly I did not mean to be so long, but I return triumphant. We can leave England as soon as you are strong enough."

Ambrose kissed him with a hard desperation, groaning into his mouth as his member swelled. "God, Fleury, let us make it sooner rather than later; I want you so very much. But how have you achieved this finery? I thought you were only going to *seek* work? You have already found it?"

Fleury pulled out Alvisi's purse and scattered the money onto Ambrose's lap, watching his love as the expression changed from amazed to worried and then finally to distrustful and concerned.

"What is this?" he questioned. "It's not...you have not..."

"Ah stop that now. I swear on my mother's life that this is not the spoil of any highway robbery. Let's just call it a debt owed and leave it at that."

Ambrose noted that he did not say where the money had come from, and it seemed obvious to him that Fleury was up to his old tricks. He tried to put the thought from him, but he was uneasy in his heart. He now knew that he could not trust Fleury not to resort to robbery or prostitution whenever the need arose, and it worried him that the need would arise quite often in their new life.

"So, how are you feeling, *luran*?" Fleury stroked the blond hair, pleased to see that Ambrose had more colour in his face and had lost the hollowness in his cheeks.

"Much better, and eager to be gone, to put everything behind us. I feel that we can leave here in a day or so, if you will make the arrangements."

"Your wish is my command, Sir, but first let's have one or two nights of freedom, shall we? I fancy being for weeks in steerage on a ship at sea will be almost as bleak as Newgate. I may have been free this past week, but you have been shut up for far too long. I fancy the theatre. What do you say?"

"Can we afford it?" Ambrose asked.

"Can we afford it!" said Fleury, pulling the man to his feet and kissing him. "Aye, lad, we can afford it. Tonight we enjoy the town like noblemen. We've missed too much this year — the Coronation and the Queen's funeral and everything."

Ambrose nodded. He did feel caged and eager to be off, but the thought of weeks shut in another cell-like environment did not appeal to him. It was the promise of a new start that drove him to it. They spent the morning talking and planning, and joined the Dunstans for luncheon. Ambrose could see that they were as concerned as he was by Fleury's obvious increase in fortune.

Later, Fleury escorted Ambrose down the stairs and into a hired carriage. He had bundled Ambrose up against the cold wind, fussing over him so much that Ambrose almost became impatient with him. "I'm not made of glass, Fleury!" he laughed. They drove through the city to Hyde Park, circling the park with the other carriages in the Fashionable Hour. Due to the lateness of the year and the chilly weather, though, most fashionable people were sensibly inside. Fleury took him to Fladong's Hotel for an early dinner, where, hidden beneath the long tablecloth, he shamelessly touched Ambrose whenever he had his fork away from his mouth. Ambrose tried to relax, to enjoy himself, but he could not help but worry about the source of the money Fleury was spending.

After dinner, they drove to the Covent Garden Theatre to see Sheridan's *The Rivals*. Ambrose looked forward to this the most. He had never been to the theatre, indeed had never seen any productions except extremely amateurish tableaux performed in private houses in Dorset.

As they pulled up outside Fleury said, "I don't know about you, but that building reminds me too much of our last lodgings. I hope it's better inside."

Ambrose laughed. The theatre did bear a striking resemblence to Newgate at least from the outside, and his mirth set the tone for the evening as he was swept away on a tide of laughter. The play was much funnier on stage than it was on the printed page, and at one point Fleury was startled when one giggling fit made Ambrose cough so hard his eyes started watering.

Their merriment was not unobserved. Dunstan, worried about Fleury's absence, had sent Rafe word of it. He had also informed him of Fleury's unexpected and affluent return and of their plans to sail at the first opportunity. Rafe had been unable to keep away and had discreetly followed them all evening. He had to see Ambrose once more before he left the country. He had to look him in the eyes, to speak to him, even though he had no idea what he was going to say. If he did not act tonight, it was more than likely he would never see his heart again.

He watched them like the bird of prey for which he was named, his eyes never straying from where they sat in the stalls. He sat in darkness in a box, slightly back from the edge. He saw Ambrose's every smile, noted every time he turned to Fleury with a laughing comment. His hands dug into the red velvet edge of the box when Ambrose began to cough, and his face contorted when he saw the look of concern and love on Fleury's face. His own crisis was past; he had made his decision. With a heart more peaceful than it had been in over a year, Rafe watched them for the rest of the play. As the actors took their curtain calls, he rose. It was time to make his.

On their way out through the crowded, mirrored foyer, Ambrose turned to Fleury to share a line in the play when he bumped into someone coming from the other direction. Ambrose looked up, an apology on his lips, but the words froze in his throat when he saw Rafe standing there, so solidly real, so clearly remembered. It seemed so natural for him to be there that Ambrose forgot himself and reached for him in a pure reflex action, as if to pull him close, to kiss him. His hand, half way to the black clad form, stopped, and a look of confusion covered his face as he remembered where he was. Rafe's eyes tore into his, and an unbidden feeling, like a long buried memory, surfaced in the pit of his stomach and bored through the walls of his guts until it reached his loins. Rafe smiled, but it was the wolfish smile of old, the polite sneer Ambrose had first encountered not the soft, warm black welcome he had come to know so well.

All this happened in a heartbeat, although it had seemed to last an hour, at least. Ambrose was certain everyone must be staring at them, but no one was, except Fleury, who was anxiously examining both their faces.

Fleury watched them, with a sinking heart. To his eyes there seemed to be a duel going on between the two men, the words spoken were not the words that were being meant.

"Standish," said Rafe, inclining his head. Ambrose flinched

inwardly at the unaccustomed formality. "I trust you are recovered? An unexpected meeting; I was not aware that you were fond of *The Rivals*?"

Rafe's eyes flickered from Fleury and then back to Ambrose, and Ambrose realised that Rafe was speaking the silky subtext he had used the first time he had met him, the one he used for strangers. Ambrose was not the same man as he had been sixteen months earler, although he remained as proud as ever. "I appreciate theatre, Sir, although I have not before seen it in such an enclosed setting." He gave a brittle smile as he thrust back at Rafe with a similar riposte. "I must admit, I find that tragedy is a little wearing after a time. One would almost call it confining. Comedy is so much more liberating, do you not agree?"

"True, but I would not have thought that your tastes would have leant towards such down-to-earth entertainments."

"I found that more recently my entertainments are preferred in the real world. The lofty idealism of the Greek theatre is stimulating and heady, but the truth and honour they depict are as mythical as the tales themselves."

"Perhaps you ask too much from your higher literary ideals," Rafe countered, his eyes narrowing, "No one can live up to those expectations, certainly not mere mortals. Even the gods were flawed."

"As you say, Sir. Perhaps I have expected more and have been disappointed in the past."

"I find that I give most literary genres more than one chance. It would be careless to do less, as so much can be missed on a first reading, do you not think? However, I can understand your viewpoint, and we must agree to differ. I hope that whatever you read next is more rewarding, and more faithful to your exacting tastes."

The man bowed, his eyes never leaving Ambrose's for a moment, and Ambrose longed to hit him, the azure fire of hatred he had displayed on their first meeting, now blazing at their last. Then Rafe had stalked away and there was a long silence as Ambrose recovered himself, swallowing fiercely in his anger.

"People are staring, lad," Fleury said. He led the way out of the main doors back into the street. Both men were silent on the trip back to St Olaf's, but Fleury held Ambrose's hand tightly beneath his coat. From time to time, he stole a look at Ambrose but saw nothing but a furious, controlled face and eyes that were angrier than he had ever seen in the man before. They each went to their separate beds with hardly a word between them, merely a swift distracted kiss from Ambrose and a reassuring embrace from Fleury.

Much later that night, Ambrose's door opened silently and a slim, night shirted form slid in with him, silencing his protestations with a deep kiss. "They are sound asleep, I promise you. I had the strangest feeling you needed me. Let me only stay a while, just while you need me." Ambrose said nothing, but clung to Fleury with a desperation he had never shown before, as if he were attempting to meld them together into one being. His eyes dark and thoughtful, Fleury held Ambrose until his breathing slowed and his clutching arms relaxed. Certain his love was asleep, he kissed his hair, savouring the scent of it, then tore himself from the one place he loved to be and left his love peaceful.

Back in his own room, he sat at the small desk and wrote for a very long time, in a rounded untutored hand, stopping many times to uncramp his wrist or to burn pages and start again. Finally satisfied, he left the envelope on his pillow, dressed, and silently left the house. Any Runner seeing the man walk swiftly away from the house at that time of the night might have suspected him of some nefarious deed, but the tears on his face were not the usual hallmarks of a burglar.

As the morning lit Ambrose's room with a grey winter light, there was a knock and Constance entered the room. Ambrose woke with a sudden gasp, like a man surfacing from drowning. Seeing her in the doorway, her face pale and her eyes wide and pained, he clambered out of bed and took the letter she held out to him, his hands shaking. She left him alone to read, and Ambrose sat on the edge of the bed and tore the envelope open with desperate fingers.

Dearest Ambrose,
You are just waking, and I am on that ship we spoke of so often, heading for that fair wind.

A soft sobbing expulsion of breath and a whispered, "Padraig...no..."

I am sorry to do it, and more sorry than I can say to leave you behind. I should have said this to your face, but for the first time in his life, Fleury is branded a coward, unable to look you in the eyes, knowing you would convince me not to leave you behind, as I must.
The past few days have brought me to this, with all that has happened, some of which you do not know.
Firstly, I am again, or will be very soon, a wanted man, and the Americas are the safest haven for me. You healed many places in my heart and soul, Ambrose, but you could never really erase the villain. I have had too many years of badness and only a few months learning the good. I am not a good scholar like yourself.
I do not regret the reason for my warrant. I killed a man two days ago. This will shock you, but I am not sorry for it. His name, I learned after the event, was Count Achille Alvisi, and he was the

man that you found in Goshawk's bed, so cry no tears for his death. How he and I met and the manner of his dying, I will not describe to you, luran. Just be glad that you are avenged, as am I.

Secondly, we can have no world together, you and I, no common place where we can ever be happy. Even in the New World we were to head for together, our social spheres are too far apart to meet. You could never flourish in my world, and I would never be accepted into yours. How ironic that the one place on this earth where we were equal was Newgate. How strange it was to be so happy in the dark.

Thirdly and most importantly, you have to examine your heart. I know it so well, and you, seemingly, do not. You have places shut up in there and you need to open them, let the sunlight back into them. You are too young and too precious to let bitterness claim you forever, lad.

Last night I saw something very rare. Two people, who despite everything they had been through, love each other beyond all measure and are tearing themselves apart denying it. He has never stopped loving you, I am certain of that. Whatever his mistakes, he has done his best to make them right. Since his betrayal, he has been truer to you than you know. You have never stopped loving him, (I know me boy well enough to know he is shouting a denial as he reads this) and if you sat down and thought about him without the bitterness in your heart you would see it as clearly as everyone else who knows you well.

You have the name Rafe etched into your heart. I tried to scratch it out, and replace it with Padraig, but he was never in any danger from me. Despite his love for you, he was willing to step aside and let you come with me to the ends of the earth, if that was what made you happiest. That's love. Pure and simple.

Remember those levels of love we spoke of? Well, with him, you have them all; with your Fleury, we only managed two at best. The way forward for you is forgiveness, Ambrose. Forgive him. But most of all, forgive yourself for still loving him in spite of his faults. After all, he loves you with all of yours.

Keep safe, be happy and forgive also your,
Padraig.

Chapter 32

Ambrose stood up and, without a word, gently escorted Constance to the door and placed her outside it. As he dressed, the anger kindled the night before rose in flames within him until it finally reached a hot and maddening crescendo as his mind ran through Fleury's letter over and over again.

Rafe. Would it never end? Rafe had done this. Maybe not deliberately, although Ambrose found it too much of a co-incidence that the man had just happened to be present at Covent Garden, but Rafe had caused Fleury to leave as effectively as if he had carried him up the gangplank and put him on the ship himself.

He tore the letter into pieces, threw them to the floor, and hurled himself against the wall, his fists either side of his head, forearms and forehead against the surface, his breathing shallow and fast. Then, starting slowly, he began to punch the wood panelling as hard as he could, as hard as he had wanted to hit Rafe with his sneering superiority and his sly insinuations, as forcefully as he felt he should punish Fleury for his desertion. He connected with the wall again and again, crying out his rage, the searing pain in his fists spurring him to harder violence.

The door flew open, and then Constance was behind him, holding him, turning him as he sank to his knees and clutched her waist, not crying but gasping in pain and fury, blood from his damaged knuckles smearing on her skirt as he gripped it, burying his head in her softness. She sank down and cradled him in her arms, held him as he never remembered being held, rocked him as he had never been rocked.

She clasped him there for a long time — as the day began, as the blood dried on his knuckles and his breathing slowed. Then he rose, awkwardly, and without a word held the door open for her again, his eyes on the floor, his face immobile. She moved to take his hand, but he pulled away from her, and she could not reach him. As the door shut behind her, she saw Christopher waiting in the hall, and she flew into his arms to be comforted as she had comforted Ambrose.

What surprised Constance more than his anger was his sang-froid when he came down for breakfast. It was almost as if the last twenty-four hours had not happened, as if the last six months had not happened. He took his place at breakfast and made small talk as he had the previous morning, before Fleury's return. He was neat, tidy, polite, and considerate to his companions, the only evidence of his recent lack of control being the clumsy bandages on his hands.

"I have decided to go home," he said in a perfectly normal tone. "I have a little money and some good friends in Dorset. I will not be able to teach again, of course, but I can do some other labour, enough to keep us at least. After all," he gave them a cool look that frightened them, as his eyes were blue emptiness, "farm labourers can support whole families; I should be able to support three people."

"Your sisters were eligible to a charitable pension," Christopher said, attempting to reassure Ambrose. He hoped that God would forgive him for the falsehood, if it was meant for the best. "I did not mention it before, as I thought you might object — but you are welcome to stay here as long as you need."

Ambrose listened impassively, but he was adamant. "No. You have been more kind to me than I can say, more than I can ever repay, but I must go home if my sisters will welcome me. If I may stay until I hear from them?"

"Of course you will stay," Constance said. "We would not let you leave without a destination, and if there is anything we can do—"

"Nothing more," he answered. "You have done more than enough. I will never be able to repay you. Although," he said, standing and giving a stiff bow, "I shall certainly attempt to."

A letter was written and dispatched to Dorset, and Ambrose waited. He was not himself, though; the other two could see that. He seemed to have developed a hard protective shell, like that of a chrysalis. He was calm and unchanging on the outside, whilst on the inside there was torment, a holocaust of anger which razed his world and rebuilt it. Whether he emerged unscathed this time, stronger or damaged irreparably, no one, not even Ambrose could tell.

He spent hours in his room sitting on his bed, his legs tucked up, turning the possible futures over in his mind. What he longed to do was to use the money Fleury had left him and to sail after him. He knew that was hopeless. He knew his Fleury well enough. He would not go to New York as they had planned, or if he did, he would vanish completely into a world Ambrose could never penetrate. He wondered if he could truly be happy with Fleury again, even if he found him. Could he love a man who had killed so easily? Alvisi had been instrumental in his unhappiness, that was true, but Ambrose was decidedly uneasy with such a severe retribution. It made him wonder how many others Fleury had killed.

Ambrose even thought seriously about sailing to America to make a new life for himself alone, but he knew he would not. To be on the same continent as Fleury but without him was as bad as being in England without Rafe.

As he had allowed himself that terrible traitorous thought, his mind attempted to rebel against it, but the thought kept returning, over and over. He reached into his pocket and pulled out the torn letter, piecing it back together as he lay on the floor and re-reading it again and again. "Forgive yourself for still loving him," Fleury had said. *No Fleury,* he had thought, *you are wrong.*

Then he remembered a hot summer's night in Newgate, when they could not sleep and they had sat up talking in the moonlight, Fleury had sat in front of Ambrose, with Ambrose's arms and legs wrapped around his lover's naked body. Fleury had talked that night as he never had before or since, of the man he had loved two years before, of whom he had given the merest hint once or twice. Fleury never mentioned his name, but he told Ambrose that he had been convicted of practising as a doctor without qualifications and had been sentenced to five years.

"He was a good man," Fleury had said, with the brightest of eyes. "This was his cell. He earned it by looking after the prisoners' and warders' ailments. In some ways he was better than the so-called real doctors. He was in the army before his conviction, and he had saved so many lives. Money meant nothing to him. All he ever wanted to do was to help people, and they punished him for it. Then I arrived and I was so bold; I would not submit to the rules and I received flogging after flogging. My back became so bad that I was taken to him, unconscious and infected. He healed me, but I was still too troublesome. I got into so many fights that eventually he gave me a mattress and let me sleep in here, let me help him mix his potions, and I would tell him tall tales and make him laugh. He was such a melancholy man, and I liked to see him laugh."

Fleury had paused a long time after that, and only continued when Ambrose kissed his shoulder and said, "Go on."

Fleury sighed, kissed Ambrose's hands, and continued. "He taught me about life, and manners too. Society, he said, was founded on good manners. If they went, then the society was doomed, and we all might as well cut our throats. Then one day he kissed me and I did the worst thing I could have done — I ran away. He cut his wrists that afternoon, but someone found him straight away and I healed him as he had healed so many others. After that day, he was sadder than ever, and after that day, and far too late, I realised how much I loved that gentle man. When I told him so, he would not believe me, *luran.* He thought I was just saying it out of pity, to save his life.

"He was such a great soul, and yet he could not believe that anyone could love him; he did not think he was worthy of affection. He never tried to kiss me again, although every day I wished he would, and the next time he cut his wrists, he made sure there was no one around to see." The tears in Fleury's eyes did not fall, but made his eyes bright and fierce. "I loved him so very much. I still do. I will never stop. And maybe I caused his death, but I have had to forgive myself for that, as I do not think anything I could have done would have saved him in the end. I loved him, yes, but that does not stop me loving you, nothing ever will. Do you see what I'm saying to you, *luran*?"

Ambrose had not, then, but now he was beginning to. How could a man such as Fleury, with no education, be so much wiser? He had not even met Rafe at that point, and yet he had looked into Ambrose's heart as if it were a clear glass and had seen what Ambrose could not. He pushed the pieces of the torn letter about on the floor abstractedly, deep in thought. Finally he picked them up and gently put them back in his breast pocket.

The next morning, the letter from his sisters came. It was three words only: "Please come home." Ambrose's angry heart calmed at last. He was welcome. He turned to the Dunstans and they could see that the man they both cared so much about was back. His eyes were older, and his face reflected his turbulent year, but he was himself again and more handsome for his maturity. Now he had leave to go, he was reluctant to do so, frightened that he might never again see the friends he had made in his darkest year. He stayed two more days before he took his place on the post chaise. As they waited for the coach to be readied, he held his hands out to Constance and kissed her gently on her cheek, then embraced Christopher like a brother. As the coach pulled away, Ambrose remembered their arrival and could hardly see them waving at him through the tears in his eyes. Still, he kept his face turned towards them until the coach turned aside in its route.

The journey home took longer than he would have liked. The roads were terrible, and he had been travelling for five days. It was raining when he arrived, freezing horizontal rain which stung his face and hands. He walked from the village, after having arranged with the coaching inn that his trunk would be sent along in a day or so. He was tired and dirty, but even so his heart was lighter than it had been for many days. Every step he took toward his home, each remembered landmark that came into view made him happier. Half way up the drive he came to the sweep where Standish lay, half hidden in the murk of the rain. He only glanced at it, borne on by the small white house before him. Out of the murk came a booming bark and a lean grey shape came tearing down the drive toward him; Aries nearly knocked him over in his enthusiasm. Ambrose gave him his portmanteau to carry and the pair of them raced toward the house.

He opened the door, and Sophy flew into his arms while Maria waited to hold him next, tears streaming down her face. There were not many words spoken, but Ambrose was left with no doubts about how welcome his return was. The house was much the same, but different in an almost indefinable way. It seemed smaller, yet brighter and sunnier, in spite of the darkness of the rain outside. Ambrose realised that there were small touches here and there, tiny luxuries, once unheard of, that enlivened the house so — a jewel-like cushion here, a drape of fabric there, a new mirror, a freshly wallpapered room. It was all proof to Ambrose that the sisters were using their annuity carefully.

After intial greetings and the tears of reconciliation he said,"Is it right that you should continue to claim this pension, now I'm here?"

Maria smiled, "There is no cancelling it, I've been told," she said. "It's a lifetime annuity. I think that more prisoners do not come home than otherwise." At this, both sisters wrapped their arms around him and cried afresh.

"It does not seem right," he said, when they had quieted down a little, "when another family could be making use of it, and I am here to earn a living."

The ladies fell silent before his unassailable logic, and he kissed each one. "I will speak to Crabtree when I call on him. It is about time that I took control of the family's fortunes, such as they are," he said. "Whatever our finances are, we will face the problem together, all of us. I will not allow you two to carry me again."

The next morning he set off with Aries to see Crabtree. The weather was cold but dry, and Standish was visible across the park. Ambrose did not linger at the normal spot. He threw stick after stick for Aries to distract himself. Although he was happy to be home with his sisters, he was beginning to wonder whether he could live so close to Standish. Could he return to the rhythm of the life he had once had? Would his restlessness fade in time?

Crabtree greeted him with familiar warmth. "My boy, my boy," he blustered, shaking Ambrose's hand hard and long. He waved for him to sit.

As he complied, Ambrose looked up expectantly at the lawyer, who was pacing in an unaccustomed fashion. In all of his life, Ambrose had never seen the man less at ease.

Crabtree glanced down at his guest. *Young Standish. Hardly that any more, though.* All of his life he had called the fellow Young Standish to himself because of the great friendship he had had with his father, but the man sitting in his office today was not a youth anymore. The difference between him now and the last time he had been there was so marked it was startling. *Older, world weary. A look of agelessness about the eyes; Caroline's mouth, just slightly saddened. But overall the look of a man who has been through his own fire and will no longer be daunted by life.*

Crabtree hesitated; his task was a difficult one. "Standish," he began. "Ambrose. Forgive me, it seems so strange to think of you as Standish. I have known you all of your life, and your father for most of his. Standish to me will always be your grandfather. But a Standish you most certainly are."

Ambrose was beginning to wonder what this unnecessary talk was of and why the lawyer seemed so agitated.

"I have here," Crabtree went on, reaching into a desk and pulling out a thick goatskin parchment, "an agreement. In essence, it is a draft agreement, but I have already examined it in great detail and can find no fault in it. It needs no revisions; all it needs is your signature." He looked at Ambrose and saw nothing but confusion in his face. "Are you saying that you know nothing of this? I assumed you knew. Why else would you have come here today?"

"Forgive me, Sir, but I only returned from London last night. If there is something my sisters should have apprised me of, I am unaware of it. I came to discuss the family's income only."

Crabtree wiped his red face with a large handkerchief. "Perhaps then, you may wish to read this before we proceed any further."

He pushed the parchment across the desk, but the medieval writing and archaic language defeated even Ambrose after the first few sentences. "All I can ascertain is that this is something to do with Goshawk." His voice was impatient and guarded.

"This document, simply put, assigns to you all interest in the estate known as Standish." Ambrose was still frowning, so Crabtree elucidated further. "Goshawk is giving you Standish, and my advice to you is to accept it. The terms of the Agreement are quite clear. The house, the contents, the livestock, the grounds and £15,000 per annum are to pass to you utterly, with one proviso, that if you and your sisters are to die without issue, then the entire estate is to revert to Sebastien Goshawk, his heirs or assigns. I assure you, it is quite watertight." He watched Ambrose anxiously as the man attempted to read the words again.

He looked across at the lawyer with an unbelieving expression. "Can he do that?"

"There is no reason why not. The estate is not entailed, nor was it, of course, when your grandfather owned it, or he could not have wagered it in the first place. It is Goshawk's to do with as he pleases, and it appears it pleases him to give it to you." Crabtree paused. He was aware of the history between the two men, and Ambrose was not taking the news as he'd expected. "There is no reason for you to sign it straight away, of course. Perhaps you would like time to think? It is a huge responsibility." Crabtree watched the young man with Caroline's face struggle with himself. "I do not often give personal advice, my boy," Ambrose's eyes flickered upwards at the lawyer's sobriquet, "but do not think that Goshawk is offering you charity. He is giving you something that he does not need, something that no one in this world would deny belongs rightly to you."

Ambrose looked down at his lap, the anger he had held for these two weeks ebbing, almost to his own disgust. Rafe, giving him the house they both loved so much, had won again. Ambrose knew exactly what Standish meant to Rafe. What game was he playing now?

"I'll need to think about it, Sir," he said, his mind whirling. They shook hands, and Crabtree sent his respects to Ambrose's sisters. Ambrose walked into the High Street and strode furiously through the village towards the White House. As he reached the bend in the driveway, Aries was standing by the fence, waiting at the spot where he knew Ambrose habitually paused. Ambrose stopped this time, leaned against the fence, and allowed himself to look at the house. He found it had changed subtly in his perception. There were now three houses in his mind. The first was the remote mansion he had lusted after all of his youth — an exterior only, untouchable, hallowed, belonging to a spectre who had cheated him of it. The second — explored and loved, but bitter with memories and belonging so completely to Rafe. And now? The answer was irrefutable. As he looked at it, the windows gleaming in the light, it was as if the three disparate images were merging before his eyes, and he saw the house as if he were seeing it for the first time. Standish was his. It always had been his. Even when he could not imagine how it would ever happen, he had known it. He had known it when he had taken over the reins of running the estate the previous year; it had all seemed so natural. It belonged to him. And just as Rafe belonged to Standish, Rafe also belonged to him. He could not take one without the other.

Standing before the Tavistock Square house, Ambrose steeled himself. He felt that perhaps he should have written, but a direct refusal would have been difficult to deal with, and he might have been refused entry. A footman let him in, and before even he had a chance to have his greatcoat removed, there was a choked cry from the hallway and a taller, slimmer Sebastien bulleted into him, wrapped himself around his waist.

"Ambrose," the boy muttered in a muffled voice. "By all that is wonderful, you have come back to us when we need you the most." Ambrose brushed the hair from Sebastien's face. He was growing up; the little boy was becoming a young man. "Papa is not well. He has not been out of the house for weeks. He will hardly even allow me into his rooms. He will not speak of you, but I know he misses you so very much, we both do. Please say you are back for good?"

"I don't know." Ambrose's eyes were dark with emotion as he looked down at the boy, so desperate for reassurance. His father had been his foundation for all of his life, and his tragic face made it clear that he felt it was all slipping away from him. "That is up to him. He's been sad for too long, and he needs time, time to heal himself, time to love us both again. I am going to see him now, to see if...he wants to." He kissed the boy gently and walked up the stairs to Rafe's suite, his heart pounding with uncertainty.

The rooms were unlit, the only source of light being the sun which was nearing the horizon, spreading a blinding light in shafts through the long, tall windows. He could not see Rafe at first, then saw a large winged chair, facing the windows, the unmistakable head leaning back onto it. He stepped up next to it and put his hand on Rafe's arm.

Rafe jumped as if he had been burned, and his wolf-like eyes looked up under suspicious brows. "You. I was expecting you, eventually. Whatever it is that you want, ask it, take it, and go."

"I..." Now that he was there, Ambrose felt inadequate. How could he make Rafe see the truth? His heart broke to see how hollow he looked, empty and hopeless. "I came to thank you."

"For ruining your life? Yes, yes, I think we have played that scene." His voice was sarcastic and bitter.

"No. Truly. For Standish...for everything."

"Everything." Rafe gave a mirthless laugh. "You stand there and thank me for what I have done to you?" Rafe's eyes narrowed. "Get out, Ambrose, and leave me be, I deserve torment, but not from you. I have enough of my own. Get back to your precious house. I ask only one thing of you — that you destroy the fountain, if you have not already. Take your Irish happiness back to Standish and leave me be."

"He has gone."

"So, what is this? I merit second prize?"

"He seemed to think you had won." Rafe gave a short bitter laugh at this. Ambrose took a deep breath. "Do you know what Standish means, Rafe?"

"I know what it means to you," growled Rafe. "And may you have joy of it, for it has meant nothing to me but my destruction."

"That is the house, not the Standish name. Standish is another name for an inkwell. I had one at ho...at the White House. It is a simple silver inkstand, but in the hands of someone who knows how to unlock it, it holds the whole world.

"Before I met you, my life was a blank page. I had studied; I had learned facts from books, languages from books, but I had experienced nothing, nothing except a longing for a pile of bricks that I had never even entered. From the moment I met you, that virgin parchment was marked indelibly with your seal, and writing crept upon the page. First, with a hesitant childish scrawl, badly blotted with dark black ink, as I hated you for simply being the son of your father; then, with an elegant sloping hand, as you dazzled me with sophistication and sarcastic charm.

"Then at last, the dam gates opened and you released a torrent of words, page after page of love and tenderness. You opened my eyes to myself, to my capacity for sensuality and emotion. Not only love, but all that tempers it: jealousy, anger, repression, and fear."

"Stop...for pity's sake, stop it." Rafe got out of the chair and strode to the windows, looking down on the street, where long ago, he had watched another life destroyed. "I am well aware of what I put you through, Ambrose. Do you think that whatever you have suffered, I have not?"

Ambrose smiled sadly. "You already knew what it was to suffer; I did not. You had suffered long before meeting me; your early life was shaped by pain. Every feeling of light and happiness should have been quenched by the darkness of your years in Paris and in this house. It is a miracle to me that you had any love within you, let alone such a wellspring as that which flowed for me.

"Love is worthless without the baser emotions that feed it; it is only those that make it worth having. At first, I could not see that. I thought only of the perfection that you had written. I thought that all had been scored through in Paris and Venice, ripped and torn, spoiled with jealous green ink, destroyed forever. I was wrong.

"I did not realise that it was only the Introduction, the Preface. Love without pain, sorrow, and jealousy is a false love, a sickly idolisation. If one can take that love and read on through the heartache and the tragedy that comes with it, then the writing is clearer and the meaning truer because of it."

There was no sound from Rafe, but he was leaning against the lintel and breathing deeply, as if having done some heavy activity.

Ambrose went on, more urgently, attempting to get some response, "We have come through now, Rafe. We can stand together and read the tale of our love and see how strong it is. A better man than I taught me the truth of my soul in a soulless place." Rafe stirred at the mention of Fleury. "He taught me that simply because one loves anew, it does not necessarily extinguish a deeper, greater love, which may have been set aside or lost, and that one can, if invited, come home at last. We both deserve that. We have no home except with each other." Ambrose's voice broke but went on desperately. "Rafe, you once gave your heart into my keeping, and I have kept it with me through every hour since our parting, even if I did not know that it was there. Now, either claim it back, or take mine in return," he choked. "For without you writing the story of my life, I have no need of it."

Ambrose stood there for what seemed like eternity, watching

the sun set on the black shadow of his life before him. There was no response. Eventually he straightened and took a deep breath. He had done what he could. Leaving his hope in the last rays of the setting sun, he left as quietly as he had entered.

The door closed behind Ambrose, and Rafe stood staring into the street. He was sixteen again, the window was open and he was screaming into the rain. Through the glass he saw, not Quinn being dragged into the gutter, but a slim blond man standing by the pavement gate holding Sebastien in his arms, then the man walked slowly across the square as if the weight of the world were on his shoulders.

He turned, his eyes blank, but this time there was no Gordian, no horsewhip, no rain, no Mauvaise, and no future.

Turning back, he threw open the window.

Erastes lives in Norfolk, UK. If he has any ambition it is to bring homosexual historical romance more into the mainstream. He's had numerous short stories published by Alyson Books, Cleis Press, and Starbooks to name a few. He believes in the Great Dark Man and bases his dodgy morality on R.A. Heinlein's Notebooks of Lazarus Long. His website and blog can be found at www.erastes.com